*"Hurt is a masterpiece. Easily one of the best books I've ever read.
I will never forget it."*
—New York Times Bestselling Author Pam Godwin

"A Home Run!"
—Author Michelle Windsor

"Raw and Beautiful! Hypnotic and Haunting! Hurt will absolutely WOW you!"
—Blushing Babes Are Up All Night

"A Masterpiece!"
—Author Haylee Thorne

"This is Lydia's first dark romantic thriller, and I pray it will not be her last!"
—AJ's Book re-Marks

"A devastatingly beautiful story!"
—Author D.D. Lorenzo

HURT

A Dark Romantic Thriller

Hub,
#Its Going to Hurt
xo
Lydia Michaels

LYDIA
MICHAELS

www.LydiaMichaelsBooks.com

BAILEY BROWN
PUBLISHING

Bailey Brown Publishing
Thriller | Dark Romance | Suspense

©Lydia Michaels

HURT
Copyright © 2019 Lydia Michaels Books, LLC
Editor: Allyson Young
Cover Design: Lydia Michaels
Photographer: Luis Louro

USA | CANADA | SPAIN | EUROPE | NEW ZEALAND | AUSTRALIA

eBook ISBN: 978-0-9995236-2-9
Print ISBN: 978-0-9995236-3-6

www.LydiaMichaelsBooks.com

Before we begin...

Special thanks to Amo, who helped bring my settings to life. Thank you for putting up with my countless questions and letting me view Scotland through your eyes and hear the culture through your ears. It was an absolute pleasure chatting, and your input has been *pure dead brilliant*.

This book wouldn't exist without the encouragement of my dear (sinister and brilliant) friend, Pam Godwin. You opened up your twisty mind and inspired me to be a little scared of the things my pen can do. You encouraged me to push a little harder—until it hurts. My admiration for you is huge, and yet my adoration is bigger still. For you, I do it *ducimo*.

And lastly, I must acknowledge the beauty that is our First Amendment. This story took several years to finish. Its weighted message chipped away at me and required moments of reprieve. Sometimes the characters were so bruised and battered, they needed days away from my pen to heal. And sometimes there wasn't time.

My muse barreled in like a mechanical bull, breaking everything in sight without flinching, without feeling, leaving me, the author, emotionally scarred in the end. That seemed the cost of honesty, the price of genuine truth. Fiction has an inextinguishable actuality to it, the shadows between the lines.

Tragedy does not end in a courtroom or a closet. It is not selective of its setting, which is why I chose to set half the book in a place so picture perfect, standing in the town feels like stepping into a postcard. The crisis isn't *where* this story happens, but *that it happens everywhere*, leaving infinite scars, as unending as Pi. But we are more than numbers, and we cannot abbreviate the pain. HURT is told as, I believed, it needed to be told. Honestly, unflinchingly, and raw. But know, it's going to hurt.

WARNING: This story is categorized as a *Dark Suspenseful Thriller* and contains multiple scenes of graphic violence, non-consensual sex, and torture. *It is also a love story*.

<u>Songs that Inspired HURT</u>

Sound of Silence by Disturbed

Possession by Sarah McLachlan

Stay by Rhianna

Enter Sandman by Metallica

Uninvited by Alanis Morrisette

Quiet by MILCK

Bruises by Lewis Capaldi

Personal Jesus by Marilyn Manson

Psycho Killer by Talking Heads

I Know You Care by Ellie Goulding

Almost Lover by A Fine Frenzy

Young and Beautiful by Lana Del Ray

Nothing Compares 2 U by Chris Cornell

Rise Up by Andra Day

Love Reign O'er Me by The Who

May It Be by Enya

Shape of my Heart by Sting

HURT

<u>Dedication</u>

To my quill, my sword, my shield.
To every Jane and Emily Doe who waited for a hero that
did not show.
For the voice that goes silent, not in fear, but in shame,
My quill knows your name.

For the knowledge that *we* can handle *it*, but they cannot,
we swallow it down.
You are fragile. You are strong. You are brave. You are
not broken.
And we hear you, though you do not make a sound.
Your story remains unspoken.

The casualty of a system flawed,
We write, we hurt, we heal.
The darkest fiction, printed in truth,
We flinch away,
We tell ourselves it isn't real.

For every silent sorrow swallowed, screams an infinite
pain.
For all the voices hollowed, that spoke only in vain.

For you, my quill bleeds across the page in tragic,
truthful rage.
My quill. My sword. My shield.
The fictional beast I slay,
The monster we know is real.

HURT

HURT

THE HURT SERIES

Lydia Michaels

HURT

Chapter One

Glasgow—Scotland

Callan's teeth clacked with a horrid smack. Precise pain exploded behind his eyes as a fire bloomed under his stinging skin. His face caught the brunt of the assault, flesh splitting and bones throbbing with familiar distress. Thick blood mixed with sweat as rivulets poured down his face.

He spit onto the cement floor and waited for his vision to clear as the beast of a man pounding him like raw mince shuffled back to catch his breath. The buffeted sound of the crowd returned, their hungry cries surrounding the makeshift ring from all angles.

Callan's throbbing ears siphoned the droning noise in and out to the rapid tempo of his heart. *Womp—womp—womp—womp...* His skin pulsed to the beat.

His head snapped back. Another blast to the skull. Blood gushed behind his nose, choking off his airway, drenching everything in the metallic flavor of defeat.

Tripping over his feet, he forced his knees to bend, rewarded by several knocks to the ribs. Voices collided in a drunken slur of bloodthirsty chants.

Launching forward, he dodged a fist and blasted a punch into the tender solar plexus of his assigned enemy. The blood-drenched tape over his knuckles did little to protect his hands, each crushing hit pulverizing his brittle bones and weakening his wrists. At this point, they swung like numb ham hocks.

Adrenaline thrummed through his veins. He bunched and bounced like a bobbin on a spool, tethered by a thread to the unknown outcome of the match, prepared for anything—even death.

Heart hammering like a bodhrán, he maneuvered closer, blinking through the opaque film of blood and sweat coating his eyes. No time to wipe it away. Even blinking cost him.

His head snapped back, jaw vibrating, as pain exploded in his ears. The sharp burst spiked through his brain, blowing open his sinuses, and drilling to the base of his spine—tripping him on thin air.

He spit again, never taking his eyes off his opponent.

The dank air mixed with the tang of whisky and desperation. Boarded windows kept the moonlight out and a stale scent of abandonment in.

Everyone in that deserted mill had something to lose. Or everything to gain. But no one had more riding on this than him.

No guarantees. Win, lose. Live, die. So long as the right people got paid, no one gave a fuck who got hurt.

A hasty lunge and a miss—bad timing on his part. A solid fist to the ribs whacked the wind from his lungs. It was the only warning before a storm rained over him. His opponent pelted him with fists, caving in his chest and hemming him to the line.

While he'd always been a notably large man, his rival was fucking huge.

They loved to do this, to cut off his oxygen, hoping he'd black out. If they couldnae get the knockout, they'd go for a collapse. But his ability to take a hit—the sort of hit that would drop an average man—had made him a legend.

Stumbling. Battered. Breathless. He let his rival—and the crowd—assume he was done. The roars of excitement echoed every hit as they fell in a flurry.

The enemy weakened with each blow, slowed with each swing. Callan gasped through it, wearing his opponent down as he gathered his strength like a tidal wave sucks into the ocean before letting go.

The abuse chiseled away the man until only an animal remained. And then...

Snap.

Like a phoenix of rage, he rose from the ashes. Nimble, with unexpected agility, he drew back, wheezed in a breath of blood and hate, and hurtled forward, rushing his rival and lobbing his ravaged knuckles into his meaty face.

When a man had nothing to lose, he'd do anything to win. No longer shackled by strategy, Callan unleashed.

His skull throbbed with the beat of his pulse. The bastard tumbled into the crowd, tripping over his own feet, only to get hoisted back into the action.

Tasting victory, Callan bared his bloodstained teeth like the devil about to take his prize.

Something dark and inhuman shifted inside of him. Limitless. Unredeemable. Hungry. He cleaved into the enemy, throwing haymakers, ballistic and desperate. *It's him or me.*

A blow cuffed his ear, delivering a stunning swirl of black behind his eyes as the roar muffled. Swarming figures blurred.

From the depths of his pain, buried beneath every ache and injustice, he scraped the filthy floor of his soul for every jagged piece of broken determination he could find. He unleashed everything.

"He's done!"

"Knock him oot!"

Jumbled chaos scattered his thinking like sparks flying from a blowtorch.

"Finish him!"

A calm stole through him as his civility disintegrated, sinking into the dark abyss of his soul where he dinnae like to dwell. Barbaric determination took savage hold of his actions, demanding he finish this.

"MacGregor, destroy that scunner!"

16

His family needed this win. But they also needed him.

Gavin's elfin face wavered in his mind, too gaunt for a boy of ten, but so hopeful. Innis's beauty shined like a beacon, her ebony waves framing the delicate angles of her ivory face.

Incarnate hate for every suffered uncertainty spewed from him in a primal rage. The body beneath him slackened and stopped flinching.

"MacGregor, yer gonna murder him!"

The hushed shock of the crowd's alarm penetrated his haze of savage fury, and his arms slowed. When nothing came at him, he staggered back, his heaving sides pumping like a bellow feeds wind to a flame, only the fire in his opponent's eyes had died.

He swayed back, panting and confused, as the world took a moment to spin to a stop. The other man lay bloody and still. Callan's panic and paranoia churned into a frenzy of doubt, waiting to see him breathe.

Balanced on the sharp prick of a needle's edge, his existence teetered on his opponent's breath. Though they were enemies in the ring, outside, they were the same.

Unlike the spectators, they came from nothing and would do anything to survive. But if that breath dinnae come, Callan would have to live with that sin for the rest of his life.

The gurgling rise of the man's chest released Callan's detained breath, and the crowd screamed.

"MacGregor wins!"

Disembodied logic gradually returned, each coiled muscle too tight to unravel, needing time to unwind. Over. It was over.

Relief hit with the hardest punch that night. He shut his eyes, thanking Christ it was done.

The medics rushed to the man on the floor, waving salts under his bloodied nose. Rhys pushed through the encroaching mob, shouting at those in his way, "Give us space!" He unzipped his backpack and hosed down Callan's face with cool water. "You were fuckin' magnificent."

Callan groaned, panting with shallow breaths, each one wheezing past his parched throat. His mate tended to the most urgent injuries, frowning as he examined the gusher above his brow.

"Aye, yer gonna need some stitching."

Callan shut his swollen eyes as Rhys got to work. "Was it a good purse?"

"Aye. And ye earned every pound. They're all waitin' te congratulate you. Already talkin' about who ye'll clobber next."

"No more for a while—if the money holds out."

Rhys paused from winding gauze around Callan's ribs and gave a gapped-toothed grin. "Good luck tellin' them that. Greedy bastards are already hankering for more."

It dinnae matter what they wanted, only what his family needed. He dinnae fight because he enjoyed it. Violence went against his nature. Or perhaps it was more honest to say violence was the part of his nature he'd rather ignore.

Callan fought because nothin' else paid as well. His pain bore a worthwhile profit, as a wealthy man's crumbs could be a gutter rat's feast. And he would feed his family well tonight.

"You'll need te ice those fists soon as ye get home," Rhys warned, carefully peeling back the ruined tape from his swollen, split knuckles. The raw flesh seemed to tremble over the bone.

"Help me up."

Rhys took his arm and pulled. As his cracked ribs pushed painfully against his chest cavity, he winced and tried to offset the pain with softening knees.

The moment he was upright, the spectators assumed he was fair game. "Bugger of a fight, MacGregor."

Gazing at the blurred figure, he only recognized the faint and fuzzy outline of a man. "Aye."

"Bring yourself by the pub later, and we'll get ye a pint on the house."

Money could buy a lot of things but not his trust. With the push of gravity came the rise of bile. He tightened his lips and turned, vomiting a mix of bitterness and blood, hardly missing a set of leather shoes.

He dragged his forearm over his wet lips and groaned. Rhys shoved a water bottle into his swollen hand.

Callan swished the pungent taste away and spit. "Get me out of here."

"Aye."

Taking pay for voluntary acts of violence tarnished a man. He'd done such vile things inside this mill, even the *polis* feared approaching him. But it was all a means to an end, the cost of peace of mind.

What a flowery crock of shite. As if his morality could be somehow spared. Sooner or later he'd either kill a man or get himself killed trying to win.

Crushing Rhys with his weight, he leaned heavily on his mate as they navigated the crowd.

The so-called gentlemen that ran these fights capitalized on pain. He hated and respected them. Lost a wee bit of respect for himself each time he fought, too. But at least he had a choice. *His* choice.

Rolling his shoulders, he gingerly straightened his spine. A river of shame washed through him at the sight of winners celebrating the utter thrashing of another man. His gaze sifted through the throng, seeking the payout area. Those hollow holes left by rage would be patched with the money earned, money his family needed.

"Another stellar win, eh, MacGregor?" As the high waned, the slightest pat on the back landed like a sledgehammer to the spine. Rhys saw it in his eyes with every wince, but couldnae force the crowd to move any faster. They all wanted a piece of the glory.

Sucking his swollen lip between his teeth, he grunted at the renewed taste of blood. Tomorrow, he'd be painfully stiff and equally tender.

"I dinnae think ye had it in ye, but ye came back like ye always do," a man with sharp eyes and a glinting diamond earring praised. "Yer a machine."

Even nodding cost him.

Finally, they approached the payout table. "I'll be takin' my money now."

"Aye." The bookie's eyes measured him. "Yer not one for talkin', are ye?"

His stony silence was answer enough.

Rhys handed him his jacket, but he was still too warm to put it on, and dinnae want to move his body more than necessary.

Registering the sum of his wounds, the man slid his money across the table. "I knew it'd be a close fight, but well worth the pay, aye?"

Callan briefly examined the contents of the envelope and stuffed it in the pocket of his jeans. "Let's go."

"Ye'll be hearin' from us again real soon, MacGregor."

Disenchanted, he silently admitted, aye, he'd be back.

His wounds would hardly have time to heal before he returned. That was the way of it. His family needed money for food and shelter. His siblings needed school fees. Sooner or later they'd have enough to buy a house in a safer area.

The cost to his health and conscience dinnae matter. It never had.

Violence was a stubborn cancer of the soul, and the profane brutality of such a vicious fight did not easily wash away. Every time Callan unleashed his temper, the gaping hole inside of him grew grander and filthier, like a tarnished cup marking his ill-gotten victories. Trophies of shame collected in the shapes of scars.

As they trudged the unlit streets, neds, junkies, and thieves loitered in every darkened alley. Brooding clouds snuffed out the glow of the moon. Soon the reddening dawn would come, and the world would awaken while sinners slept. A time to repent. A time to forget.

The weight of a thousand pounds planted in his back pocket hustled them past the drunkards in the streets. Callan retained his threatening presence, but tonight's fight had wrung him out, and he had little strength left to defend himself if anyone approached.

Watchful eyes glinted like windowless souls. He'd fought damn hard for the money in his pocket. He was grateful for Rhys's gun—an unlicensed relic of a pistol he'd won in a card game and never fired to see if it worked. In a pinch, neither of them would have the bollocks to pull the trigger, but it was a good scare tactic. Strip away the undefeated reputation, and they were just boys trying to be men.

Rolling his shoulders in an effort to uncoil the tension, he sought a sense of satisfaction.

The stitch on his eye wasnae holding. Squinting through a trickle of blood, he dabbed the swollen, torn flesh. "I need a rag."

Rhys glanced over his shoulder and stopped walking. Reaching in his bag, he pulled out a roll of tape and tore off a strip with his teeth, doing a quick examination of the gash.

"We gotta pick up the pace. Ye got a real gusher. I shouldae done more than one stitch before we left."

Callan winced as Rhys pulled away the ruined suture, pinched the wound, and pressed fresh tape tight to his skin.

"If I let ye stitch me up all the time I'd look like Frankenstein's patient."

There weren't any beauty pageants in his future as it was, but Rhys sucked with a needle and thread, and he'd rather risk bleeding out on the way home than let his mate sew him up like a voodoo doll. Once they got home, Innis could do it nice.

Rhys's green eyes flashed as they dropped from studying the gash to meet his stare. "Aye. Well, I'm sorry if I don't have the delicate touch of Innis. She's got those wee female hands."

Any mention of his sister's body—even her wee hands—earned a scowl. Innis was undeniably beautiful. Even blind men knew it for a fact. But it wasn't something they spoke about.

As her older brother and caretaker, he'd always been overly protective of her. She was too damn pretty, too damn innocent, and too damn fragile. And wee hands or not, the girl should know how to throw a punch. He tried teaching her, but she always laughed his concerns away.

He bet she forgot to lock the damn door again. That's how seriously she took his warnings that the world was a dangerous place.

Their da had been a monster. But Innis had been too young to recall much from that time. Callan had often made a game of quietly hiding with her whenever their da had been on a tear. Sheltering her, even then, from things that went bump in the night.

He winced as a sharp zing pinched his eye. "Don't fuckin' squeeze it!"

"I'm tryin' to tighten this stitch. It's comin' apart." He let go, and warm blood trickled from his brow. "She'll have to fix it when we get there. She'll be up."

Most of the time, Rhys and Innis bickered like children, but they were no longer kids. Innis, now a seventeen-year-old young woman, could not afford to be naïve. And Rhys couldnae afford the thrashing Callan would unleash if he ever put his hands on his baby sister.

"Stop scowling. Yer makin' it bleed more," Rhys fussed.

"How is it ye know when she's up and when she's sleepin'?"

His mate paused, his gaze shooting to the road. "I'm sayin' she'll be up soon enough. It's a school day and almost dawn."

Rhys might care for her in a tender, harmless way, but Callan dinnae want him confusing things for her. "Don't be an obstacle blocking her future. I want more for her." It was a hard but honest truth.

24

Like the wasted moments of deafening clock bells, they were just marking time for her. She was destined for a better life. And Callan wouldnae let anything—including his best mate—stand in her way.

"Aye. I want better for her, too," Rhys agreed.

Their life had been a culmination of hollow joys and dense tragedy, but their bad luck was coming to an end. His soul thirsted for a home. Not a ramshackle dwelling surrounded by the scent of rotting potential, but a true home, a place to bury bleak regrets and sew honest dreams.

Once they escaped their impoverished start—which they would—he'd repent for his sins and start anew. No more violence. No more pain.

Gavin would grow into a fine young man and Innis could attend uni, fall in love, raise a family—all the things their mother never mastered.

The fading memory of their ma brought only a whisper of grief. Life got harder after she died, and mourning seemed too indulgent for three wee kids trying to keep a roof over their heads, shoes on their feet, food, heat, and everything else that always just appeared.

He'd never resent his mother. Through all the depression, addiction, and abuse, she still managed to deliver the necessities. But love … love was a luxury.

By the time Gavin was born, she dinnae have it in her to hold the baby. Luckily, Innis possessed a maternal heart.

Maternal, and never squeamish—thank God, because his eye wasnae lettin' up.

The first time she stitched him up after a fight, she argued that she had no experience sewing people, only fabric. He gave her a few slices of ham to practice on, and since then she'd been a regular medic.

They cut across an empty pathway to a sundry of vacant buildings. The metallic tang of blood faded as the cool morning fog misted his face.

Not much in this section of Glasgow as far as commercialization. It resembled a modern-day apocalypse. Lifeless structures, once beautiful but now soulless, hung on the abandoned streets like prostitutes on their last fuck. The far-reaching decay of this place infected more than the vacant buildings, and he ached to escape.

Chapter Two

Glasgow—Scotland

The house was dark when they arrived. The rotting porch creaked under their combined weight.

Sliding his key into the lock, he jerked the deadbolt free. A wave of satisfaction hit when the inside chain caught. Dim light caught in the eyes of a scraggly dog slumbering in the corner, slightly sheltered from the misting rain.

"What the fuck is that?" Rhys shifted behind Callan.

He shook his head. "Innis keeps feedin' it. We barely have enough to feed ourselves. She's probably lettin' the bloody thing inside when I'm not here."

"It's ugly as sin."

Callan grumbled and hissed through the cracked doorway, "Innis." He tried not to wake Gavin who likely slept on the sofa closest to the fire.

The dry-rotted awning did shite for shelter against the damp Scotland climate. Rhys's shoulders bunched against the cold mist as he impatiently crowded the stoop to get out of the rain, his untrusting gaze shooting back to the watchful dog. He probably worried the stray might take his place.

His sister's willowy form approached the other side of the door like a silent shadow, and the chain slid free. They bustled inside, kicking off their muddy boots and relocked the door.

"Fuck, it's bloody freezin' in here," Rhys complained, immediately moving closer to the fireplace. "Warmer outside in the rain."

Innis ignored him and assessed Callan's face. "Yer late. And you look like shite."

"Ye should see the other guy."

"Did ye win?"

Pulling the money from his pocket, he dropped it on the table with a thump. "Aye. Put that in the tin, will ye?" He moved closer to the fire and hauled the sofa back from the hearth. "Innis, ye cannae let him sleep so close to the flame. An ember catches in the blanket, and he could get hurt. The whole place could go up."

She pulled the corner of the blanket over Gavin's scrawny shoulders. "Yer eye looks atrocious. Is that sad stitch supposed to be doing something?"

"It was a temporary fix," Rhys said defensively. "The patch is doing most of the work."

She clicked on the lamp, already sorting through her little box for a needle and thread.

"Come have a seat then, and let me see what I can do."

Callan pulled out a chair from the table. "Do ye want me te wash up first?"

"That'll only start the bleedin' again. We'll clean ye up when I'm done." She tsked, getting another glance at Rhys's shoddy work. "I dinnae ken why ye let him by yer face with a needle. He's only addin' te yer scars."

Unaffected by her insults, Rhys warmed his hands by the fire. "Why's it so cold in here?"

"I couldnae get the storage heater on. The timer's shot and I was too frozen te keep messin' with it."

Callan took the hint and stowed it away with a sigh. It had to be damn near freezin' for Innis to complain. She already put up with drafty, uncovered windows and bare floors. When it got really cold, she'd fill a glass bottle with hot water from the kettle and wrap it in a towel to keep warm. But she wouldnae tolerate a broken storage heater as well.

Two grimy bare feet dangled from the sofa. "Is Gavin warm enough?"

"He's too young te mind the cold. The fire's enough for him."

"I'll take a look at the heater when yer finished stitchin' me."

"You'll not do anything until ye get those hands in some ice." She disappeared into the kitchen, returning a minute later with two buckets.

She set them down and tsked. "Look how swollen. You shouldae tended to them sooner."

He gingerly submerged his hands, and his shoulders flinched as the cold cubes ground against his torn knuckles and swollen fingers. The brutality of the evening stayed with him like a foul stench.

Using a match to sterilize the needle, she then snapped off a length of heavy thread. She and Gavin were too desensitized by the regular sight of blood. Guilt churned in his gut, reminding him this wasnae how normal people lived.

"We made a good profit tonight," he said as a way to ease the guilt.

Innis tsked, her eyes focused on threading the needle. "A profit at what price? Where else are ye hurt?"

"Nowhere that willnae heal on its own." Her worry cost him in ways he couldnae afford. He wished Rhys was a better medic, wished Innis dinnae see him directly after a fight.

He sat silently as she worked, his eyes watching hers as they focused on the task. Rhys settled in at the table with a mug. "Drop of whisky te warm yer blood."

Callan eyed the cup. He'd wait until Innis finished stitching his eye to have a nip. "Anything happen tonight?"

She pulled the needle slowly, closing a neat seam along his torn flesh. "Spent most the night fussin' with the heater."

The poor condition of their house played as a constant reminder of all they'd suffered and continued to sacrifice. Still, it was better than living on tick and falling deeper into debt.

They dinnae have much, but what they had was theirs. And the tin in the kitchen hid enough notes that they'd soon be rid of this drafty gaff for good.

"I'll fix the heater," he promised, taking one worry away from her for now.

"Good." She pushed the needle through the tender edges of his tattered brow, dragging the thread slowly, so as not to rip the skin. He remained still and tried not to wince.

"*Doctor* Innis. It's got a nice ring to it," Rhys teased. "No clue how ye keep yer hand so steady."

"Ye just shut everything else out—includin' chatterboxes who cannae respect a peaceful silence." She glanced over her shoulder at Rhys then back to Callan's gash. "Stay still. Almost done."

Innis had been bullied, so he transferred her and Gavin to private school. But to see her now, one would never know she'd been a victim. Fragile but fierce. She was his masterpiece, the beneficiary of all his sacrifices. She and Gavin were the sum of his pride and the whole of his heart.

"There." She clipped the thread with a pair of shears, cleaned the needle, and tossed the items back in the box. "I'll get a damp rag and clean you up." Closing the sewing box, she disappeared into the kitchen.

Callan longed to fall into his bed and sleep for days. Rhys looked ready to pass out as well. "Feel like helpin' me take apart the heater te see what's wrong with it?"

Tired emerald eyes flicked to him. "Hardly."

Callan stretched, his shoulder adjusting with a pop. "You'll help."

Innis returned with a steaming rag and wiped the dried blood from his face. "You'll be a picture once these bruises darken."

"I like te think my beauty's in the flaws."

She scoffed out a laugh. "Beauty? Yer nose's been broken so many times it's no wonder ye cannae smell the bullshite yer spewin'. Yer skin's nothin' more than raw mince. It'd be nice if ye gave yourself time te fully heal for once."

She was right, but he couldnae make any promises. Too late anyway. While Innis was great at stitching up wee nicks, his face had paid a hefty, permanent toll for so many victories. After the bruises faded and the swelling went down, he'd still be ugly.

"Brat," he teased, knowing she regretted the irreversible damage he'd done to his face. But if they couldnae laugh about it, there was no sense in mentioning it at all.

He stood and stretched, wincing when his ribs reminded him to move a wee bit slower. He followed her into the kitchen. "Have ye seen my tools?"

Rinsing the bloody rag in the sink, she gave him a stern look that reminded him of a natural born mother but nothing like their beaten down ma. "Rest first. I know yer exhausted, Callan."

Ignoring her concern, he found his screwdriver in the pantry from when he fixed the latch. "I think I left the rest of them in the basement."

Worn floorboards creaked as he took the stairs, and his battered back envied the soft groans.

Simple acts like mending a broken hinge or tightening the faucet helped him rein in his unraveling sense of self. His humanity slipped further away with each fight, but doing things like fixing the heater for his siblings felt normal, grounding. Vigilance kept his mind rooted, even when the violence sometimes let his innate nature dangerously loose.

Their father had been a nasty bastard, and Callan felt him in his DNA. While every man was capable of vile acts, not every man had the genetic makeup of a monster.

He did.

But the fights were a temporary solution. One he hoped to be through with soon. It was best to not think of what was. Survive the present. And when the time came to sever the now from the then, he'd start anew.

There was no salvaging the heater. By the time he'd given up trying to fix it, Gavin had woken. Innis set him up with a bowl of beans, hot off the stove, and went upstairs to dress for school.

"I knew you'd win," Gavin announced, laying out the paper notes and handling each one with awe in his wide eyes. Money was a respected thing in their household—rare and respected.

"Aye. And I asked yer sister te put tha' in the tin. Why don't ye put it away when ye wash yer bowl? It's gettin' late."

Gavin's wee fingers clutched the bank notes in two hands, counting them out in manageable piles. "Do ye think we'll finally have enough?"

Though Gavin never complained about their circumstances, Callan made sure the boy believed things could always improve. "Soon."

His brother's youth limited his experiences and narrowed his view of the vast world. Callan told him tales of a better life, a faraway home they would someday own. And Gavin gobbled up the fantasies like children cling to the magic of Saint Nick or Superman.

Callan savored the last of his brother's childhood years. Soon enough, Gavin would mature into a mouthy teen, and all that trust and innocence would fade. He wasnae ready. They needed a wee bit more time, and then Callan could set them up in a better area where a boy wouldnae be surrounded by so many bad influences and a girl wouldnae be surrounded by as many bad boys.

He tossed another log on the fire and collapsed on the sofa.

"Gavin!" Innis appeared, dressed in her uniform for school. "I told ye to get dressed as soon as ye finished breakfast. That was forty minutes ago."

Gavin rushed up the stairs. Innis sighed and bent to gather the scattered money.

Rhys watched her from the chair by the fire. "You look nice, Innis."

Callan frowned, wincing as his stitched brow pinched.

"What is it yer after, Rhys?" Innis's clipped tone echoed with suspicion.

"Just payin' ye a compliment."

A distrustful laugh burbled out. "*You* don't pay anything without expectin' somethin' in return. Did ye not have enough to eat?"

There was never enough to eat, yet somehow they always managed to feed Rhys, too. Innis seemed to take pity on him, like that scraggly, old, stray dog.

"There's nothin' I'm after. Just bein' gentlemanly. Can a man not be nice once in a while?"

"A man can. You cannae."

The two of them were making his headache worse. His fingers pressed to the bridge of his swollen nose, and he groaned. "Hold yer wheesht, the both of you."

"He started it."

"I was bein' nice!"

"I know exactly what ye were doin'," she argued.

Callan growled and snapped, "Christ, Innis, he was payin' you a compliment. And Rhys, find another girl te look at before I rip out yer eyes. Now, both of you, shut the hell up so I can rest."

That did the trick. The den quieted, and he sank deeper into the thin cushions of the couch. The heat from the fire finally penetrated the chill in his bones, and his concern over their bickering disappeared.

Resting his eyes, his mind slowly drifted like an unanchored ship at sea. Placid calm consumed him, and his aching body seemed to exhale one tired muscle at a time.

The cool press of lips to his brow had his eyes wrenching open, the tight skin pulling under his stitches. Gavin grinned, his childlike breath a fragile tease over the stubble on Callan's jaw.

"Bye, Callan. Love you."

"Ye have all yer books?"

"Aye," Gavin whispered.

Callan cupped his small face, the contrast of his delicate features thrown into stark relief against his battered knuckles. "Love you."

Rhys snored softly from the chair as Innis buttoned her jacket at the door. She nudged Gavin out of the house. "Go back te sleep."

"Have a good day at school."

The moment they left, the house seemed too still, as if the circulation was cut off at the foundation. A fresh draft seeped into the emptiness left in their absence.

He preferred when they were all together, but knowing they'd be at school meant he could rest easy for at least a few hours. Easing back into the sofa, his body quaked with relief, muscles throbbing.

He longed for the days when he'd only know tiredness, not this chronic, bone-aching exhaustion he battled now.

Drawing in a slow breath, he released the last of his fraught strength. But he never fully unloaded it. And knowing, after all he'd been through, that he still banked a reserve of strength, left him unsettled in ways he couldnae explain. Ways that gave him a healthy fear of himself.

Chapter Three

Glasgow—Scotland

"The payoff is ten thousand pounds, Callan. That's more than you've ever made in a fight." Rhys paced through the kitchen as Callan pieced together a sandwich and took a bite.

"It's crooked. I might not have a dignified job, but I have my dignity."

"Is this about keeping yer undefeated record?"

He scowled, the pith of his abilities sheered down to naked purpose by even his best friend when the right price sat on the table. "I dinnae give a piss about the titles those twats pin to my name. I just care that they pay me on time and that the fights are fair. Being undefeated keeps me in demand. It keeps food on the table and a roof over our heads."

"You'd still be in demand. They bleedin' love you."

"They dinnae fucking love me," he sneered. "I'm nothing to them but a dog in a fight."

Rhys shoved into the empty chair, green eyes crazed with greed. "Then why not take the payoff and be done with them once and for all? Ten thousand, plus what ye already have saved, could get us all out of here."

His stature was damn tired, crippled by the weight of his responsibilities. Rhys sometimes climbed onto the pile, forgetting he could make his own way. "I'm not a fuckin' sponge to squeeze. I'll fight for a fair purse, but I'll not tarnish my integrity. And fuck you for suggestin' I do. It's my name out there, not yours."

Genuine hurt flashed in his friend's face, and he drew back. "I love ye like a brother, man. I'm only delivering the message, letting you know what they're offerin'. It's one fight, Callan. One fight and ye could score enough to never fight again. I promise, my thinking is only about you and Innis and Gavin. I dinnae give a fuck about those setting up the matches. I'd never betray ye or cross ye. Tell me ye know that."

He believed Rhys wanted to believe that, but the older Callan got, the harder it was to trust others. Sometimes people did fucked up shite whether they agreed with it or not.

"I trust ye dinnae want to betray me."

"I would not. Not ever."

He finished the last of his sandwich. "I'm not takin' a payout. If they want a fight, that's fine, but it'll be an honest one."

Rhys's shoulders hunched, perhaps in disappointment, but he accepted Callan's decision. "You know, there's a chance he might wallop you. The Mountain's a fuckin' beast. Merciless."

Callan knew the guy's reputation. He was a foot taller than his six feet, and a good five stones heavier. Of course he had a chance of getting his arse crushed.

The man hailed from the travelers, a batch of lawless gypsies even the lowest of neds had the common sense to avoid. They stuck together, like bees to a hive. To them, life was about savage survival and clan pride.

The Mountain had been known to bite off men's ears, lips, and noses in fights, and swallow them whole. They said he did it to mark his victims, leaving nothing to be sewn back on.

"There's always a chance I'll get beaten."

"They say the last sorry bassa lost an eye."

One did not fight The Mountain without understanding the risks. He wouldnae leave the ring unscathed, whether he won or not.

The men who trained him and traveled with him also sanctioned deathmatches. Deathmatches led to bodies, legal hang-ups, and pricey cover-ups. They might have very few rules in the ring, but no one ever died under Callan's fists.

He wasnae a killer. That needed to stay true for his sanity to stay in check. But fighting The Mountain might very well destroy him, leave him in a way that death would be a blessing.

He should turn down the fight. Take the smaller ones and keep squirreling away his nuts. But inescapable leverage came with booking a dangerous fight—fixed or not.

"I'll accept no less than thirty-five hundred for the win." It was less than the payoff to throw the fight but much more than an ordinary purse. They'd hear that number and know he would deliver a fight worth witnessing. Sort of a *fuck you* to whoever thought they could buy him off and a taunt to The Mountain at the same time.

Rhys balked. "They'll never pay tha'."

"They will." Once he said it, he felt it. Vile curiosity would insist they made it happen now.

"If ye want that much, why not just ask for the whole ten thousand? At least then you'd be guaranteed to walk away, just take enough lumps to make it look real."

"Because I'm not gonna throw a bloody fight. Thirty-five hundred to the winner. They can take it or leave it."

The crowd for a fight between him and The Mountain would be huge. The price wasnae too improbable.

Rhys stared into his eyes, his concern working out like a math problem across his face. "Do ye think ye can actually beat him?"

"I think I'll try my best and that's the best I can do."

Honestly, he wasnae sure. The offer for a payoff to throw the fight—though from an outside party— made him wonder how many other opponents The Mountain had beaten fairly and how many were paid off. Perhaps his record wasnae a true measurement of his actual abilities in the ring. But Callan's record dinnae lie.

"He's a fuckin' beast," Rhys muttered, rubbing a hand over his face.

"We're all beasts."

Any man that stepped into that ring understood that. Being nearly bludgeoned to death on a regular basis had a way of stripping down a man and revealing the animal within. Strip them enough and the skin never truly grew back.

The unsettling truth that he'd been doing this too long and had been stripped to muscle and bone too many times told him everything he needed to know.

The Mountain might be a son of a bitch, but the darkness shackled by Callan's bones, that shallow puddle of strength even he never wanted to dredge, that was worse. Whatever lived inside of him could win this fight. If he needed to, he'd wake it up and let it off the leash.

"Book it. Thirty-five hundred one week from tonight."

Rhys got on the phone and made the arrangements. Within one hour they took the offer, realizing a high stakes fight might be just as good as a fixed one.

The seven days that followed revolved around high protein, portion controlled meals, grueling circuit training, and rest. Some days he'd spend hours simply meditating, trying to get his head into the game and clear away the stress of life. Others he'd spend sweating out his worries.

Innis and Gavin always fretted before a fight, but never tried to talk him out of it. But this time, once Gavin saw a picture of The Mountain, his unflinching confidence visibly shook.

"He's a tree, Callan."

"And I'll be yellin' *timber!* when I drop him like an oak," he teased, exaggerating his self-assurance to bolster his brother's.

He dinnae have room for doubt. Doubt invited other negative thoughts, like maybe he should have taken the offer to throw the fight, guaranteed an outcome, and secured a sure profit.

No.

There was still a chance he could win this way—dignity intact. He'd be able to look himself in the eye, no matter the victor. Though he might be a little disfigured and hard to recognize.

The day before the fight, Rhys pushed him to the point of exhaustion. He got a full eight hours of sleep and, once he woke, his heart pounded ahead of normal speed.

Anxious to get the match over with, he said goodbye to Gavin and Innis and reminded Innis to lock up after him.

"I will." She poured some chopped vegetables into the broth warming on the stove.

"I mean it. Do it now, Innis. I willnae be back until late." And who knew what condition he'd be in.

She rinsed the cutting board and counted out potatoes to peel. "As soon as I'm finished starting the soup."

He gritted his teeth and pressed a kiss to Gavin's head. "Mind your sister."

"Can you bring me back a lock of The Mountain's hair?" he asked excitedly, earning a scowl from Innis.

Callan dinnae know how to outwardly respond to such a request. Inwardly, he cringed, hating how desensitized Gavin had become and how easily he requested the maiming of another living soul.

"Say yer prayers before bed." Leave the Almighty to field that one.

On the long walk to the mill, his lungs seemed steadily short of breath and his steps sluggish. His ribs still werenae completely healed from the last fight, but his range of motion had recovered.

His strategy tonight would be speed. Like a bullet, he'd plunge in with force, attacking every vulnerable inch he could reach, and then pull back like a slingshot only to unleash again. If he kept his motions precise and unpredictable, the fight shouldnae drag too long.

The sight of bodies overflowing from the main entrance had both him and Rhys slowing their steps.

"Jesus." Rhys's eyes widened as the roar of idle chatter reached a deafening rumble.

Callan's heart vibrated up his neck into his skull. The place was fuckin' mobbed. "Come along. Let's get my hands taped."

As they cut through the crowd, men *and women* turned to stare. Once they were recognized, the excitement built like a wave, a growing tsunami climbing and sucking everything out of its wake and clearing their path.

"This is new," Rhys mumbled, a deep S curved along his forehead as he raised a brow at all the fuss.

A definite sense of importance floated in the air, making this fight more significant than all the rest. "We should have asked for more money."

Rhys laughed. "Bastards. Who knew this many people would show?"

Someone knew. That's why they wanted it thrown. Someone hoped to score a fine payout at the expense of their pounded flesh and spilled blood.

The swollen crowd had his ego clawing to the surface. Their chants and excitement for the coming fight infected him with a mix of shame and glee. While he loathed the idea of thrashing another man, he was human enough to desire the win. But no matter who won, they'd never be on the same level as those in this room.

They slipped into a private room, and the noise muffled to a distant drone. Using his meditational practices, he quieted his thoughts and let Rhys take charge.

Layers of clothing slipped off, and his laces were tightened. Water and fruit were shoved in his face, and he drank, taking intermittent bites.

"Ye gotta move around," Rhys said, once all the prep was done.

Callan paced over the cement floor, his head down and eyes unseeing as he psyched himself up for the battle. Rhys left to check the start time. As the door swung behind him, the echo of anxious spectators chanting something seeped into the private space.

It was too muffled by other noise to tell if they were shouting *Mountain* or *MacGregor*. Probably a mix of both.

The air thrummed with anticipation and promise. His flesh drew tight, damp with sweat, taut over muscle like the skin of a drum.

Rhys returned, opening and shutting the door with another wave of muffled sound. "Holy shite, there are so many people here."

"How long?"

"Ten minutes."

Time to check in. "Give me yer phone."

Rhys handed him his mobile and Callan dialed his sister. The service in the mill was shite, so he shifted closer to the broken window. Wind cut through the glass, regardless of the hole.

"Hello?"

"I've got about nine minutes. Just called to check in."

"We're fine. About to eat."

He let out a breath. They were why he did this. They were worth it.

Sensing his tension, she clucked. "You've got this, Callan. No point in givin' up yer cockiness now."

He grinned. It was her way of calling him dramatic. "Aye. I suppose not. Let me speak to Gavin."

"Come home to us in one piece."

"Aye. Love you."

"Love you, too. I'll get Gavin."

The certainty in his sister's voice dropped his anxiety a few notches. A dangerous cocktail of doubt and fear mixed in his gut. But Innis was right, he did better when he was cocky.

"Callan?" The sound of Gavin's wee voice stifled his fear.

"I'm about to go in, but I wanted to tell ye to expect a win."

Gavin laughed. "Really?"

"I'll do my best."

"Destroy him!" His baby brother yelled with enough hero worship and blind faith to shove the last of Callan's doubts out of reach.

"Consider him destroyed." He ended the call, and his heart bounced with impending energy. Time to let some of this lightning out of the jar. "Let's get this over with."

Rhys grabbed his bag of medical supplies and a few water bottles as they headed out. Additional lighting had been brought in, and a long banner with a picture of The Mountain hung down the rotted, far wall.

"We forgot to do your photo shoot," Rhys teased.

Callan frowned at the level of promotional material flung across the decrepit walls. Who was endorsing this? Typically, these fights came with a *how do you do* and nothing more.

"MacGregor!"

Identified, the crowd again parted, making a clear path between him and the ring.

48

"MacGregor, I need a word!" An older man approached, panting for breath. "I was told to deliver this to ye." The man's eyes bounced under the brim of his hat, his motions sketchy.

Callan frowned and took the thick envelope. Cracking open the seal, he peeked inside, spotted a hefty stack of bank notes. "Who gave this te ye?"

"I'm not te say. There's ten thousand there."

Aggravated, he flung the envelope at the man's chest. "Tell whoever gave this to you I'm not interested. See it gets back te him."

The man lifted his cap and wiped away the gathering sweat on his brow. "I strongly suggest ye take it." His rotted teeth delivered each word with a cutting stench.

"I strongly suggest ye get the fuck out of our way," Rhys snapped, in full guard dog mode.

The man glanced over his shoulder and Callan did a quick scan of the area. Whoever gave him that envelope was in the crowd.

Rhys gave the man a shove. "Get."

With a final huff, he turned, and the mob swallowed any trace of him.

"The pay off?" Rhys asked.

"Aye. I thought ye—"

"I did," he said, hands up defensively. "Tenacious bastards."

Rolling his shoulders, he shook off the incident, but Rhys held on.

"Stupid tits. Do you know what this means? It means whoever they are, they're scared."

Callan dinnae care who they were. People who tried to fix fights werenae decent people, and he wanted no association with them, mistaken or otherwise. "Let's get this over with."

The conciliator greeted him, going over the general rules and verifying the thirty-five hundred pound purse to the winner. Everything had been arranged.

Callan paced, waiting for his opponent to show. The crowd erupted, and he turned, certain The Mountain finally arrived, but not yet able to set eyes on him. He dinnae have to wait long.

Speakers, that were not typically present, pounded from brackets on the wall. Heavy drums and screaming metal guitars built in a crescendo, announcing the start of something unstoppable, promising the delivery of an unforgettable thrashing.

It might have looked like it was for the crowd, but Callan felt it in his spine, tingling through his gut. This was a gift from his opponent to him, a method of intimidation. It was working.

Gritting his teeth as tight as his fist, he ignored the propagated display, blocking out the music and roaring crowd. He wouldnae be distracted. A switch went off inside of him. Physical preparations had been made. It was time to mentally get in the game.

Then he saw him.

Towering two stories above the masses, The Mountain's black eyes shone flat like the surface of a lagoon. His hungry stare latched into Callan with a physical chokehold. Depthless, soulless eyes.

A socket of a mouth. A neck the size of Callan's thigh. And shoulders the breadth of a man.

Veins crowded his flesh, forming canyons on swollen muscle. Tattoos belted his bare stomach, twisting with sinew. Twin gutters angled down his carved hips, interrupted by a blue kilt with a bold white X. Scotland's national flag.

Legs, thick as logs, bunched with strength as his bare feet ate up the distance between them.

Callan swallowed, his gaze encompassing the entire beast of a man. The patch of hair twisted atop his bald skull was a blatant *fuck you.* That knot represented confidence. No one could touch him.

Rhys swore, but the precise curse disappeared in the thunder of the crowd. The Mountain spread his arms wide, like a peacock flaunts its feathers, and circled the sparring area, fists thumping his inked chest as if this was *his* show.

Callan waited like a lamb before the sacrifice, as inconsequential as an appetizer before a feast. And when his opponent's soulless gaze latched onto him again, he flashed a grin of rotting teeth, snapping as if he could taste the blood before the meal. The crowd exploded at the taunt.

Callan handed off his water bottle to Rhys and shoved past The Mountain to the center of the ring. He dinnae come to perform. He came to fight.

A priest approached with the conciliator, pinching a rosary cross between two fingers. The Mountain crowded in, breathing hard and rolling out any last kinks of muscle before the bell sounded.

The Conciliator yelled so they could hear, "No biting. No finger snapping. No throat punching. No hits to the bollocks. No shoving into the crowd. When the fight's called, you stop and back off. Understand?"

They both nodded, and the priest took over, lifting a hand and holding out the cross. "In nomine Patris et Filii et Spiritus Sancti."

Callan dropped to a knee and bowed his head, never one to turn away a free blessing. When the priest called *amen,* he sprang to his feet and clenched his fists until his knuckles popped.

Those precious seconds before the bell narrowed his focus to the point of a pin, rendering him momentarily deaf as everything in his peripheral vision disappeared. His heart thundered like a steady tribal drum, and then the bell clanked, propelling him into action, flinging him at his enemy.

The rush of noise slammed through him with physical force, roaring loud enough to thicken the air. Callan MacGregor no longer existed. There was no him, no ego, no hunger, no thirst. Only the necessity of survival and animal instinct to conquer The Mountain.

He threw the first punch, jarred by the solid, meaty wall of flesh that greeted his fist. The Mountain laughed, and Callan braced, drawing back and keeping his footfalls feather-light as he skirted his opponent's first heavy blow.

He jabbed, landing another punch in The Mountain's solar plexus. He might only be able to land quick jabs, but if he peppered him with strategically placed hits, striking critical zones, he could weaken him and go in for the metaphorical kill. Hit just right, he could contract the diaphragm.

He dropped a spattering of wisely placed jabs, thinking he'd made progress. But The Mountain tolerated him like the Queen's guard would ignore a fly.

Then The Mountain's fist slammed into his temple, jostling the world out of focus and throwing him to the ground. Gravel and soot scraped under his palms as he blinked his eyes back into focus.

The kick to his stomach lifted him off his hands and knees, tossing him to his side with a thud as he gasped for breath. Fire burned through his constricted lungs like fire.

Screams of excitement were the only thing that brought a reprieve. The Mountain was a bit of a crowd pleaser, and couldnae resist parading about whenever his fans applauded.

Callan's arms shuttered close to his sides as he shoved to his feet and charged. He launched himself at the other man, climbing onto his back like a wild animal and using all the strength in his legs to constrict his breathing. He locked an arm around The Mountain's thick neck, sealing his wrists in a tight hold, and squeezed.

Punches rained over him as The Mountain tried to knock him off. He flailed and scratched, but Callan's body had become a vise. Just a few more seconds and he'd pass out, and it would be over.

The Mountain staggered, and the crowd roared. Like an ancient oak, he teetered and swayed. Then … *timber*.

There was no amount of bracing to protect Callan from the impact. The Mountain dropped, his full weight smacking onto the ground with a booming clatter of meat and bone, trapping Callan underneath. But it wasnae over.

The second he loosened his grip, The Mountain had him. Callan couldnae throw him off or grapple across the floor. Crushed under the immense weight, his lungs fought for breath, claustrophobia setting in.

His jaw locked as meaty fists reached back and closed around his throat, tightening like a tourniquet. Gravel clung to his sweaty arms. His legs flailed, his hands clawing at those strangling him.

Circulation cut off. Blood rushed from his gashed eye, the old wound reopened by The Mountain's punishing fists.

His face bulged under the building pressure, his eyes protruding, and his hearing winking in and out. The fucker was gonna rip his head off with his bare hands.

"He's got him now!"

Numbness teased his fraying consciousness, the roar of spectators fading to a low drone as his vision tunneled and flickered with blotches of black.

"MacGregor! Get up, you cunt!" The screams sounded miles away.

If he blacked out it would all be for naught. His palms slid over sweaty sinew as heaviness compressed his trachea. His ears popped and his eyes bulged from their sockets.

Pinned beneath the heft of his weight, his upper body useless, he kicked and twisted his legs. Crushing weight slammed down on him, knocking the wind from his lungs until they contracted around hollow nothingness.

Callan clawed for breath in a frenzy. The Mountain slammed down again, emptying every crevice of air until Callan heard death trying to slip through his dry throat. His thoughts spiraled, and panic choked him as his brain fought for oxygen.

Drowning on arid, breathless nothingness, he struggled to break free. His need for oxygen was so frantic and overwhelming, he couldnae finish a single thought beyond the need to breathe.

Fire burned in his hollow chest cavity as three hundred pounds of solid muscle crushed the literal life out of him, and his vision flickered more black than alive.

His flailing limbs slowed, and his palms tingled, heavy and weak. His unhealed ribs splintered with every crushing slam.

It was over. He was going to lose. He couldnae hold on, and the ability to tap out seemed to have escaped his flimsy control.

Sliding his hand free to reach for the ground, he stilled, as his fingers caught on the knot of hair atop The Mountain's head. Gavin's words flickered through his oxygen-starved brain. The task of closing his fist seemed impossible.

One finger at a time, he locked down his grip. And once he had ahold of his sweaty strands, he jerked with the last of his strength. Hair split from the root, tearing with a shredding pop of snapping follicles and punctured flesh. The Mountain released an unholy growl and spun off of him. But Callan wouldnae let go.

The first gasp of air gave him the strength to roll to his side and protect his battered front. Wheezing in a lungful of air, he blinked hard, forcing his vision to clear.

Fire corroded his airways, and his throat burned as if sliced by a thousand razor blades. A strange crackle filled his lungs, fluid choking him from places he couldnae cough up. Punctured lung? Not enough time to think.

The Mountain screamed. Callan staggered to his feet, crumbling under his own weight. He needed to turn, to protect himself. Gasping for oxygen, he tried to find his opponent, tried to find balance.

Gravity threw him like a tornado spawns wind. He gripped the fenced walls of the ring, his fingers the strongest appendage at his disposal. A horrid sound ripped through him as he forced a lungful of air down.

The screams. Loud. Deafening. Pained. Gasping and panting, he clung to the fence and coughed hard.

The Mountain flailed, marching and clutching his bleeding head, howling in delirious pain. Only then did Callan feel the tickle of hair knotted within his fist.

Bellowing as crimson tears beaded on the surface of his head, the gigantic man cradled his skull and wobbled from heavy foot to heavy foot. It was now or never. Callan had no choice but to see this to the merciless end.

He charged and unleashed like an automatic weapon, letting off punch after punch until the towering giant fell like Goliath, shaking the earth in a crash that vibrated the world with shock.

In the brief silence of awe, Callan recognized his own surprise, but dinnae let it distract him. He pummeled flesh until bone lost shape and nothing but a sack of meat slapped under his fists.

Wet punches landed, again and again, relentlessly stealing the victory. He couldnae stop until he'd ensured it was over.

The announcement came like a whisper at the fringe of his mind, scrambled by rage and speckled with the beating sound of his fists. The Mountain was a slap of blood and tenderized muscle bleeding beneath him, but he couldnae stop.

A bell rattled like a rushing freight train, and the conciliator caught his arm, flinging it into the air. "MacGregor wins!"

Labored breaths sawed through his lungs and spectators poured forward, crowding and congratulating him. Shaken by the rushing need to survive, an unfit rage peeled through him, making him flinch away from the slightest touch.

Too many people. Too many strange faces. He jerked into a corner, but more people crowded him, touching and congratulating.

"Rhys?" He searched the sea of strangers, seeking familiarity.

Blood slicked down his arms, coating his knuckles and crusting into his fingernails. Blood of another man.

"Rhys!" Why was he not rushing to his side?

"MacGregor the Conqueror!" Voices called, victorious excitement punctuating their praise.

Panic welled up inside of him. The crowd made it impossible to see The Mountain. Was he alive? Had he killed him? *"Rhys!"*

"Callan!"

He spun, eyes as frantic as his rapidly beating heart. "Rhys?"

"Callan, over here!"

Spotting him, Callan shouldered off the hands stroking down his bloody arms and back. "Move!" He needed space.

Rhys's wide-gapped grin greeted him, a wild mix of thrilled shock on his face. "You were pure dead brilliant! Un-fucking-believable! I thought ye were done and then this animal came out of ye!"

He gripped his shoulder. "Get me out of here."

"Ye destroyed him, ye magnificent beast!" He laughed in an almost maniacal, disbelieving way. "They'll be talking about this for years!"

His grip tightened, and he hauled him close and hissed, "Get the money and let's go. Now." Intoxicated by relief and joy, his words werenae penetrating Rhys' euphoric haze. "Innis can stitch me up when we get home."

Rhys shook his head. "Callan, you daft cunt, there ain't a mark on you!"

He glanced at the rivulets of red sweating off of him. Not his blood.

His ribs were going to need time, but... He glanced at his fists and stilled. Locks of hair still tangled between his battered knuckles. Jesus.

"The money."

"I hear ya. Come along." Once they were moving, Rhys looked back. "Would it kill ye to be a little happy about the win?"

He'd be happy once he had that thirty-five hundred pounds in his hand. Got it home and into the tin. They might finally have enough for a down payment on a house, enough to start over.

Then the rest would come. He wanted to remember what it felt like not to physically ache from fighting. It would feel damn good to declare tonight as his last fight—go out the undefeated champion.

"Outstanding show tonight, MacGregor!" A hand clapped down on his back. "I doubt anyone will have the bollocks to fight you now."

He tasted the words before pushing them out. "Tonight's it. I'll not be fighting anymore."

Rhys pivoted, another look of shock stealing over his face, this one robbing him of his smile. "What?"

"I'm through. But I'll be thankin' ye for my money." He held out a hand, and the startled clerk slid the heavy envelope into his palm.

"Are you certain? Maybe ye just need a break."

Having heard the words out loud, he never wanted to pull them back. It was the first time he truly admitted how deeply he hated the violence he'd welcomed into his life. He wanted simplicity and peace. He wanted to have the time and normalcy to know a woman and a soft touch, things his circumstances hadnae allowed so far.

"If I never have to fight again I'm certain I'll be a satisfied man."

"What the bloody fuck does satisfaction have te do with it?" The clerk scowled. "You want te be satisfied, find a whore te fuck. Then come back here and do what God intended you te do."

Callan glared at the man. Leaning close, he hissed, "Don't assume to know anything about my God and His intentions for me."

They wouldnae be satisfied until he wore a mask of disfigurements and spoke in slurs. His life needed to be worth more than that.

Rhys grabbed his arm, tugging him away from the clerk's desk. "Come on."

Good thing, because fury still boiled close to the surface. He snagged the envelope and shoved his way outside.

The second they made it away from the smothering crowds his friend turned on him. "What the fuck, Callan? You're already tellin' people you're never fighting again? Maybe wait until yer head clears."

"This is it. I'm done."

The incredulous look on Rhys' face wasnae worth the small commission Callan shared with him. "Were ye plannin' on telling me before ye told the world?"

"No, because it's not yer decision and I willnae be talked out of it."

He shook his head. "Callan, ye just destroyed the most renowned fighter out there. Ye took the bloody title, and now you're just gonna quit?"

"Think of it more along the lines of retirement."

"You've lost yer mind. You're in higher demand now than ever before. They'll pay whatever you want."

"I dinnae enjoy having the pulp beat out of me. Nor do I enjoy hurting other men. This isnae the life I want."

"But Callan—"

"I said no," he snapped. "I've said my piece, and tha' is the end of it. You dinnae ken what it feels like te split someone's flesh open with yer bare hands night after night, te taste their blood on your lips and breathe it in for days. Ye cannae imagine the feel of having yer eyes nearly pushed from the sockets. I've done what I've set out te do, and it's over, Rhys. I want te live a life I can be proud of, a life where Innis and Gavin dinnae have te hide behind locked doors or fear I'll come home bludgeoned out of my mind. I'm through living in the shadows. Do ye understand?"

He looked like a petulant child who just lost his balloon. "Aye."

Though they walked home side by side, they seemed to experience polar opposite journeys. Callan felt ten stones lighter, as if he'd been given an insurmountable gift. Rhys seemed to be traveling the last mile of death row, carryin' the weight of the world on his shoulders.

Callan's head was clear. So clear, even rogue thoughts lacked purchase and flitted in and out without tamping down in the hammock of his mind. His worries seemed to be mentally lounging for what felt like the first time in a long time.

Then something caught in the damp air, a fizzling tinge that dinnae belong. His nose twitched, pulling him out of the comfortable nothingness and luring his glance to the darkened roads ahead.

Smoke. It billowed in a black funnel, camouflaged by the navy blue sky. A glow of light wavered low to the ground, hidden by buildings, but illuminating the black clouds billowing like heavy smog about the moon.

The scent burned so strong the taste of blood in his sinuses disappeared. Rhys's concern mirrored his own, and their pace doubled.

Callan's blood caught a chill. "Jesus." His tired legs were suddenly running, racing down the familiar blocks that lead to his home.

His knees pumped. A foreboding, errant thought drifted through his mind, this time anchoring down hard, but Callan dinnae want to think it. Couldnae think it.

"Callan, wait!" Rhys raced after him, but the crackling air called like a siren and Callan couldnae slow his steps.

His worst nightmare spilled out before his eyes as he turned the corner. Enormous flames clawed at his home, licking and swallowing the walls with such intensity the place was almost unrecognizable.

"Innis! Gavin!"

Flames beat over the walls of his house, engulfing the peak of the second floor and billowing out of every window. The noise was like nothing he ever heard, hissing and spitting like roaring hellholes hungry for life.

He shoved his way through the people gathered on the road. Why was everyone just standing there?

"Innis!" He searched the neighbors, jerking women to face him and shoving every unfamiliar face away. "Gavin?"

The stench and heat beat at his back. Faces deformed under the flicker of red and orange. They werenae there.

"Have you seen my brother and sister?" His gaze hunted through the crowd "Gavin! Innis!"

Sirens blared, as lights smeared the houses in a hideous blend of glowing reds. Rhys raced to his side, more frantic than Callan had ever seen him. "Where are they? Where's Innis?"

"I can't find them!" Callan screamed for them until his voice broke. He raced onto the front porch, immediately pushed back by the intense heat.

Firefighters dispersed, falling into action and hauling him back from the burning house as they readied their equipment. Not fast enough.

"My brother and sister are in there!"

"Stay on the street!"

He shoved them off, yanking his arms free and planting his feet on the ground. "I have te get te them!"

"You need te get back!"

Hoses snaked onto the yard and aimed at the house. The roof on the left collapsed, the frame melting into the flames. The fire moved so fast and the men so slow.

"They're in there!" Unthinking, he lunged past the men and raced into the heat. Shielding his face, he squinted through the smoldering clouds, his eyes cooking out of his skull.

"Callan, no—"

Flames scorched his face. His crackling lungs heaved and coughed. Thick, black smoke choked the breath out of him.

"In—" He hacked through her name. "Ga—" His voice scraped past his vocal cords in a painful scratch. *"Gavin!"*

Dropping low, he tried to escape the clawing smoke, but there was no dodging it. It was everywhere, hot and dirty. Creeping death and blinding heat.

He grabbed a doorknob and jerked back, the metal white hot and blistering his palm. Water hissed like steam, raining into the flames as if angering them. The smoke liquefied into muddy tar.

Pain grabbed him, eating through his clothes, searing into his flesh.

Delirium. So much pain. Scalding, agonizing, overbearing. The worst enemy he'd ever fought, and it was swallowing him whole.

"Innis! Gav—" Choking, he spewed out blackened phlegm. His eyes were on fire from the heat and his ears deafened by the screaming flames and whining structure melting around him.

Everything happened so fast. Water doused the inferno. He searched for any sign of them. Did the fire tip over the chairs? Why was the door to the basement broken? Scorched, in the middle of the charred floor, was the tin where they hid their money.

"Innis! Gavin!"

Hacking painfully, he collapsed. No choice but to cover his head and suck filthy breaths. The heat was inescapable, everywhere.

His entire universe shrank to a delicate fleck of burning dust. Eyes closed against the burn, he watched his world blow away like ash.

Tears burned his skin as he wept for them, calling in silence, unable to make a sound no matter how hard he screamed.

Angry flames climbed the walls, melting the wallpaper and lifting the charred curtains. The power and wind of the fire held him down. The stairs creaked and collapsed without warning. The whole house would fall, but he couldnae leave without them.

He rolled to his side, needing to move. The moldings bubbled. He mouthed their names. His last illusion of finding them crumbled to unchartered depths as the ceiling collapsed.

Flashes of his sister as just a wee girl racing down the hall stole through his mind. The ground burned his back, the fine fibers of his clothes melting into his skin.

Barren regrets ripped from his heart in a brutal harvest that promised nothing else would ever grow. They'd been so close. The bitter taste of loss choked him as much as the smoke and tears.

He surrendered to the merciless heat. He cupped the collar of his shirt over his mouth, sucking in a long draught of thick, hot, polluted air. He wanted to give in, but he couldnae. Not until he knew they were safe.

"Ga—vin!"

Hacking hard, he covered the back of his head. The flames were so hot. Too hot. His flesh would soon melt from the bone. How could anyone survive this pain? There was nowhere to hide.

The smoke overtook every crevice, creeping up from the floorboards, in from the walls, and pressing down from the crumbling ceilings.

"Innis!"

A crash and explosion of raging flames. Unbearable heat burst around him and something heavy crushed his legs.

Flames caught at the frayed cuff of his jeans, biting into his skin, on him, gnawing, but he couldnae roll away. He screamed in agony, his heart tearing in two.

Lost in the delirium of pain and grief, there came a humming stillness, a moment of isolated time when he realized this was how he would die.

Blackened flecks of cindered ruins feathered through the flames and he could no longer draw in enough breath to call for them or feed the need to cough. His throat collapsed, crumpling like a crushed can and the pain existed as only excruciating numbness. He gave in, embraced its vicious power, let it take him from this place.

His lungs filled. Black blood sputtered over his lips. Tarnished sweat colored his arms as he twitched and thrashed, but there was no escaping the pain. Blistering agony, inescapable torment. Scared and alone.

Trapped in a burning coffin of fire, he roared as the rubber soles of his boots burned into his feet. Even kicking frantically, there was no evading the agony. It was so intense, so overwhelming, he went mad.

Something grabbed hold of him, and he fought. Claws digging into flayed flesh, tender and blistered, skin falling away at the touch.

Blind. Deaf to all but the pain. Chaos ripped into his mind. A merry-go-round of images that made no sense.

His da smiling at him kindly. His mother's praising grin. The first sight of Innis wrapped in a baby blanket. The scent of her hair. The feel of Gavin's fingers locking around his thumb. The first time he saw his da hit his ma. The second time. The twentieth. The way his da looked at him like a stranger the day he left. The sight of his ma leavin' their home in a black body bag. The inconsolable way Innis had cried when she understood there was no reversing death. The sound of his promise to always protect them. The crack of his heart breaking with that vow.

The agony of too much hurt flooding in…

Chapter Four

The Royal Infirmary
Glasgow—Scotland
Four Weeks Later

Searing pain, more excruciating than any injury he'd suffered before, reigned over him. He welcomed it. Favored it to the stabbing grief gouging through his heart. A heart that no longer existed, punctured into nothing, shredded, hollow tears worn into his empty chest where hope once lived. He prayed for death.

His ravaged throat seemed nothing more than a dry, narrow tube, too small to squeeze a breath through. The entire trunk of his body ached from the inside out, each brutal inhalation pushing his lungs against splintered ribs.

No escaping the sting beaten into his flesh. No escaping the hurt.

He'd lost them. Lost everything.

Investigators were still working to identify the cause of the fire, still searching for his siblings' remains, but with the close of each passing day, the useless catalog of every week, the truth became inescapable.

His home lay in a puddle of mud and ash. Rhys had searched long after the flames had cooled leaving rotted cinders of soot and decay. No traces of Innis or Gavin. Nothing left to live for.

Everything he was and all he'd ever known had vanished. Nothing but pain. Nothing but hurt. Not even a merciful end to the gnawing grief.

No family. No relics from his childhood. No photos. Nothing. Just the aching, inescapable hurt of being turned inside out and left broken in the ruins.

He'd lain in this wretched bed for a month, a prisoner to his weakened body, counting down the days until he regained his strength. But then what?

Every conscious minute his mind tortured him with things that could have been, things that would never be.

He should have been home with them, watching over them. Everything gone. And for what?

Rage boiled inside of him, singeing the last of his humanity with agonizing regret. It should have been him to go. They were innocent. He'd have burned for a thousand years if it saved them, died a thousand deaths. But he'd failed.

He failed. And nothing he did would ever bring them back.

It should have been him. He was already dead inside.

No warmth. No happiness. No love. Just misery. All the good died with them. And he couldnae afford a proper burial, couldnae find their ashes or the strength or…

He had nothing.

The door creaked, and Rhys crept in, his face a mask of misery, but his pain only a fraction of what Callan felt. He wasted hours here every day. There was no point. Callan dinnae want company. He dinnae deserve visitors.

"Yer lookin' good today."

He turned his gaze to the opposite side of the room. He just wanted to be left the fuck alone.

In the days after the fire, he'd been trapped in some sort of nightmare, too medicated to make sense of things and too delirious on morphine to recall what had happened.

The polis found bones in the ruins, mixed within the rubble. Small, like that of an animal or young boy. Since then, Callan hardly spoke, and dinnae want any more reports. They were gone. He dinnae need the gory details driving the point home.

All other reports fell on deaf ears. He simply couldnae bear the emotional pain. And he internally raged at the physical pain that kept him grounded to this earth when he desperately longed for death.

Third degree burns on his legs and hands. They had to graft skin from his arse and thighs to fix the damage, but he'd never be fully right again. If only they knew the damage inside.

There would always be significant scarring. The rubber soles of his boots had to be cut away from his blistered skin.

His ravaged throat twisted as unshed tears seemed to crush his windpipe another degree. The grief was simply too much.

Poor, wee Gavin. Who knew what sort of man he would have grown up to be? He was young enough that Callan might have been able to replace the shite memories with good ones.

And Innis, she'd never know love or what it would have been like to have a family of her own. Such beauty and brains lost to a chanceless existence, stolen by miserable conditions and disadvantage.

He longed to join them. Planned to, as soon as he regained his strength. He dinnae have to be in perfect condition to toss himself off the Squinty Bridge down the River Clyde.

If he had a gun handy, he'd end it now. But Rhys fell apart when he asked him where his gun was. Sooner or later his friend would look away, and Callan would do what needed to be done.

"I've gone through most of the rubbish by now," Rhys said, filling the silence with unnecessary chatter. "I've found a few things that might be of interest to ye."

Rubbish? Was that what they were calling it? His siblings' ashes tossed to the wind. Rubbish.

The tick of a zipper coming undone told Callan he'd brought the items with him. He dinnae want to see singed memorabilia. He wanted his fucking family back.

"This looks like a ring. Maybe your ma's. Maybe Inn—" Rhys's voice cracked. "I know she wasnae much for jewelry, but maybe she planned te wear it one day."

Callan's chest caved in a little more. Moments like this, the pressure was too much. Keeping his gaze on the far wall, he ignored the tear that rolled from his eye, let the pain pierce him through. Maybe if it stabbed hard enough, it would finish him off.

A long silence unfolded. Rhys eventually pulled out another item. "This looks like a toy plane. I think it was probably Gavin's."

Not even morbid curiosity could draw his gaze. His face locked, every muscle refusing to look.

"This might have been a hairbrush of—"

"Go home, Rhys."

He couldnae stomach it. Nothing in him wanted to see proof that they were gone or a reminder of how they were taken from him. He could smell the singed items he'd brought. His clothes wore the charred scent of death and destruction.

"Do ye not want these things? These pieces of them?"

"No." He wanted to die.

"Callan, I know you're hurting—"

"Ye know nothing about my pain!" His chest constricted, drawing a sharp hiss of air through his bared teeth. The burned skin on his face tightened. He welcomed the ache. Locking his jaw, he growled, "Ye want to bring me something? Bring me yer fucking gun so I can join them."

"Callan…" His name was a plea, a whispered breath so full of pain it carried the intensity of a scream.

There was nothing more to say. His life had been a series of sacrifices with very few choices. In death, he should have a choice.

"Leave me alone," he rasped.

The sound of clothing shifting and a zipper closing was the last he heard of Rhys for some time. After that day, Rhys dinnae visit for a while.

Chapter Five

The Royal Infirmary
Glasgow—Scotland
Four Months Later

It had been months of grueling physiotherapy and endless waiting. So much effort put into healing when Callan's goal never wavered. The second he got out of this hospital he was going to find his siblings the only way he knew how.

Every day he had the nurses help him down to the infirmary chapel. His skin, especially around his calves and ankles, lacked the elasticity it once had, making it painful to stand for longer than a few minutes. Painful to sit, too. Painful to live.

Since having the bandages removed from his feet, he had little sensation where the grafts had been transplanted. The doctors said sensation would come back with time, but never feel exactly the same.

Movement of any kind was difficult. A numb man walking was like a deaf man talking. A lot of times he got it wrong. And every time he fell, the world got a glimpse of the rage he kept bottled inside.

He spoke to the visiting priest, confessed his sins, and begged for penance. He wasnae sure if God had a place in heaven for a man like him, but he was certain that was where his brother and sister were.

Taking one's own life was a mortal sin. Callan had to believe God would take mercy on his tortured soul. Christ's blood should cover all matters of sin, but his greatest fear said it might not save him.

Rhys knew his intentions. "You'll wind up in purgatory."

"Anything is better than staying here." No point in denying the inevitable.

"You would trade a moment of suffering for an eternity without them? You're thinkin' like a Godless man. A mad man. You're stronger than this, Callan."

His grief had eviscerated the last of his sanity months ago. And while killing himself might violate one of the commandments, it was his only option of escape. This excruciating healing process, always knowing he'll never be fully well, that was the penance for his sins.

"I'm already in hell. Purgatory would be a welcome reprieve."

"I'll not let ye do it."

"You're selfish to try and stop me."

"Bullshite! Yer my best friend and all I got left in this world! I know they were yer family, but I lost them too! Do you think it doesn't kill me te know I'll never see her face again? Never hear her laugh…" His voice broke under the weight of palpable sorrow. "Yer the selfish bastard thinking all this grief belongs te you and you alone. And now you plan on killin' yourself as well?" He snatched his coat off the chair and jerked open the door.

"Rhys, wait."

"Fuck you, MacGregor!" The door slammed, and cold silence enveloped him.

He didn't return for a week, but when he did, Callan immediately knew something was wrong.

"What is it?"

Rhys paced, wringing his hands and avoiding eye contact. "How strong are you right now? Honestly."

Callan frowned. "I think I can tolerate more than a kitten lick, but if someone hit me I'd probably shite myself. Why?" His fighting days were over, so he didn't understand the point of the question.

"The polis have been tryin' to reach you."

Everything inside of him tightened to an agonizing point of awareness. All the reports were done weeks ago. "About?"

"There's new information. They know the cause of the fire."

Of course. The fire.

He swallowed, unsure if he was ready to hear this. There had been so many rigged outlets in the house, and he told Innis not to use the iron anymore because the cord had frayed.

What if it was something he could have prevented? More guilt. More heartache.

Impatience filled him with the urge to vomit. "Out with it."

Rhys pivoted, his eyes boring holes into him. "It was arson."

Callan sat up, ignoring the pull of his tight leg muscles and the ache in his back. "What? How did they determine tha'?"

"I heard whispers and finally got the polis to question the neighbors. Apparently, some people on your street heard a … commotion. Glass breaking and furniture being thrown around. Someone broke into your house, Callan."

His skin tingled, waking forgotten nerves. He shivered at the strange chill. His brain cleared in an instant, his mind more alert than it had been in months.

His words escaped in a low growl. "Who was in my fucking house?"

He hadnae been able to picture his home since the fire, but now he was taking a mental stroll up the front steps. He could hear the creak in the porch, see the fine cobwebs fossilized around the moldings. He was always on her about locking the door.

"Jesus. She probably let them walk right in."

The color in Rhys's face drained. "The reports…" His gaze dropped to the floor. "They could hear screaming."

"And no one called the fucking polis?" But as the words spat from his mouth, he recalled all the times they'd ignored nearby shouting, and how angry his da would get when a neighbor would report him after one of his battles with their mother.

"They called when the fire started. Callan, they said it started with a Molotov cocktail thrown from a car. And they have the plate number."

He couldnae catch his breath. The need to spring out of bed mocked his broken body.

Too many questions bombarded him at once. Who would do this? Why? Had Innis and Gavin suffered? They must have attacked the wrong house.

His sweet baby brother. His beautiful sister. He couldnae stomach what could have happened before the fire if someone truly wanted to harm them. The briefest hint of a scream cut through his mind, and his entire body jerked. Someone intentionally hurt his family. Stole their lives.

Sweat beaded on his brow. His fingers closed into fists. "Who?"

"The car was stolen. The driver's a nobody—"

"*Who?*" A hot uprush of hate poured out of him. "Someone did this!"

Rhys's face pinched. "I asked around. He works for a man named Oscar Riordan."

The name nipped his violent agitation, some form of recognition poking deep. "Who is tha'?"

"Most know him as Rory."

He gave Rhys a baffled stare. "The kingpin?"

Rhys looked over his shoulder and quietly shut the door. Pulling a chair closer to the bed, he lowered his voice and said, "He was at the fight tha' night. I think he's the one who wanted ye to throw the match."

The blade of guilt pressed deeper. He dropped his back to the bed and stared at the overhead light.

"My family's dead because I refused te throw a fight?"

Rhys's hand hesitantly brushed his arm and settled, squeezing tight. "There's more."

"More?" He dinnae know how much more he could take.

"When I got the name, I started asking around. This Rory fella's a nasty prick, a real dangerous cunt. Drugs, black market crime, women, gambling, sex trade, he's got his filthy fingers in everything. He's got an underground army workin' for him, men like the one who showed at yer place that night. Not someone ye wanna be messin' with. I'm *only* tellin' ye because ye said yer too weak te retaliate."

"I'll heal."

Rhys met his stare. "Sometimes it's best te know when te walk away, Callan. This isnae someone you could take to the ring. You're in no position te fight anyway. This man's powerful. He'll destroy you—"

"I've got nothing te fucking lose. He already robbed me of everything."

No matter what he'd done, he dinnae deserve to see his family killed. And for what? Refusing to throw a fight?

"This doesnae make sense. They were innocent. If he wanted me, he should have come after me. I was there! He could have—"

"If we hadnae left so fast, he would have found us. According to others, he was looking for you. Only when he heard ye left, did he send someone to yer house." Rhys's face tensed. "Do ye remember the old man who offered ye money just before the fight?"

His vision glazed with savage rage, the need to kill chewing at his insides, breathing fire into his veins. "Vaguely."

"He told Rory ye took the payout."

The blood rushed from his brain. If he hadnae already been reclined, he would have plummeted to his arse. *"What?"*

Rhys nodded quickly. "Told him it was a done deal, which led te a lot of money shifting in favor of The Mountain. And if ye think about it, it really did look like it was over for a moment there. But then—"

"I won." His face numbed.

"You won."

He couldnae breathe. Couldnae think. Couldnae swallow. "I need … water."

Rhys filled a cup and handed it to him. Callan chugged it down and crushed the plastic in his fist.

"I want the name of every single person involved. The people at the house, the old guy from the fight, anyone who works for this Rory bastard. I want every fucking name of every fucking prick whoever paid that son of a bitch a compliment. I

81

want his mother's name, his children's. I want the fucking name of his dog. And I want the address te his fucking home because that's where I'm going te murder everyone he's ever loved."

"Callan, you can barely walk—"

He gripped his friend by the front of his shirt, the tight skin on his knuckles pulling painfully as his fist closed over the material. "And I want you te bring me your fucking gun."

Rhys plunged back into the chair. "Ye cannae go after this guy, Callan! He's not a street fighter. He's more powerful than anything we understand. He's got real mafia ties, crooked politicians te wash his balls, dealers te dress his estates in gold. This is bigger than the ten thousand pounds that old prick stole. Ye saw how many people were there tha' night. High rollers. Major money was lost, and he thinks ye stole from him. Be grateful he hasnae come to find you—"

"Enough!" Callan's eyes lit with vengeance. "No more excuses."

"This isnae your game, Callan. You cannae beat a man like tha'."

"I dinnae intend to beat him. I plan te murder him. And I'll be doin' it with or without yer help, Rhys."

His brow twisted with concern. "How're ye gonna go after a man like tha' when ye can hardly lift yer own dick te take a piss?"

Frustration choked him as the truth of his friend's word burrowed into the cracks of his hollowed shell of a heart. Why was death so easy and life so hard?

Blinking up at the ceiling of the infirmary, the goddamn ceiling he'd been staring at for almost half a year, he accepted he couldnae leave this world until he avenged his brother and sister.

"Get me what I asked. I'll get better. Stronger. And when I do, I intend to slaughter every single person who played a part in their deaths." *Then it'll be my turn to die.*

Chapter Six

Glasgow—Scotland
Seven Months Later

Sweat poured into his eyes leaving a puddle on the floor beneath his face. Every press of his nose to the ground drew a grunt of exertion, a taste of hard-earned satisfaction.

His muscles screamed for relief, but Callan mercilessly pushed himself harder. The relentless beast in his gut demanded every pound of flesh and needed him strong to act as a vehicle for vengeance.

Every day he grew more savage than the last, more bloodthirsty. *Rory.* The name played like a taunt in his mind, a target for his rage and pain, a final hope in this unending hell called life.

Rory was going to look into his eyes and feel true pain. Callan would make him hurt until he begged for mercy. He would make him pay. They would all pay.

He kept his growing rage bottled inside of him, boiling so hot it singed every thought. His injuries were inconsequential when it came to his need to destroy those who murdered his family, burned down his only home, annihilated every tangible memory, leaving nothing but pain and ash.

The memory of Gavin's innocence steered him. The robbed potential they stole from Innis galvanized him. The hollow ache in his chest starved him. And the bloodthirsty hunger inside of him focused him.

The pain was real. The pain was unflinching. The pain was dependable. The pain drove him.

When he was through with Oscar Riordan, and the geezers who worked for him, the world would know what he'd done. Callan MacGregor would have the last word.

An eye for a fucking eye. He'd take his eyes, his balls, his teeth, his fucking limbs. He'd eat his fucking heart. Mothers would cry just from hearing rumors of what he'd done.

Soon. It would all happen very soon.

"Callan!" The music cut off as Rhys stood in the doorway, looking none too pleased with being woken up. "It's five o'clock in the fuckin' mornin'."

"I was up." He hardly slept anymore. And when he was awake, he was focused on his goal.

He switched arms, balancing on the scar tissue covering his knuckles, fist planted in the wood floor, as he did another set of one-armed push-ups.

"So ye wake the rest of Scotland? Bleedin' Christ, I have neighbors, Callan."

Panting through his teeth, he counted down then rolled to his back. He grabbed a medicine ball and hissed out fast breaths as he twisted from side to side in a circuit of Russian sit-ups.

"Let them complain." One look at him and they'd shut up quick.

"Can ye see past yer anger for one minute and remember what it is te not be such a fucking cunt? Ye used te be a decent man. At least save yer anger for those who deserve it."

Cutting a scathing glare to his friend, he dared him to go on. "Seems te me, I'm the only one who fucking cares."

Rhys's chest lifted. If he challenged him, he'd lose. "Fuck you, Callan. This isnae you. If they were here, they'd hate the bastard you've become."

He counted out another set of reps. "This is who I am now."

"I liked the old you."

He rolled to his feet, picked up the sledgehammer and swung, whaling down on the massive tire. His skin protested, but his muscles tingled for more.

"Old me's dead, Rhys. Sorry, you missed the wake."

"Innis and Gavin would have wanted you te move on. They'd have wanted you te find peace."

He spun, tossing the hammer and gripping Rhys by the throat, backing him into the wall. "*Don't fucking assume to know them better than me! Do not fucking dare! They're dead, Rhys. Fucking dead!*"

Rhys caught his wrist, his anger spitting into Callan's face. "Ye know I'm right! She'd hate seeing ye like this!"

He jerked his hand away, letting Rhys fall to the floor, gasping. Hoisting up the sledgehammer, he pointed it at him. "Dinnae come up here tellin' me what they'd fuckin' want when they cannae want for anything anymore. This is about what *I* want. Me. What I fucking need. I want to hear that bloody cock scream in pain, beg for mercy that will never come. And when he breathes his last fucking breath, I'm going to whisper my name in his ear so he can tell the devil himself Callan MacGregor sent him."

All color washed from Rhys' face. "Yer fuckin' mad. I think you need to speak to someone, Callan—a priest maybe."

"I dinnae need a fuckin' priest. I've made a deal with God." He tossed the sledgehammer on the ground and grabbed an armful of thick rope, hauling to the far wall.

"God or Satan? I honestly think you believe you're going to kill people."

He laughed without humor. "Not just kill. Slaughter."

Rhys watched him like one might watch an absolute lunatic. "I'm worried about ye, Callan. This isnae justice. You'll find no peace—"

He scoffed. "Justice cannae touch monsters like Oscar Riordan. Only greater monsters can."

"And that's what yer becomin', a bloodthirsty monster."

No choice. Rory had authority at every level from the wealthy to the impoverished. He had syndicates in Glasgow, Edinburgh, and even some tucked away in the Highlands.

Wealth was his poison of choice, and for the right price, he'd commit any manner of sin. There were no limits to his ruthlessness. Women werenae safe, children werenae safe, no one was. He needed to be put down, and only a fearless maniac could do it.

Callan intended to dismantle his entire empire, one piece of scum at a time. He had nothing left to lose. Death would be a welcome rest, but so long as he was still breathing, he planned on collecting souls.

He might be morally bankrupt by the time he finished, but he wouldnae stop until he stole every life Oscar Fucking Riordan loved—including that of his own.

The fool should have come after Callan and killed him as well. But he'd left him in a world of misery where his only purpose seemed to be assuring evil men reaped every bit of what they sewed.

Hooking the ropes to the heavy grommets in the wall, he turned. The doorway was empty. Good. He dinnae need anyone telling him how to fucking feel.

Maybe Innis and Gavin wouldnae approve. More likely Innis would have something to say about his new philosophies. But what he'd said was one hundred percent true. They werenae here. What bloody difference did it make guessin' if his intentions were right or wrong when they'd never know for sure?

Never know.

Never.

He would never know what they were thinking or hear their voices again. He was already starting to forget little things, like the shape of Gavin's ears and the sound of Innis's laugh.

He had no photographs, no keepsakes of any sort aside from the burnt relics Rhys had saved. Ashes to ashes.

The only memory of their existence now lived in his broken mind. So when anybody, including Rhys, assumed to know them better than him, he grew very territorial, as if they might steal away the last few memories he had left of his precious family.

Aye, there was definitely a touch of madness wreaking havoc in his head. But he preferred lunacy to sadness, found purpose in its relentless nature.

And soon it would end. Soon the fucking monsters of this world would reap the justice they deserved. He'd bathe in their blood, baptized, reborn, forgiven. Or not.

This wasnae about saving his soul. It was about taking theirs.

Chapter Seven

Saratoga Springs, New York—America
Four and a half years later—Present Day

Emery Tanner averted her gaze as Wesley, professional athlete, and guest at the hotel, eased his limber form against the edge of her reception desk, his exposed arms tan and roped with sinew from vigorous training.

"That's a great name. Emery." He spoke the three syllables as if they tasted like his favorite food. "Sexy."

Born with an abysmal inability to take a compliment, exacerbated by overly critical parents, she flushed. The marbled countertop acted as a shield, hiding her shifting legs, as her toes bunched in the tips of her navy blue work pumps. "Thanks."

Managing the reception desk at the Imperial Regal Hotel and Spa of Saratoga Springs meant catering to a variety of privileged, upper-class guests who retreated to the charming country of upstate New York for weekend getaways. Saratoga

Springs was a stunning town to visit but a boring place to live.

"You got a boyfriend? I bet you have at least five guys dying to go out with you at any given time."

Yeah right. Men weren't usually so direct with her—at least not the man she wished would notice her, the only man she'd consider dating. "No, I'm single."

She wasn't unattractive. Just … average. Mousey blond hair that, without highlights, was completely dull and unremarkable. Average weight and height. No overly striking features that made her stand out in a crowd in a good way or a bad way.

She was just an ordinary girl in her early twenties. She could get a boyfriend but had her heart set on a specific man. So she remained single by choice.

"Do you ever stay here?"

His strong jaw and straight nose gave him a Kennedy appeal. Or perhaps that was the magic of his confidence working overtime. Entitlement wafted from him as much as the stale scent of top-shelf bourbon.

She shook her head. "I live about a mile away. Not a far commute." Ugh, her banter sounded so lame.

His sandy blonde hair wanted to curl at the ends, and a dimple flirted with his smile when he turned on the charm. He fit the perfect definition of masculine beauty for New England *WASPs*—lean, flawless, safe … not at all edgy.

His gaze skipped from the cuff of her blazer to the lapel, landing on her breasts, and her chest tightened.

Sliding the checkout forms in front of her, she used the stack of printouts like a shield, a rush of inadequacy making her fidget. She should be delivering the forms instead of fondling them and practicing her flirting skills on a random guy who got lost on his way back to the bar from the men's room.

But chatting with guests and acting hospitable was also part of the job. "Where are you from?"

"I live in…" He might have said Chicago. Or maybe Georgia.

Movement in the bar across the lobby caught her attention, and her gaze drifted past his shoulder. Her breath hitched as her heart tumbled in a delicate flip when her stare fell longingly on the most beautiful man alive.

Callan.

Her soul sighed under the unmovable weight of her crush. Wesley's voice faded to a distant drone as her senses bathed in all things Callan MacGregor.

He was her heart's compass, her obsession, her reasoning for so much, including this job and the late hours she kept.

So gentle and so kind, but also terrifying for reasons she couldn't understand, reasons that warned she should fear him but fed her addiction all the same. He was a stunning paradox, a mysterious tapestry of secrets she longed to unravel. Watching him, her insides melted. She ached to examine every stitched inch of his soul.

Wesley continued to prattle on about his hometown, selling it like a travel brochure, but with the success of a failing time-share.

"Is it nice there?" she heard her distracted voice wonder while her thoughts drifted elsewhere.

Various athletes lingered at the bar. The most rambunctious groups were oversaturated men, cut loose by their coaches and managers for the last night of the conference.

"Definitely. And the view of the lake is choice."

She resisted the urge to crinkle her nose at his tragic vocabulary. Not everyone could have a lexicon of language and a voice that teased every nerve in her body like Callan had.

She often fantasized about Callan's deep timbre, imagining the feel of his accented words wrapped in that thick Scottish burr breathing over her skin. The greedy way each letter clung desperately to the next, teeming with lush, rolling elocutions as the broad brogue of his tongue tormented her with sensual secrets only the two of them would ever share.

But it wasn't just his mouth tormenting her. Callan also spoke with his eyes, and when he sometimes looked at her like she was the only woman alive, she existed purely for him.

Her heart fluttered at the mere thought of his attention, her insides pulling with languid heat. His soft-spoken gentleness contradicted his rough edges, yet she ached to touch him.

Not that he'd ever come close enough to whisper sweet nothings, but, in her fantasies, he gave her everything—every secret, every sigh, and every syllable.

"Do you know what I mean?" Wesley asked, a look of expectation telling her he'd wait for her answer.

Crap. What did he just say?

She blinked. "Um, yeah," she agreed, hoping her response worked.

"It's a total buzzkill, but that's part of the job…"

If she tipped her head, she could keep her eyes angled at Wesley, but still watch Callan as he wiped down the tables.

He moved like poetry, rhythmic and smooth. So graceful. So agile. So strong.

Yet, at times, she caught him unconsciously massaging his muscles or favoring one leg over the other. Perhaps he'd been a soldier in Scotland, or in some sort of accident.

Three years of working across from him and she still didn't know his exact age, so she'd likely never find the courage to ask the cause of his injuries. His dark hair and distinguished jaw made her guess he was somewhere between his mid-twenties and early thirties, but his eyes seemed much older. Crystal blue, and hauntingly sad, as if they'd seen a million untold tragedies.

He was a far cry from traditionally handsome, but still the most beautiful man she'd ever met. His flaws were the makings of a masterpiece, even his crooked nose, which looked like it broke more than once and had never been properly fixed. His face was a battleground of scars, each one a story she longed to hear.

She'd never seen him clean-shaven but suspected he left the scruff to cover the nicks along his jaw. But such blemishes never mattered to her. Once she'd asked how he got the scar above his eye, and his gaze turned distant.

"Scotland has good areas and bad. I don't come from the good," he'd said, hardly explaining anything at all.

She glanced at Wesley's unblemished face, then dropped her gaze to his phone as he slid through pictures from a recent vacation. Why did people torture other people with slideshows of things that were only interesting when seen first-hand?

His thumbnail looked bitten painfully short. "Here's our last trip to Aruba. You ever go scuba diving?"

She shook her head.

After graduation, she'd gone as far away from home as financially possible, but the distance between New York and Kentucky cost her. Her independence came with expensive responsibilities.

Lavish vacations and deep-water excursions weren't in her budget.

"You'd love it." How would he know what she loved? "You're not supposed to touch anything, but last time we went down I couldn't resist snatching a piece of the reef as a souvenir. It's *that* pretty."

She frowned. "Doesn't coral die if you touch it?"

"Who's gonna know?" He dragged his thumb through another slideshow. "Here we are on the catamaran."

Entitled people bothered her. Here was a golden Adonis, everything a woman should want in a man, and yet she felt nothing. The implied assumption that she should care what he looked like on a catamaran cruise only enhanced her disinterest.

He was one of many athletes staying at the hotel for the annual conference, refined specimens who had golden futures in the next Olympics. There had to be something wrong with a woman who couldn't appreciate all that beauty in one place. There was definitely something wrong with her because every single one of them couldn't hold a candle to Callan MacGregor.

But it was her job to politely converse with the guests who approached her desk, so she smiled. "I guess, as a swimmer, you're at home in any body of water."

"Definitely. Been taking lessons since I was a baby. Competing since I was ten. How about you? Any sports?"

"I ran track one year in high school."

His gaze dropped, measuring her in ways that made her uncomfortable. "You look like a runner." Blond lashes fringed his hooded gaze. "So, anything fun happening around here tonight, Emery?" He tacked on her name implying a sort of familiarity they didn't share.

"Things shut down pretty early in town." She adjusted the checkout forms, tracing her finger over the corner of the stack until every sheet fell perfectly in line.

The back of her neck tingled and her fingers fluttered to where a wisp of hair slipped free. Her gaze shifted past Wesley, and all sound fell away.

Warmth bloomed in her chest, bursting like champagne bubbles, as Callan's gaze collided with hers, piercing her composure from a hundred feet away. Sometimes, when he looked at her like that, she felt so connected to him she wondered if he could hear the catch in her breath from all the way across the lobby. Her trembling fingertips gripped the marble countertop as chills danced over her skin.

He gave a subtle nod, and a smile spread across her face, too emphatic and too genuine to disguise. Drunk from one simple glance, she flushed and dropped her gaze.

Wesley, noting her grin, looked over his shoulder and frowned. "It must get pretty boring around here then," he said, vying for her attention and winning it out of pure hospitality.

"Not really." Her attention flicked back to Callan, but he was no longer smiling. Unease darted through her as he glared at the reception desk.

Her fanciful heart wanted to believe jealousy formed that scowl. Callan's possessiveness challenged at the sight of another man speaking to her. But that was insane, being that she and Callan only ever shared polite, co-worker small talk.

But she wanted to play along with the fantasy—even if only in her own head. "I should really get back to work."

She had a lot of slips to deliver. One hundred athletes and their coaches, managers, trainers, and physical therapists put the hotel at maximum capacity. And they were all scheduled to check out tomorrow.

"What time do you get off?"

She logged out of the open computer program. "I'm here until four." She wanted to look back at Callan, but not until Wesley left.

He checked his phone. "So, in two hours?"

Her gaze jumped to the computer clock. Was it already that late? Callan would be leaving soon. "Around then."

"We should meet up."

Not expecting an invitation, his words caught her off guard. She quickly camouflaged her surprise with a soft laugh so he wouldn't take her rebuff personally. "You'll be asleep by then."

"I'm wide awake. Maybe I'll hang out and keep you company."

Impatience gnawed at her insides. On Friday nights, Callan left right after two when the bar closed. Today was Friday.

So much energy went into anticipating his visit to reception, missing that exchange would be a devastating loss. She'd have to wait twenty-four hours for the opportunity to talk to him again. And she had a feeling, if Wesley didn't leave, Callan wouldn't approach.

Her cheeks pinched with a polite smile. She needed to get rid of him. "Aren't your friends waiting for you?"

"They're fine." He rolled his eyes. "They're all wasted anyway."

It wasn't just his friends who had been drinking. "The bar's closing. They'll probably be looking for you."

"I'd rather be here, talking to you."

Right on cue, a gaggle of tall men shuffled into the lobby, their athletic agility skewed by too much liquor. Their voices echoed off the marble walls, profanities and rowdy laughter punctuating every sentence.

A knot tangled in her belly. Callan was already wiping down the taps. "I have to deliver these soon." She adjusted the stack of forms.

"What are they?"

"Check out slips."

His head cocked, his clipped blond curls staying perfectly in place. "Can I come with you?"

Take a hint! Her smile fit like waxed lips over her mouth, artificial and stiff. "It's really boring."

"We can talk. Make it fun."

"Sorry." She bit her lower lip and lied, "I'm not allowed to do that."

Hooded, hypnotic eyes looked back at her. "I won't tell."

Just like the coral reef he stole...

His lack of respect for rules pissed her off. He wielded his charm so easily it would surely open doors for him—probably already had. He'd grow up to be one of those men who needed little words like *no* spelled out every time.

"Sorry. Cameras." She pointed to the computer, knowing he couldn't see the screen. "My boss would see."

"There aren't any cameras in the halls."

"S—sure there are." How did he know that?

He smirked as if silently calling her a liar, but too polite to speak the accusation out loud. And it wasn't necessarily a lie. There were *some* security cameras around the doorways and in the stairwells.

His teammates stumbled toward the elevators, tripping over their own feet and fumbling as they tried to navigate the open space. It was time for them to go. All of them.

She took a step back. "Sorry. I don't make the rules."

An obnoxious burp ripped through the air, pelting off the walls with ripping acoustics, and the group of drunken athletes laughed. "Wes," the burper yelled. "Where you been all night, bro?"

She glanced at the bar. Callan was stacking chairs on top of tables, swinging each one up with one hand as if it weighed no more than a feather.

His glare drilled into the group of men, and her heart jolted with a spike of urgency. "You should go. And maybe tell your friends it's quiet hours."

He chuckled, a strange vide ricocheting between them. "Wouldn't want the hotel police to come after us."

Did he know the worst that would happen was a call from the front desk—from her? If things got too out of hand, which they never did, she could call the police. But guests would have to be belligerent and damaging property to go that far.

Flies with honey, she thought, reinforcing her smile. "Hotel police can be very threatening." Not a trace of vinegar in her tone.

He winked. "I better see that they make it to their rooms quietly then."

He stepped away, his arm stretching as his fingers clung to the marble countertop as long as possible.

"See you later, Emery."

"Goodnight."

She silently counted to ten, holding her fake smile, as Wesley rejoined his friends. His gaze found her one last time as he huddled into the elevator, and something tight and sharp pinched her chest, gone before she had time to examine it.

The elevator doors glided shut, cutting off the obnoxious shouting, and finally severing her from her hostess façade. She sighed and rolled her shoulders. Big groups like this one always made the nights longer than they actually were.

Her head turned toward the bar, finding Callan's familiar blue eyes watching her again, and all her tension melted away. When she smiled with true emotion, so did he.

His striking size and battered beauty rendered her mute on most days, but she welcomed their quiet method of communicating. It saved her from babbling like a first class idiot, and he never seemed bothered by her shyness.

They were both reserved—Callan sometimes painfully so, as if *afraid* to speak to her at times. While masculine men weren't supposed to have obvious fears, there was something achingly fragile about Callan. One look in his soulful eyes and she was lost in a sea of vulnerability. Stark. Afraid. Alone.

He was her dark secret, a consuming part of her life no one knew existed. A decadent treat she never wanted to share. Crumbs of his attention were worth a feast from other men. Exactly why she emotionally starved herself for this moment every day, hoping to eventually get a taste of all that was Callan MacGregor.

Emery patiently waited for him to wrap up. She discreetly checked her makeup and snapped the compact shut, tucking it in her purse under the counter.

A shaky exhalation trembled over her freshly glossed lips as the bar lights dimmed then flickered to black, extinguishing all the shadows. It was her favorite and least favorite moment each night, those last few seconds of his shift when they shared more than a few stolen glances and actually talked.

Her fingers smoothed down the front of her blouse as she tried to calm her nerves. Anticipation tumbled like a freefalling summersault into the pit of her stomach—heady with excitement and deaf to any instinctual fear.

Maybe she was a fool for wanting him. Callan's secrets, whatever they were, were dark. His reserved mannerisms seemed a deliberate mask meant to hide a savage nature, a shield that protected him from the world as much as it protected the world from him.

But she sensed his innate goodness, a defining code that guided his moral conduct on the safe side of right and wrong. His kindness called to her, promised he'd respect her and never hurt her. So while something warned Callan MacGregor was a man to be feared, the most she could dredge up was a respectable degree of caution.

And despite the brutality she sensed hiding under his surface there were also hints of vulnerability, and he treated her in an almost protective way. On the nights he stayed, he always walked her out. And when it snowed, he cleared off her car.

Callan claimed to hate the heat of the sweltering summers in the States, but never minded the cold—said the rain reminded him of Scotland.

And ever since the night he straightened the buttons on her coat, she loved winter, too.

"It's cold," he'd murmured, his sure fingers gently fastening the clasp. So simple and strangely natural, yet probably one of the most erotic moments of her life. A button. *"Has no one taught you how te properly button a coat, Em'ry?"*

Her heart stuttered every time he dropped the middle syllable of her name, the first half pulling from deep in his throat, the R rolling over his tongue like a passionate kiss.

The few words he'd spoken to her over the years could be collected and kept in the palm of her hand. The small number she had, she treasured, each little moment as subtle as a breeze carrying the vigor of a tornado, sweeping her clear off her feet.

She sometimes worried he had a woman, perhaps a family, back in Scotland. Irrational jealousy could burn a hole through her belly, but three years and a button hardly gave her possessive license.

Last New Year's she'd thought he might kiss her, but as always, something held him back. That had been nine months ago, and nothing since. Like a boxer pulls a punch, every time he reached for her, he drew back.

It messed her up because sometimes longing seemed all she could read in his eyes. But after all this time, those silent, hungry stares never amounted to more. Yet here she was, balanced on the threshold of desire and need, wanting him again. Still.

Her heart lurched as she watched the dark cavity of the bar, waiting for the moment he'd reappear. Tugging at the hem of her blazer, she did a quick inspection of her skirt and sucked in a deep breath. Awareness tingled low in her belly, and she swallowed a shallow breath, her lungs twice as tight as usual.

Unlike other nights, he left immediately after his shift finished on Fridays. She didn't know where he went or what his life outside of the Imperial entailed, but the thought of him possibly meeting a lover tortured her on a regular basis.

And there he was.

Her breath held as his dark figure sliced into the light. Denim-clad legs and heavy black boots contrasted with the lobby's white marble floors. His black T-shirt blended in with his black, wool coat, but neither disguised his bulk.

With the strap of his bag crossing his broad chest and his hands wedged into the pockets of his coat, his attempt to make himself appear smaller showed. He failed.

Her breasts pressed against the thin fabric of her blouse as she breathed deep, waiting for that precise moment when she could hear the rasp of his clothing over his skin, the air pulling through his lungs, the smell that only belonged to *him.*

His gaze held her in a tight grip as he crossed the lobby, a long-practiced goodbye she waited for every day from the minute she first opened her eyes, akin only to the first smile he gave her when she took her post at the desk each night. As his purposeful strides closed the distance, she balanced on the razor-sharp edge of desire, exposed and thirsty for a mere taste of him. A sip. A drop.

Locked into those eyes, powerless under his spell, she always let him speak first. "I've come te say goodnight te you, Em'ry."

Her entire being shivered. His gravelly voice penetrated her senses, sending her nerves on a rollercoaster ride of endorphins and desire. He withdrew his hands from his pockets, resting them on the counter, and she breathed deep.

His hands fascinated her. Strong. Large. Nails clipped to the quick with broad fingertips and strangely blunt thumbs.

Black ink always stained the first knuckle of his index finger, as he constantly wrote in the leather-bound book he kept with him. Wide, somewhat deformed knuckles, bleached of pigment, pressed into the countertop separating them. Her pulse thumped wildly as he grinned at her in all his unrefined glory.

Sheer masculinity. A wallop of capability. A taste of sorrow. A hint of roughness. A touch of danger. A heap of carnality.

She wanted to know how hands could get that way but never dared to ask. More than her discovering the cause, she wanted permission to touch the scars, trace the discolored spots, soothe any painful memories. An impossibility, when she'd never been invited to hold his hand.

"How was your night?" Her voice always came out a little breathy at first.

"I did well enough. Should be a slow weekend once the conference clears out."

Her lips trembled as she tried to retain her smile without appearing overzealous. Sometimes when he spoke to her she smiled at the wrong times, so she learned to filter her emotions. "The bar was packed tonight."

Thankfully, the athletes were mostly men. There was nothing quite as wretched as watching beautiful women throw themselves at Callan—*not* a rare occurrence.

"Aye. I've got a banger of a headache. It'll do me lovely te get some rest."

She loved his unique vernacular and phrases. Despite his sometimes unfamiliar words, Callan spoke slowly enough for her to understand, and often more eloquently than American men.

"They *were* loud."

His gaze shifted from her eyes, dropping lower and quickly returning. When he watched her the way he was now, she grew painfully self-conscious of her flaws, wondering if he noticed how her lower teeth were not quite as straight as the top ones. Or if he found her face unremarkable. If only he knew how much he invaded her routine at home, how every stroke of mascara over each lash was placed for him.

"I saw ye had company."

Recalling the way he'd glared earlier, she made light of the situation and rolled her eyes. "I thought he'd never leave."

One dark brow quirked higher than the other, a clever trick of face muscles she wished she could mimic. "Did the bugger ask ye out?"

The territorial tone of his voice spoke of implication, and it became harder to breathe, thinking he might stake some territorial claim. "I … wasn't interested."

His eyes darkened to sapphire. "Good ye chased him off then. A rammy lot. They must've drunk twice their weight."

The backhanded warning stung. Was he implying Wesley only talked to her because he was wasted?

"The guy talking to me wasn't drunk." Though he'd been drinking.

He leveled her with a piercing, perceptive gaze. "They were *all* wrecked. Aside from me servin' them, I suspect they were dabbling in somethin' upstairs. I cut some of them off."

Maybe he was right. She dropped her gaze to the counter, not caring about the man who was there earlier and wondering why it meant so much to the man here now.

Her breath caught as the tip of his finger brushed her jaw, lifting her chin, barely making contact. The swipe of a feather would have left more of a physical impression, yet his brief touch somehow reached into her lungs and stole her breath.

Her gaze lifted and her heart raced as those soulful eyes watched her, possibly seeing all the insecurities she tried to hide. His head cocked, and he frowned, unspoken words chasing between them.

"I dinnae mean to offend you, love. Drunk or not, I think every man tha' walks through tha' door wishes he had a right te speak te you."

Her fingers clutched the cool lip of the counter as her knees softened. A flurry of wings tickled the inside of her belly, low and warm, soft and sweeping.

A hollow ache yawned inside of her, desperate to feel the gentle caress again, hold his hand to her body, and beg him to continue touching her. But the moment was over a second after it began.

Frustration clogged her lungs, making it hard to take in a full breath. Mixed signals were shooting everywhere. He didn't like when men lingered at her desk, yet he did nothing to mark his territory.

Because she wasn't his territory.

"It's okay," she lied. She had to look away— had to stop torturing herself like this.

He was as reliable and as teasing as an echo, always coming back but never lingering long enough to be real. Swallowing hard, she took a step back from the counter. The longer her ruined heart pined, the more her heartache became her own fault.

What was wrong with her? He clearly wasn't interested in anything more than a work friendship.

Her desperation hit her with the force of a hurled brick. Not the first time the obvious struck her hard. Right on time, the sadness swallowed her whole.

If he wanted her, he could have had her a thousand times by now. It was amazing she remained standing. Three years sacrificed for a disinterested man cumulated into a stunning weight. Guess that was why they called it a crush.

Her gaze skittered to the elevators, looking anywhere but at him. Like any addiction, coming down from the high was the worst. Reality was always waiting. "I have to deliver the checkout slips."

"Aye. It's gettin' late."

And you have someone waiting for you, don't you?

Other nights he stayed until four, not driving away until she safely started her car. But not tonight. Not on Fridays. Where did he go?

The elevator bell pinged, and the doors parted, drawing both their attention and stretching the opening for him to escape. Marco, the evening maintenance man, pulled the buffer onto the marble floor.

She nodded a silent hello and tried to smile. Maintenance waxed the floors every night, and the machine was loud, so she usually used this time to make her deliveries.

Callan knew her routine by heart, just as she knew his. At the sight of Marco dragging the plug to the outlet, he adjusted the strap of his shoulder bag and stepped back a pace.

"I'll see ye tomorrow night, Em'ry."

The ache bloomed. Tomorrow. Like a glutton for punishment, she'd wait for this moment all over again, no matter how much the repetitive end result slayed her every time.

"Goodnight, Callan."

"Be safe."

They were the last words he said to her every night. She lifted her hand and watched him walk away.

When the automatic lobby doors closed behind him, she shut her eyes. Three years and her courage failed her again. She blamed herself.

Having been raised in a Christian Science home, she still struggled with any sort of direct confrontation. It remained an ongoing battle to prove to herself that people were not victims of circumstance, as her parents believed, but independent thinkers in possession of free will.

But that decision had come with a fair amount of pain. Her family believed pain and suffering were necessary parts of life. Emery preferred a more anesthetized approach, one that avoided discomfort whenever possible.

Rejecting her family's faith meant sacrificing her family. And that, unfortunately, hurt no matter what the differences were in their beliefs.

Her fingers paged through the forms, checking one last time that they were in graduated order by floors and hallways. Her eyes blinked hard when they glazed at the sight of so many room numbers. She was getting sleepy and welcomed the excuse to take a walk.

She'd taught herself how to be an independent, modern woman. Eventually, the rest would come. Relationships were always the most complicated, as the nature of her upbringing left her short on confidence and common ground. But every day she grew a little bolder.

The guys she met since leaving home didn't know her family's background. They saw her as basic. Basic was better than sheltered or strange. Basic was closer to normal, and that's all she really wanted to be. But to Callan, she wanted to be more.

She might never be woman enough to parallel Callan's potent virility, but she wasn't ready to surrender the dream. Gripping the stack of checkout forms, she ambled to the elevators. Tomorrow she'd try to find her courage all over again.

Marco smiled as she passed, lifting his headphones off his ears. *"Cuidado con el cable,"* he said, pointing to the power cord running along the floor.

She stepped over it and offered a polite grin. "I'll be back in a little while." She flashed her larger than usual stack of forms.

He nodded and waved. *"Hasta luago."*

Once inside the elevator, she reached into the pocket of her blazer and removed her earbuds, thumbing on her cell.

The gentle piano of Rhianna's *Stay* matched the downbeats of her heart, every lyric representing everything she wished she could say to Callan. Every begging wish she hoped to one day voice.

HURT

114

Chapter Eight

Saratoga Springs, New York—America
Present day

Making her way to the second floor, Emery double-checked the numerical order of the forms. At least she was getting in her daily cardio. By the time she finished she'd have done roughly two hundred squats from sliding papers under guestroom doors.

Strolling through the empty corridor, she zigged and zagged in a serpentine pattern, slipping receipts under the dark cracks of each listed door. By the time she reached the top floor, her thighs were burning pleasantly and her skin warm.

At the far end of the hall, her ears perked at the distant ping of an elevator, though it was hard to hear through her earbuds. Sometimes guests ran out to their cars at night. Plucking her headphones free, she scanned the empty hall but didn't see anyone.

Just hearing things.

She worked her way through the remaining slips. As she bent to deliver the last form, the hair on her arms prickled.

A soft click jerked her gaze to the opposite end of the hall, but again, no one was there. Freaking herself out, she left one headphone dangling while the other played in her right ear.

When the icemaker gurgled, she let out a breath. Cubes rattled into a bucket, and she shook her head at how paranoid she could be sometimes. Ridiculous. She popped her earbuds back in her ears and headed to the elevator.

Pressing the button for the ground floor, she lifted her heel and flexed her ankles. Checking her phone to see the time, she cued up Fine Frenzy's *Almost Lover,* her mind going right to Callan, filling with unfinished fantasies. Un-started fantasies.

The doors parted, depositing her adjacent to the lobby. The loud hum of Marco still buffing the lobby floors overpowered her music. Time to put it away and play the game of how long could she go without thinking of Callan.

Killing the music, she coiled the cord around her phone and slipped it into the pocket of her blazer. She stepped into the ladies room.

They were almost out of toilet paper in the middle stall. She made a mental note to let Marco know.

Righting her stockings, she flushed the toilet with the toe of her pump and unlatched the stall door—"*Jesus!*"

The somewhat familiar smile wasn't enough to settle her nerves, and when she staggered back, nearly tripping over her own feet, his appearance in the ladies room registered, startling her even more.

"Boo," he teased, and she frowned, utterly thrown by his presence.

"Wesley? What are you doing in in the ladies room?" *Seriously?*

"Found you."

His smile had the opposite effect he intended. Or maybe it had exactly the effect he hoped. Either way, she understood in that moment there was something very unsettling hiding behind his grin. Something that scared her enough to automatically know it was in her best interest to play it cool and not show him he'd startled her.

Straightening her shoulders, she tried for firm yet friendly. "You shouldn't be in here."

He shrugged.

Schooling her expression, she eased her hip away from the toilet paper dispenser and blew out a frustrated breath, her heart whipping against her ribs as she stepped within his reach and quickly moved to the sink.

"I saw you on my floor and followed you. Everyone else is passed out."

Her brow pinched as she skated her hand under the foam soap dispenser. "You followed me?" Her gaze bounced between his reflection and the sink.

"I wanted to talk some more."

Her lips flattened, unease poking at every nerve as he watched her through the mirror. She quickly rinsed the suds from her hands.

His persistence was disturbing on so many levels. "I have to get back to work." Maybe she'd ask Marco to play cards with her so no one else would linger at the front desk.

He shrugged. "I'll keep you company."

She didn't want his company. Pulling a paper towel free from the dispenser with a thunk and a whoosh, she tried to think about how to politely yet firmly decline.

Nothing like this ever happened before and she didn't know how to graciously ditch someone who excelled at inviting himself where he didn't belong. Maybe Marco could get rid of him. How could she casually let the custodian know this guy was bothering her?

Her gaze shifted to the door. She could still hear the distant hum of the buffer.

Taking her time to dry her hands, she watched Wesley through her lashes. His previous charm appeared overtaxed by booze and ego, and she now found him the opposite of attractive. He ranked creepy more than anything else. She needed to get back to the lobby.

Enough. She tossed her crumpled towel in the bin.

Who did this guy think he was? And why was he still smiling like that when she'd done nothing to make him think his presence was welcome?

She tried for politeness, but her tone contained impatience. "Excuse me. I have to get back."

Thankfully, he stepped aside and let her pass. The hairs on the back of her neck lifted when he brushed a finger down her arm. Even through the sleeve of her blouse and blazer, her skin revolted at the caress.

"Wait." His fingers curled around hers, and when she jerked her hand away, he laughed as if it were a game. His other hand pressed into the tile wall, blocking her way.

"Let me pass." Her agitation bled into resentment. This wasn't funny.

"Why do I get the feeling you're blowing me off, Emery?"

She wasn't doing this. "Please move." He was freaking her out, and if he got any closer, she'd shove her way out the door.

"I wanna talk." Fraudulent charm dripped from his watchful eyes, melting his smile into an insincere smirk. He didn't move his arm. Didn't touch her. He even let go of her fingers, but the way he looked at her, the weight of such unwanted charm, the infringing prickle of a threat, it violated her personal space without ever encroaching on the distance separating them.

Her heart tripped out of beat. She never considered how blurred the fine line was between panic and pride. Fear that she might make something out of nothing had her vocal cords paralyzed. But a small voice inside of her said now was the time to scream.

"Please let me pass," her voice whispered, unrecognizably weak.

Fear choked her, fear she wasn't sure should exist. She couldn't scream. Dreaded embarrassment kept her quiet, despite her terror of pain—or something worse.

Muzzled by the worry that she might humiliate herself by overreacting, she despised the soft request. Wondered where her strength had gone. Her courage was likely hiding off with her voice.

The distant buzz of the buffer still vibrated from the lobby. Would he hear her if she yelled?

His fingers closed over the lapel of her jacket, lifting it away from her body and stroking the seam without actually making any contact. Her mind worked like a scoreboard, weighing every move, tallying which touches actually crossed a line. She wasn't sure.

They all did. Maybe not. Maybe she was tired, and this was just—

His finger flicked the stiff fabric right at the slope of her breast. Intentionally.

"Open the door, Wesley." She used his name in hopes that it might encourage cooperation.

"What's the rush?"

"I think I hear the front desk phone. If I don't answer it—"

"No, you don't." He shifted his feet closer.

She couldn't catch her breath. The door was right there, but he was blocking her path.

"Please."

He casually dropped his arm from the wall and stepped aside. Something untrustworthy hid in his eyes as he waved a hand, inviting her to open the door.

She didn't care what game he was playing. She just wanted to get the hell away from him—possibly call her boss or Callan. Ask someone to wait with her until the end of her shift. Even Marco, who hardly spoke English, would do.

Two quick steps and her fingers closed around the handle. She yanked the door open, and a heavy hand slammed into the wood beside her head. Something hit her back, and pain exploded in her face as her cheek whacked the door.

Fear spiked and vibrated inside of her, making it hard to worry about the injury. She tugged at the handle, but he jerked her away, lifting her feet clear off the ground and shoving her roughly into the counter.

"Stop—"

His larger body forcefully wedged her against the rigid edge of the counter. "Dumb bitch."

He was fast, faster than she anticipated. He pushed her against the sink, shoving her shoulders down, crowding her body, and pinning her wrists behind her back, crushing her hand.

The scream she'd been holding ripped from her throat, painful and hoarse as he twisted her arms grotesquely, wrenching her body back.

"Shut up!" He bent her wrist, hitting some sort of pressure point and her knees buckled. Her

weight fell into the sink, the cold, damp surface unforgiving against her chest.

"You're hurting me!"

"Shut. Up." The fist in her hair jerked hard. Tears sprang to her eyes.

Her scream fizzled to an agonized whimper as he wrenched her neck back, and then panic shrieked through her in a furious sob as his hands tugged at her clothes.

"Get off of me! *Help!"*

His heavy fist thumped the back of her head, and her jaw cracked the countertop. Her teeth clacked. Precise pain exploded in her skull, leaving her momentarily deaf and blind. Metallic blood coated her tongue.

No one had ever purposely hurt her before. The shock had her body quaking. Enveloped by panic, she jerked and thrashed.

He hit her again. His fist locked in her hair, smashing and grinding her face into the counter. Her feet slipped over the tile floor, one shoe flinging off her foot as he shoved her roughly against the damp surface, smacking her head against the metal faucet.

The lip of the counter wedged into her stomach with bruising force, knocking the breath out of her. His knees jammed between hers, forcing her off balance.

"Somebody help me!" Tears burst from her eyes as he pinned her down and hiked her skirt over her hips.

Her body vibrated, jittering with fear and denial that this was happening to her. Absolute terror rushed through her when he tore at her stockings. The thin shield shredded from her skin, tearing away in ribbons.

"Please... Stop! *Help!*"

"Shut. Up." He hit the back of her head, enunciating each command, and her face smacked against the porcelain sink, pain bursting in her cheek as tears stole her vision.

Bile rose, burning her throat as his hands pawed her. His aggressive seeking scratched her tender parts. She clenched her body, but his strength seemed indomitable.

She shrieked and thrashed, kicking at him as hard as she could. He twisted her wrists higher, and sharp agony shot through her arm.

"*No!*"

Her panties tore away, his nails scraping bare flesh, ripping up skin and leaving burning tracks scored into her flesh. The brunt of his weight crushed her against the vanity with bruising force. Her hips stung from the impact of his shoving.

Heat. She felt the burning heat of his body pressing against hers. Her feet scrabbled along the floor, seeking purchase and finding none.

"Please, stop," she sobbed, voice swallowed by terror, the pain choking her as he twisted her arm.

He yanked her thighs apart, ripping a wail from her throat.

"Bitch." His hand fumbled between their bodies, clumsy and urgent. "Open your fucking cunt!" His vile words spilled like acidic threats, burning her on impact. "Fucking slut."

The first brush of his engorged flesh against her tender folds unleashed a blood-curdling scream that had no end.

His fist slammed into the side of her head, and her lungs collapsed as he entered her with brutal force. Her inner walls burned at the intrusion, but he didn't relent. Impaled, her breath filled her like water, wheezing, suffocating, choking. She was drowning. There was no air.

Empty yet full. Shattered yet trapped. He gored a permanent hole in her, punctured every part. He split her in two, stabbed so viciously that when she finally felt the slightest moisture soothe the pain, she feared it was blood.

Her eyes squeezed shut. Her mouth gaped in silent horror. How long would it go on? Time no longer mattered. He was killing her, yet she breathed, groaning through the agony, as he took what could never be returned.

Why? No, no, no, no…

The world silenced, but it had always been a lonely place. His disgusting grunts as his body sawed into her filled her mouth with vomit.

She choked on her own bile until it dribbled over her lips into her hair. Harder he pushed, like he hoped to kill her.

Her vision blurred into a siphoning hum. Blood or puke trickled from her nose, clogging her throat in a bitter mix of disillusion.

"Please," she sobbed in a voice she didn't recognize. "Please…"

Her arm went numb, only sharp shafts of pain with each jolting thrust.

His hissed breaths beat against her neck, covering her in an invisible filth she'd wear the rest of her life. He was going to break her arm if he pushed any harder. He was breaking *her*.

Already broken.

Her mind fractured, splintering into shards that cut away at her sanity. Gouging, cleaving, stabbing.

Again the rollercoaster of pain gutted her, and this time when she vomited, it went everywhere, spraying into her eyes and drowning her cries.

Her legs gave out, and her body sagged. No more…

"Stay still!" Something slammed into the back of her skull. Her jaw collided with something wet and hard, but her eyes wouldn't open. Couldn't open.

He pried her body apart when it fell limp, the searing pain cutting right to her heart. Her broken cries ricocheted in the shrinking room until she couldn't scream anymore.

Her world narrowed to the point of a pin. The bones in her hand snapped with an agonizing crunch, but she was too beaten to do more than whimper and spew the burning saliva she could no longer swallow.

Excruciating pain blasted up her arm. The fire he put in her scorched her womb where her babies should someday grow. He burned through her like acid, a hot poker, lurching the contents of her hollow stomach until another bout of vomit burst past her lips.

Her hair and face lay in her own waste as she tried not to choke on her cries. Cruel, intrusive, piercing thrusts bulldozed through her with relentless stabs until every fragile objection withered into dull acceptance.

Tissue scorched and countless invisible scars formed, each one carving deep. His ruthless force desecrated her soul. Annihilated her dignity. Eviscerated any future of intimacy.

He violated every sacred inch of her being.

He ... *raped* her.

Forced into a quiet corner of her mind where denial grew, she somehow found a safe place to hide. Her body broadcasted every cruelty, but she wasn't there. This wasn't happening to her.

And as his body jerked hard, grunting and spoiling her to the last drop, annihilating her sense of security forevermore, smashing the lingering pieces of her that still thought like a little girl, and snapping the reed-thin confidence that allows women to rise, he let her fall to the floor like unwanted garbage. He demolished her. No longer human, just a receptacle for pain. His filthy finish seeped past her swollen abused folds and wet her battered thighs.

Shame enveloped her, more agonizing than any physical ache. Eyes unfocused, her tongue silently caressed the word *no.*

No.

No.

No...

The hollow mantra offered no protection.

The phantom weight of his body still clung to her as she folded like a broken doll, a marionette cut from its strings. Lifeless.

She wrapped her arms protectively around her gored center, unsure if this was the end or the beginning. Perhaps he'd murder her next. He'd already stolen the life out of her.

His shoes squeaked over the marble, pointing in her direction. She cowered like a beaten dog. Would he kick her? Humiliate her beyond what he'd already done?

If she thought of what he'd done, the pain became unmanageable. She didn't know how to navigate it, how to not think it, not feel it.

Pressure crushed her chest as her heart slammed against her ribs. Her body shook uncontrollably. Her unsteady hands closed around her head as she whimpered like a wounded animal.

Breath jerked in and never seemed to let out. Her throat and eyes welded shut as she braced for whatever he planned to do next.

He won. She couldn't beat him. She had no defense against such savage brutality. She just didn't want to hurt anymore.

"No more," she begged. "Please." Face wet with tears, she repeated the plea. "N—no more…"

Sometime later the silence registered in the stormy aftermath of her tremors and fear.

Time passed in immeasurable chunks of confusion. Not seeing him was somehow as terrifying as seeing him.

It took a long time to trust he was truly gone. And then the fear of being alone tortured her anew.

Her dungeon now protected her from every terrifying reality on the other side of the door. She wished she had the strength to block that door, but it was so far.

Bile and wasted tears clung to her hair and clothing. Her stomach roiled with regret, sadness suffocated her, snuffing out any flicker of logical thought.

She mourned things she couldn't name, things she didn't remember but innately knew a girl should always protect. They were all gone. She was gone. Just a husk of a woman left behind. Desecrated.

Everything hurt. Her thoughts, her body, her lips, her feet, her nail beds, her teeth, her gums. Flesh held her together, broken bits shattered within.

Her sluggish mind took its time to form a chain of necessity, simple enough for her body to follow.

Find help. Call the police. Get somewhere safe. Her thinking had never been so naked. Stripped. Bare.

Rolling to her hands and knees, her tender stomach lurched, her crushed hand a useless claw, incapable of supporting her weight. She tried to crawl and crumbled.

A pained sob tore from her ravaged throat, and she collapsed, protectively cradling her battered fingers. Her shaking arm folded against her chest as she rolled onto her back and swallowed down the ache.

The metallic taste of blood bloomed in her sinuses. She pressed her cheek to the floor, cool and calming, and simply breathed.

Determination to escape winked at the periphery of her mind. Stillness won. Time passed in uncountable measures. She needed to move, but her fear and wallowing shock kept her down.

Some innate part of her commanded she rise. Beneath the wreckage of her body and soul, an indignant voice shrieked for her to pick herself up off the floor and find help.

Dizzying pain engulfed her, but somehow she crawled to that door. Somehow she rose to her feet. Somehow she stood and stayed standing. Somehow, she got the hell out of that bathroom.

Find help...

Chapter Nine

Saratoga Springs, New York—America
Present Day

Callan gripped his face and growled, staring through his fingers at the hotel entrance where Marco dragged the buffer over the marble floor. The car was warm. He should just go. She was perfectly capable of taking care of herself.

Jealousy. That's what this was. He was behaving like an utter tit.

He wanted to slaughter the fucking prick who'd been hovering around her reception desk most of the night, but he had no right to stop anyone from speaking to her. No claim to her time or her beautiful smiles. And he never would.

"She doesnae fuckin' belong te you." His glare narrowed as he stared at his battered reflection. "And she'd be crazy te waste a single smile on you."

If he knew how to shut off this volcanic upheaval inside of him, how to mute the imprisoned passion, he might be able to one day let her go. For now, he was trapped.

She was everything. The essence of delicate grace. Skin as soft as a summer peach. Body as lithe as the baton of a willow. And he was nothing. Lost to her perfection like a candle to the sun.

He shut his eyes and sighed. Time to drive away.

He shouldn't have touched her tonight. He was getting sloppy when he needed to be stronger. He'd been so good about keeping his hands to himself. Nothing since he'd slipped last New Year's Eve. But tonight, when she cast her eyes away from him, he couldnae bear it. *He* was the one who had a claim to shame, not her.

He'd forgotten himself, forgotten his vow not to touch her. And in a moment of weakness, lost in the endless voyage of barren opportunities that was his life, he caressed her.

As his hideous fingers appeared against her flawless skin, rage filled him. He wanted to break his own hand to save her from such filthy contact. She was clean and pure, and his hands had been washed in blood.

It wasnae totally his fault. When she spoke, the air turned to wine, and his senses drank her in until all inhibitions were lost.

Locking his molars, he pulled the gearshift to reverse but left his foot on the brake. His glance returned to the lobby doors. Marco still had the buffer going, which meant she'd already gone to deliver her papers.

132

He threw the car into park and hesitated, his eyes flicking to the rearview, scanning the overflowing parking lot. They were at maximum capacity.

Something wasnae sittin' right in his gut. Perhaps it was the awareness that so many drunken men rested under one roof.

His gaze skipped to the dashboard clock. 2:52. He should have been home by now.

He gripped the key in the ignition but left the engine running.

"And what excuse will you have for comin' back te work after the bar closed and you've already left?"

He banged his head into the seat. He could tell her his battery was dead or maybe that he forgot something. He could pull a few wires to make it look legit—

"Jesus."

Shutting his eyes, he tasted the desperation of his thoughts. But what if his hesitation was a sign he should stay?

Or maybe it was just his dick, wantin' what it would never have. "Fuck!" He slammed his hand onto the steering wheel and yanked the keys free.

Climbing out of the car, he crossed the parking lot. The lack of empty spaces added to his concern. These were special circumstances.

The moment he stepped under the carport, he pivoted, marching back to his car. "Idgit," he mumbled, still gripping his keys. "What the hell are ye thinkin'? Go the hell home where ye belong. Yer fuckin' pathetic is what ye are."

His hand fell on the handle of the car door, and he paused, his gaze again pulled to the illuminated doors leading to the lobby. His stare lifted to the numerous guestroom windows. The majority were dark, but some were still lit.

Marco pushed the buffer across the tile. Still no sign of Emery. And why would there be? He'd seen the size of her checkout pile tonight.

"Fuckin' Christ."

Pocketing his keys, he stormed back to the hotel, not stopping until the automatic doors parted and he had no choice but to show himself or look like a total dolt wandering back and forth in the cold.

Marco spotted him and pulled his headphones off one ear. "¿No vas a casa?"

The few things Marco said to him, Callan could usually translate. *Casa. Home.* "I forgot something at the bar."

"Ah. Bueno." He covered his ear with the headphones again and returned to buffing the floor.

Callan pulled a chair from a table and removed his journal from his back pocket before sitting down, body angled toward reception. Lifting his hips, he unearthed a pen but did nothing more than tap it on the leather cover of his book and stare at the elevator doors.

This needed to stop. She'd turned into an addiction, and that was never the plan.

He wanted her more than his next breath, but he would never have her. To lay even a finger on her would be a sin.

His gaze dropped to his deformed hands. Burned. Broken. He'd bludgeoned, strangled, and snapped countless bones with these hands. Covered mouths as they desperately pleaded for mercy. Stolen several last breaths.

A crimson sea of carnage lay in his wake, and to invite her into his life, risk sullying her perfection with his vile past would be a greater crime than any other he'd committed.

It was his honor to watch over her—no one else seemed to take the job. But it was also his duty to keep his distance.

Of course, he wanted to slaughter anyone who looked at her. But he'd resisted so far. Blind men noticed her beauty. And his jealousy got a nightly workout every time some hard up fuck glanced her way. They even smiled when their wives were with them.

Looking out for her was one thing. Stalking was another. She wasnae even at her desk and yet, here he was.

What the bloody fuck was he doing there? One night. He gave her one night a week that belonged completely to her. Friday was that night.

The rest of the week she was stuck staring at his mangy face while he waited for her shift to end just to see she got safely to her car. She dinnae seem to mind him lurking, but she also never—*not once*—asked him to stay.

After the New Year's slip, he'd made the Friday rule, promising each month that passed he'd add another night until he eventually followed his schedule and left her to fulfill hers. But winter melted into spring and spring warmed into summer, and here he was, already in fall, and not keeping his word to leave her be, even on Fridays.

"Fuckin' pathetic," he mumbled, flinging his journal open and paging' through the ramblings and various sketches that kept him sane.

His gaze fell on a doodle of Emery and calm washed over him. His thumb traced the inked lines of her profile.

He dinnae know what it was about her. But the moment she walked into his life he was gone, enchanted, trapped under some sort of spell.

She was a wisp of a woman. Naturally slim with fair skin and the eyes of an angel. Soft brown hair with blonde threaded through. She always wore it twisted into intricate styles, and he loved trying to figure out how she held it in place. When he sometimes spotted a hairpin, his fingers itched to pull it free.

Her legs went on for days. A wee thing next to him, but womanly. She was what inspired artists to chisel into rocks. She was a masterpiece of immeasurable beauty and soft-spoken sweetness.

She was good and kind and patient with everyone that walked into the hotel. And when she looked at him, he could feel her stare before he even met her gaze. She was magnificent. But she was a woman.

136

Women were delicate. They were breakable. They made a man vulnerable.

He'd loved two women in his life and lost them both. But his feelings for Emery were far from familial. He had no comparison. His life before moving to the States overflowed with violence, lacked everything else, everything tender.

He dinnae know what to do with his feelings, dinnae want to chance finding out. He knew better than to get close to someone as fragile as Emery.

Women were breakable. Men, unfortunately, were not *as* delicate. He'd have died a thousand deaths for his sister, Innis. Perhaps he already had. Not a single one actually killed him.

He knew how to hurt. He knew how to maim. He knew nothing about touching a woman and had even less business experimenting with one to find out.

He dinnae have any decency left. His crimes were too many to name. His sins too evil to forgive. His mind too dark to open. And his heart... His heart was far too battered to love. Emery deserved to be loved, right and proper.

Marco killed the floor buffer, and the lobby silenced. Callan's eardrums vibrated with the brash echo of the machine's droning buzz. He glanced up from his book and frowned at the elevators. What the hell was takin' her so long?

He watched Marco wind the long cord. Time slowed to a snail's pace. Pushing up the sleeve of his coat, he checked his watch. It was already after three. She should be back by now.

137

His gaze traveled to the scars on his arm. Each carved tick denoted a tallied secret. A vindication. A token. A receipt from Satan himself for an evil soul collected.

His eyes returned to the elevator. Marco was gone.

Callan thought he heard something down the hall, probably the custodian onto cleaning the restrooms. Who knew what Marco did when he wasnae polishing the floors?

An elevator pinged and his head snapped around with short-lived relief. Not her. He dinnae catch the face, but the broad build sliding into the lift definitely belonged to a man.

His fingers returned to the sketch. He should go. This longing needed to fade before it swallowed him whole. Maybe it already had.

He never wanted anything the way he wanted her—so much so that it scared him, kept him at a distance he'd probably never cross.

The dichotomy of his longing could be paired down into two parts. One that was lush and pure and devoted to Emery. And another that was dark and vile and fixated on revenge. It would be impossible to have both.

His laughable inexperience was another reason to keep his distance. In the three years he'd known her, she never once spoke of havin' a boyfriend or lovin' someone. When men paid attention to her—which they often did—she played coy, claiming she wasnae interested. The thought that she might be as untried as he only endeared him to her more.

A fantasy. Emery was far too kind and pretty, and he was far too scarred by reality to practice naiveté. But, in this case, he allowed the foolish assumption—if only to calm his own lust and ego, subdue his often-raging jealousy.

She was younger. Just past twenty. And while he wasnae delusional enough to believe a woman as beautiful as Emery might be a virgin, she still struck him as somewhat innocent.

To kiss Emery one day, truly kiss her... It would be... A description escaped him.

The sour tension in his gut returned as he glared at the elevators. Did she stop somewhere? Perhaps she met up with...

He ground his teeth. She was delivering receipts just like she did every night. The hotel was full, that was all.

He glared at his watch as the minutes ticked by. His gnarled hand slapped the leather cover of his journal shut, his thumb pressing over each knuckle and popping the joints in a practiced *click*, *click*, *click* as his eyes bored holes in the elevator doors. He stood to stretch his legs.

The soles of his feet flattened into the floor, and he focused on his core rather than waiting for his legs to captain the ship. His toes spread inside his boots, an old trick to retain his balance. The flesh on the back of his calves pulled.

"Fuck it."

He pocketed his journal and removed his keys. It was probably best that he got out of there before she realized he'd come back.

Returning the chair to the table, he rounded the marble pillars and crossed the lobby when something caught his eye. In a flash, not even half a second long, he understood something terrible had kept her. The blood rushed from his head, and he knew when he saw her stumble along the wall, it was the beginning of the end.

Chapter Ten

Perth—Scotland
Four and a Half Years Prior...

"Let's try this again." The lamplight caught on the sharp blade of Callan's knife as he tightened his grip around Finlay Campbell's throat.

Campbell's eyes bulged. Callan's hand pressed hard into his trachea. Blood trickled from his nose, his frantic mumbles pleading jabbered fear.

Callan's booted foot pressed into the bedding just beside the man's head, his weight distributed heavily over his lungs. Campbell had no chance to run. The short demand for him to open his fuckin' eyes had been his only wake-up call, and by then Callan already had him.

"I'm going to ask ye a question, and you're only going to speak the answer. If you're lyin', I'll know. And if ye scream, I'll snap your fuckin' fingers off one by fuckin' one. Understand?"

Campbell nodded as much as he could, his heavily browed eyes squinting in the dim lamplight.

141

Beads of sweat gathered on his nose, his ruddy flesh a chewed up bubblegum pink that provoked the urge to spit.

Callan switched his hold to the man's hand, crushing the small bones. Keeping his knee buried in Campbell's chest, he hissed out his questions with a hushed demonic force.

"What's yer name?" He knew exactly who the cocksucker was, but wanted to make sure the fucker told the truth.

"F—F—F—inlay Campbell."

"What do you do te make a living, Finlay Campbell?"

"I manage a launderette—*ach!*"

Like crushing a finch, several delicate bones in his hand crunched painfully. "Dinnae lie to me!"

"I swear it! A little place on Ash Grove. Please dinnae break my hand!"

Callan's glance swept over the flat. No manager of a launderette could afford such luxuries. "How do ye know Rory?"

"I dinnae ken no Rory. *Ahh!*"

The finger snapped with little effort. "Oscar. Riordan. *How* do ye know him?"

"What did ye do te my hand? I'll not be able te work!"

Callan gripped his brittle fingers, several already broken and hanging cockeyed from the tendons. He dug his knee deeper, pushing Campbell harder against the bedding.

"Answer the fuckin' question!"

Campbell sobbed. Spittle coated his lips as he blubbered like a wee baby over a few broken bits. "I did a few jobs for him," he rushed out. "Nothing major. I swear I've not seen him in over a year. Please dinnae hurt me no more."

"What *kind* of jobs?"

"Shite work. Sometimes I'd run a delivery for him, pickin' up a package or droppin' messages."

"How would ye deliver the messages?"

"However he told me."

His grip tightened, and the man whimpered like a toddler. "Be. More. Specific."

"I dinnae ken! Every time was different. *Ahh! Fuck! All right!*" Sweat poured profusely from the man's head, leaving a dark stain on the pillow. "If someone owed him money, I'd shake 'em up a bit so they'd make a payment. But I never really hurt no one. Only thieves and people who owed him. They mostly all deserved it—*Ahh! Christ!*"

Callan released his shattered hand and climbed off the bed. Campbell pulled his arm to his chest, sniveling, and too distracted by the pain to make a run for it.

Callan cinched a rope around his feet.

"What are ye doin'? I told ye everything I know!" He kicked and tried to sit up, but Callan cuffed his ear, dropping him back to the bed.

He yanked Campbell's hand back and tied it to the bedpost, twisting the rope extra tight around the shattered bones. He struggled in vain.

Pulling a flask from his jacket, Callan sprinkled the contents over the man. When the

143

decanter was empty, he twisted the cap on and returned it to his pocket.

The heady scent of gasoline filled the air with unmistakable promise, leaving Callan both giddy and nauseous. So came the truth of his irrevocable past and unreliable future. No fear. Only promise. Only vengeance.

"What are ye doin'? Let me up! I dinnae ken anything else to tell ye!"

Mockery crept into Callan's tone. "I'm deliverin' a message."

Campbell likely recognized the scent of liquid death saturating his clothes. He screamed in frantic desperation for someone to help.

Callan slapped him hard, and he silenced. If anything, a man should have the dignity to die like a man. At least he'd be relieved of the exquisite burden of living, while others were sentenced to stay and face the ceaseless continuation of time.

Leaning close, he gripped Campbell's face with punishing force and held his stare. "A year and a half ago ye took a stolen car to the dodgy end of Glasgow with a man named Fraser. Ye threw a bottle bomb through the window and left, burning the house to the ground with everything I loved inside."

The man shut his eyes, but not before Callan read his guilt. There would be no denying it either way. Fraser had confessed everything just minutes before breathing his last gurgled breath.

Callan's life existed here, now, in the vestibule of death, chaperoning evil souls into hell.

Perhaps *he* was the devil. No amount of begging and pleading could distract him from his purpose. His entire existence, his every breath, channeled into destroying those who thought to destroy him.

And there was also the issue of his rage, which needed a target. *"Open yer fuckin' eyes and face what you've done!"*

Breath shook out of the man as he flinchingly forced his eyes open.

The beast prowling beneath Callan's surface preened and purred, sharp claws flexing and teeth chomping for the savory taste of vengeance and enemy flesh. His voice vibrated with sadistic promise as he stood over the bed. "My name is Callan MacGregor. My face will be the last thing ye see before looking into the eyes of Satan himself. Yer life is the price for those I loved. Yer sins are the toll tha' shall deliver ye to hell."

"Please! I need a priest!"

Callan cocked his head, a wooden match pinched tight between his finger and thumb. "I deliver evil, not mercy." He struck the match and dropped it to his chest.

Flames engulfed the bed. Screams ignited within, a lunatic trapped with no sense or hope of salvation. The thrashing shadows of frantic suffering heightened the stench of burning hair and flesh. And Callan watched.

But no measure of peace came.

When screams finally silenced, the heat of the burning bed and cindered body toasting his chest and shins, he withdrew his knife and pushed up his sleeve. There, beside the nine lines just starting to scab, he sliced another tick.

Chapter Eleven

Saratoga Springs, New York—America
Present Day

His gaze jerked to her face, his heart lurching, as his entire existence came to a shuddering halt. Emery. Staggering down the hall, leaning into the wall... What the hell was he seeing?

His eyes blinked hard. Unwelcomed fears—the worst sort—took shape before him as her battered face and ruined clothes tripped into view.

And as she braced herself against the wall still several yards away, arms clutching her ribs, hair tumbled in damp snarls, his mind registered the unmistakable scent of blood.

"God, what have Ye done?" The words breathed past his lips as his gut hollowed with sickening dread.

No. Not her...

The stench of vomit threw him into a dead sprint.

"Who did this to you?" His sweet, precious, gentle Emery.

She flinched, and he shook with the effort to contain his fury, the need to take her into his arms and protect her from such a hideous world.

Fuck, her head was bashed and bleedin'. Her lip split at the soft pillowy crease where a dark bruise already formed.

A hard lump choked him. Vomit and blood soiled her skin, hair, and clothes. Her torn blouse hung like wet gauze, soaked with vomit and clinging to her skin. Buttons were missing, and her bra strap showed. Her skirt hitched beyond modesty, beyond Emery.

He'd watched countless men die, beat others within an inch of their death, but he could hardly look at the vileness marking her. The sight of her damaged body too much even for him.

His hands hovered, palms out as if he could somehow offer comfort without touching her. She dinnae seem to register his presence.

He quickly removed his coat. "I'll not touch you. Just…" He gently draped it over her shoulders. The weight seemed too much for her as she sagged closer to the wall. "Tell me what happened, love."

His hands frantically ached to adjust her clothes but touching her seemed a graver crime than usual. She shook so intensely. Or was that him?

His breath hitched as he spotted her shredded stockings bunched beneath her knee. His stomach lurched as his gaze locked on her thighs where blood and…

"Jesus H. Christ," he rasped, his voice trembling on a shallow breath.

She slid down the wall, and a sob broke from her battered lips. He had no choice but to catch her, to save her from crashing to the floor. Her unfocused eyes looked past him, gasping breaths sobbing inward as she fell into a state of broken panic.

He clutched her shoulders, and her body jerked, an animal response so unrefined her fear shattered him. "Em'ry, it's me."

"No." Her eyes screwed shut as her strength gave out and she moaned, "No more…"

It killed him to have to calm her with strength, but once she stilled he gently cupped her cheeks and put his face in her view. "Em'ry, look at me. Look into my eyes and know that yer safe. I've got ye, love, and I'll not let ye out of my sight. I'll not let anyone hurt ye."

She'd already been hurt. His mind swam in a squall of regret. He should have been there. He should have kept a better eye on her. The scent of sweat and tears and every other bodily fluid stung his nose, and he nearly tossed. He needed a phone.

"Can I lift ye up?"

Something sparked in her eyes, perhaps recognition, but the lingering dazed look terrified him. He had no idea how badly she'd hit her head or the extent of her other injuries. Rage unraveled in him at the speed of light.

What if he moved her and she flipped out? Sometimes, when adrenaline ran so close to the surface, human contact was intolerable.

He searched his pockets for his phone. Nothing. "Do you have your mobile on ye, love? I dinnae want to leave you. We need to call for help."

Something shifted in her eyes, as they widened for a split second. Beneath the smeared makeup and blood, the color leached from her skin.

She'd been cradling her right hand to her chest, but when she let go of it, he diagnosed it as broken. He'd slaughter whoever did this to her.

She reached a trembling hand into the pocket of her blazer and choked on a sob as she pulled out her phone tangled in a nest of headphone cords. Her shaking fingers gripped it, handing it over as her face collapsed like a pricked balloon.

He carefully removed it from her trembling fingers, trying not to focus on the broken, chipped nails that had been perfect an hour ago.

"It's all right, love," he said softly. "You're safe now."

His fingers shook so fiercely he struggled to dial the correct numbers. As he waited for the call to connect, he tried to keep her communicating. "I willnae hurt ye, Em'ry. Let me see your hand."

Slowly, her arms folded out from her shuddering body and he glared at her dainty fingers, noting the red bruises taking shape beneath swollen joints. Definitely broken.

The second the dispatcher answered, he gave them the necessary details to get there *right away*.

Then ended the call and pocketed the phone. The immediate call back vibrated against his leg, but his full focus returned to Emery, distracting him from all else.

A scarlet smear of blood beneath her fluttering nostrils caught his eye, and he wanted to scream and kill someone. *Who?*

His forearm burned for another mark. He'd sworn the last tally had been carved, but this changed everything. Berserk rage threatened to shatter his well-practiced calm, revealing everything he never wanted her to see. Only her current state kept him in check, her need for his calm more significant than his inner turmoil screaming to unleash. He buried his thirst for vengeance, training his focus on her wellbeing.

But there would be a reckoning.

"Help's on the way, *leannán*. The polis are comin'." His fists clenched at his side. He wanted to comfort her, but every time he lifted a hand to her she tensed. Of course, she didnae want his hands on her—at a time like this or any time at all.

Her teeth chattered, a sign that her body was going into shock. He needed to keep her alert for when the authorities arrived. "Do ye know who did this to ye, Em'ry?"

Her body twitched, her shoulders shaking with a forceful shiver. Crazed fury seethed under his skin, but he tamped it down.

His eyes searched the empty hall. They were too far from the front entrance. He hated having to move her but wanted to get her right where the

EMTs could find her. She was in bad shape and they couldnae waste time.

"We need to take ye to the lobby. Can ye walk?"

Her head tipped in a jagged nod but she dinnae stand.

He wasnae sure of the extent of her injuries—couldnae let his mind imagine more than what he saw. Cognitively, she only seemed about a quarter there, the rest of her trembling in shock.

The dark centers of her pupils swallowed the color of her eyes, and her teeth continued to chatter. A thousand years passed as he debated what to do, no solution good enough.

"I'm gonna help ye stand, but first I need ye to tell me what hurts." He dinnae want to cause more damage. "Can ye tell me, love? Can ye talk to me?"

She blinked her unfocused gaze coming to rest on his face. "E—e—everything," she mouthed, the word coming out on a whispered breath, enough for him to hear how hoarse her voice was.

Dear God, she'd screamed... She'd been callin' for help, and no one fuckin' heard her. His eyes closed for a brief moment as agonizing regret washed over him like razor blades and salt.

His jaw cracked as he gritted his teeth. He'd murder the fucker that did this to her. Slaughter him. Make him suffer a million times over for every hair harmed on her body. How dare anyone think they could lay an unkind finger on her?

Taking a long breath that hardly reached his lungs, he kept his voice low and measured. "I'll be as gentle as I can, love. Take my arm."

She slowly latched her arm around his, her touch as fragile as a bird's wing. She kept her damaged hand tucked to her chest.

He stood slowly, careful not to jostle her in any way, but she gasped in pain the moment her weight shifted off the wall onto her legs. Her knees buckled and her grip slipped, her body collapsing too fast to consider the consequences of catching her.

He scooped her into his arms, pulling her protectively to his chest, and stood extremely still, giving them each a moment to adjust and trying not to focus on how right her weight felt in his arms.

"I've got ye. You're safe."

She met his gaze, her big eyes looking up with uncertainty and far too much innocence. The tension in her body eased as her eyes rolled back.

"Em'ry."

Her head lolled to his chest, her entire body limp.

"Fuck." Perhaps this was best. Unconsciousness might save her suffering.

With agile steps, he carried her to the lobby and situated her on his lap as he settled onto a seat directly across from the main entrance.

Breathing through the panic, he swallowed convulsively and rasped, "Em'ry. Love, I need ye to open your eyes."

He hated that his need to wake her stemmed as much from selfishness as it did concern. He couldnae have her unconscious when the polis arrived, couldnae have them assumin' he had anything to do with what happened. Most of all, he couldnae have them nosin' around in their computers with his name.

His crooked, scarred knuckle grazed the delicate arch of her cheek. "Em'ry. Please, love, open yer eyes for me."

Her face drooped against his chest, her weight utterly insignificant in his arms. She was so wee, so delicate. He should have never left her alone. He wasnae sure he'd ever be able to leave her alone again.

Her brow pinched, and he sensed her coming to. He rocked her gently, humming a lullaby his ma used to hum to him, the same one he'd hummed to Innis, and she'd hummed to Gavin.

She moaned, soft and shifting into a sigh of pain. Damn how she must hurt. He loosened his hold but somehow cradled her closer.

Her eyes screwed tight, her body tensing. He wanted to tell her to try not to tense. Her muscles were overtaxed as is. Poor thing.

"You're safe. I've still got ye, love." He wasnae sure what he might do if she left his arms. The slight weight of her body kept him from spiraling into a bloodthirsty manhunt.

He stared at the glass doors because it was easier than seeing the evidence of destruction cradled in his arms. Red flashed against the pillars as a squad car pulled into the carport.

How much would they need to know? How much could she actually tell them? How much did she remember and how soon until they figured out who he had to kill?

Unblinking, he watched the doors, his rocking body soothing him more than it seemed to register with her. "The polis are here."

They'd want her coherent. He needed information as well. The more she could speak for herself the better off everyone would be. But he also dinnae want anyone pressuring her.

No one was going to make her do shite that she dinnae want to do. If this was the most she was capable of, this was it. His first and last concern was Emery.

He swayed, holding her securely but gently in his arms. "They'll want to ask ye questions before the ambulance gets here. I willnae leave yer side."

The doors parted, and a female officer entered, making a quick scan of the area and spotting them in the seating area of the lobby. A quick assessment of the situation registered in the firm set of her slender jaw.

Her spine straightened as she approached, but Callan dinnae miss the flutter at the base of the officer's throat as she muttered something into the radio strapped to her shoulder.

The passenger door of the squad car opened. A male officer entered the lobby but kept his

155

distance, seeming to guard the door, eyes searching the area.

The female officer crouched in front of Emery and glanced at him. "What's her name?" she asked softly.

"Em'ry. Em'ry Tanner."

Her dark brow etched with sympathy and her full lips pursed. She nodded her comprehension of the situation.

"Ms. Tanner?" She waited for Emery's eyes to open. "I'm Officer Banks, and that's my partner, Officer Knowles. Can you tell me what happened?"

Emery's lips compressed. Tiny heaves shook her chest, building like an avalanche. She dinnae seem capable of answering, but then her shattered voice emerged, hoarse and soaked with emotion.

"I was attacked."

Callan's composure slipped, but he dinnae let go. An ache formed in his hollowed heart, seeping into every cold cavity and choking the breath from his lungs. He wasnae prepared to feel the things her pain made him feel.

Her verbalized confirmation accentuated every horrific mark on her body. It told him there was so much more to the wreckage he could see.

Officer Banks kept her tone gentle and pressed on. "Were you sexually assaulted during the attack?"

Emery gave a tense, clipped nod. Her confirmation slammed down like an ax striking his heart, shocking him all over again despite the evidence clinging to her battered body.

He must have made a sound because the officer's gaze jumped to his face, but quickly returned to Emery.

"You're safe now, Ms. Tanner. There's an ambulance on its way. Do you know the man with you now?"

Emery's eyes closed, a concave divot forming in her throat under her soiled collar as she nodded.

"Are you okay with talking to me here, Ms. Tanner? Do you feel safe with the man holding you?"

She nodded again, and Callan breathed a sigh of relief.

The officer kept attention focused on Emery. "Where were you attacked, Emery?"

Tremors radiated from her body into his chest. "The ladies room."

Before he could wonder how he had not heard a sound, he recalled Marco waxing the floor, the auditory memory so clear it was all he could hear for a split second.

"Can you tell me which one?"

She whimpered, and Callan lifted his gaze to the other woman. "I think the one down that hall on the right. I found her just outside the door."

It was the one she always used during her shifts. So close and yet…

"Is that correct?"

Emery nodded again.

"Did you recognize the person who did this to you?"

He held his breath, his ears attuned to every shift of her clothing, every swallow of her ravaged throat.

A tear escaped her swollen eye and rolled into her hair. "Yes."

Callan's hard gaze fastened to Emery's face, his nostrils flaring with a heavy, shaken breath. He knew. He knew who it was before she even spoke the fucker's name—not that he knew his name. But he knew who it was.

It hit him then, like a bullet spearing his heart. No matter what name she gave, no matter what he did to the motherfucker, nothing would erase what was done. Nothing would save her this suffering, but he wanted to slaughter him anyway—*needed* to see her avenged.

"Can you tell me the person's name?" Officer Banks casually waved her partner closer.

"W—Wesley. He's a guest. He … visited my desk earlier…"

He knew it. The same man who'd been hanging around her. The same build of the man he'd seen slip into the elevator not thirty minutes ago.

He inwardly raged. So close, and he'd just walked away. He could see his face clear as day— hear the echo of his drunken friends yelling his name. *Wesley.*

Every muscle in Callan's body locked, vibrating as he shook violently with the need to find and destroy. He focused on the fragile weight of Emery in his arms, as it seemed the only anchor keeping him from a homicidal rampage.

"Do you know his last name?"

"N—no."

"Did he use a weapon?"

Her eyes closed, more tears seeping through her damp lashes. "No."

"Was anyone else present?"

"No."

The second officer moved closer and quietly announced, "The ambulance is about five minutes away, Banks." Officer Banks nodded, but dinnae react to this information.

"Do you know where the assailant went?"

"He's staying here," she whispered, and Callan's stare followed the second officer toward the reception desk where he spoke into his radio.

"Can you describe what happened?"

"I was using the bathroom." Her words slurred, as they whispered past her barely parted, swollen lips. "He followed me. Sn—n—uck up on me. I told him to leave, but he wouldn't. When I tried to... He..."

"Take your time."

"He threw me into the wall," she murmured, and Callan wasnae sure he could handle the details. "I ... I tried to fight him. I screamed. I kept screaming. But he kept hitting me." Her face crumpled. "He wouldn't stop..."

Her words fizzled to nothing. Silence imbued the large space, and no one dared to fill it.

More lights flashed. Officer Banks spoke in simple sentences. "The ambulance is here, Emery. They're going to help you. You're going to a crisis center where they can treat your injuries. Once I'm finished here, I'll meet you there. Would it be okay with you if we talked some more then?"

She nodded weakly.

"Would you like your friend to go with you?"

He held his breath, unsure if he'd be able to leave her, certain if he stayed at the hotel he'd have one more death on his conscience before dawn, and the polis would be carting him away.

But he also feared he might not be strong enough to go through this with her. Someone needed to call Matt, the manager. Marco could fill him in.

His mind moved as if she'd already agreed. He needed to stay with her, no matter how hard it would be because he absolutely wasnae strong enough to stay here.

Her delicate nod sent a thunderbolt of relief and fear to his heart. The officer's gaze lifted to Callan and he quickly agreed, "I'll stay with her."

Officer Banks nodded and stood. "Thank you for talking with me, Emery. I'm going to hurry the EMTs along."

Emery rolled her face to Callan's chest and shuddered out a sob. His arms tightened protectively.

"Thank you, Callan." Her thready whisper gutted him.

"Dinnae thank me, love. I shouldae been there when ye needed me."

Her good hand tightened subtly over his arm. "You're here now."

Chapter Twelve

Riordan Private Estate
Lower Whitecraigs, Edinburgh—Scotland
Four Years Prior

"Now, what do we have here?"

Callan's heart raced as three large guards yanked his head back by his hair and held him immobile. Blood gushed from his cheek, his skull still rattling from where they subdued him with the butt of a gun. His kidney screamed, still throbbing from where the one guard whacked him with a cudgel.

The one that fisted his hair let go and wedged his fingers into the side of his mouth, wrenching back his lips and baring his teeth. "Ain't goin' anywhere now, are ye, ye cunt?"

Saliva gathered faster than panic as his lips pulled painfully over his gums and he stared at the man responsible for his misery, the man he'd come to kill.

Oscar Riordan—Rory to most—paced the room as if he had no care in the world. "Callan

MacGregor. You're just as impressive as I remember."

His spiked hair and narrow eyes gave him a shrewd appearance, but his build was all together unthreatening. Still, it never escaped Callan's mind that this was the most dangerous man in Scotland.

The tight skin at the corners of his mouth tore as the guard subdued his struggles. Grime from those fingers washed to the back of his throat on a gathering puddle of drool, and he groaned, unable to shout *fuck you* like he wanted.

Rory peeled away an unruly fingernail and cocked his head. "You killed my chauffeur."

He'd killed a lot more than that. Thirty-two cuts marred his arm, one for each evil soul he cleansed from this earth, each one tied to this man's corruption, and guilty of harming innocent people.

Not all of them were amateur crooks. Many were seasoned killers. Trusted assassins within Rory's most intimate circle of colleagues, a circle Callan had penetrated.

Tonight's misstep wasnae part of the plan. But when Rhys had shown up, unexpectedly following him, he'd tripped the alarm and seconds later they were being chased down by the hounds of hell, dragged into what he assumed was some sort of holding cell built into the estate basement, and beaten into submission.

Callan was only catching his breath. Let them assume they had him. They were all going to die before the night ended.

Except goddamn Rhys. He should have never followed him. If Callan got hurt, he dinnae care, had nothing to lose. Rhys was a liability.

"I'll admit," Rory chuckled as if genuinely amused. "It took me a while to figure out who would have the bollocks to go after my men. Once I realized who you were, I pieced it together." He stepped closer, the saccharine scent of licorice puffing from every word. "You never took the payout, did you? And then you went and killed ol' Ramsey for lyin' about it. Killed Fraser and Campbell, too." He slapped the side of Callan's neck twice as if praising a job well done. "Campbell's poor wife hardly had a tooth left to bury."

Saliva continued to gather in the back of his throat, aggravating his breathing. His lips were bone dry and starting to crack.

"Let go of his face, Brooks."

The moment the fingers left his mouth, he stretched his gaunt lips over his teeth and spat on the cement floor. Two men still held his shoulders to the chair where they'd tied his arms. And he was pretty certain that was a gun jabbing into the back of his skull.

Rhys was unconscious, which was probably for the best at the moment.

Rory massaged his angular chin, pacing slowly around the chair. "What, exactly, is the end game for you, MacGregor?"

The eloquent pacing of Rory's speech and deliberate elocution spoke to an educated background. But Callan was no fool. He saw through every practiced and mocking pronunciation and recognized that a small man like Rory would use every tool at his disposal to intimidate others, including language.

Articulations dangled from his words like jewels on painted whores. Artificial distractions pasted over something damaged Oscar Riordan dinnae want the world to see.

Callan saw through the veneer. Well-bred diction did not equal a well-bred man. And beneath those fine clothes and all that fancy speech rested an animal undeserving of trust—an animal he wouldnae let intimidate him.

Callan bared his teeth and sneered, "It's over when I cannae take a piss without hittin' the graves of all yer men."

"Ambitious." He lifted his brows and nodded. "But that will never happen."

"Not in your lifetime. I'm afraid that ends tonight."

Rory chuckled again, appearing truly tickled by the threat. "Dinnae be so sure."

Callan already loosened the rope around his knees. If he could sink his teeth into one of the guards, that could buy him enough time to distract the others and—

"I'm one hundred percent certain whatever you're planning is not going to happen. As much as I'd love to see you try, I'm afraid I must insist otherwise." His gaze dropped to Callan's chest. "But I would love to postpone our playdate. So much hostility blazing inside of you. I can almost taste it."

He'd savor the moment he beat that smirk off that disturbing face. Some men wore menace in heft and breadth. Oscar Riordan had an unremarkable, spindling, effeminate build, but something in his eyes, something that promised he dinnae flinch easily, warned he could probably watch a man die with unblinking fascination.

The unnatural way his angular face lifted with giddy enthusiasm at the idea of others suffering, proved an unhinged psychopath lingered close to the lunatic's surface. He likely practiced his first kills in the garden, catching furry little creatures and spooning out their eyes just to see if they would still live.

Callan never met someone who set off such alarm bells, but they struck with a roaring, soul-shaking clang the second Rory looked him in the eye. Callan would murder him before the night was over. He was merely regaining his strength.

"Oh, smell the determination wafting from you." Rory tipped back his head and sniffed the air. "So close to desperation, but there is something heady about it." He paced closer, an almost euphoric anticipation to his tone. "You'd like nothing more than to kill me. What a lovely sensation, having all that raw, animal focus directed squarely at me."

His fingertip trailed up Callan's throat to his jaw, and he jerked his head away.

"Easy now." Oddly, he pulled out a handkerchief and wiped his fingers clean of any invisible filth. "You see, MacGregor, I find myself intrigued by your capabilities. I've watched you fight, but this…" He waved a hand, gesturing to the dark fatigues and the weapons on the table that they stripped off him. "This is a brand new side of you I've never seen." A crooked smirk pulled at his lips as he waggled a brow. "Why, I'm almost twitterpated."

He picked up Callan's scythe and turned the long handle, slowly rotating the hooked blade through the air. "Our ancestors would be proud. Such a fine barbarian."

He'd gutted a man by the name of Baird with that one. He'd been paid a hundred pounds to give up Callan's address, leading Rory's men right to his home.

"Here's what I know, MacGregor. Any man with the bollocks to come to my private residence isnae playin' with a full deck. Did you come here to die? Typically, I'd accommodate you, but I'm rather amused by your presence, so I must decline."

Callan licked the dried blood coating his teeth, his arms stretching the rope with each slow breath. "I came to kill ye."

"Well, we've determined that is not happening." He laughed. "At least not tonight." His lashes lowered as his thin lips formed a smirk. He winked at Callan. "I wonder if it *will* be you in the end. Something poetic, I hope."

He couldnae wrap his thinking around Rory's. What sort of man takes pleasure in their own demise? "I promise ye, my face will be the last thing ye see."

His hands clamped tight. "Marvelous. I almost cannae wait." He seemed to savor the promise. "Almost."

He fished in the pocket of his suit and withdrew a mobile phone. A terrifying smile bloomed across his face. Despite being a grown man, his grin was made up of underdeveloped baby teeth.

"You're going to love this." He brought the phone to his ear. "Yes. Good. Good. We're in the back."

Muffled grunts came from the corner as Rhys stirred. The guards kicked him hard enough to launch him at Callan's feet. Rhys peered up at him, face spattered with blood, green eyes wild and terrified.

Callan gritted his teeth. He should tell him it served him right, but he couldnae. Rhys was his best mate and the only family he had left. He'd trade his own life to save him, but he had people, bad men to kill. Rhys interfered with his objective. His presence complicated everything.

"You see, I'm well aware you're not afraid of death. We've already established that you had a death wish the moment you came to my home. But your friend here is a great incentive. I'm a real believer in behavior modification by finding the proper motivation, aren't you? With the right…" He cocked his head. "...source of persuasion, I find anyone will do anything."

Rhys rolled to his side, groaning and spitting blood and saliva onto the floor. Fetid dampness seeped from the cinderblock walls marking how deep underground they were.

Callan met Rory's gaze with narrowed eyes. "Aye. I'm listening."

"I'm a collector of weapons. As you know, I deal with all sorts of people, and one can never be too well armed."

"Fuck this, Callan. Dinnae negotiate with this cunt."

A guard kicked Rhys in the side, lifting him off the ground and sending him skidding into the wall. In a flash, Rory had Rhys gripped by the jaw, a shiny blade protruding from his fist.

"Now, now. If ye cannae remember yer manners and refrain from interrupting, I'll have no choice but to cut out your tongue. Grownups are talking."

Callan jerked against the ropes and shouted, "Dinnae lay a fuckin' hand on him!"

Rory turned, eyes bursting with barely contained excitement. "And there it is." He sheathed his knife in the breast pocket of his jacket and stood. "As I was saying. Incentive."

The wavering patterns of his speech swayed from proper to mocking. No matter how he pronounced his words, every one was intentionally delivered, purposely measured like a caress or a slap.

Callan leveled his stare on Rory. "Let him go."

"Of course," he pouted. "But nothing's for free."

Murder suddenly seemed too merciful for this cocksucker. "What do ye want?"

"You're so much more than a bare-knuckle boxer, MacGregor. You're a force of nature, the devil incarnate, and I want you to work for me."

Callan spat, a knee-jerk response brought on by his repulsion to have any association with this animal. "I'll never be on yer payroll."

"Uh, uh, uh. Never say never." Rory spoke with cumulating flaccid gestures that only added to his unnerving aura. "Everyone has a price."

"I don't."

"Oh, I believe ye do, my boy."

"I'm not yer fuckin' boy."

"Well, of course not. You're a vigilante, and vigilantes are rarely children. Aye, you're all man. I think we'll be great friends over time."

His molars scraped. "We're the opposite of friends."

Rory chuckled. "If life's taught me anything, it's that hate can motivate a person almost twice as fast as love. You can hate me and still work for me. After you hear what I propose, I imagine that'll be the way of it, no matter how much every cell of your being objects. Like I said, every man has a price."

He was growing tired of the dramatics. "Do you plan on tellin' me what ye want? Or are ye gonna continue blowin' yourself for another hour?"

The lunatic truly laughed this time. "Oh, my apologies. Am I keeping you from a prior engagement?"

"Aye. Slittin' yer fuckin' throat."

Rory tsked several times in a row. "That's no way to speak to yer superior."

"You're not my fuckin' superior. You're a worthless shite who'll never have my respect, least of all, my loyalty."

Rory tipped his head back and sighed. "Oh, I'm going to enjoy watching you eat those words. Pick up his friend. *Gently.*"

The guards lifted Rhys off the floor. Rory removed a roll of tape from the table and hesitated before placing it over Rhys's mouth. "Behave, and I willnae let them hurt you. Misbehave, and I'll let them do their worst." He covered his mouth and pointed to the wall. "Hang him there."

The guards stretched Rhys's tied hands above his head, hooking his arms on a peg in the wall, high enough to leave his toes twisting over the ground.

Callan's heart hammered with uncertainty. "You can let him go. He's not who ye need to worry about."

Sweat gathered on Rhys's brow as he groaned a garbled swear, shooting off muffled threats at the guards who slung him up. Callan glared, silently ordering him to shut the fuck up.

"Easy now," Rory warned. "He's not any concern."

Callan frowned. Then why not let him go?

Rory typed something into the phone and crossed his arms over his chest, cupping one elbow in his palm and flipping back the hand holding the mobile. "I apologize for this next part, but you understand I must protect my men, especially after you left me so short-handed these last few months."

A heavy chain clinked and dragged from the wall. The guards twisted it around Callan's neck, cutting his airway down to the width of a pin. Tape covered his mouth, and a blade pressed into the soft flesh under his eye.

"Move a muscle and my man has permission to remove yer eye."

Callan seethed, his head bent at an unnatural angle due to the weight of the chains. But the point of the blade made sure he dinnae shift a muscle.

"Now, we can talk business."

Rory pulled a chair across from him and sat, crossing his legs. Callan's vision blurred as sharp pressure poked beneath his eye. Head tipped back, he watched Rory through his lashes as his eye watered.

"You're going to act as my tax collector. Twitch the fingers on your right hand if you understand what I mean by tax collector."

He balled his fist. Rory smirked at the challenge. "If your hands are not working, perhaps you'd like to borrow your friend's. I could cut his fingers off and bring them to you—one by one."

Callan's nostrils flared with boiling rage. His fist loosened and his fingers twitched.

He knew what taxation was. It was said to be the perfect crime. No authorities intervened when thieves stole from other criminals like drug lords, sex traffickers, and weapons dealers. But Callan wasnae a crook, and he'd never work for a man like Oscar Riordan.

"I'll expect you to be ruthless. I want you to make me a lot of money, MacGregor. You'll be well paid for your service. But the job's permanent."

The man was off his rocker if he thought the threat of losing an eye was enough to broker such a deal. He wouldnae share his fucking toilet to take a shite. No way would he go into business for him. He could have both eyes. Callan would still kill him in the end—blind or not.

"I see we're still not in agreement."

He stood and moved to the metal door outside of Callan's view. Two firm knocks, and then he returned, but dinnae take a seat. He smiled like a sadist about to take his victim's balls.

Callan couldnae see who came in the door when it opened, but he could see Rhys. His friend's eyes widened like white saucers as a muffled shriek peeled against the taped gag. He thrashed against the wall, and Callan's heart jackhammered at the unknown.

Should he turn, say fuck his sight? He roared against his own gag. *What's happening?*

His eyes bulged, straining to see, wincing as the blade pressed into the soft flesh above his cheekbone. He blinked rapidly at the prick to his tender tissue.

Rhys kicked and screamed, bucking wildly against the wall. Panic welled. Rory grinned like a lunatic, holding out a hand to whomever had entered while watching Callan.

Callan roared with impatience, his feet jerking against the ropes. And then he heard nothing. The world silenced. His pain vanished. The earth fell out from beneath him, rolling right off its axis as his sister stood before him.

A wave of chills chased up his body. Was he dead?

Everything he knew to be true shifted into a blatant lie.

But there was one thing Callan knew to be true. Rory had him by the fucking bollocks. He'd do whatever the man wanted because he'd found Callan's price, had the perfect incentive to motivate him. He had Innis.

HURT

Chapter Thirteen

Saratoga Hospital
Saratoga Springs, New York—America
Present Day

The fraying threads suspending Emery's sanity unraveled, thinner and thinner with every question. Words were flung at her like bullets, no matter how soft-spoken, and her broken mind struggled to provide even the slightest answer without feeling her guts bleed all over the floor.

These things, these facts they wanted to know... They were her most shameful secrets, freshly inked tattoos marring her soul. The pinprick still burned and the stain had yet to set, but they all waited for her to pull it together and regurgitate the horrific details.

But shame wouldn't fit into a tidy box, and it certainly would never go by one name. It was slippery and sycophantic. As much as they all wanted to help, not a single one of them could ever understand her pain.

The female police officer came to the hospital to follow up and completed the report. Emery gave as much information to the cops and nurses as she could manage, her words clumsy and basic. Recalling the simplest details hurt her brain. Hurt her body.

Question, after question, after question... She was a once full object now shaved wafer thin. And then ... nothing. Her voice just quit.

Her stunted mind suffered too much trauma. The finite details of her memories scattered like chaff to the wind, pieces of her womanhood cremated and lost without a proper goodbye.

All she wanted to do was sleep. Shut off the broken record in her head that stunned her with every turn. Mute the ache in her body and silence the recurring thought that this had happened to her.

Strangers hovered. People she didn't know, expectantly waiting for her to hemorrhage excruciating details from her ravaged soul. Every memory was too humiliating, too intimate, too fresh, but if she wanted a scrap of justice—knowing it would only be a crumb compared to what he stole—she had to divulge every painful part.

Her conscience whispered constant reminders that these strangers were not the enemy, but it wasn't always easy to hear through all the screaming in her head.

Their determination to salvage something that wasn't there overwhelmed her. No matter their efforts to comfort her, they couldn't ease the trauma. If anything, their professional proficiency neutralized the severity. They were so calm she wanted to take offense. Didn't they understand what he did to her? But then again, if they acted hysterically instead of professionally, she'd never get through this.

There was one person who got it, one person whose eyes reflected the shock that swam in hers.

Callan...

Maybe he understood, because he found her, or maybe because he didn't hear her scream. But she placed no blame on Callan. He was the first to come to her rescue.

She'd been in enough danger that her needs now included words like *rescue...* Her spine softened, denial and acceptance seesawing inside of her as she tried to find some sort of balance.

Her gutted insides pulled in ways she didn't want to feel. She should have fought harder. She should have bitten him and clawed out his eyes. Why hadn't she?

I thought I had, but then...

I lost.

I lost everything.

It seemed impossible that another human being did this to her.

Not a human being. A monster.

Without Callan's strength and resolute presence, she'd be lost in a sea of statistics, swallowed down with so many other women who suffered the same. One nurse, trying to calm her, whispered that they dealt with this every day as if the commonality of assault might soothe her aching heart.

Every day? How was that possible?

She had to trust them, let them do their jobs. She was on autopilot, lifting, scooting, opening, obeying… Better if she just shut off for a while.

She was mad at the world. Crushed. Physically and emotionally.

While her pulverized insides ached, her outsides itched to be scrubbed raw. Her mind shattered like a one-dimensional piece of glass, broken shards reflecting the last few hours and mocking her in some distorted mutation of the truth. Repeating and fishing for answers that weren't there only confused her more.

How had this happened? *To her?*

Dull acceptance eased in like a glacier splitting from the place it rested for a million years. This would be her life now. This was who she was, now.

This day, this horrific time would become a defining point in her future. Every other man would be judged harshly. And might judge her. Would judge her.

No matter how optimistic she'd always been, from now on, skepticism would always precede trust. She could feel herself chilling into a frigid person, measuring others in a forever skewed light. Maybe that was the only way to ice her injured soul.

Her shoulders hunched. Now that the worst of the examinations were over, Callan returned to her side. An anchor in a storm.

"Hey."

Her gaze lifted. He hovered a few feet away, hands buried deep in his pockets, eyes haunted by the inescapable truth of what brought them here.

God, it hurt. Beyond the physical, beyond the shock and shame, it hurt to see him look at her that way. This would always be between them.

Her chest quaked as an unexpected sob tore out of her. He was there in an instant, crouching in front of her dangling legs, fists braced on either side of her hips, pressing into the paper cloth.

"Hey. Look at me."

She blinked through her blurred vision, her lungs burning with each expelled, shallow breath. There was a hole inside of her, preventing her from breathing right. Maybe she'd never draw a full breath again.

"Right here, love." Keeping his touch feather light, he lifted her chin until her eyes met his. "In. Out. Nice and slow. In … and out."

Her gaze dropped to his lips, her body mimicking the rise and fall of his shoulders. He dropped his hand but continued to hold her with his stare. She wished she could swim away in the blue of his eyes, disappear like a sapphire fleck, lost forever in a sea of beauty, far removed from all the ugly of this world.

"That's it. Just breathe. Yer only job right now is breathing."

He watched her for a few more moments as if a sort of reluctance to turn away held him close. Once her breathing regulated and she no longer seemed on the verge of hyperventilation, he retreated to the nearby wall.

As they waited for the nurse, he kept his head bowed and his focus mostly on the floor. But when he did look at her, his eyes shimmered more than usual.

His stoicism proved she'd been right about him all along. Callan was one of the great ones.

Anger rushed through her. She was suddenly furious with herself. Why had she never told him how she felt? She'd waited too long, and now she was broken.

A fist locked around her heart, squeezing mercilessly. Shutting her eyes, she trapped her tears until too many built and seeped through her lashes.

Her shoulders trembled to hold it all in, as if she'd swallowed a tornado, each tumultuous and traitorous thought left a trail of devastation in its wake. All her focus poured into containing the storm inside of her.

Stillness helped her silence the thoughts she didn't want to think. As long as she didn't move, she could almost forget that she hurt, pretend this happened to someone else. Almost.

"Em'ry? Do ye need me to call for a nurse?"

She blinked, heavy tears skating down her cheeks as she met his gaze. How was he so aware of her up and down turmoil?

"No. I was just thinking… Or trying not to."

His brow creased, that long, jagged scar carving a divot in his skin. "Do ye pray?"

Of all the things she expected he might say, none had to do with faith. Her shoulder lifted. "Not since I was a little girl."

He took a slow step closer. His hands reached into his collar, coming away with a beaded rosary. He held it out to her. "Take it."

"I don't know what to do with it. I'm not Catholic."

"Just hold it."

Her fingers closed around the long chain of beads, still warm from the heat of his skin. He sidled closer, his voice low. "The crucifix is for the *Apostles' Creed*. Then the *Our Father*. All these little ones are for the Blessed Mother. And at the chain, ye say the *Glory Be*. Ye do it all the way around until ye get te here, the *Hail Holy Queen*."

She blinked at him, his voice soothing in itself but his words going right over her head. "I don't know any of those."

He adjusted the beads, closing her fingers over the cross. "It starts like this. *I believe in God...*"

It didn't matter what he said, only that he kept speaking. The quiet, baritone burr of his voice cocooned her in a familiar rumble. The way his mouth formed every memorized word made her feel stronger simply by listening to him. And when his tongue rolled over the R in Lord, she felt a shiver as if God Himself had reached down to touch her.

To her, they weren't prayers. They were beautiful distractions, and she clung to them. Part of her believed he knew she would, as if he spoke them to simply give her something to hold.

Her hand turned, her fingers releasing the cross to close around his rough fingers. "You're one of the great ones, Callan."

His gaze devoured their entwined fingers. His words cut off and his brow pinched, the jagged white scars around his eye emphasized by the look of confusion twisting his face. He untangled their hands, leaving the rosary draped over her empty fingers as he took a step back.

"I think yer medicine's kickin' in."

They'd given her something to relax and ease the pain. She did feel a little calmer, but it wasn't the pills. "You don't have to be embarrassed." A breath of laughter punched inside of her chest as she glanced down at her bare legs dangling from the disposable hospital gown. "I think we're past that now."

"Em'ry, please don't mistake me for a decent man. I'm not one of the good ones."

"But you are. You're good and decent and kind—"

"A decent man would have been there when ye needed him most."

"You were."

His face pinched. "I was late."

Her heart broke for the regret shimmering in his eyes. "But you were still there. In the end, that means more to me than I'll ever be able to explain."

His gaze broke away, and he swallowed hard. "Try to rest. I'll see what's keepin' the nurse."

He didn't stray far. And even when he stepped out of the room his presence somehow lingered, the

182

heavy timbre of his voice and distinguishable thump of his boots always within earshot.

He was a rock. A life raft in a stormy sea.

Tonight, he saved her. She'd been shattered, nothing but jagged edges jutting out every which way, but he collected all her broken pieces and kept her together. He kept her stable. Human.

Her eyes grew heavy, and she drifted in and out of sleep, only partially awake when they moved her to a bed. The physical aches numbed to dull throbs. Whatever they gave her was magical, a buffer against the psychological damage unraveling on the inside.

Guilt washed away, teasing in the periphery of her mind, but never creeping close enough to sink its claws in. She was a passenger. Maybe a hostage. At the moment it didn't seem to matter.

They'd stitched her up like a puppet, yet she still felt severed from her strings. Broken.

Her mind floated on a cloud of opiates and whatever else they put in her IV until there was nothing. Just … emptiness. Robbed.

"Em'ry? You all right, love?"

She dashed away her tears, not sure why she was crying, only then realizing she was awake and staring blankly in a sort of numb daydream of silence. Her fingers felt like they were on someone else's hands. She frowned at her broken nail. Her mind flashed to the hotel bathroom, the sound of wet Formica scraping under her clawing fingers, the feel of her nails bending back.

Callan cursed and jolted into action, thrusting a bedpan under her as she vomited. "We need a nurse!"

A flurry of people surrounded her, mopping her up with wet wipes and sweeping back her crusty hair. She cried, apologizing for making such a mess of herself after they'd cleaned her up once already. Then she puked again.

"It's the meds," she heard a woman say.

"She needs water and a new gown," Callan ordered.

Her sobs ricocheted off the shallow bowl, its swirling contents producing a sour stench. "I'm sorry," she choked.

"Stop apologizing. It's not yer fault, love."

She shut her eyes. A firm, warm hand brushed down her back with long soothing strokes. The bowl disappeared and a cloth pressed to her lips. She winced as it brushed over a cut.

"Sorry." A plastic cup appeared. "Take a sip. Not too much."

Her lips closed around a straw, and she swallowed down the cool water. She moaned. "This sucks."

She didn't know what else to say. The drugs numbed the pain, but she couldn't even get high successfully. She suspected, once the drowsy effects evacuated her system, all the hurt would return—descending like a freight train.

She admitted defeat before it happened and folded onto her side.

Callan excused himself, and a nurse helped her change.

From then on she blinked in superficial awareness. Her mind became a placid lake with DO NOT DISTURB signs planted around the perimeter. The slightest sound a cannonball, wrecking her momentary peace.

They collected her clothing as evidence, treated the last of her injuries, and reviewed her x-rays. A shaft fracture in her pinky and articular fractures in her other three fingers. Plus, a number of breaks in the small bones of her hand.

It meant nothing. It was all nothing. Letting it be more than nothing meant it was something.

More pills were offered as a precaution against pregnancy and other possible aftermaths. She swallowed them without question.

The orthopedic surgeon wrapped her hand in plaster, offering advice about care. She shut her eyes and nodded, not hearing a single word.

When everything finally quieted, it seemed the stillest silence in the universe. That was when the truth came out.

"I should have paid better attention."

Callan shifted against the wall. If anyone should witness the blame, it might as well be him. Like poison, she needed to get it out.

"I thought I heard something when I was upstairs. And earlier... I sensed something *off* in him. I should have trusted my gut."

"Evil people masquerade as regular people, Em'ry. Ye couldnae have known what he was until it was too late."

But part of her did know. Her instincts told her to scream, but she didn't listen. "I was afraid of making a fool of myself."

She'd entertained the entire *what if* scenario in her head, all while drying her hands under a predator's watch. If she'd screamed and Marco heard her, he'd have come running. But it could have turned out to be nothing, and she'd have been humiliated and offended a guest of the hotel.

She frowned. But he'd been in the women's bathroom.

Did *she* let this happen? So what if she yelled for nothing because something inside of her didn't feel safe? That should be enough of a reason to call for help, but she'd hesitated. Why?

She thought of all the stories on the news. Were they women who waited too long, too? How long had she actually hesitated? How long had he been in that bathroom before hurting her? One minute? Two? Did it matter?

"I let this happen."

His eyes narrowed, his gaze hardening to a scowl. She'd never seen him look at her like that and instinctively drew back, wincing as her injuries protested.

"Ye listen to me, Em'ry," he said, voice low and threatening. "*Nothin'* about what happened tonight was yer fault. You willnae put the blame on yourself. Dae ye hear me?" His accent thickened and his eyes flashed with haunting menace.

She nodded nervously. "I'm sor—"

"And no more apologies."

Unsure how to respond, she jerked her head in a tight nod. He paced to the opposite end of the room, dragging an unsteady hand through his dark hair. Seeing how upset he was, and not understanding why, filled her with the urge to apologize again, but she'd just agreed not to say *sorry* anymore.

He turned, his face once again a mask of composure. "I dinnae mean to yell at ye. You've been through enough."

"It's okay." It was strangely welcome. Like his fraying nerves made hers more normal.

Silence stole through the room. Something raw and haunting seemed to vibrate within him. She stared at his hands, wishing she could ask how they got that way.

There was so much she didn't know about him, so many signs that he might be a dangerous man, yet he seemed the only person she felt safe around at the moment.

HURT

Chapter Fourteen

Riordan Private Estate
Lower Whitecraigs, Edinburgh—Scotland
Four Years Prior

The childlike laughter that chirped from Rory as he steepled his fingers close to his face with barely contained excitement was perhaps the second most disturbing thing Callan had ever seen or heard in his life. The first was the condition of his sister—and her silence.

The breath rushed out of him. The tension in his body sapped away, leaving his bones hollow and his heart untrustingly full. He was almost grateful for the bindings that tied him to the chair, otherwise shock would have surely knocked him down.

Innis.

Her name washed through him like a sacrament. Her clothing was pure and clean, confusingly vintage. Delicate fringes of white cascaded to the floor from an elegant, mid-century dressing gown. But she was alive. An angel from heaven, come to rescue him.

Her hair shaded her face. He willed her to turn and fully look at him. She showed absolutely no reaction to his or Rhys's presence.

He tried in vain to say her name, but the tape distorted the word. His grasp on reality tumbled as he questioned the authenticity of her presence. It might be a trick.

He forgot the day, the year, when he ate last, where he slept. There was no beginning and no end, only scrambled fractions of truth he dinnae trust.

Rhys floundered against the wall, his muffled grunts wailing against the tape. Callan's heartbeat thundered in his ears.

Then his heart broke all over again. Where was Gavin?

Hurt bloomed anew. A wisp of hope and he'd invested in a tortuous lie. A promise broken before spoken. He suffered his brother's death all over again, his eyes blinking hard to clear his vision, his sister's willowy figure wavering before him.

It was the cruelest trick, giving her back to him but putting her here. She dinnae belong near this filth, these people. How long had she been here?

More than a year. His stomach dropped. What sort of hell had she endured?

Eyes pleading, he looked at the man holding him. Pride disappeared, his need for revenge withered to a silent plea. A truce. He needed to hug her, speak her name.

"Is it not brilliant?" Rory purred. "All this time, ye assumed she was dead. And she was right here—alive. Had I known you were searching for her, I would have sent a message, but I'm afraid you, like all vigilantes, are not in the book." He clapped, delighted. "What a wonderful turn of events!"

She dinnae look at him. Would not. Something wasnae adding up.

While her flesh appeared rosy and her clothes and hair appeared clean—her figure bent in too delicate a way. Her jaw, where it peeked past the curtain of her dark hair, seemed too gaunt, too slender for even Innis.

This wasnae his sister. It was a look alike. Had to be.

"Come, my little trinket." Rory held out a hand, and Innis shuffled closer, her posture subdued but guarded, the way a loyal dog obeys but cowers before its cruel master. She showed no hesitation to lay her hand in Rory's.

He pulled her close so that her back filled Callan's view, Rhys's muffled moans now resembling wounded cries as his brow pinched as he looked at Innis.

Rory watched Callan as he whispered into her ear, loud enough for him to hear. His fingers gently clasped the delicate tip of her chin.

"Head up, Trinket. There you are." He giggled and licked his lips, salivating in anticipation for whatever came next. "Now, look at your brother."

Rhys's muffled screams grew louder and more frantic. Rory's hands closed over her shoulders and slowly turned her to face Callan.

Rhys cried, miserable and stuck to the wall. One of the guards thumped him in the stomach, momentarily silencing his wails to guttural whimpers.

"Look what I've brought you, Trinket." With a delicate hand, Rory lifted her face and tucked the ebony waves behind her shoulders, and the blood rushed from Callan's veins.

His sister's face turned, but she dinnae look at him. One eye lazed, angled toward the floor, hidden by her fringed lashes. The other socket sank into her beautiful face, empty.

Callan's roar filled the silence as he bucked against the chair, a force of rage barreling through him like a stampede. The tape over his mouth did nothing to filter his wrath. The blade by his eye gouged, possibly piercing the tender skin.

What had Rory done to her? Why? He'd massacre him! Make him suffer a thousand deaths without coming close to letting him die.

The guards wrenched his head back, and he seethed. The tension in his shoulders bunched, the chains cutting off his oxygen as the ropes ate into his flesh, strangling his circulation.

He couldnae uncoil the need to break free and destroy. The putrid sight of Rory's hands on his sister's narrow frame did things to him he couldnae bear.

He growled, and Rory smiled. "Now, I have your attention."

His cheeks swelled over the constricting tape covering his mouth, saliva and sweat coated his lips beneath the adhesive. His eyes bulged with vehemence, silent threats of retribution too dark for his enemy to imagine.

The way the bastard handled her, deferentially rather than aggressively, spoke of a fondness Callan couldnae tolerate. Possessive rage ripped through him, igniting a burning fury deeper than any hate.

She still wouldnae look at him. Could she see him? Did she retain the sight in her other eye? Did she not recognize him? There was no measure of the damage already done to her.

His brow pinched as he wheezed hard. He turned his pleading gaze on Rory, silently begging him to remove the gag and let him speak to her.

"Did ye want to say something?" Rory asked in an indulgent tone. He nodded to the guard. "Go ahead then."

A guard ripped off the tape. Callan sucked in a breath and panted. His lips trembled, wet with sweat.

"Innis," he rasped, voice ravaged by emotion. "Innis, love… Look at me."

Though she held herself stiff and straight, her narrow shoulders trembled fiercely at the sound of his voice. Rhys's heavy breathing overpowered the silence.

"Innis, love, say something," Callan begged. "Do ye not know your own brother?"

Rory still held her hand, her dainty fingers resting in his open palm. The monster's mouth twisted, gliding into a smile, slick lips pulling back over all those underdeveloped, sharp teeth.

"I'm afraid you've upset her. You may go, now, Trinket."

"No! Innis!"

Rory watched him closely as he pressed a kiss to her cheek and nudged her toward the door.

"Innis!"

Rhys screamed and earned another silencing blow from the guards. Callan struggled to breathe under the weight of the chains, revolting as their weight restricted him from turning and watching her leave. Stark separation from what he'd already lost choked him.

When the door rammed shut, Callan felt his heart close to the world. Defeated, he wanted to wave his white flag and give in. Just stop fighting and go back to how things used to be. But there was no backward. Only forward.

"Now," Rory said, brushing his palms together as if dusting away crumbs. "Shall we discuss your new position?"

Something dark and feral trembled under his flesh. His voice tore through the room, a raw plea drenched in despair. "What did ye do to her?"

"Trinket's fine."

"Her name is Innis!" he snapped with ferocious rage.

Rory tsked and shook his head. "She's no longer your Innis. She's my trinket. You'll have to respect that."

He flexed every muscle, his body fighting to break the bonds until the rope burned his skin and the chains dug into his bones. Out of breath, he released his weight with a frustrated roar and sagged into the chair.

His chest heaved with the need to sob. He was weak. Useless. The weapons that had been trained on him earlier no longer posed an imminent threat, but the cocksucker had him by the hairs of his bollocks.

"Here's how this is going to work." Rory paced casually as if dictating a letter. "You work for me, as of tonight. Your life will be a revolving door of taxation. Any syndicates in Scotland will pay a fee. I claim a cut in all trafficking—drugs, sex, money—I'm entitled to all of it. Anyone refusing to pay, answers to you. You will report directly to me. And let me warn you now, ye beautiful beast of a man, I'll know the second you think to betray me. And while you might not care about your own life, I know you care about hers. There are worse things I can do than kill her. She understands that. Do you?"

Impotent rage stormed inside of him, churning his stomach into acid and burning away the last of his humanity. Innis was alive, but now death seemed a touch more merciful. How had it come to this?

"Do we have an agreement?"

There would be blood on his hands, the blood of men he dinnae know, men he had no issue with. By the time Rory was through with him, his sins would be too many for the Heavenly Father to forgive. This place would be his end.

His focus shifted. He needed to get Innis out of here. Once she was safely somewhere that Rory couldnae get to her, he'd carve out the man's heart and make him eat it.

His life whittled down to a debt he dinnae owe, but one that would ruin him to pay—until his sister was safely away from this place.

But in the end, he would collect. He'd take everything from those who stole from them. But first, he needed to know if he should expect any more surprises.

"Where is Gavin?"

He held his breath, afraid to hope, afraid to uncover a worse fate.

Just … afraid.

"The boy? Too young for my taste. Trinket, on the other hand, her beauty appeals to me. Much like yours but in a slightly different way."

"Men…" The word hung with implied curiosity. He hated to ask anything of such scum, but if his instinct was right and Rory preferred men, Innis might be safer than she seemed.

Rory lifted a shoulder. "Men, women. Hell, I'd fuck a dog if it did it for me. Depends on what sort of day I'm having." He approached the chair and dragged a tapered finger over his thigh. "I collect beautiful things as devotedly as I collect weapons. You, MacGregor, are a beautiful weapon. And now, you're mine."

Callan jerked his knee away from his touch and Rory laughed.

The ache in his chest spread like wildfire. Did they take Gavin? Kill him? Had he died in the fire?

Maybe it was better if he dinnae know. But what if they let him go?

He tried to keep his mind moving forward. No matter what, he'd see this vendetta to the end. His vow was solid. He would be the last person Rory saw before leaving this world. Everything from this moment forward would determine how much Callan made him suffer.

"What happened to her eyes?"

"Oh, that." His lips twisted in what seemed genuine regret. "A bit too much sass, but we worked it out. She's quite obedient, now, as docile as a doll." A dreamy glaze covered his eyes. "My trinket."

His stomach rolled as he mentally searched for explanations. Any graphic details might push him, and he was already past his breaking point. "What do ye want with her?"

"She's my toy," Rory said as if that explained everything. "She's whatever I want her to be."

Perhaps the flamboyant tells he'd spotted were more than a hunger for the same sex. Maybe effeminate hobbies also came into play. "I don't understand. Explain it to me."

"There's nothing more beautiful than a woman. The delicate bone structure, the fragility, the soft tickle of a female voice... The ease with which they scream." His eyes rolled closed, and he shivered as if titillated. "Fascinating creatures."

The ease with which they scream...

Working hard to keep his voice from breaking, he asked, "Do ye hurt her?"

At this, he scowled. "I take care of my toys so long as they behave. Trinket knows what I need. She likes being in my care. I dress her, brush her. I make her pretty."

That dinnae answer his question. "Can she see?"

No matter what Rory claimed, he'd disfigured her.

He waved away Callan's concern. "She has her vision in her good eye."

He had the empathetic capacity of a psychopath.

"Is she on drugs?"

Rory chuckled. "There are things much more powerful than drugs, MacGregor. Human resolve, for instance. Trust me when I tell you, your sister's here of her own free will. I don't lock her in, and yet she chooses to stay. She thanks me for allowing her to live here every single day."

Rhys groaned, reminding them of his presence. The guards had done a number on him, and his body was likely numb from hanging on the wall.

Rory plucked up a small blade from the collection of weapons on the table, using the tip to scrape the dirt out from under a manicured fingernail.

"Do you know anything about pelicans?"

Callan scowled, sick of the theatrics. "When do I get to see Innis again?"

"When I say so. Pelicans. Do you know anything about them?"

His molars locked. "No."

"Impressive creatures, solely devoted to those they love. They'll do anything for their wee hatchlings."

He returned to the table, opening a leather duffle and dropping the weapons inside one by one.

"Pelicans are so intensely led by responsibility they've been known to pierce their own breast and sacrifice their lives to save those in their care. They bleed from the heart, literally, to deliver sustenance to their young when food is scarce, even if it eventually kills them."

He handed the bag to a guard, delivering quick instructions for the others to gather the weapons that wouldnae fit. Two men left the room.

Rory folded his arms over his chest and leaned into the wall, facing Callan. "Spiritually, pelicans are the tortured heroes. Patient and wise, with an intimate knowledge of suffering. But like Jesus to the cross, Socrates to poison, and Joan of Arc to the flame, mortality remains an insoluble failing. Do you understand what I'm telling you, MacGregor? Do you know why the pelican bleeds?"

He drew in a measured breath, reminding himself that he was at this psychopath's mercy as long as he wanted to see Innis again. "Duty and love."

"Yes. And the moral of the story, my darling boy, is that love will always be fatal. *You* are the pelican, MacGregor. And I own everything you love. For them, and for me, ye will bleed."

HURT

Chapter Fifteen

***Saratoga Springs, New York—America
Present Day***

"Thank you. I'll let her know."

Emery came awake, reluctance keeping her eyelids pressed tight, but it was too late. She blinked, still at the clinic.

"Good morning," Callan said, voice soft. He'd finally settled into a chair, but pulled it back from the bed. Maybe he was afraid to get too close.

"Morning." Good was up for debate.

"That was Officer Knowles on the phone. They have him in custody. No issues."

The subtlety of his words vanished with crushing significance. The earth didn't shake and time moved on, but somewhere in the midst of her sleep, they'd apprehended the maker of her nightmares.

And he went quietly, like a sinking pebble into a placid pond. Hardly a ripple at all.

A thousand little needles punched through her skin as she tried to make sense of the hush-hush way this monster drifted into custody when, to her, he'd been the most unstoppable force she'd ever met.

She expected a bigger splash. It didn't seem real without one.

"He's been arrested? He's in jail?" She hadn't expected it to happen so fast—so easily.

She frowned. Why hadn't he run? Was she just another broken piece of coral shamelessly stolen from an otherwise perfect reef that he'd take no accountability for destroying?

"They want you to sign a statement. So they can charge him." Purple shadows showed beneath Callan's eyes.

"Have you slept?"

He shook his head. "I'm not one for sleepin' much."

Yet, exhaustion showed in his face and posture. "You don't have to stay."

"I know it. I'm here because I want to be."

Despite her gaping sorrow and guilt for hijacking his night, she smiled. "Thank you."

"No need to thank me. When we leave here, I'll go with you to the station."

She felt like she was missing something. "Is something wrong?"

His lips formed a grim line. "If a judge grants him bail, they can only hold him for a short time. Statistically, white, privileged men escape legal situations with … leaner consequences than most in this country."

"Oh, God." Betrayal stabbed into her heart. "How long can they hold him?"

"He'll need to go before a judge, and maybe—given the medical report—they'll hold him without bail."

She shook her head. At this point, even emotional coddling abraded. "He'll get bail, and someone will pay it." He seeped charm, privilege, and entitlement. Those things came with connections.

"I'm sorry, love. It's just the way of things no matter how wrong it is."

She sat up, her body protesting in ways that felt foreign. "But it just happened. We haven't been to court." She knew very little about the justice process, but this felt innately wrong. This was a dangerous man they were letting go.

"Until convicted, he's technically innocent. They can hold him on charges, but most likely a judge will grant him the right to post bail. They'll get him on charges of battery and aggravated assault, too, but this is his first offense."

Fury boiled inside of her. Like he was some sort of a boy scout! "Did they send over all my medical reports?"

"The polis have everything."

Her brow tightened, the sense of fighting a losing battle overwhelming her before the war even began. "It doesn't seem fair."

"No," he agreed, but it was clear there was nothing they could do.

Her head hung. "I guess I need a lawyer."

"They'll supply a prosecutor, but having an advocate on yer side is always a good idea. We can ask around for a recommendation."

Her side? "Everything's moving so fast." And yet, she felt like she'd been waiting in this room forever.

"Ye have time. First, he'll have an arraignment. The trial willnae come until later, dependin' on how he pleads."

How was he so informed about the legal system? He wasn't even a natural citizen. "Did you have to learn about our legal system when you got your citizenship?"

He shifted in the chair and folded the coat draped over his thighs. "Something like that."

She ate some crackers and drank a glass of apple juice for breakfast. She couldn't bring herself to touch any of the other food they brought.

Her appetite wasn't the issue, chewing was. Her jaw pulsed and her eardrum kept clicking and crackling. The doctors said one of the blows had ruptured it. Callan said it would hurt less in a day or two. It was only one of her injuries, but enough to make her miserable.

Pushing her breakfast tray away, she huffed. "I can't eat anymore. My face is killing me." She pressed on her ear. Nothing helped.

"You're lucky it burst. The pressure's the painful part. Now, it's just gotta heal."

"Are you also an ear expert?"

He pointed to the side of his head. "Ye dinnae get ears like this without learnin' a thing or two about the pain."

It was the first time she ever really looked at his ears. At a quick glance, they looked like everyone else's. But now she saw the misshapen curve and the way the center swelled unnaturally.

Her breath hitched. It looked painful. "What happened to you?"

He faced her, eyes creased with a forced smile that seemed plastic. "I used to get into a lot of scraps in Scotland."

"Fights?"

He nodded but didn't elaborate.

"We don't have to talk about it."

His gaze shifted away. "Maybe someday."

She bit another cracker. As her stare dropped to his hands. "Is that..."

He looked at her, and she swallowed, remembering her manners.

"Never mind."

"What were ye gonna ask?"

She tried to make something up, but couldn't bring herself to lie to him. She tipped her chin. "Your hands. Are they like that from fighting?"

He closed his fists. "Some."

Her gaze traced the scars on his face and neck, knowing each one by heart. She glanced at the thick muscle roped around his forearm. Heavy veins and corded sinew, under a masculine dusting of black hair.

Just beneath his elbow, stretching only a few inches from his wrist, was a sort of scarred band, little markings forming several columns and rows, wrapping around his arm. Unlike his other scars, these appeared intentional.

"What's that?"

The misshapen fingers of his right hand covered the tracks. "These are off limits."

His words chilled the air between them. She instantly regretted her curiosity and knew she'd never ask about the band of scars again. But her mind wouldn't stop wondering.

Had someone done that to him? Was he abused as a child? They looked too … new. What did they mean and why did the last row stop in the middle? The pattern looked unfinished.

Eventually, a daytime nurse arrived delivering a jogging suit. The police had taken her other clothes for evidence. She didn't have shoes with her, so she slipped on a pair of hospital socks, the good kind with the foot grips.

When it was time to go, a sense of displacement overcame her. They didn't have a car, because they arrived by ambulance. No shoes, no car, no purse. She was a balloon let go from its string, and gravity had no hold on her.

Callan's hand brushed to her back, hardly touching but enough to keep her moving. "I've called for a car."

Thank God he was there. She could barely find her way out of the clinic.

She'd never used an Uber, and it felt strange sitting in the back of someone's family van, baby books stuffed in the pocket behind the seat, the scent of dried Cheerios and artificial strawberries suspended in the air.

The entire drive was surreal. She didn't have to talk. Couldn't think of words.

Callan sat beside her, the empty middle seat wearing a dusting of crumbs from the family that owned the car. She kept her head down and studied him, staring under her lashes at his thick thighs and long legs.

He could be so still. So powerful.

She drew so much from his strength. This nightmare could have been a thousand times worse if he hadn't been there. And he was still here, by her side.

Without thinking, she reached across the middle seat and turned her palm upward, opening her hand.

He glanced down, and then back to her face, a silent battle unraveling in his eyes. She peeked down, and back to him.

His chest lifted on a slow breath.

He moved in slow increments, his crooked fingers coming to rest in hers. Warm. Secure. Right. She managed a tiny smile and closed her fingers around his.

HURT

Chapter Sixteen

Riordan Private Estate
Lower Whitecraigs, Edinburgh—Scotland
Four Years Prior

"**I** want to talk to her—alone," Callan barked.

"What do you suggest I do with your friend?" Rory asked, seeming not at all surprised by his demand.

"He can stay."

He drew in a breath and gave Rhys a measuring, seemingly unimpressed look. "Wonderful. Another leech." He waved a hand at Callan, addressing the guards that returned, "Remove the chains."

As they stripped away the weight of heavy metal, his body sagged with relief. Rory folded his hands at the base of his back and stood in front of him, placing his face directly in his.

"You understand what's at stake. Betray me, and I'll make it hurt in ways you've never imagined." He let the warning settle over him. "I'll hurt *her*."

He wanted to spit in his face, bite off his nose. "I understand."

"Good." Rory unfolded his body and removed his knife, cutting away the ropes.

Callan's body thrummed. He could attack, take his knife and ram it into Rory's jugular. Disarm the remaining guards, snapping each of their necks then rescue Rhys and go find Innis.

"Dinnae be foolish," Rory warned, meeting his gaze. "I welcome a reason to make her scream."

He squelched his murderous desires and forced his will into submission. A silent beat passed where they all seemed to hold their collective breath.

Finally, Rory nodded—satisfied. "I'll leave ye alone now. Have fun."

The second the door closed, Rhys screamed behind the tape. Callan's stiff legs protested as he stood. His body wobbled, the blood rushing into his limbs and out of his brain. The scarring on the soles of his feet hindered his balance as he staggered into the cinderblock wall.

Rhys grunted, urging him on. Clinging to his prone body, Callan ripped the tape off Rhys's mouth.

"Bleedin' Christ! Get me off this fuckin' wall."

He shoved a shoulder into Rhys's stomach and hoisted him upward, stretching to unhook the rope from the peg. His full weight toppled them to the ground.

"I'm going to kill that dirty fuck!" Rhys hissed, moaning and wincing as the blood likely flooded his extremities in a storm of stinging pins and needles.

"Not before I do." Callan shoved him off and caught his breath. He dinnae have a knife to cut his mate's hands free.

They worked together to unknot the rope, unraveling it quickly, and then they both stilled. Reality crashed over them at exactly the same time, wiping them clear off the grid of sanity and leaving them stranded on an island of lunacy.

"Did you see what he did to her?" Rhys breathed, a tortured glaze overtaking his green eyes.

"He'll pay."

"He took her fuckin' eye, Callan. She was perfect, and he ruined her."

He shoved his friend. "He dinnae ruin her! She's still Innis." A vise closed around his chest. "She's still…"

Had he broken her? How much of her actually remained?

"We need to speak to her. Until we get her talkin', we dinnae ken anything."

"Aye," Rhys agreed. "He's got to be holdin' somethin' over her. Why else would she stay?"

"He's full of shite. He'll not let her leave. She's a fuckin' prisoner here." He forced his legs to bend and slowly stood, helping Rhys off the ground.

"Do ye think he was lyin' about Gavin?"

Callan swallowed. He couldnae fool himself into hoping his baby brother was still alive. And if he was here, that wasnae exactly a better status than death. "I dinnae ken."

Rory was a psychotic son of a bitch, but he seemed dangerously candid. Brutally honest and unflinchingly cruel. If he said he dinnae have Gavin, Callan was tempted to believe him. And he despised that fine thread of trust, hated that he already knew the man well enough to believe anything out of his mouth.

"I dinnae think he's here," he finally said. "Wishin' he was, is a selfish wish. What good would it do him to be trapped in this hell? God took mercy on his soul when he removed him from this world. Nothin' but ugliness."

Rhys quieted.

"When Innis gets here, we'll find out what we can," Callan said, not wanting to get overly introspective about Gavin at a time like this. "Then I want ye to take her away from here. Go as fast and as far as ye can get. Just keep runnin' until ye hit the ocean. Take her where even I cannae find her. That way we know Rory willnae."

"I have no money te go anywhere."

"Under my mattress, at yer place, there's about eighty pounds and some quid. That should get ye as far as Dublin. Do whatever ye need to do to get more, but do it quietly. No matter what, dinnae use your real names." Her missing eye would give her away. "Try to keep her out of sight."

"What names do we use?"

"Fergus and Uma Stewart." It was their parents' names, their mother's maiden name.

"Aye. That'll work." Rhys rubbed the tension out of his neck. "Will ye be far behind?"

"I'll do what he asks for a time. Then, when he least expects it, I'll slit his fuckin' throat. Only when he and all his men are dead will I come for you and Innis."

"Maybe we should just run—the three of us. If ye kill him, people will be lookin' for ye."

"They'll all be dead."

A shuffle sounded from the hall, and Callan held up a hand, silencing Rhys. He reached for his knife, forgetting his weapons were gone.

Pressing a finger to his lips, he motioned for Rhys to get to the other side of the room, the better to defend themselves against anyone wishing them harm. The heavy door creaked, and he held his breath. Pressure, with the weight of an anvil, slammed into his chest as Innis's lithe form filled the doorway.

He exhaled roughly, and she flinched when he crossed the space in two strides. Her face angled toward the floor, and her hair, again, struck him as surprisingly clean for a hostage.

His raw voice sliced down to a thin breath as he rasped her name. "Innis." But she still wouldnae meet his gaze.

Rhys moved forward, his courage to touch her outweighing Callan's. Hands shaking, he lifted her chin and stared into her damaged face.

A tear carved a wet track down Rhys's bloodied face. "Oh, Innis…" A patch now covered her missing eye, and he traced a finger over the black canvas. "What has he done to you?"

Her lips compressed, and her good eye screwed shut, tears dampening her lashes. Her shoulders quaked, and her sorrow brought him bitter relief. If she heard and recognized them, the damage might only be on the outside.

"Easy, beauty." Rhys pulled her close, but her arms dinnae lift from her sides.

This moment, it wasnae his. She was his beloved sister, but as she leaned into his friend's arms, Callan understood the truth of things he never wanted to acknowledge. He finally saw the heartache of all the pain and hurt Rhys had suffered since the fire.

Innis's weak sobs tore at Callan's heart. Rhys pressed his lips to her hair, breathed promises into her ears, and held her with such gentle possession Callan could only see the purity of his friend's love.

"My heart hasnae beat right since I lost ye."

Her delicate sniffles pitched in a strange tenor like she'd somehow forgotten how to cry. "I couldnae get away."

"Hush. You did what you needed to do, beauty. I'm here now."

She nodded, edging away from Rhys but his grip noticeably tightened. "It's not safe."

"I dinnae care." He kissed her again, and Callan drew back, feeling like an unwelcome voyeur and drawing Rhys's attention. "Your brother…"

She reached for Callan, and he stumbled forward, the tightening knot in his throat crushing his windpipe. His arms itched to close around her, but he trembled so fiercely he feared the slightest contact might turn him to dust.

She untangled herself from Rhys, and the invitation for any contact was silently rescinded.

Her arms hugged her ribs. "You have te leave. I know Rory convinced you te stay, but you have te go. The both of ye."

"I'm not leavin' ye here," Rhys snapped. "And Callan can handle himself."

"Do ye not get it?" Her face crumbled, her hands fisting in front of her chest. "He doesnae have an off switch. He doesnae care who he hurts, and he willnae hesitate te hurt ye if it gets him what he wants."

"What does he want?" Callan still couldnae accept that this was about a human doll and taxation.

"Power. Loyalty. Toys. It's all a game to him. He's demented, and he'll use ye against me."

Or maybe use her against them. "We're gettin' you out of here."

"No."

"Aye. Tonight. You'll go with Rhys, and I'll stay behind."

"No, you're not listening! I'm safe until I leave."

"*This is safe?*" Callan yelled, not expecting an argument. "Were ye safe when he did tha' to your face?"

Her body noticeably stiffened. She silently gathered herself, straightening her spine and raising her chin. "I'm not a child anymore."

Rhys took a step closer. "Innis—"

She jerked away when he tried to touch her. "Of all people, ye should be on my side, Rhys."

"I am on yer side," he snapped. "Leavin' is the right thing to do! Callan will catch up with us."

"No." She shook her head, taking several steps back. "I'm not a prisoner here. I havenae been for some time. He knows I'll never leave. I cannae betray that."

"Jesus. He's gotten in yer head." This could only be some demented form of Stockholm's. "Innis, we're yer family."

Her mouth pressed tight. "I'm staying. I have to."

Callan's mind scrambled. "Does he have Gavin—"

"Gavin's dead." She held his stare. "They drowned him the night of the fire. He never made it out of Glasgow."

He staggered back, his entire body gone cold.

"Do ye not see?" she pleaded. "He knows how to get what he wants. He's ruthless. They all are. But he's the boss."

She dinnae know the things he'd done since losing his mind. "Innis, I can protect you—"

Her head shook. "No! Ye have te go. I cannae spare the worry, and I cannae stomach the thought of anything happening te either of you."

"You're out of yer fuckin' mind if ye think we're leavin' you here!" Rhys snapped. "Enough of this. There's nothin' he can do te hold ye here if we leave together."

"Ye dinnae ken! Ye think that, but ye dinnae have all the facts. I assure ye, he can keep me here. There's nothing ye can say to make me betray him."

"Why?" Callan all but snarled.

She looked up at him, tears swimming in her eye. "I'm sorry," she whispered. Her head lowered and she turned to Rhys, her tears dripping down her face in defeated resignation. "I have to stay because he has our daughter."

HURT

Chapter Seventeen

Saratoga Springs, New York—America
Present Day

Officer Banks met Callan and Emery outside of the station and escorted them inside. Her powerful polis presence cast an invisible shield around Emery, and he appreciated what seemed innate protectiveness.

They were led into a private room with a table and four chairs. Officer Banks sat across from them and slid a stack of stapled papers over the battered tabletop.

"You can take as much time as you need. You'll want to read over everything carefully. If you recall new details or find any errors, we'll correct the information. At the bottom of each page, there's a space for you to initial. Only initial pages that have accurate information. And let me know if there's anything you'd like to add."

Emery stared at the thick packet, her hands resting in her lap under the table. "I have to read all of this, now?"

"I know it's overwhelming," Officer Banks spoke in a tone that made Callan grateful she'd been the officer on duty last night. Empathy and exhaustion reflected in her eyes, a testament of her dedication to the job. "But we need an exact statement in order to press charges."

The room grew so silent and cold he could hear Emery's breath skating into the air. Slowly, she lifted her left hand and turned over the cover page. Time suspended as she stared down at that first page listing her name and personal details.

"Pen...?" she rasped, and Officer Banks slid one across the table.

Emery lifted it like a foreign object, limited to her left hand. She took a moment to adjust her hold in her less dominant hand, another long moment to read over the first page, which verified logistical details.

Her initials scraped onto the bottom of the sheet with unsteady curves. A long huff filled the silence as she turned the page.

Black, heavily inked words crowded the white space. His eyes glazed over as several terms popped off the page. *Victim. Intercourse. Bathroom. Pushed. Pulled. Said stop. Repeated. Penis. Forced. Evidence.* Blunt and matter-of-fact, the words carved into him, yet lacked all accountability. It was as if these events had happened to an object, not a person. They read like stereo instructions, yet each offensive letter processed like a lead bullet, lethal enough to rip a person open.

There were roughly twenty-some pages, and she initialed one about every five minutes. Some she seemed to only stare at, not reading a single word.

Many times he wished to help her through, but his voice abandoned him. He couldnae say those horrific truths out loud. It would hurt too much. Just watching her struggle through this moment gutted him.

Somehow, she made it to the last page where she signed a sloppy version of her name and gently put down the pen. Officer Banks attempted to speak when she finished, but Callan held up a hand, silencing any further discussion. It was enough. Emery had suffered enough.

They waited outside for another car to collect them. Ten, possibly twenty minutes in the cold and neither he nor Emery spoke a word. What was there to say?

The ride to her home seemed an out of body experience. He could only imagine what she was feeling.

Emery lived in a wee house with a red door, twin planters beneath the front windows and a large tree in the front. It sat like a postcard on a picture perfect street. The driver dropped them off and realized they dinnae have keys.

Knowing one hid under the planter, he waited for her to disclose its location. She stared at him as if she dinnae recognize her own home.

"The door's locked," he said softly, and she blinked.

"Oh." Bruises had started to darken on her face. She nudged the planter aside, its need for water making it light, but she still winced.

"I can—"

"Here." Her discomfort showed in the set of her mouth and the way she coddled her side as she bent down.

He silently took the key and opened the door, following her into the house. It was the first time he'd ever been *invited* inside.

"Can I get ye something?" He knew she liked chamomile tea sometimes, and there was that mangy, stuffed dog she slept with. "Tea?"

He needed a distraction from his thoughts. Before they left the clinic, the doctor gave a rundown of all her injuries. The length of the damage gutted him.

Contusions on the front of her hips, slight tearing of flesh, numerous lacerations on the backs of her thighs, multiple shattered bones in her hand... He couldnae think of the more intimate details without losing his mind, so he blocked out several. Her biggest scars would mark her heart.

"You're probably starving," she said, drifting into the kitchen.

He frowned, not worried about his needs. He knew her jaw was hurting. And her ears. "Do ye have soup? I could put some on, get something in yer stomach. Broth willnae pain you te eat."

"Hello, sweet baby."

He turned, drawn by the soft pitch of her voice. Little begging mews filled the quiet as her cat rubbed her legs. She crouched down, but it cost her.

"Where do ye keep the cat food?"

"In the cabinet next to the fridge."

The cat followed him to the cupboard, jumping into the open cabinet. It butted its furry head against his arm, and Callan laughed. "A wee lion."

"He likes you."

A relationship that had taken time to cultivate. He grinned and scratched the wee beastie's head. When he poured the food into its bowl, it purred, munching with eager bites.

"What's his name?"

"Ernie."

He cocked his head. "Like the puppet?"

"Like the writer. It's short for Ernest Hemingway."

He crouched in front of the counter, studying the hungry critter. "Hemingway's a good name— one of my favorite authors. I doubt you appreciate her callin' ye Ernie though."

"You read Hemingway?"

He stood and searched for a pan to heat some soup. He helped himself to whatever was in her cabinets, finding a few options and the necessary utensils in the drawers.

"He's one of the best. Wastes no time gettin' to the point, and he has an eloquent way of describing life's ugliness." He dragged a hand over the cat's back, and its spine hitched. "Hemingway believed cats were the souls of a house. Tomato or chicken noodle?" He held up two cans.

Her lips twitched into a semblance of a smile. "Tomato. In a mug please."

He got to work, searching out a can opener and figuring out the controls of her stove. She disappeared into the other room.

A bang ripped his attention from the soup, and he rushed toward the sound. "What do ye think you're doin'?"

Her face flushed, her breathing unsteady. The sofa cushions were on the floor, and a metal frame protruded from the couch.

"I'm opening this for you."

Pressing his lips tight so not to yell at her for taxin' herself on his account, he crossed the room and pulled the accordion frame free. "Just … sit. The doctors said no heavy lifting." And he dinnae recall asking for a bed.

She lowered into the chair, and he regretted raising his voice.

Her gaze dropped to the floor. "I don't know how to do this."

He frowned. "Ye dinnae need to do anything, Em'ry."

"They all know, don't they? Matt, Marco, Christine…"

He lowered himself to sit across from her, and the mattress whined. "There's nothin' to be ashamed of, love."

A deep V formed between her brows. "I know this wasn't my fault, but the humiliation keeps getting bigger. And the audience keeps getting wider."

"No one's judgin' ye."

Her head turned to the side, face pinched with tension. "I don't know if I'll be able to go back there."

His heart stuttered. He couldnae imagine working at the hotel with no Emery. She was the reason he kept the job. "Give yourself time."

How much time? Before he could think of something more comforting to say, the soup hissed in the kitchen, and he cursed.

The pot had boiled over, and he had a fine mess on his hands. He pulled the last paper towel from the roll and searched for napkins.

"Will you stay?"

All concerns washed away as he pivoted.

She stood in the open doorway looking nothing like herself. Purple and yellow bruises shaded her face, and her hair was twisted back in a ponytail that made her look a decade younger than she was. The baggy sweats they'd given her swallowed her womanly figure. She looked absolutely innocent and terrified.

"Aye. I'll stay as long as ye need." He'd just have to make a phone call.

Relief loosened her spine, and she leaned into the wall. "Thank you."

He fixed her a mug of soup and cleaned up the mess while she sipped it silently. They dinnae speak, but neither of them seemed to mind the silence. Silence meant not crying.

Her eyes wore a hundred years of exhaustion when she looked at him.

"You need sleep," he whispered.

"I need a shower."

His stomach turned. They'd sponged her clean at the clinic, but he couldnae bear to imagine what her body felt like, the sort of invisible filth she'd been trying to ignore.

"I'll wrap your cast. Do you have a bag?"

She pointed to the cupboard, and he remembered one of those dainty bag socks.

His hands shook as he unwound the crinkled plastic. Guilt, for not realizing this would be her first concern, stole through him, followed by the painful awareness that another man had touched her. More than touched her—*violated her.*

He gripped the cabinet door, catching his breath. His legs shook with unsure steps as he staggered to a chair.

She held out her casted hand, and he covered it carefully with the plastic bag. So trusting. So gentle.

A delicate groove tightened at her brow, just above a yellowing bruise. She blinked at him and frowned.

"You…" She paused and looked at him in question. "You came back to the hotel."

"I…" He shifted, self-consciousness jostling his usual confidence. She deserved his honesty where he could offer it. "I couldn't leave. I tried, but I had a feelin'—stronger than usual."

"Stronger than usual?" she repeated.

He swallowed and nodded. "I try hard not to get in yer way, but I'm not perfect."

"What are you saying?"

His lips pressed into a thin line. His gaze shifted away at the discomforting sense of exposure.

"Callan?"

He couldnae do it. Terrified he might scare her, he couldnae tell her how much he thought about her when they were apart. "We'll discuss it another time."

"I thought you met someone on Fridays. Isn't that where you go?"

His gaze jerked back to her. Is that what she thought? Nothing could be further from the truth. "No."

Confusion dominated her bruised face, but he sensed relief. Did she not realize how fond of her he was? Of course, she dinnae realize. How would she?

In that moment, it became everything to pay her a compliment. Something she could hold onto and take with her into tomorrow and the next day as the dust settled, something that told her he *saw* and *respected* her.

"You're very strong, Em'ry."

Her jaw quivered, a fresh sheet of tears shimmering in her eyes. "What other choice do I have?"

"Not all women would handle this so well."

"You don't *handle* it. It handles you."

Cradling her broken hand in his, he sighed. "Dinnae underestimate your resilience, love. Ye never know how much ye can take until ye reach a point where ye can take no more."

"I think I'm there."

He shook his head. "No. You're still breathin'."

A tear tripped past her lashes, the gentle fall nicking his heart. It seemed like a sin to let such sorrows escape. He caught it with a trace of his thumb, and she stared at him, not in fear or repulsion, but in some sort of awe.

Her uninjured hand lifted to his face, and he held his breath. Her eyes squinted, and she traced a finger over his temple. The scar there cut clean through his eyebrow. He'd had it for nearly six years, but it never felt healed. Not until her fingers touched it.

With a soft caress, her caress feathered down his cheek, the delicate pads treading over the stubble of his beard.

"You're so beautiful," she whispered.

He dinnae know what to say to such a misdirected comment. His breath quickened when she outlined his lips with her fingertips. "Em'ry."

She blinked up at him as if just realizing what she was doing. Her hand dropped to her lap, and she looked away. "Sorry."

He should go, but he'd never be able to leave her in such a fragile state. "I'll make ye tea for after yer shower."

Her eyes closed and she sighed. "You're so kind. You'd never hurt anyone."

He looked away. He'd turned a deaf ear while men begged for their lives. He'd made them suffer until they pleaded for oblivion. "Everyone's capable of hurting others."

She frowned as if she doubted his words. "But you respect the word '*no*'."

From her? Always. "You never have to fear me, Em'ry." He'd always protect her.

"They give us these words, little, tiny things like *no* and *stop*. They tell us they're weapons, but they're useless. He hardly flinched when I screamed."

His gut twisted. "You dinnae have te talk about it."

"That's the thing. I can't stop thinking about it. He's turned my body into a prison, and I'm stuck inside for the rest of my life. Soap isn't going to wash this away." She dropped her gaze, hiding her eyes. "I don't want to be me anymore. I'm trapped in my skin, and all I want to do is escape myself."

His heart broke. His hands lifted, seeking a place to hold, and hesitating. "You feel that way now, but I swear to you, this ache will heal." He gently cupped her shoulders. "Your body is yours, Em'ry. Not his. Not anyone else's. It may feel foreign right now, but it will become familiar again. You have to give yourself time, love."

The breadth and depth of her injuries cut him open.

"You're not what he's done to ye, Em'ry."

He had to believe that. Because, if she was the sum of someone else's sins, he'd be the poison that infested the world.

Chapter Eighteen

Riordan Private Estate
Lower Whitecraigs, Edinburgh—Scotland
Four Years Prior

"Daughter?" Callan repeated.

Innis met his stare head-on, wearing the stone-cold certainty of a woman who knew her worth and dinnae appreciate having to spell out the facts of her life to anyone else.

"That's right." She glanced at Rhys who wore a shell-shocked mask.

"Who's the fuckin' father?" Callan snarled, ready to kill.

She scowled at him. "Who do ye think? It's Rhys's."

He glared at his friend, forgetting all the sentimental whispering Innis and Rhys shared only minutes ago. "Ye touched her?"

Innis caught Callan's hands, jerking his attention back to her. "I named her Uma, after Ma."

231

A smile trembled to her lips, and she glanced behind her to Rhys. "And she's got wild green eyes like her da."

Wrenching his hands free, his fist flew into Rhys's face, dropping him like a sack of potatoes.

"*Callan!*" She shouted, following Rhys to the ground, catching his face in her hands. "Rhys!"

He groaned, still in shock, and she glared up at Callan.

"What did ye hit him for, ye doaty bassa? You're twice his size!"

Callan rolled his eyes. "It's what he deserves for puttin' his hands on ye! *Pregnant*? Christ, Innis! How did ye expect us to take care of a baby on top of everything else?"

The scowl she sent him could have chiseled glass. "I figured it dinnae much matter. Since bein' abducted, and tortured, and seein' my brother thrown off a bridge in a sack while I screamed in horror... Havin' the screams slapped out of me..." Her shoulders moved with each heavy breath. "Well, I guess by then I thought, just havin' some wee piece of what my life used te be, somethin' good, and pure, somethin' tha' only knew love... Something tha' gave me a reason te keep on breathin'... Well, I guess I figured it dinnae much matter what *you* thought."

By the time she finished, she was standing at her full height, glaring up at him with stone cold fury.

He swallowed hard, his head dropping in shame. "If..." He cleared his throat when his voice failed to make a sound. "If I'd known ye were here, I would have come for ye."

"I know ye would have. But ye dinnae. I was here six miserable months before I had her, and the mornin' my water broke, I prayed I'd die in labor."

His heart shattered, the fractured pieces withering to dust and blowing through the tired bones of his hollow chest.

"But then I held her in my arms, and I felt stronger than I had in ... ever. I found the strength te keep breathing, te stop fightin' a battle I'd never win. All my energy went into protectin' her. My daughter." She glanced at both of them and took a step back. "She's my first and last loyalty in this world, and I'll not let either of ye put her in harm's way. I'll fight ye with everything I've got if it means keepin' her safe."

He mistook her for a victim when he first saw her here. But now her strength filled the room. This was no longer his sweet, wee sister, but a fierce woman who chose courage in the face of fear and, despite everything, she still stood proud.

He regretted ever doubting her ability to handle things he clearly could not.

Dropping his head and his voice, he softened. "I'm proud of ye, Innis."

"I don't need yer pride. I need ye te leave here before it's too late. Let me handle everything else my way. I know how te maneuver Rory."

"I cannae do tha'." She was so strong, and he hated to clip her wings, but it was for the best. "We can get you and the wain someplace safe."

She took a sharp step back, closer to the door. Her head shook. "Why can ye not trust me te know what's best here?"

"What you're suggesting is insane. This place is poisoned."

Her eyes flicked to the door. "He's coming."

He paused, hearing nothing. Then... Distant footfalls—softer than those of a man wearing boots. "We'll protect ye and the baby, Innis."

"I'm not leaving ye here with my child," Rhys said, his mouth a hard line of determination.

Callan shot him an incredulous look. The second Rhys agreed to stay with her she'd feel vindicated. "No," Callan argued. "You're leaving with her. I'll follow."

"We'll figure out a different plan," Rhys argued. "I'm staying."

Everything was crumbling around them. "No one's stayin' here," he hissed.

The steps drew closer. Panic flashed in her eye just before a mask of tranquility fell into place.

He wasnae sure how she did it. It was like watching her disappear, turn into an inanimate object. Human and then ... vacant.

The door pushed open, and Rory appeared. "Did we have a nice reunion?" He held out a hand, palm up, and Innis, once again, draped her fingers across his. The side of his mouth curled into a smile, overflowing with conceit.

It would be so easy to snap his neck. But guards were everywhere, and they had no weapons.

Callan's knuckles popped, his hands twitched with the urge to maim.

"MacGregor?" He pulled Innis to his side, combing a hand through her dark hair that tumbled down her back and arms. "Do we have an agreement?"

"Aye. I'll do the job ye want. But I ask that ye set Innis and the baby free."

"Trinket's always been free to leave." His fingers slowly coiled around her hair, the strands raveling around his knuckles like a boxer tapes his hands. "The wain, however..." His taunting gaze drifted to the other side of the room where Rhys seethed. "She looks to me as a father."

Rhys lunged forward, and Callan caught his shoulder, hauling him back. "You're not the child's father!"

A placid grin matched Rory's flat eyes. "The child stays." He yanked his hand free from Innis's hair with enough force to make her flinch. He shoved her aside. "Perhaps I need to find a new toy—less ... damaged. Maybe you should go, and Uma and I will find a better mommy."

Innis notably trembled, her hair a shiny curtain of black as she turned her gaze away. This was how he got her absolute obedience.

"No," Callan said, saving her the humiliation. "She stays where the child stays, or none of us stay."

"So be it." He clicked a finger at Innis as if she was nothing more than a dog. "Go away."

The sight of her cowering transformation disturbed him to the core. His list of those needing to be saved continued to grow. A foolish friend who put them in harm's way, a terrorized sister, and a baby. He dinnae care about saving himself, but he'd see to it that they were able to get away from here. With or without him.

He was indeed the pelican. His heart bled for those he loved. But before the last drop of life escaped him, he'd be gouging out Rory's eyes and feeding them to him with a chaser of his balls.

Chapter Nineteen

Saratoga Springs, New York—America
Present Day

The water sloshed in the tub, leaving Emery painfully aware of how quiet the house was. She should have put music on. She'd taken an extra-long shower, but still hadn't felt clean, so she decided to take a bath as well.

The thought of drowning flitted across her mind—by accident—but also on purpose.

The low rumble of Callan's voice penetrated the wall, at odds with the silence. She never had male guests. Who was he talking to?

Of all the times she fantasized about Callan's first visit to her home, none of them came remarkably close to this. More tears. Her raw eyes burned from leaking.

Her shoulders sank under the surface. Water lapped at her jaw.

She blinked like a gator in the bayou. Waiting. But for what? Strength? She had no power. She was not the predator, only the prey.

"Em'ry?" The muffled voice preceded the rap of his knuckles on the door. Her body jerked painfully to attention, emerging from the blanketing water. "Ye all right in there?"

"I—I'll be out in a minute." Drops of lukewarm water gathered on her pruned skin, and she shivered.

"No rush. Just checkin'."

Gratitude for his presence warmed her. "Did… Did you make your call?"

Who did he phone? A friend? A lover? A roommate? Someone had been expecting him if he needed to let them know he'd been detained by a terrified co-worker.

"Aye." The floorboards in the hall creaked. "I'll be just out here if ye need anything."

"O—okay." She could hear him hesitate before walking away.

Keeping her hand elevated, she dropped her face under the surface, muffling all sound until her lungs burned for breath. A piercing calm punctured the panic, and she considered letting go and swallowing a lungful of water.

Not realizing she'd made a decision to live, her gasps filled the silent bathroom as she caught her breath. Living had never been so exhausting.

Climbing out of the tub and drying off with only one functioning hand proved more challenging than expected. Winded, she haphazardly tied her robe and sat on the lowered toilet seat, combing her hair.

The backs of her thighs hurt. Her scalp hurt. Her face hurt. Her gums hurt. Her hands and ankles hurt. Her insides hurt. And her heart hurt.

She shut her eyes, willing all the hurt away. If she focused hard enough she might escape it, be able to stop feeling it for a few seconds like when Callan had said those prayers.

Her eyes opened, and she gasped. A tangled nest of hair wrapped around the teeth of her comb, enough to shoot a jolt of alarm through her system.

She ran a hand through her hair, and more damp strands pulled free, weaving between her fingers. "Oh, my God."

She got up too fast, pulling her tender insides. Mopping the condensation off the mirror, she stared at her scalp through the foggy glass. No bald patches, but the more she fussed, the more strands fell out, dropping to the porcelain sink like lost wishes into a well.

Panicked, she gathered the evidence and shoved it into the wastebasket. Those weightless strands tipped the scales of her sanity.

Bruises would heal, and the worst of her injuries were on the inside, but her hair was her shield. It would take months—*years*—to grow back.

Was this the result of stress or more proof she'd been violated? How many more marks would she wear?

Her gaze dropped to her hands. One casted and wrapped in a Price Chopper grocery bag. The other wearing a sad manicure with two broken nails.

Her name mocked her as she read it off the hospital bracelet still circling her wrist. Who *was* Emery Tanner?

Certainly not me...

She searched the medicine cabinet for scissors, but couldn't hold them in her broken hand. She used her teeth to tug the bracelet off, but it only added to the marks on her body.

"Damn it."

She needed sleep. And vitamins. And a new body. And a new life. But mostly sleep.

Callan sat silently in the living room, his profile outlined by the mid-afternoon light seeping through the curtains. His head bowed in pensive thought as his elbows braced over his knees. He looked as tired as she felt, but his exhaustion seemed collected over years where hers was still brand new.

As she studied his stunning size and wide physique, she examined her feelings for him. No fear. His strength called to her but didn't frighten her.

Something silent and tortured pressed like an invisible weight into his broad shoulders. What would it be like to soothe away that unseen ache? What would he do if she touched him?

What would *she* do if she touched him?

Her mind slammed down a wall. Maybe she made a sound, because his head lifted, turning to face her.

Sorrow swamped her. Grief for an opportunity lost. She might always want him, but everything inside of her said she'd never have him. Her obstacles were bigger now, far beyond silly shyness.

Like an egg cracked open, she seeped messiness that could never be put back. Cracks and pieces so fragile the lightest touch could turn her to dust.

She wanted him. Loved him. But would never have him.

Broken.

All the hunger remained, but her appetite disappeared. The thought of lying next to a man, opening herself up, letting her vulnerable underbelly show, turned her stomach. She was a starving man with his lips sewn shut. A pianist without her hands. A woman violated.

Raped.

She'd been *raped*.

The full extent of the word stabbed into her. Each letter a little sharper than before. The pointed meaning a dagger in her mind.

Flinching away from the knifing truth before it gutted her, she buried the reality behind the hurt, stuffed it down angrily, but on the outside, she didn't make a sound.

Just Emery. She just wanted to be the old Emery, not this new, broken version incapable of hosting the slightest intimate thought.

Her hand lifted, and she looked at Callan. "Can you help me cut this off?" Yes. Normal. As soon as that bracelet disappeared all traces would be gone.

241

That was a lie. The cast, the bruises, her hair...

I just want the fucking bracelet off!

"Please," she choked, and he stood.

"Do ye feel better from yer shower, love?"

No. She nodded.

She followed him into the kitchen and watched silently as he unraveled the plastic bag from her casted hand, still wet with drops. He used a steak knife to cut away the hospital bracelet.

Her eyes stared at it, resting on top of the garbage in the can. Items she'd thrown away yesterday, before...

Once again her name mocked her. Gone to the trash. Wasted.

She flinched as he came up behind her. He rarely touched her, but sometimes his presence carried more weight than any physical contact could.

"Ye should sleep."

Funny how sometimes the motions got lost in the ordinary pattern of things. Next thing she knew, she lay in her bed, covers drawn to her chin, Max, her stuffed dog, wedged under her arm. She blinked up at Callan, wondering what he thought of all this.

Would he ever see her as a woman again and not some shattered, sharp edge left behind, a broken piece of what once was whole? Did it matter?

"Try te get some rest," he whispered, leaning down to shut off the bedside lamp.

I love you… I have for years. I love the way you're looking at me now, but I hate whatever you see… But… I love you.

"I just wanted you to know."

His brow creased. "What did you want me te know?"

"Nothing. It doesn't matter." *I would have loved you deeper than any woman should. But I can't now.* "Just … thank you. For being here. For staying."

She blinked, her eyes so heavy she missed the moment he left the room.

Sometime later she awoke and the sun no longer filtered through the drapes. When she got up to get a drink of water, Callan's form carved a lump on her couch. She tiptoed closer, barely breathing, and watched him sleep.

Time moved like fog, rolling more than ticking, passing but never lifting until it was suddenly clear and she stood at the coffee pot staring out the window the following morning. Callan was in her house. How bizarre. How awkward.

The necessity of his presence was inescapable. His reason for being here taunted her, as if making a mockery of her fragile little crush while the circumstances of reality pulverized her. He was here, but not the way she wanted him.

Did she want anything anymore?

They danced around each other in an awkward ballet of surreal circumstances for most of the morning. How long could they hide like this, pretending he didn't have better things to do?

They struggled to talk about normal topics, their crude insignificance paling in comparison to her situation. But they both avoided the reason he'd slept over.

Mute. Her life played like a familiar movie without sound, and no matter how she puzzled over it, she couldn't guess the words.

But they were there, ringing in her head. She just didn't want to voice them.

"You should probably go."

He stilled as if the same thought had been taunting him all morning. They both knew he couldn't stay. Maybe he'd wanted to leave hours ago, and her pitiful silence held him hostage. She couldn't take advantage of him any more than she already had.

"I really appreciate your staying with me last night. I'm better now." A lie.

When she was a little girl, her gran had bought her a paint spinner. You poured globs of paint in the center of a paper in whatever colors you liked, then you shut the lid and turned it on. The puddles of paint spiraled into an instant work of art that one could just as easily call a disaster.

She'd been spinning for almost two days. Two days that moved with the speed of shifting continents, yet filled her with sickening dizziness. Her pretty world just a spatter. A disaster.

Who was she kidding? Those paintings were lies. Their messiness a far cry from an accidental work of art. They were trash.

"I don't mind keepin' ye company."

A splatter couldn't spin back into a blob. "That's okay. I think I need to be alone for a while."

She wanted to roll in the ugly. Drown in it. Swallow it down until it suffocated her. Spin until there was nothing left, until all the colors blended to black.

There was truth in the pain, honesty in the hurt. She'd been trying not to face it head-on. Trying to hold herself together when everything inside of her wanted to spin out of control. But it would feel so good to let go.

Shut the lid and let it spin into a splatter of shit. Let the ugly seep out. Fall apart. Fall and never get up.

With unspoken doubts and false promises that she felt stronger than she was, Emery walked him to the door.

He crushed his wool coat in his fists as he stared back at her from the other side of the threshold. She couldn't bear the look in his eyes, couldn't bear the thought that he might see through her façade to all the ugliness hidden below.

"Th—thanks again."

"Em'ry…" Concern carved deep lines of worry into his brow. "Let me—"

"Goodbye, Callan." She closed the door with a shaky hand and locked it behind him, swallowing a breath before it turned into a sob.

The sound of silence bludgeoned her ears. The sudden emptiness of her home choked her like water filling her lungs.

She passed through the house like a ghost, her fingers tracing familiar relics of her life. The paper bag from the clinic crinkled as she removed the bottle of pills. If she took enough, she'd sleep, maybe suffocate on her own pain if they upset her stomach again.

She watched as her casted fingers failed to untwist the childproof cap. The taste of the lid against her teeth seemed more upsetting than the pain. She cried as her pulsing jaw ached, her mouth biting into the lid until it flung out of her hand and rattled across the counter.

A wretched sob of frustration ripped from her, so raw it scraped out of her throat with the tang of blood. She had no control over anything!

Then the pounding registered. She blotted her eyes and swallowed hard against the boulder in her throat.

Callan's silhouette blurred behind the glass of the front door. She caught her breath, tried to appear more put together than she was, and unlocked the deadbolt.

His sharp blue eyes locked on her with enough intensity to push her back a step. "I'm not leavin' you. I dinnae care if ye fall apart a hundred times. I'll catch ye. No matter how broken ye feel right now, Em'ry, ye cannae cut me. And ye cannae scare me away or push me out because ye think I'll see something that's not so pretty."

Her breath jerked in as he crossed the threshold. His hands gently gripped her upper arms as he looked down into her wet eyes.

"Let me watch over ye. Let me be yer eyes so ye can rest, yer hands so ye can heal, yer ears, so ye don't have te worry. Let me be there for ye. I'm strong and I…"

Her face pinched, every delicate muscle trembling as tears fell past her lashes. The inarticulate echo of her longing ripped from her lips in a broken sob, scraping past the lump in her throat.

She couldn't do this alone, but it belonged solely to her. "It hurts."

"I know. And tha' is why I cannae walk away," he rasped.

The tragic intensity that sustained the agony washed her away, but he pulled her from the tide.

Strong arms wrapped her in borrowed strength. The hollow joy of his touch burned a cold blaze through her broken heart. It was the first time he'd ever touched her so intensely, and she couldn't bear it, but also couldn't bring herself to reject it.

Her tears seeped into his chest, his warm shirt thawing the chill she couldn't shake as she clung to him like a shield. His whispered words poured over her like a baptism.

His lips pressed to her hair, speaking softly into her ears, promising not to let go, swearing she was safe, vowing to collect every piece of her that fell.

They moved to the living room, sitting on the large upholstered chair in the corner when her sobs finally quieted. She blinked with poignant clarity, a strange sense of awe creeping through her.

Callan rocked her slowly, like he'd done at the hotel, only now his hands touched her in a way they never had. The closeness choked her, but also saved her.

The gentle way he caressed her face, the weight of his lips pressing to her hair, the curve of his arm under her legs... They melded together so tightly light wouldn't pass through the space between them.

It was the most intimate position she'd ever been in, yet...

She blinked up at him, her lashes spiked with tears. His gaze moved over her face, seeking.

The give and take of that single glance tied them in an eternal knot a lifetime apart couldn't undo. She'd never forget how his support cocooned her. She could feel his soul welding to hers, and she welcomed the burn, invited the heavy permanency.

He wasn't leaving. He vowed to stay, not out of pity or a sense of obligation, but out of something neither of them could name, something tender and delicate. And she believed he would stay until she no longer needed someone there. It seemed the only belief she held in that moment, and it was enough to save her from herself for a while longer.

Whatever this was, she couldn't fight it. She didn't know how she'd tolerate it, but the sad light in his eyes belonged to her as much as it did to him.

Some of the crushing weight on her shoulders lifted as if he took the heaviest bits of her thoughts—like he could somehow carry the pain for her.

The strangest feeling crawled through her, foreign and more animal than human. Less thoughtful and therefore easier. She didn't question it. Didn't want to.

Her hand cupped his jaw, and their breath mingled. Her mask fell away, and the ugliness inside of her showed in bright exposure, but he didn't flinch. She recognized the flutters of affection, but her vehicle to transport those feelings had been totaled.

He didn't seem to mind. So much of him spoke in silence, communicated without expectation.

A bubble of misplaced laughter tickled her belly, as she finally understood what she felt from him. Acceptance.

She could be her worst, and he wouldn't run away. "Why?"

"Why what?" His head tipped closer.

"You could have anyone…" It was a foolish thing to say, out of context and undefined, but somehow she sensed he'd understand what she meant. All the feelings she'd kept bottled up over the past three years now spilled between them, mixing.

Her deepest secrets splattered to the outside in a beautiful accident, a masterpiece of trash. But even at her worst, she'd never been more certain. He cared for her.

"I dinnae want anyone else. I'll not let ye run me off because ye think I cannae handle yer pain. I've hurt before, Em'ry. I've suffered alone, in agony. I'll not leave ye te do the same."

His fingers trailed to the underside of her jaw, stroking the soft skin of her throat in an extremely intimate caress. Her breath hitched, not in fear but with impotent longing.

"I can't…"

"I know."

But she wanted to. She wanted to be who she was two days ago, but that girl was gone. Humpty Dumpty was a lie, and love proved an agonizing torture only ever tangible in the shards of fairytales, lies she'd been sold as a child.

Princes weren't charming, and big bad wolves would always clean their teeth of little girls no matter what the moral.

Her plans of happily ever after swept away in the devastation. All that was left stood naked and raw, a woman carved of bone and truth, held in the arms of a man who didn't need her to lie.

He didn't need her pretty. And he didn't need her whole. He just needed her to trust he wouldn't let go.

The tension in her arms wilted and she rested her head against the warm wall of his chest, hearing the steady beat of his heart, counting the repetitions, as if they marked the strokes of a threaded needle sewing her back together again.

For the first time in days, a sense of peace washed over her, enveloping her in an impenetrable shell she could hide behind for as long as she needed. She might always be as delicate as a butterfly, but so long as she stayed in her cocoon of Callan's arms, she would be safe.

Even if he eventually left her, she'd always have this moment.

Chapter Twenty

The River Nith
Dock Park, Dumfries—Scotland
Three and a Half Years Prior

The singe of burning paper competed with the whisper of frantic prayers as Callan pulled a long drag from the smoke clamped between his lips. The glow of the cherry-red tip and the moon made up the only light for miles on this side of the River Nith.

He let the man plead to a God who would not come. Took his time collecting himself before he got to work on what needed to be done.

The switch of a man's humanity could flip with shocking ease, Callan had come to learn over the past six months. After the first few kills, he'd abandoned his senses, snuffing out the lives of anyone who disrespected the living, anyone who devalued or abused innocent bystanders, anyone he deemed evil enough to thrust into hell.

As the ticks on his arm collected, each one a cataloged life he'd taken, his mind further untethered. Rhys had Innis. Innis had Uma. Callan had no one. Nothing but time. Time to kill.

The only way to shut off the pain was to shut off his compassion. Stop feeling and live by an unbreakable code. Easy. Empty. And eventually, the guilt slid away.

Pain had been anchoring him since boyhood, since the day his da walked away leaving his ma crumpled on the floor. Letting go of the hurt liberated the beast he'd kept locked inside. It freed the knots of tension that tightened over the years. And releasing those reins, embracing the truth of all the hurt, set him free.

No guilt. No shame. No regrets.

Truth and hurt. Pain would always be more dependable than people. It was a relief to finally embrace something of permanence.

"It's time." He snuffed the smoke out against the sole of his boot and withdrew his blade.

The crunch of leaves littering the forest floor made a bed of decomposed life. It swallowed the heavy footfalls of his steps, disguising his intent and giving his companion false hope.

"Please, MacGregor." Craig toppled back on his hands, crawling away like a scurrying crab. "I've got a daughter and a pregnant wife at home."

Deaf to excuses, numb at heart, he yanked the man to his knees by his hair, exposing the soft side of his throat where his beard stopped. "The understandin' was twenty percent. Was I not clear the last time?"

"I know what I owe ye, and I swear to pay it—with interest. I just need a little more time."

He whacked him in the temple with the butt of his knife. "Do ye think I like draggin' ye out to the middle of nowhere to break your bones? I should beat ye just for makin' me go te the trouble."

Flinching against the rivulets of blood seeping into his eye, Craig whimpered like a baby. "Please..." He sputtered in pathetic fear. "The last time ye did such a number on my legs, I couldnae make my deliveries. If I cannae move my products, I cannae collect, and then I've got nothin' to pay ye wit."

The sheer volume of excuses he heard every day desensitized him like a drug. "Enough! This is the second time you've been late."

He'd pay a debt once for the scum who he held no personal quarrel with, a courtesy to his conscience, but this one was makin' a habit of dickin' him around. Takin' advantage of his patience and his pocket.

Though he wouldnae know Callan had covered for him with Rory. And his ignorance angered him more.

Now, he was in the hole, wastin' his personal time. And there would be more. Every week the commission owed to Rory by these scumbags grew. It was the cost of makin' a profit in a country his lunatic boss believed he owned.

There had to be a consequence. "I'll give ye the choice between yer ear or yer finger."

"MacGregor, please! I need—"

"Many think the ear's worse, but ye'll still have some hearin', just not as much. A finger— even the wee one as humble as it might seem— holds half yer hand's strength."

Craig ducked his head and wept into his palms. Callan gave him a moment, removing his flask to take a swally of whisky. He debated lighting another smoke, but dinnae want to waste the time.

"Clock's tickin', Craig."

"Will ye knock me out, first?"

Callan blew out a long breath. "Which'll it be?"

The man looked up at him with the eyes of a lost boy. "The ear's the right choice, in'it?"

He shrugged. "The Lord gave ye a backup." He dinnae see the point in mentioning God also gave him ten fingers. In the end, he was takin' a piece of him either way.

"Aye." His breath shook out in shuddered rasps. "The ear then. But I beg ye te knock me out."

Callan circled his kneeling form and cut away the ropes tying his hands. "This is the last time ye'll be walkin' out of these woods, Craig. Next time I see ye, ye'll be payin' the full debt."

Not waiting for an answer, Callan walloped him in the back of the head, dropping his unconscious body to the soggy ground.

"Idgit." He crouched, pulling his head by the hair and angling his limp neck before making a quick slice. He tossed the ruined flesh into a riot of leaves and pine needles then rinsed his knife in the river.

Whistling a tune that had been stuck in his head for days, he lit a fresh smoke and stepped over the prone body, heading back toward Edinburgh.

The second he stepped away, his mind moved on. Over the last six months, he'd learned more about the underground crime in Scotland than he ever wanted to know.

His ability to trust others had disintegrated to nothing, and every day the numbness that infected him spread like an aggressive cancer in his bones. Death seemed the only cure.

Though he despised Rory more and more every day, he'd come to accept they were both monsters. Rory was the broken mind, Callan the hand he used to squeeze the life out of those he controlled. And Rory controlled *everything.*

The man had little self-restraint, especially in moments of disappointment. His infantile response to the word *no* brokered too many *yes's*. And years of cowards satisfying his sadistic needs only inflated his sense of grandeur.

Such narcissism simplified Callan's vow to never look at himself. He'd burnt out on self-examination and shame months ago, and this was who he was now. No better than the rest.

But a flicker of the hatred that drove him still kindled inside. A low light others wouldnae see, but it remained the beacon directing him through the darkest hours, lighting his purpose like a fuse to his

257

hidden rage. It patiently flickered as he bided his time, knowing that sooner or later he'd kill them all.

Sliding into the shadows at Dumfries Railway Station, he waited for the train. The station was empty. He boarded, taking a seat at the far back.

The unrefined psychopath who employed him desperately wanted to believe in a bond that wasnae there. Rory often waxed on about trust and loyalty. Callan felt nothing but hate for the man.

Rory was incapable of remorse. And while he'd manipulated loyalty from his sister, thereby evoking the same from Rhys, Callan would never give him the satisfaction.

To this day, he promised his employer to bank on nothing more than the vow that he'd kill him. Of course, Rory accepted the ongoing threat with perverted amusement and twisted anticipation.

Callan's distaste for violence only fed the sadist in Rory. He took great pleasure in flouting his authority and demanding wretched acts of evil— some Callan figured out ways to avoid, others he had no choice but to commit.

He consoled himself with promises that these were evil men, making money off the innocent. They peddled drugs in once clean towns, forced acts of prostitution on unwilling young men and women, and wouldnae hesitate to slit his throat if they got the upper hand.

A janitor of Scotland's most vile creatures, that's what he'd become. Yet it all boiled down to serving the vilest of all.

At first, he thought to lie. Men were one thing, but women... Callan couldnae hurt what he'd always been afraid to touch. Women were fragile, breakable. He'd watched his father destroy his mother again and again with barely any effort at all. He couldnae do the same.

But when he'd lied to Rory, promising he'd roughed up the woman who owed him a debt, someone had ratted him out. The following night her head had been waiting on his dresser, lifeless eyes watching him through slits of sagging, wasted beauty.

No whispers of who did it. No offer to help bury the severed head. But the message rang loud and clear. Rory would always know when he lied, and there would always be others less afraid of violence to tidy up behind him. He also had people close to Callan to abuse.

When Callan had placed that woman's lifeless head in a box, he saw Innis looking back at him and slammed the lid shut. That was when he realized the only way to ever beat this place and break through the wickedness that rotted it from the inside out was to let his own darkness seep through.

But the second he untethered the snapping beast that growled inside of him, his world washed in shades of red. He welcomed the carnage, swearing he and Rory were not the same, but knowing they were more alike than he ever wanted to admit.

Pent up rage spilled from him like a tidal wave during that first kill. Once he came to terms with the inescapable entrapment, he embraced the darkness, became a dark passenger to the violence inside of him. A masterpiece carved by malevolence.

The naked truth of his corrupt soul became an inescapable echo, calling back to him in the silent hours of each night. And soon, Rory's list wasnae enough.

Men like Craig dinnae commit crimes deserving of death and something inside of Callan needed a target to kill. It was the only thing keeping him together as he awaited Rory's turn.

The downfall of Rory would surely be his boastful ego. He loved to brag about all the disgusting monsters he knew. Callan had become one of them, a twisted puppet in the toy box of a psychopath.

But every name Rory mentioned, Callan remembered. And one by one, he collected their souls, fed the beast.

These were not kills sanctioned by anyone other than himself and what he believed was God's whispers. He needed a purpose, some good to temper the evil, and this was the toll he needed to pay.

Graham Sùdrach.

The name embedded in his mind the moment Rory uttered it. He'd practically preened with admiration for the sixty-eight-year-old retired bookkeeper who'd spent thirty years working for Rory.

His admiration told Callan affection existed between Rory and the bookkeeper. And affection was the counterpoint of grief, the thread that led to attachment. Callan planned to mutilate the things Rory loved—steal them away in a manner even a psychopath would feel.

Sùdrach was a master at molesting financial records and little boys. During Rory's drunken blathering, he bragged of how some of Sùdrach's victims would cry. But he always enjoyed the pain.

"The tenderness would tear away..." Rory recalled with almost dreamlike awe. "Rip."

Who knew the degree of torture that turned a young boy into the sort of monster Rory had become. At some point, he'd stopped squirming and started craving the pain. Then he took the reins and decided to deliver some of his own.

Rory saw no harm in taking. He never hesitated over consequences, and he often marveled over others' empathy, watching with a peculiar envy for the feelings he was too broken to have.

Sùdrach had played a key role in the making of a monster. And tonight was the night one of Rory's makers was scheduled to die.

Over the three-hour ride back to Edinburgh Callan rested, though it had been months, perhaps years, since he'd truly slept. When the train arrived at his stop, he was the last passenger.

Clinging to the shadows, he remained mindful of the CCTV cameras stationed throughout the city. The night was, for once, dry, and that made for an easy trek.

The school campus stood in open emptiness. But in a few hours, it would be alive and bursting with innocent minds as the students spilled from the dorms.

Perched just beyond the property line, sat a picturesque home. Someone had lovingly planted flowers along the walk, making it an inviting place to visit, a well-disguised place of pain, a memory for so many, entrenched in guilt, shame, and silent blame.

He lit a smoke and studied the dark windows of the house. The all boy boarding school seemed the picture-perfect backdrop to such carefully designed lies. But beautiful things often hid the worst ugliness inside.

Sùdrach purposely chose this home. He used it like a portal to hell, luring innocent boys into the basement under the pretense of being a math tutor.

It was where he taught Oscar Riordan the formulas to collect interest and the profits that could be made from commissions and fear. It was where he showed him what pain truly felt like, the inescapable surge of hurt that ravaged the weak and spewed the shattered pieces back into the world.

It was where Rory first fell in love. Not with Sùdrach, but with the ease of agony. It was where the innocent little boy had died, and the monster was born.

Sùdrach showed him first-hand the power of cruelty. It must have seemed so vastly opposite from the fragility of everything good that little boys were.

Callan could almost sympathize with why a young Oscar Riordan would make a conscious decision to let the hurt in. Embrace the pain. Horns would always be sturdier than feathers.

The evil born in that house broke wee Oscar and built Rory. And the man who sired all that damage, taught the monster, a budding, young sadist, how great other's pain could be, was overdue to die.

He flicked his smoke into the grass and crossed the lawn. His glare fastened to the front door, as his strides swallowed the distance. The house was dark, its inhabitants likely asleep, so he knocked loudly.

Sùdrach had three daughters, all off to uni and out of the house. His wife was a minor concern, but not a deterrent.

Callan knocked again, this time harder, and a light flickered on at the second floor. The porch bulb clicked, illuminating the cement step. The vase surrounding the light entombed countless moth corpses. This place reeked of forgotten innocence and stolen joy.

Sùdrach wouldnae recognize him. He hardly had time to see him when the door finally opened.

Callan's hand flew out, his fingers popping the underside of the man's nose and sending his head back with an explosion of blood. It was a messy but quick way to disarm an enemy.

Sùdrach cupped his face, dark, oily blood seeping through his fingers. Callan gouged his finger into the soft skin beneath the eye and sent him to the floor, shoving a knee into his chest.

A light flicked on at the top of the landing. "Graham?"

"I—"

Callan's knee pressed harder, forestalling him from answering. Then he applied pressure to the carotid artery, cutting off the oxygen feeding the brain and Sùdrach's body went limp.

Callan dragged him into what looked like a dining room.

"Graham?" Soft footfalls descended the stairs. "I thought I heard—*Oh!*"

Covering her mouth, Callan performed the same move on the wife, touching down on the same pressure point but with more care. He gingerly laid her on the carpet, slipped a little something in her mouth to keep her asleep, and adjusted her head so she'd not waken with a stiff neck.

"Stay," he whispered.

Grabbing Sùdrach's ankle, he dragged him through the hall toward the basement Rory had described. Hauled the piece of shite down the stairs feet first. He groaned as Callan hoisted him up by the wrinkled scruff of his neck and threw him over the back of the sofa, facing the double paned bow window that looked out on the schoolyard. Heavy, light-blocking drapes hung to the sides ready to provide privacy.

Reaching in his bag, he removed five extra-long zip ties and a roll of tape. He tied Sùdrach's arms behind his back, fastening the ties at the elbows to make it as uncomfortable as possible.

"Wha—"

Callan cuffed him in the back of the head and shoved him forward over the sofa. "Shut yer fuckin' hole."

He bit off a length of tape and slapped it over Sùdrach mouth, wrenching back his head by the thinning hair. He hissed close to his ear, "This is yer favorite room, is it not, old man? Do you think yer fear's as sharp as all of theirs?"

A panic, muffled cry answered back.

"No, me neither. But I'll get ye there." He released his hair with a hard shove and secured his ankles to the feet of the sofa, spreading him nice and wide.

According to Rory, the room was soundproofed from the upstairs for the Missus' sake, so he dinnae worry about his cries or screams carrying. He tightened another zip tie around Sùdrach's neck, using his wee finger to keep it loose enough for air to wheeze past his windpipe.

"Don't want ye passin' out and missin' it, now do we?"

He cut away the man's pants and tossed them aside. Sùdrach jerked hard enough to shove the couch, but Callan kept him down.

"How many times have ye sat here, lookin' out tha' window, playin' a game of who's next?"

He forced him to look now. The black night was dotted with security lights throughout the campus. The landscape invited eyes, but Sùdrach had done more than just look at all the pretty trees.

"Did ye think ye'd get away with it? Tha' no one would ever know?" His voice lowered another degree. "What did ye do to them to keep them quiet? Did ye threaten their families? Their pets? How did ye get them to come back, even when it hurt?"

He released his hair and rounded the sofa. A frantic, possible apology muffled against the gag as tears gathered in the clouded whites of his eyes.

The skin around Sùdrach's eyes had thinned to crepe, softening the windows to the soul in a dangerously misleading way. He had the aged eyes of Santa Clause but the appetite of Lucifer.

Callan glared into those lying eyes. "You're not sorry. Only sorry ye got caught."

Once Sùdrach understood what Rory was, he'd taken the boy under his wing like a protégé, taught him the art of cruelty the way a totalitarian teaches obedience—exhaustively and unflinchingly until it corrupted every private thought.

Together they fed off the agony of others, the pain of those weaker than them. Rory loved his trinkets, loved to save pretty little treasures to play with again and again. A collector of weapons, beauty, and nostalgia. And he learned that from this man.

The room had several filing cabinets and a dusty desk in the corner. Callan jerked a drawer open and removed a file. It appeared nothing more than financial statements.

"Where are they hidden?"

He yanked open another drawer, spilling documents all over the floor and Sùdrach groaned. Sweating profusely, he watched in horror as Callan ransacked his papers. Only when he stopped groaning did Callan know he'd found the right drawer.

"This one?"

Sùdrach shook his head, confirming his suspicions, and Callan flipped through the files. *Eureka.*

Disgusting photos of young boys in every which position, several showing Sùdrach's face. It was all the evidence the world needed to see what kind of animal this man was.

He dropped the file on the coffee table, leaving it open. Sùdrach's brow kinked with deep lines as he sniveled and looked away, the back of the sofa still wedged under his ribs as his tied body bowed over the cushions.

"Open yer fuckin' eyes, you godless piece of shite and *look at what you've done!"*

A tortured whimper choked through the gag. More tears gathered in his deceptive, soulless eyes.

Callan revealed one more zip ties. "This next part's gonna hurt."

In one quick pull, he cinched the tie around Sùdrach's cock and bollocks. The man bucked like a raging bull and screamed bloody murder. The sofa jerked under his thrashing and rammed into the coffee table, knocking some of the photos onto the floor.

Callan popped his fist between Sùdrach's legs, delivering a brain-scrambling blow that belted out an agonized sob.

"Ye love the pain, right? Is this enough for you?" Callan removed the blade from the holster at his thigh. "Nah. I think ye still got a ways te go." Crouching down, he looked him in his now bloodshot eyes. "No one can hear ye cry. Ye made sure of tha', dinnae ye? Now, they'll all know what you've done."

Another broken cry. Sagging over the back of the sofa, drowning in his own misery, Callan gave him a few minutes to wallow. His dangling bits darkened like rotting fruit, the fight draining out of him as the circulation cut off.

"Dinnae quit on me yet," Callan taunted, rising to speak so closely to the man's ear he could smell his sweat. "A man's entitled to his weapons, so long as he respects the power they wield." He stared into those frantic eyes, tipping his head in the direction of Sùdrach's tethered cock. "Ye ignored their screams when they begged. So I've come to relieve ye of your sword."

He shrieked against the muzzle, begging for mercy. Callan flashed his sharpest blade, examining the curved point and lethal edge. He waited for Sùdrach's cries to quiet.

"The things you did te those boys... They carry the scars as men. So many lives ruined."

This place bred monsters, and Callan's inner beast preened as it woke, licking its jowls for its next victim, hungry for other's suffering of those who deserved to die.

Callan was not as monstrous as the rest of them. He was merely the instrument of a brutal form of justice.

"I'll give ye a choice. One, ye can live, but without yer cock and balls. Two, I do the world a favor and end yer pathetic life now. Either way, everyone will know the monster ye are by morning—the polis, yer wife, your family … yer daughters."

He wept, and Callan leaned forward, ripping away the tape.

"What'll it be?"

"Please," he sobbed. "My family! My wife is upstairs…"

He rounded the couch. "I ken exactly where yer family is. Mentioning them willnae earn ye any mercy. If ye cannae make up your mind, I'll choose for ye."

"Please! God, please, no!"

Callan wrenched back his head and hissed, "Then choose. Three seconds. One, two—"

"Kill me!" he sobbed. "Oh, God, just kill me."

Callan yanked his head, exposing his throat. A blue line crowded the zip tie cutting into his flesh.

"When ye meet the devil, tell him Callan MacGregor sent you." The blade sliced across his quivering gorge, tearing into tender tissue with a flood of scarlet.

Gurgles faded to silence as a puddle of blood seeped into the cushions. Dead. The monster was dead and the beast temporarily sated.

When he passed the dining room, the wife was still out cold. He had no guilt for what she might find when she woke. Chances were she'd had her suspicions all along and turned a deaf ear to the cries below. He'd spare her life, but not her conscience. In the end, she'd square away with the Almighty, and He'd decide where her final resting place would be.

As for the polis... Once they discovered Sùdrach's crimes, they'd be grateful for Callan's services. Any investigation would only draw attention to the predator they missed.

As for Rory... The side of Callan's mouth kicked up in a satisfied half-smirk as he left the house, taking the pretty flowered path into the shadows and pinching a smoke between his lips.

Sùdrach was Rory's hero, his malevolent sire, his companion and the closest Rory could get to love. His death was a crumble in the foundation upon which Rory so arrogantly stood. Soon, his entire empire would fall.

Chapter Twenty-One

Saratoga Springs, New York—America
Present Day

Wesley Blaine was born during a December snowstorm, twenty-one years ago. It was the last white Christmas on record. His father was a successful commercial architect and his mother a dental technician.

He attended Bay Cove Day School and served three years on the student council at Bay Cove High School West in the affluent suburbs of Ansley Park, Georgia. He still holds several swimming records there. His picture's still displayed in the trophy case of his high school, just across from the main entrance.

Those were the things being reported about Wesley Blaine on the news, the things journalists thought the world needed to know. The things that were slowly overshadowing the fact that this gently bred, upper-class, future success story was also a vicious rapist.

His bail had been made and the court date set. Emery returned to work but could hardly make it through a shift without having a breakdown. Matt had hired a guy by the name of Peter, saying he felt better having two people at the desk at all times—safer.

She didn't talk to Peter because she didn't know him and had no interest in getting to know him. She answered the phones and confirmed reservations, but she couldn't leave the lobby without breaking into a cold sweat or falling apart.

She was a mess. But good old Wesley Blaine—handsome, high school hero whose life fit like a charming Norman Rockwell painting over a crack in an otherwise perfect wall—yeah, he was doing fine. That's what mattered, right?

She'd never given a statement to the press, and her silence angered the media. Forget that she'd already been violated in the worst possible way. Reporters lurked around her community like sharks fishing for chum, scenting the blood in the water and wanting more.

As if leaving the house wasn't already stressful enough, now she had to race to her car and dodge random people hurling questions at her? Questions that hit like bullets. And when Callan saw the media sharks, he revealed a threatening side of himself that left her in awe. Once the sharks realized she had a killer whale at her side, they backed off.

As her silence screamed on, the rumors and assumptions started to rumble. She almost contacted a reporter when she read Wesley's lawyer's diatribe of how needy she'd been, begging for attention and determined to get it. The liar even posed the possibility that she'd used a door to break her own hand.

The newshounds visited the hotel disguised as regular guests, trespassing into her life, into the place of her employment and nightmares. She had no defense against their intrusive observations, as they were paying customers like every other guest staying for a visit.

She'd thought privacy was her right. What a joke.

Frustrated by her silence, they doubted her unspoken conviction of an otherwise perfect man. Suddenly, she wasn't the victim anymore. The mood of the stories shifted as more artistically designed elements of Wesley Blaine's impeccable life slipped into the public eye, and suddenly she was the villain of the piece. A hysterical woman out to destroy a good man, tarnishing his clean record with her filthy accusations, and depriving the country of what might be the next Olympic gold medalist.

Her fingers clutched her phone like a security blanket that never left her hand, as she watched the reporters detail more pretty pieces of Wesley Blaine's life. A text came through, the slide of the banner startling her out of her daze and interrupting the video.

She closed the report and opened her messages.

Stop watching the news.

Her gaze drifted across the lobby to where Callan sat. The bar was empty, closed since midnight, but he waited for her to finish her shift. Lately, he felt like her only friend.

Were they friends? Were they more?

"I'm back."

She startled as Peter returned. She hadn't realized he'd gone somewhere. She needed to pay better attention to her surroundings.

She didn't say anything but managed a jerky nod.

Everyone knew. Callan had no choice but to explain the situation to Matt, who then passed along the information to the owners of the hotel—corporate people they never saw. A business card with an HR rep's name on it appeared in her mailbox the day she returned. Did they want her to call the number? Was it required?

No one told her what to do. Everyone sort of watched her, waiting for her to flip out. Sometimes she did, but never the way they expected.

She'd almost wet herself during her first night back. Not until Callan realized she'd been avoiding the bathrooms, did he insist she go. He went in before her, inspected every stall like a mom checks under the bed for monsters, and guarded the door so she could pee. No one could hear her scream, but

274

the acoustics of her urinating carried the subtlety of a gong.

The one thing about Callan, she was coming to realize, was that he didn't embarrass easily—or ever. If him hearing the tinkle of her pee was the only way she could go, then so be it.

The paradox of their relationship could be defined in boundaries. Strange walls remained between them that might never be breached, and gaping openings left no room to hide. He confined her the way a basket gathers fragile eggs, but he also gave her room to breathe.

They didn't have to be friends because they were trapped in something more. Something adult, but not at all sexual. Yet an undeniable sense of intimacy surrounded their every encounter.

Were they dating? Could two adults date and never fondle or kiss? Never ... fuck?

She watched him, his hand scribbling over his book as he journaled in the pale light. When she asked what he wrote about he said the journals were filled with wind, as if that was all *he* was full of.

She highly doubted the books were filled with nothing. How much space could nothing take up?

Callan was always writing. Every night he'd spend hours, sipping a whiskey and jotting down his thoughts. Something more than wind filled his mind and those pages.

Perhaps he had a story to tell. Or maybe he was trying to rewrite the past.

"We cannae rewrite the past," he'd said to her in the days that followed the assault. "All we can do is learn from it."

She didn't know what kind of lesson a woman took away from rape. The things it taught her were uncomfortable facts in her own head.

No matter how strong she was, a big enough man could always prove her weak.

No didn't mean shit.

If she shared too much of her pain, her healing could quickly become an inconvenience.

And rape might be a forgivable offense if the guy acted entitled enough and possessed a pretty enough background.

Those weren't any lessons she needed to learn. And while they were true, she rejected every one.

She was going to lose this case. Not that she would be on trial, but he was going to walk away with a slap on the wrist. Everything she read about similar hearings pointed to the same disappointing end.

His lawyer knew what he was doing, leaking charming little tidbits out to the press about her attacker's life. She didn't have a picture or a trophy in her high school. She wasn't born to a picture-perfect couple on a postcard-worthy winter day. And she didn't seep charisma the way she recalled it pouring from him the night he approached her desk.

He was a horror novel wrapped in a taffy-colored book jacket. But in the end, his story would tell mostly of his redeeming qualities, not the cruelties hidden between the lines. He'd slide safely back onto the top shelf, while her ragged, war-torn pages ripped at the seams.

His sentence would be a blink while hers would last a lifetime. These were the truths of the aching hurt she struggled to carry.

She'd been counting down the days to get her cast off, for the last bruises to heal. But scars were forever.

She glanced up from her phone as Callan crossed the lobby, coat on. Her gaze shot to the time. 2:34. Panic welled in her chest as she feared he might have to leave early, but she swallowed it down.

Her shoulders tensed as he approached. She didn't want to stay here alone with Peter. She couldn't catch her breath.

"Let's go, love. I think Pete'll be fine finishin' out the night on his own."

She blinked and turned to Peter who barely looked up from his spy novel to mutter a "See ya."

She scooted off her stool and gathered her coat and purse from the back. Callan took the jacket and held it open, helping her slide her cast through the sleeve.

Her gaze lowered, watching his rough, crooked fingers slide the flat, pearl buttons through the narrow holes.

"I thought of this, the first time you fixed my buttons. I thought of it every day, from the day you did it." But she hadn't thought of it since her life turned upside down.

He grinned. "Well, I've seen how ye struggle to button yourself up properly—even without the cast."

A smile teased at her lips. It was stupid and simple, but she loved that he helped her with her coat, adored that he put some sort of importance on the order of her buttons.

Her hand squeezed over his, which was like third base for them. His pupils darkened, and he swallowed. "I'll walk ye to yer car."

Every night, he followed her home and stayed until she fell asleep. In the morning she always awoke alone with the door locked. It had been five weeks, and she wondered if she'd ever reach a point where she felt safe without him there to tuck her in.

Their days were their own, but their nights kept them together. Even on her nights off, he'd come by, sometimes bringing take out or suggesting they order delivery.

When they reached her car, he opened the door and buckled her seatbelt, turning the key as she pressed the brake, since her cast made twisting small objects impossible.

"I'll be right behind ye."

She waited for him to get to his car. Twenty minutes later they were in her home.

Changing out of her clothes was a one-handed nightmare, but she'd picked up some creative tricks over the last few weeks. Once in her favorite flannel pants and a loose-neck sweatshirt, she met Callan on the couch.

He held out his arm, and she nestled into his side, resting her head on his shoulder. Ernie pounced onto the cushion beside her and purred, mashing potatoes into the pillow with his little paws.

"Ready?" Callan's thumb held their place in the book resting on his thigh.

"Ready."

The spine creaked as he opened it, the scent of the pages piercing the air with that fine fragrance of well-loved paper and tired ink.

"Where were we?"

"His letters to Fitzgerald."

It seemed they shared a fondness for Hemingway, but having both read and enjoyed his greatest works, Callan thought it fitting to get to know the man behind the masterpieces.

"There's nothing more honest than a man's personal conversations with himself and friends. The truth rests in the belief that such things will never be punished, the trust that our privacy is sacred," Callan had said.

Knowing he was a writer himself and journaled religiously in those leather-bound books of his, she was immediately intrigued and captivated ever since. And there was truly nothing more pleasant than listening to his thick Scottish accent strum over the private musings of Ernest Hemingway.

"Forget your personal tragedy," he read. *"We are all bitched from the start, and you especially have to hurt like hell before you can write seriously. But when you get the damned hurt, use it—don't cheat with it."*

Her brow scrunched at the tone of the letter. "I thought Hemingway and Fitzgerald were friends."

"I'm not sure a man like Hemingway knew how te be a gentle friend," Callan mused. "He reveled in brash masculinity, was a hard drinker, and wasnae known for mincing words. I bet the man had an enormous ego tha' needed frequent stroking. Fitzgerald was more of a social charmer. But they worked in the same setting, and sometimes tha' is all ye need te form a friendship between two people who couldnae be more opposite."

He gave her a pointed look, and she smiled, knowing he was comparing Hemingway and Fitzgerald's friendship to theirs. She liked the comparison, finding Callan quite close to a Hemingway hero in that he was enduring, honorable, and always appearing to hide a secret sort of pain.

Her heart warmed. "You got all that from this letter?"

He shrugged. "Ego's the heart of every man. The nature of the beast. But every man needs a friend."

She nestled closer, and he draped his arm around her shoulders, pulling her into the nook. It was becoming her favorite place to be.

He continued reading, going back to the line where he'd left off. *"But when you get the damned hurt, use it—don't cheat with it. Be as faithful to it as a scientist..."*

They read close to five letters before her eyes grew too heavy to keep open. Television couldn't hold her attention lately, and the news was a tempting torture she couldn't always resist. But books, no matter how heart-wrenching the stories, were safe because she could close them at any time.

The soft thud of the cover shutting only teased the slumbering edges of her mind. Her weight shifted, and she nestled closer to his warm chest, the soft drafts of the house plucking at her clothes as he carried her to her room.

Covers pressed to her shoulders as he tucked Max by her ear. "Goodnight, *leannán,*" he whispered, tracing a gentle finger down her cheek.

"Goodnight, Callan," she whispered, knowing it was only a matter of time before she'd ask him to stay—unsure what would happen if he did.

HURT

Chapter Twenty-Two

Riordan Private Estate
Lower Whitecraigs, Edinburgh—Scotland
Three years and four months prior

Callan entered the main room of the house to find the evening's affairs at the height of depravity. Music pumped from speakers and piles of cocaine dusted every surface. Used up women serviced the men, while Rory sprawled at the center of it all, a corrupt king reclining on his decaying throne.

"MacGregor, come in here," he called. Only then did Callan notice the naked, masculine back of the man with his head between Rory's legs. "Did I tell ye to stop suckin' my cock?" he snarled at the young man, shoving his head back down. He lifted his chin to Callan. "Any trouble tonight?"

He shook his head. The less he said, the sooner he'd bore Rory and be able to escape to his room.

"Then help yourself to a whore for a pummel."

Innis, sitting just beside him on the couch, glanced up at him, moving only her eye. Like he'd ever take Rory up on such an offer. He wouldnae touch a single houk in the place.

He dropped a fat stack of euros on the table. "I'll pass."

"Your loss." Yanking the hoormister off his knob, Rory slapped the man across the face. "Do I have te knock yer teeth out te stop ye from rakin' my fuckin' cock?" He kicked him away and tucked himself inside his pants. "Trinket, make me a drink."

Innis stood, dressed to the nines like a porcelain doll, and went to the bar. She never reacted to the vulgarity that infected this place. Rhys was nowhere to be found but was most likely with the wain while Rory demanded Innis's presence.

Callan turned to leave.

"Hold it, MacGregor. Where's the rest of it?"

Grinding his teeth, he turned, but dinnae step any closer. "Stewart's men need another week."

"Oh, another week? That's fine," he said, all too easily. "I'd thought I'd explained quite clearly about the requirements of your job, but I guess ye misunderstood." He tossed the banknotes on the table, his easy tone at complete odds with the irritated spark in his eyes. "And what did you do te them when they claimed they couldnae pay on time?"

Callan drew in a slow breath, refusing to be baited. "I told them they had better pay up next week, or they'd regret it."

Rory smiled slowly, taking the glass from Innis. "Did ya, now? And I bet they found tha' real threatenin', being tha' you're so big and scary."

"They'll pay—"

"They were meant to pay tonight!" The glass his sister had just handed him shattered against the wall, the high proof amber seeping like tears down the damask paper. "When I tell you to get me my fuckin' money, I expect it when I fuckin' ask!"

"There were women—"

"Whores!" He jumped from the couch, kicking the table out of his way and glaring up at Callan's face. "We had an agreement, MacGregor. You work for me, and that means ye do as I goddamn tell ye."

"I give ye my word they'll pay up when I return."

His claim had no backing. But he believed if he gave the Stewarts one last chance, they'd repay him for his leniency.

"Is that so? Well, what kind of man would I be not to trust my employee's word? We trust each other, don't we, MacGregor?" He waited, eyeing him with a threatening stare. "Say ye trust me," he whispered.

Words turned to sawdust on his tongue. He'd never trust him. He dreamed of strangling him every night. Rory knew it, too, but took sick pleasure in taunting him. It became a silent guessing game of what would come first, Rory's murder or Callan's surrender.

He held his glare, noting the angry red curves of his upturned nose. It was clear he'd had it buried in coke all night.

Rory audibly seethed, a slow grin twisting his thin lips around those little teeth. "Say it…"

Callan locked his jaw. He dinnae care that he was as unpredictable as a tornado. He wasnae uttering a fucking word.

Rory laughed, and some of the tension unknotted in Callan's back. Slapping his shoulder as if they shared a private understanding, Rory's posture shifted from intense to relaxed.

"Aye. Ye might never say it, but you and I have a special bond. We understand each other—so much it makes yer insides squirm in that wriggling, delicious way that tells ye you're not sure if ye need to shoot a load or shite yourself."

Mostly, the man made Callan sick.

He paced along the fancy carpet. "But I understand a threat's only as good as the man backing it. Now, I told ye, if ye worked for me and did what I asked, we'd get along fine, and I meant it."

"I'll have the money next week."

"Dinnae interrupt, darling boy. There's a lesson I'm tryin' te teach ye here. How are you te trust my word if I break my promises?"

"I'll keep my word, Rory. I'll get ye everything that's owed. The Stewarts know they have a debt—"

"The Stewarts are sleepin' soundly in their beds, not a worry in the world. You have to show them they're dealin' with a mad man if ye want them to fear you, someone who will fly off the handle at a moment's notice, do the unthinkable, and go after whatever it is they love. That's how ye get through to them. That's how ye make them obey."

Out of the corner of his eye, he saw Innis take a slow step backward. It was the first time he ever saw her react to Rory's ramblings, and it terrified him.

He nodded. "You're right. I'll go back tomorrow and get what they owe. I'll do whatever needs te be done te make them pay."

Rory flung a hand out behind him without turning around. "Not another fuckin' step."

Innis froze, her shoulders trembling ever so slightly.

"Aye, I believe ye will. But not because of words. Words are just empty promises. You'll do my bidding because deep down you know that I'm madder than a fuckin' hatter, and you can trust that until the day ye finally get te watch me die."

He hadnae blinked in a while and his eyes burned, but he feared the second he shut them something awful would happen. The air vibrated with the silent threat. And no matter how he tried to guess, he'd never come close to knowing the depravity that danced in Rory's mind.

"Smithy!" Rory shouted. "Grab the spider gag and bring it here." He clicked his fingers the way he often did when commanding Innis's attention. "Come."

Callan's stomach bottomed out as his sister moved forward reluctantly. Smithy, a filthy drunkard who smelled twice as ugly as he looked, held out a contraption with various metal spikes, a buckle, and a ring.

"MacGregor, did ye know Smithy was the one to take the head of the woman we left you? Aye, he's a dedicated part of this operation, and I've been meaning te reward him."

Smithy's tongue slithered across his stained teeth as he sneered at Callan, as if he gave a shite who was Rory's favorite.

Rory glanced at the bloated tick of a man and held out a hand for the gag. "After the last biting incident…" He unraveled the buckles, stretching the mask for Callan to see. "We take precautions. Sit, Trinket."

Callan jolted forward and Rory's demented glare cut to him, freezing him where he stood. "One more step, MacGregor, and I'll let Smithy fuck her in the eye. Be grateful I'm only sharing her mouth."

His breath shook out of him in jagged skids. "I'll go back. Right now. I'll bring ye twice what he owes."

Depraved satisfaction glittered in Rory's eyes while Smithy breathed heavily at his side. Callan could not allow this. His beautiful baby sister…

"Please, Rory…"

His fingers tightened in Innis's hair, and he laughed, jerking her body like a ragdoll. "Too late. If anything, this will teach you te do as you're told the first time." He buckled the gag around her head, the metal pins forcing her jaw open. He dragged a tapered finger down her suspended face, rimming her parted lips. "Trinket learned that lesson long ago."

"I understand now," he said frantically, his hand circling the hilt of his knife as Smithy rubbed his swollen cock through his jeans. "Let her go, and I'll have your money by—"

"I'm afraid you're just not mad enough to make me believe you."

"I'll bring you his fucking head!" He dinnae care. He could not allow that bacterial infection of a human being to touch his sister. "Please, Rory," he begged.

He tsked. "So pretty when you beg. Though it's not a very masculine quality. Careful now, ye wouldnae want some of us gettin' the wrong idea…"

Smithy licked his lips with a gnarled tongue, his filthy hands reaching to stroke a lock of Innis's hair.

"*Rory!*" Callan begged desperately.

"Sit. Down." The command snapped the entire room into silence. Men stilled, mid-fuck, and stared at what was happening.

"Don't any of you fuckin' look at her!" Callan fisted his withdrawn knife, scanning the room.

Rory laughed. "Lay one hand on any of my men, and I'll give them all permission to try her."

The knife clattered to the carpet with a solid thump. A hollow ache ruptured poison in his gut. He held up his hands, shaking with shackled rage.

"Please, Rory. Dinnae do this to her. I beg you. Your anger's with me. She's innocent."

Rory rubbed his lips together, his small eyes missing nothing. "Look at how ye squirm to protect her. Fascinating." He sniffed the air, his nostrils stretching under a long inhalation. "Your fear's exquisite. I can almost smell it."

"Please," he choked, knowing Rory would never go back now. The pleasure for him was in delivering the pain. The emotional torture excited him. It would never be enough to stab a man in the heart, he'd always need to twist the blade.

"Your vulnerability's disappointing, MacGregor. I thought ye were stronger than that."

"Please..." His weapons were useless, his desperate humility a last resort.

Rory massaged his chin, studying him. "You'd do almost anything to save her, what, five minutes of degradation?" He glanced at Smithy. "Maybe not even that."

"Don't do this..." Callan swallowed, his disgraceful human nature wrapping him in a crushing fist. Paralyzed by circumstance. Impotent. A wasted shell of a man.

Rory's eyes narrowed, the side of his mouth hooking like the curve of Callan's favorite blade.

"Offer me something better, MacGregor, and I'll let her go—unscathed."

His blood stilled in his veins as he understood what Rory wanted him to offer. But he'd never ask for it. It had to come from Callan, a true surrender.

290

More poison ruptured inside of him, the toxic burn sloshing around his insides and demolishing his integrity. Innis stared at him from where she kneeled on the floor, frozen, her expression a tragedy he could barely face.

He couldnae do it.

Shame and dark self-hatred bled through him. In his broken mind, he consoled himself with lies, promises that she'd recover from this degradation faster than him, that this would be the last time. But the truth swilled in the pit of his rolling stomach, and he staggered back, a jagged breath wrenching from his hollow chest.

Innis was stronger than him.

His head bowed, his shame weighing down his gaze as he backed toward the door.

"I said *sit*."

He stilled at the command in Rory's voice. The depravity of such a monstrous man could only be trusted in degrees of wickedness. If Callan dinnae obey, Rory would only punish him more— punish *her* more. He could do worse things than let Smithy rut in her mouth.

Cold and empty inside, he lowered himself onto a nearby sofa. He dinnae watch. Couldnae. But he sat as he'd been ordered.

The buzz of Smithy's zipper tore through the air like a chainsaw. Callan stopped breathing as the inescapable sounds filled the silence. His eyes screwed shut, and Rory's scent crowded him, the cushions of the sofa shifting under his weight as he whispered in his ear.

"There it is. All the beauty wrought by madness. Look how prettily she cries—even with only one eye—but she knows better than to make a sound."

Rage covered him like cold chainmail as his body shook. He envisioned slaughtering every last one of them, saving Rory for last.

The violence churning inside of him served as a welcome distraction from the sounds of Smithy using her, grunting. The sounds of her gagging. The disgusting wheeze of his finish.

It lasted no more than three minutes but stole a decade off his life. Perhaps several from Innis's.

He couldnae look at her when it was over, too ashamed by his cowardice to meet her gaze. They were in hell and the longer they stayed, the clearer it became that they were never gettin' out.

That night, long after everyone had left the estate or passed out, Callan fed Rory's prized deerhounds Smithy's cock and tongue. The rest of him the world would never find.

It restored nothing, but provided the useless assurance that the swine never lay a finger on his sister again. It was paltry penance to Innis, a pathetic apology he'd never have the strength to say. But it was all he could offer. All he was good for.

The courage he'd once had now abandoned him. Shame replaced integrity, and of all those he hated, he placed himself first.

Chapter Twenty-Three

Saratoga Springs, New York—America
Present Day

Her cast was finally off, and despite the lack of mobility that remained in her hand, she felt like celebrating, so she decided to make Callan a surprise dinner.

He claimed to love red meat but said he'd never tasted filet mignon, so she wanted to make him the best steak in the world. A steak for a king.

When he called to say he was leaving the house, she admitted she might have bitten off more than she could chew. Keeping her voice calm, she scooted off the phone and surveyed the damage.

Mashed potatoes dripped off the cabinets, the corn boiled over onto the stove, and her beautiful filets were overdone. He didn't live far, so she focused on setting the table, using her grandmother's china, which she never had an excuse to use. She lit long taper candles and set out champagne on ice.

Only when she stepped back and surveyed the dining room did she realize she hadn't made a dinner for friends.

Despite the ruined food, she'd created a setting for lovers.

"Fuck," she breathed, gathering up the dishes and taking them back to the hutch. "Ah!" she hit her bad hand on the cabinet and almost passed out from the sharp spike of pain radiating up her arm.

"Em'ry?"

She spun to the door, still holding the plates to her chest.

Callan stood in the hall wearing a gobsmacked stare.

Pain still vibrated her arm, but she gave up trying to tuck away the plates. He insisted she no longer hide a key out front, so she gave him the spare, told him to use it, and he had. Now, it was too late.

"What's all this?" His gaze swept over the dressed table as he slowly entered the room.

She swallowed and set the plates down. "I wanted to do something nice for you."

His confused stare jumped to her. "This is for *me*?"

She nodded. "You've been such a good … friend to me. I wanted to say thank you. I made you a steak."

He blinked at her as if she spoke a different language. "I love steak."

"I know. And mashed potatoes and corn. I even picked up a strawberry shortcake for dessert."

His brow pinched as he turned back to the table. He lifted the champagne from the ice bucket. "Is this…?"

"Champagne." She shrank a little. "I…"

His face lifted and he drew in a sharp breath. "Ye got yer cast off today?" He crossed the room and gingerly lifted her hand, turning it carefully.

Her nose crinkled at how thin her fingers had gotten over only a few weeks. "I still can't move it."

"Ye will. You're used to keepin' it stiff. Does it hurt?"

She nodded. "I accidentally hit it just before you walked in. Instant tears."

His gaze met hers, his mouth forming a little pout. "No tears."

"I toughed it out."

He traced his thumb over the arch of her knuckle. "I cannae believe ye made me dinner."

"Well," she said, glancing to the kitchen nervously. "I burnt your dinner and the sides sort of got away from me."

"I'll savor every charred bite."

She smiled up at him, her earlier nerves washing away until a sort of buzzing vibrated between them in the air, heady and sharp enough to contract her lungs. A heavy ache formed in the pit of her stomach, rolling like a snowball, gathering everything in its wake.

It stole her breath. Tricked out her heartbeat. And her skin shivered.

"Callan?"

"Yes, love?" he whispered.

"Do you feel that?"

He nodded, his hand sliding slowly to her jaw. "I always feel it."

She wanted to blurt that this was a friend dinner, not a romantic one. She wanted to push him away and at the same time pull him close. She wanted to scream and cry, but also moan. She wanted to know what to do with her hands.

"I don't know where to put my hands," she murmured and then swallowed.

"Me neither."

Was he just mirroring everything she said to make her feel less awkward?

She tried to think of the last time a man kissed her. Her mind catapulted into a bad place. Her hands. They were there, scraping along the Formica, her screams echoing as he shattered her bones.

No!

Stop!

Please!

Useless words.

Shut up.

Be still.

Effective commands.

Can you tell me what happened?

Do you know who did this to you?

Did he use a weapon?

Stay still!

Shut up!

Shut up!

Shut up!

Callan let go of her and took a step back. "Em'ry, look at me."

Her stare darted to his face. His eyes showed deep concern. The heat between them vanished, chased away by a haunting ghost.

What was she doing? She couldn't bear his knowing stare, so she dropped her gaze to the floor.

"Sorry," she rasped, the word cut up her throat as it sliced out of her.

"Do you want me to go?"

She shook her head, unsure what she needed. A tear trickled down her cheek. "I wanted to celebrate something, but everything I do reminds me that I'm broken."

His arms closed around her, tighter than she could handle. She flinched, and he whispered, "Give it a second."

Her panic calmed, and her weight sagged into him, his familiar presence and scent sheltering her.

"Yer *not* broken."

She was sick of crying. Sick of losing it. Sick of being fragile. "You say that because you don't hear the crazy thoughts running through my head."

"Tell me what happened," he whispered. "Walk me through everything that took place in the past two minutes."

Her eyes closed and she leaned into him. "I can't."

"You can. They're just words, Em'ry. No judgment."

A vise crushed her heart, and her fingers curled into his shirt, squeezing until the threads wouldn't give anymore. "I thought you were going to kiss me. I wanted you to, but then … I didn't. It felt like he was right here. I could hear him screaming at me to shut up. Then I heard myself screaming it back."

His hand dragged up and down her spine, delivering the perfect amount of pressure to keep her anchored.

"Then I realized I didn't have my phone. It's in the kitchen."

"Dae ye want me te get it for ye?"

He was safer than a phone. "No. It doesn't matter anyway." She'd had it the whole time in the bathroom, and it didn't save her.

Maybe she should get a gun.

You had your phone in your pocket the whole time…

Three little buttons… 9-11, what's your emergency?

Safety. Trigger. Bang.

She wanted to curl into herself and disappear. "No matter what I do, I'm trapped. It's got its claws in me, and I can't get them out."

He massaged the tension at the back of her neck. When had they lowered to the floor and when had she climbed into his lap?

She shut her eyes, breathing in his familiar scent. Her fingers loosened in the twisted fabric of his shirt, and she flattened the wrinkles with her palm.

"Your dinner's going to be cold."

"We can reheat it."

Those steaks would be charcoal if they suffered any more heat. "I wanted to do something nice for you, and I ruined it."

He drew back so he could look her in the eyes. "Listen te me, Em'ry, this dinner, no matter how cold or burnt it is, it's probably one of the nicest things anyone's ever done for me. And sittin' here holdin' ye... I could do it forever."

She blinked at him, wishing there was some way to show how much he meant to her, but she didn't want to trigger another meltdown. And she certainly didn't want to force herself beyond her comfort zone.

She loved him and had no way to express everything inside of her. But just as she'd always choked on her feelings, just as she couldn't release that initial scream, she swallowed the truth down, fearful it might die inside of her, never finding its way out.

Her life felt like a locked in scream, growing inside of her until her being ached with the effort to hold it in. That unspoken scream and her taciturn love ravaged her insides, clawed at her inner walls, fighting to escape. But she feared them with equally paralyzing panic that wouldn't let her utter a sound.

The beat of his heart matched her own. So much of him fit precisely in the vacant parts of her that she had to believe, in time, they would get through this. Somehow they would make it work. Either that or he'd grow tired of waiting and move on.

"Have you ever been so scared you couldn't scream, Callan?"

A silly question. Men like Callan feared nothing. He was courage and virility and strength.

His breathing slowed, his hand stilling at her back. Their position prevented her from looking into his eyes. But she felt his pain without seeing it, heard it in the shift of his breathing before hearing his answer. Easing back, she gaped at him with wide eyes, as the truth ripped from some hidden place of his soul.

"Aye."

Chapter Twenty-Four

Riordan Private Estate
Lower Whitecraigs, Edinburgh—Scotland
Three years and Three Months Prior

The wicked rested during the early hours of the day and the Riordan estate collected dust like a tomb for the decaying morality buried within. With no reference beyond the last year, Callan could only assume the downward spiral of Rory's delinquents, and Rory himself was a normal occurrence.

Drug money, pills, and various white packets littered the common areas. It seemed a sloppy method of hiding their supply, and *everyone* had their nose in the honey pot.

Maybe he just dinnae see it before. Maybe they hid it because they thought him untrustworthy. But now, there were several newer men hanging around. They came sniffing like foxes and rats, digging out the trash and adding to the mess.

Eyes that were once sharp and alert now wore a cloud of confusion. Synthetic energy and a clumsy sense of omnipotence wafted from every loser. Clothes were askew, dishes and rubbish were left, and no one, especially Rory, seemed to have a limit when it came to being entertained by extremes.

Evenings dissolved into debasing of men and women. Orgies carried on in every corner of the house, the slapping of flesh mingling with the wasted scent of sweat, semen, and depravity.

It would be so simple to join them. Easier. Like a long-awaited exhale of breath he'd been holding since his father left. How divine it could be to just stop fighting.

His resolve overwhelmed him to the point of resentment. Always swimming against the current had worn him down to nothing, a jetty beaten to a nub. He felt himself shrinking, the temptation to swallow a few pills, grab a woman and disappear into sweet oblivion pulled hard, but he did none of those things.

Perhaps that was why he ended up with Rory. Callan could be such a self-sabotaging masochist, a tortured hero who never won, the perfect plaything for a psychopathic sadist.

As Callan lie awake in bed, the house quieted but hadnae yet silenced. The men liked to poke at him, throw women his way and take bets about when he'd give in and let go.

They knew he judged and despised them. The women were not humans to them. They were vessels, receptacles brought here with lies and paid far too little for the abuses they endured.

He would never lower himself to that level. Sex and violence seemed to dance so well. The hair tugging, the slapping, the thrusting. It scared him.

Women were simply too delicate and, despite all his efforts, he was as monstrous as the rest of them. What if he broke one?

His gaze shifted in the darkness of his private bedroom, his body alert to the creeping footfalls in the hall. Lying on his back in his unadorned bed, his fingers closed around the butt of his knife but he remained perfectly still.

The flash of shadowed feet fell outside his door, and he waited.

The handle clicked, and the floorboard that usually creaked seemed purposely avoided. Soft panting sounded, as a masculine silhouette slipped inside his cell.

A man. Was this about Smithy? Perhaps the kid he'd stabbed in the hand earlier for sassing off?

The darkness took up mass in the windowless room, and Callan waited, pretending to sleep, and letting the unforeseen space make its own obstacles for his unwelcomed visitor. One misstep and—

A foot bumped into the desk, and he sprang into action. He leaped to his feet, knowing the layout with his eyes closed, and threw his guest to the floor.

A hard grunt escaped as he yanked the man's head back, shoving his knife under the cleft of his jaw.

"Breathe, and I'll bury my blade in you. *What do you want?*" he hissed.

"Callan, it's me!"

His muscles loosened. "Rhys?"

"Yes, you twat!"

Callan unclenched his fingers fisting his hair, but held onto his knife. Rhys grunted. The familiar scent of his friend penetrated his defenses, and he backed off.

He found the light. Rhys panted on the floor, inspecting his jaw with his fingers and checking them for blood. "Damn it, Callan!"

"What the fuck?" he snapped, pocketing his knife. "What are ye doin' sneakin' in here like that? You're lucky I dinnae kill ye."

"Where's the money?"

"What money?"

"The money you're gettin' paid. And a weapon. I need several. The fucks stole my gun and never gave it back."

While Rhys stuck around the estate, he stayed mostly hidden. Rory openly disliked him, calling him a leech or a parasite or a squatter, and tossing food at him whenever he passed. For the most part, they avoided each other.

Rhys was there for Innis and Uma. So long as Innis chose to stay, Rhys wouldnae leave her.

"Dae yourself a favor and dinnae concern yourself with the arrangements between Rory and me. And whatever you're thinkin' ye need a pistol for, rethink it."

"Fuck you, Callan. He let tha' prick put his hands on her. Ye shouldae stopped him—"

He flew across the room, gripping Rhys by the throat, squashing any further accusations. "Tread very carefully, my friend. I did everything I could to save her—"

"Bullshite," Rhys wheezed, fingers scraping at Callan's hold. "You just … sat there. Let it happen."

Fury boiled over, and he jerked him with a hard shake. "Ye have no idea what I endure te protect her! Dinnae dare say I do nothin'! I've done everything! I've got nothin' left in me after livin' in this rot for her, and yet, I fuckin' stay!"

"You let that scum inside your sister!"

Callan slammed Rhys's head into the plaster. *"And where were you?"* He seethed with outrage, beyond his breaking point. "Ye lurk in the shadows, playin' judge and jury, but you're not there when it counts."

He shoved Callan with shocking force. "That's why I'm leavin'! I'm gonna kill tha' fuck, Rory, and get her and Uma out of here!"

He released him. "Ye think it's so easy, tha' ye can just leave? I've been fully armed since the day we arrived. Carelessness will get ye killed, Rhys." He tapped his temple. "Use yer head. He's got more power in his wee pinkie than you'll ever have. And if he hears about yer plans, he'll take it out on her—just like he did te punish me."

Heavy breaths beat out of Rhys as he glared at him. "This is not how our lives were supposed te go. I wanted te marry her. I love her. That's my daughter up there."

"Be grateful ye have what ye have."

"What happened te you, man? You'll fight for them, but not for us? Ye could end this, Callan. I know ye could."

At one time, he believed he could, but now...

The ugliness of this place had infected his mind. The hurt of his crimes lived like a cancer in his heart. And Rory was a monster that got bigger and meaner with every breath.

"I... It's too risky. If I mess up, she'll pay. You'll pay. The child..." He couldnae bring himself to call it by name or look it in the eye. Innis's child played the pawn, locking the other players in place while an infuriated queen reigned with vicious fire, pinning them all.

"You're a fucking coward."

Callan's growl snapped through the room. "Get out! Get out of my room and don't ye dare come back until yer ready te take at least part of the responsibility for her being here. It's *your* child that holds her te this rottin' hell. *You* got her pregnant when she was just a defenseless girl!"

"*I love her!* They stole her from me before I had the chance to do right by—"

"And what the hell does *right* look like? Yer only income's been the commission I paid ye. How the bloody fuck were ye gonna protect her with tha' pittance? She may be a lunatic's toy and a dead man's whore, but ye'll never be good enough for her. *Nothing* touching this life should touch her, including *you*."

The fight visibly left Rhys in one blink. His shoulders sagged, and his gaze fell to the floor. "I know I've got nothin' te offer her. But I do love her, Callan. I'd give my life for her—as worthless as it seems te you. I just want te protect her." His voice broke. "And I cannae. What kind of man does tha' make me?"

A hole burrowed through his chest. "Yer life is not worthless—"

"I heard what ye said!"

Regret burned hot and bitter. "You're my best mate, Rhys. The closest to a brother I have in this world. I'm hard on ye because I have te be. All of you are mine te watch over, and I cannae do tha' when you're threatenin' te do somethin' tha' will likely get yourself killed. If ye want te stay with her, then…" It was the thing he'd been fighting since the start—the reason he swam so hard against the beating current. "Then ye have te submit to this life."

"I *do* love her, Callan."

"I know. And I think—if the circumstances were different—you'd make a good husband for her."

Callan wanted to think of her as sweet Innis with her bright eyes and sarcastic wit, but that little girl was gone. This place had ruined the innocence in her, stolen it with cruel hands and filthy grabbing.

He dinnae know if normal could exist after this. Perhaps she was too damaged to find it. Rhys wanting to offer her something close to decent might be the best she could get, even if Callan would always believe she deserved the moon and more.

"He willnae let her see Uma," Rhys rasped, his heartache puncturing the words, "She hasnae seen our daughter in days. She's freaking out. We both are."

Callan's back tensed sending a line of tension straight to his skull. Everything was a game to that fuck. "He willnae hurt the baby."

Anxiety reflected in Rhys's eyes. "How do ye know for sure?"

"Because it's his greatest bargaining chip. Without the child, he loses his power over Innis. And without Innis, he loses all of us."

Callan hated to admit it, but losing the wain might be the only way they'd ever escape this place. But if that were to happen, they'd all be destroyed anyway.

"Please…" Rhys sniffed and turned his face to the shadows. "If ye willnae let me go after him, then give him whatever he wants, Callan. She's strong until he takes Uma from her. And I cannae bear te see her so defeated."

To what end, he wondered. The raw truth poked like a dull blade. Since the dawn of time, men justified violence with violence. But how many lives would be lost to save theirs? What if, in the end, they were all dead anyway?

Rory had called him a pelican. Since that day, life gushed from Callan as if his heart had been torn open, and life steadily bled out of him. Dying. He'd been dying ever since entering this hell.

His sacrifices had always been to keep them alive. Only now, he understood there would be no saving himself. He would die here, bleeding to death with his greatest enemies. A pelican stranded in the cold, sacrificing everything down to the last breath, to save those he loved.

"I'll get ye out of here. You, Innis, and the child. But it's not an easy switch to shut off. I'm not a ruthless man, yet I've done so many barbaric things."

They'd swim out of here in a bloodbath of his making. But in the end, Callan would choose to drown. The sweet exhalation he'd been holding in for so long would escape, releasing him of all he held, unlocking the crushing weight of his responsibilities, and mercifully sweeping him away.

Living in such hell made a man not want to live. But perhaps Rhys could see to Innis's future.

"Give me a few more weeks to make a plan and then…" He nodded, already working under a code of secrecy that should never be spoken aloud.

"What about Uma? Innis needs to see her."

"I'll work on Rory. Maybe I can convince him te lighten up where the wain's concerned."

Rhys nodded emphatically. "Whatever ye can do te help."

Rory, a man incapable of caring emotions, took great fascination in the human condition. Torturing Innis and the child by separating them could serve as some twisted titillation, as the more distraught she became, the more excited Rory would grow.

Innis had mastered playing the doll. While it satisfied Rory's desire for pretty things, it also protected her by hiding her emotions. She did it so convincingly at times, Callan wondered if a conscious thought remained under that porcelain shell.

He tried not to envy his friend, but Rhys got close enough to still find pieces of the Innis they loved. Callan only ever saw her as the doll. And she never let that mask slip when Rory was around.

When she bored Rory, he'd drum his thin fingers over his chin, a devious smile curling his lips while he mused at the dilemma her obedience proved. A sadist loved to watch others suffer, but sometimes his toys were too inanimate. With few emotions of his own, he feasted on the feelings of others. Innis knew how to shut herself off.

Callan sometimes wished he could do the same.

The following morning he joined Rory for breakfast to see about gettin' Innis time with her child. He couldnae act too wanting, or Rory would deny him for the perverted thrill of it.

"She seems different today," Callan observed, pitching his voice with enough indifference to draw Rory's attention but not his alarm.

Eyes on his plate, he cut into his food. Innis slouched in the seat at the far end of the table, beside Rory. She wore a peach-colored dressing gown with feathered lapels, and her hair had a freshly washed sheen.

Rory paused at the head of the table, a plump link sausage pierced by the tines of his fork, the silk sleeve of his kimono exposing his tattooed arm. Callan dinnae need to look up to know he watched him.

Head down, Callan ate, his gaze sneaking through his lashes to observe Rory observing Innis. The man sighed and bit into his sausage.

"She used to cry so much," Rory recalled, the maternal fondness of an empty nester in his voice. "And then..." He used a spoon to scoop a fat berry off the top of his porridge. "Pop." He chuckled and ducked his head to catch Innis's view. "It's a lot harder to cry only one eye." He ate the berry. "She still can, of course, but after the screams stopped, she taught herself to hold in the tears."

Callan's appetite disappeared, the few bites he had swallowed threatened to come back up. He breathed through the rage simmering inside of him, swallowed back the rising bile.

"It's been so long since I heard her scream. I almost forget what she sounds like." He brushed a finger over her lifeless arm. "When will you scream for me again, Trinket?"

Maybe if she just cried... But Callan couldnae judge her for her silence. Silence was her shield. He had no idea the pain she'd endured.

"I havenae seen the baby lately."

At that, Rory's sharp eyes turned on him. Callan never spoke of it, and mentioning the wain now might have given him away.

Rory's eyes narrowed, and his head tipped curiously to the side. "Say the child's name, MacGregor."

He met his stare, hesitated several seconds. "Uma."

Rory smirked as if he could taste Callan's discomfort. The child was a bargaining chip. Rory would leverage it against all of them if he found the proper opening.

"That's right. Uma…" he purred, his small teeth caressing the name with his thin lips. "She's named her for your mother, I believe." His brow puckered and a falsely sympathetic snick smacked from his mouth. "So much loss in one family. Tragic."

Callan dinnae respond. He wished he still had an appetite. Eating safeguarded him, and now he felt exposed. No other choice, he held his stare.

"Tell me, MacGregor, what was *Da* like?"

Callan's eyes narrowed. He measured every breath so as not to give anything away.

"Did he push you around? Pick on poor wee *Innis?*" he hissed her name. It was the first time Callan had heard him use it. "Did he hit Mother? Maybe take a belt te you?"

As transparent as glass, Callan sat there, breathing, fighting off the memories he hated to examine too closely.

"Aye, yer da was a mean old bassa, was he not? I bet ye lose sleep at night, worryin' ye'll be just like him." His lips curled into a half smile. "But Da never killed anyone, did he?"

The need to breathe disappeared. The world quieted, punctuated only by the slow blink of Rory's eyes. The crucifix dangling from Callan's neck burned a hole into his chest.

Honor thy father and mother... Thou shall not steal... Thou shall not kill...

"My sins are between me and God."

Rory's brows lifted with amusement. He peeked under the table and behind him. "And where is this god hiding?" He yelled to the man making a plate by the sideboard. "Hamish, check around! See if there's a god in any of the other rooms." He laughed and reclined in his chair. "Really, MacGregor, next ye'll be tellin' me ye plan te hop out of here on the Easter Bunny's back."

The silk of his robe separated, showing a pale flash of tattooed flesh and nothing underneath. Rory openly scratched his balls. From the deep pocket of the robe, he withdrew an antique hairbrush and clicked his fingers.

"Come, Trinket." His chair scooted back, and she rose, stepping between his bare legs and perching on his thigh. He combed through her ebony locks with an ornate brush and obscene affection.

"Your brother thinks you're upset with my recent decisions."

Her eye shifted, her solitary gaze locking on Callan. In that moment he knew this had been a mistake.

"Is tha' true, Trinket?"

Her chest silently heaved with each labored breath, and she winced as the back of the antique brush clacked hard against her skull.

"Answer me."

313

Her eye watered from the swat and she shook her head.

"I think you're lying." He glanced at the other man who now buried his face in his plate and ate as if he had the room to himself. "Hamish, bring me the black case on my vanity."

Innis's eye closed, the last bit of life inside of her severed from the rest of them as she fully became the doll.

What was in the black case? He had no idea, but Innis knew. Fuck.

"I was just makin' small talk—"

Rory held up a hand, silencing him. "You're giving me a headache, MacGregor."

Innis sat like an inanimate object, compartmentalized. She vanished yet somehow remained physically present, as if folding her psyche away for safekeeping.

The guard returned carrying a small black trunk and set it on the table in front of Rory. He lifted the lid, leaving it upright in a way that concealed its contents from Callan's view.

The soft clink of glass and delicate objects rattled in the trembling silence as Rory dug around in the box. Knives? Razors? Poison? He had no idea what was inside, and his curiosity nauseated him.

Rory set a small vial on the table, then an ornate, bulbous bottle with an atomizer pump and gold tassels. The delicate items were old, female relics from a time when movies were made of silver and women were taught that ladylike grace could garner more success than any level of education.

Dainty nail files, casks of powder, ivory handled brushes and polishes gathered in front of him. Callan suffered sharp relief that none of these items could hurt her.

Stripping Innis of her eye patch, Rory tossed it into the case. "We want everyone te see your eyes today. I'm going te make them extra pretty." He withdrew a small pot of black coal and a thin brush. "It's been a long time since we played like this. Ye remember how fun it is."

Callan's gut twisted. Maybe whatever this was would lead to her seeing the baby, but he felt certain she'd been better off suffering alone.

Rory braided her hair, moisturized her skin, and painted her face with heavy makeup. To him, she truly was a doll. A plaything. A medium for pain.

"So sweet of your brother te remind me of your feelings. If not for him, I wouldnae have realized. I've been so distracted lately, what with trying te locate some of my men." His gaze landed pointedly on Callan. "Trying te keep an eye on precious, wee Uma. Sometimes I forget she's there. Forget how quickly little ones can get into trouble…"

Callan prayed for the day he could strangle him. Innis notably paled with worry for her child.

Rory had no proof of his part in certain disappearances. But he knew. Rory always knew.

A cold chill rushed up Callan's back and he looked away. Innis sat perfectly still and limp as Rory lifted her hand and painted her fingernails.

Dark, blended khol outlined her lashes in a cloud of smoke. The hollow socket of her empty eye appeared almost normal, if not slightly sunken in. Her lips wore a sheen of red, and as he stared at the transformation, he caught the slight tremble in her jaw.

"Dae ye ken the difference between a reflex and a reaction, MacGregor?"

His voice had burrowed deep in his gut, and it took him a moment to coax it out. "No."

"A reaction is voluntary. But a reflex is involuntary. It's the body's natural response to protect itself from pain—like tears. I could pull out Trinket's teeth, and her eyes would tear, producing a natural painkiller called leucine encephalin. But her cries... They would be a voluntary reaction, brought on by her fears and anxieties. It's a beautiful thing when a woman learns te control her screams, that divine struggle between surrender and control."

He turned Innis and pinched both her cheeks, leaving rosy marks in the shape of a blush. A sheen of tears instantly sprang to her eye.

"Trinket knows how I hate it when she pouts. But I do love te see her cry." He petted the side of her head with disturbing affection. "Tonight we're going te play. You're going te be the perfect doll and not make a sound when you cry. Do that, and I'll let you see the wain."

The price of her tears snaked through his veins. Rory planned to hurt her, to bring her pain, but she'd get nothing if she let out a verbal cry. He should have never listened to Rhys.

"There now. You're as beautiful as ever."

Callan considered the time. It was still early in the day, some men still slept and had yet to arrive. But Rory was wide-awake and prepared to do his worst. Callan could only guess what that might be.

"Rory…"

He heard Rhys's pleas in his head, recalled the desperation in his eyes. Callan was prepared to die here. He'd sworn to protect her. His eyes pleaded from across the table, begging him to reconsider whatever this was.

Rory smiled, perverted satisfaction distorting his eyes as he hooked a finger in Innis's mouth and tugged her off balance. "See how she'll submit te anything I choose, MacGregor. And there's nothing you can do, short of killing me—or her—to change that. When will you accept that you're powerless here? She's not your sister anymore. She's mine, whatever I want her te be. And today I'm feeling generous with my toys."

His blood boiled as fire burned through his lungs, smothered by impotence. Rory was a master at bending others to his will. His demented taunts could abolish every moral principle from the holiest of men.

When would he learn? The harder he swam against the tide, the rougher the rapids. It became a puzzle he couldnae solve, and he wondered if he ever would.

Every man there had Rory's permission to torture and murder Innis and the child if Callan raised a hand to their boss. No matter what, he'd lose. It came down to his willingness to let go. But he couldnae do that until he was certain Innis, the baby, and Rhys would be safe.

Chapter Twenty-Five

Saratoga Springs, New York—America
Present Day

The defense seemed to be angling for a speedy trial, but nothing would save Emery the pain of testifying. It seemed no matter how much time passed or how much effort went into healing, outsiders kept forcing her to relive those horrific events.

The preliminary hearing would at least take place in a private setting, closed to the public and far away from the accused, with only the judge, district attorney, and defense lawyer. But Blaine's attorney wouldnae take it easy on her. He knew this and, unfortunately, so did Emery.

The defense lawyer would have the opportunity to cross-examine her, force her to regurgitate painful details. She'd be eviscerated by the facts detailed in cold, dead ink on the medical records and polis reports.

More than anything, he wished he could save her that pain. But the only person who could save

Emery the pain of testifying was Blaine. But that might make him look guilty.

Plea bargains were discussed, but Blaine continued to claim he was innocent. Like a thunderstorm on the horizon, they waited for the coming storm.

Emery feared she'd lose. He wanted to tell her, as the victim who'd done everything right after a trauma, a loss would be impossible. She wasnae the one on trial. It was Blaine versus the people.

But the criminal justice system let evil men walk free every day. Stroke the right judge or politician, and it was a natural reflex for them to get hard.

Wesley Blaine might walk after what he'd done. Sure, he'd serve a wee sentence, earn a slap on the wrist hard enough to prove he'd been punished, but he'd never get what he deserved. He'd never know the hurt he caused her.

And Emery would have to live with that. She'd have to swallow down the bitter truth that someone had hurt her in the vilest way and accept that the world forgave him before the injuries had time to heal—if they ever would.

She and Callan had been dancing around a relationship, neither of them emotionally equipped to launch into physical intimacy. Callan wanted her with a desperation that terrified him, but he loved her more, loved her enough to save her from the evil inside of him.

Emery, on the other hand… She dinnae restrain herself for fear that she might hurt him. She was locked in a cell of another man's making. A prisoner inside her own body and he dinnae have the key to let her out.

Wesley Blaine was guilty. The evidence of his crime lived and breathed. Yet he flouted innocence with a Soviet confidence that showed no symptoms of defeat.

This cocksucker had somehow turned into the world's Boy Scout overnight. His accomplishments were dumped into the media by the truckload, and they gobbled every bit of bullshite up.

An advocate had been a recommendation to Emery from Officer Banks. Harold Wong wasnae a sharp-dressed shark like the defendant's attorney. No, he was a recovering alcoholic with a mediocre background in law and a closet full of dated suits, a good guy who had a bad few years, now trying to resurrect his career in advocacy by assisting a client in a high profile case.

Blind anticipation burned across Callan's nerves when Emery described how the man clumsily handled the facts while offering disjointed suggestions to help her cope. The man had good intentions, but his bumbling delivery sometimes left Emery shaken and feeling without a champion.

Harold Wong was lacking in the emotional support department, but he made up for it in other areas. As an advocate, he intercepted on Emery's behalf whenever possible. He provided resources and handled a lot of the paperwork.

Banker boxes now shuffled back and forth between the lawyers, packed with details about the case, intimate photos of his precious Emery marked with the evidence of what that monster did to her.

There were enough medical records to assume Blaine wouldnae get pardoned, but the district attorney—the prosecutor against Blaine—just so happened to also have family in Ansley Park, Georgia. Coincidence?

So as those dreaded dates approached, the outcomes whittled down. Blaine could take a plea bargain, saving Emery the pain of testifying but getting away with a pitiful sentence compared to the crime. Or they could go to trial. The D.A. might go hard or take it easy on the accused. Either way, the defense would use every weapon they have against Emery. In the end, it would all come down to the judge at the sentencing.

"Callan?"

He glanced up from his journal, Emery standing in the doorway of one of the hotel boardrooms. They'd come in for an employee brunch and a meeting about the upcoming season, which had wrapped up a bit ago. "Are ye ready te go?"

She nodded. "I've been calling your phone."

He glanced at his mobile, seeing the notification of a missed call. She was getting around the hotel better these days, but she still didnae like walkin' the halls alone.

"I'm sorry, love. I had it on silent from the meeting." He adjusted the volume.

He'd picked her up that morning, seein' no point in driving separately. Any chance he had to spend time with her, he wanted to take.

He wanted a lot of things lately. Namely, he wanted to let her in, open himself up, and show her all the secrets he hid inside. But that would be a mistake.

"Matt said we could split up the leftovers. I have a box up front for you."

She was always so thoughtful of him, making him romantic dinners and picking up his favorite snacks at the store. He wished he could do something nice for her, something that showed her how much he loved her.

He tucked his journal away and gathered his phone. When she stepped into the hall, he caught her arm, a bolt of lightning striking through him like it always did whenever he touched her.

He kept his grip loose, and she looked up at him, her face a cross of hungry curiosity and anxious worry. Tenderness breathed from her. Her beauty never failed to strike him dumb, yet she remained as unassuming as a wildflower.

The dream of one day knowing her in any sort of carnal way blended into the shadows of his zealous devotion to take care of her. For her, he could be as patient as the trees.

"Would ye like te come te my home?" he heard himself ask without thinking through the invitation.

Her full lips parted in surprise, and he was once again a prisoner to the dazzling totality of her loveliness as she smiled. His hands itched to trace her serpentine curves, but he lacked a delicate touch, and that was what she needed.

Even holding her wrist took great restraint. And when she sometimes crawled onto him, as if trying to hide in his strength and seek protection, he struggled not to crush her to him. Her softness countered his hardness, and whenever she touched him, he turned to granite.

"I'd love to," she rasped. "I've been dying to see where you live, but I didn't want to impose or invite myself..."

Sometimes her joy seemed as fragile as cobwebs left in the morning dew. He never thought seeing his home might be something she wondered about.

His desire to please her hit him with titanic force. Though his home opened him up in the most vulnerable way, let her into parts of his past he preferred to keep private, he wanted to hold that smile on her face forever. He'd risk the painful, possibly dangerous exposure if it meant even a minute of her happiness.

His hand slipped to hers, their fingers entwining like children who knew no other way to care. His pulse fluttered like a dove's wing. Her cheeks flushed with the soft pink of a blushing cloud. Her smile quivered, but she dinnae pull away.

He boldly dragged his thumb down the fragile line of her finger and a flame of scarlet burned across her chest. Her breath hitched, and the jumping pulse at her wrist quickened.

Desire knotted inside him, tightening every muscle until he worried he wouldnae be able to walk. Sometimes those strings pulled so tight, he felt her body cinching closer without moving an inch.

"I've been thinkin'," he whispered, his gaze locked with hers as the fire burned up his arm.

"About?" She watched him like a fitful girl, still full of dreams, forgetting her demons for a moment.

His heart pounded in his throat. "What it might be like te kiss you."

He waited for her gaze to tear away, expected her to sever all contact. The aftermath of his confession could strangle the rest of their day in awkwardness, and he dinnae want that, but he also—desperately—wanted to feel her lips under his.

She continued to stare up at him, her eyes as unfathomable as the stars.

He swallowed hard against the lump in his throat. "Is that somethin' ye think ye might like to try, *leannán?*"

Her tongue darted along her lower lip. "Why do you call me that?"

He never really thought of it. "It's Gaelic for sweetheart."

Her hand tightened, and his soul thirsted to taste her. Her breath shook into the silence. "Yes, I think I'd like to try."

Everything inside of him twisted and released with pulsing need. His feet shifted, but his legs felt heavy. A shiver chilled him under his clothes, despite the heat of his blood.

The soft echo of his slow breath matched hers. Everything amplified the moment he traced a gentle finger down the side of her face.

He feared moving too quickly and frightening her. Worried if he botched this, it would take a million years of waiting before he found the courage to try again.

Her fawn colored lashes dropped low, as she watched him through half-lidded eyes. The raw composition of his soul, written from tragedy and wrung of blood, ached for experiences he dinnae possess.

Nowhere in his past had he learned how to touch a woman the way she deserved to be touched. The pain of inadequacy squeezed him hard. He couldnae breathe.

He'd begged for this moment a thousand times, and she'd given it to him, but now, as he leaned in close, he panicked.

His gaze cut away. "Show me how." The plea ravaged his manhood, leaving him raw and painfully exposed.

He glanced back to her, and she blinked, the sharp flash of confusion slashing the threads that bound them. He wanted to pull back, retract the last two minutes and burn them to dust.

He closed his eyes at the soft caress of her fingers to his cheek. She gentled him like one steadied a wild horse. With slow, courageous motions, she lifted to her toes and closed the distance.

The press of her warm lips to his sent desire tunneling through him like fire. His eyes squeezed shut, perhaps against tears, tears reflexively sent to numb the pain of learning such pleasure could exist. It terrified and excited him.

Damp heat traced the seam of his lips, and he opened, gasping against her tender mouth.

Not realizing he'd moved, his hand closed around her hip. He clutched her shirt in his fist so as not to hurt her. Everything inside of him clasped tight.

Her tongue swept into his mouth, and a moan vibrated from his chest. His lips instinctively tried to catch it, chasing the soft edges of her mouth with his.

He shuffled forward, his hard body pressing to her soft front. Her fingers teased the hair at the back of his neck, and he angled his head, taking the kiss deeper.

"Em'ry," he breathed, tightening his hold.

The door behind her bumped the wall with a thud as his hips reflexively ground against her stomach. A soft gasp slipped past her lips, and he swallowed it whole. Hungry for more.

Her warmth cushioned him. He wanted to plow through her, sink into every heated crevice. Bury himself so deep that he existed only through her, in her.

"Callan, stop."

He stilled at the soft plea, dizzy and taking a moment to recall where he was and what they were doing.

He immediately released her and took a step back. His gaze darted to the floor as awareness settled over him like daggers. His rock hard body pulsed with thick desire he couldnae contain, couldnae hide.

"I'm sorry."

She remained silent, and he couldnae bring himself to look at her, couldnae face the contempt he might find in her beautiful eyes.

"I shouldnae have touched ye."

"It's … okay."

His head jerked, and shock knifed through him when he saw the uncertain smile on her swollen lips. "I dinnae scare you?"

She bit down on her lower lip. "The only thing that scared me was how much I liked it."

The breath in his lungs rushed out with a shove of relief. "I liked it too." Too much.

A small divot formed between her brows. "Why did you ask me to show you how?"

Vulnerability prickled at the back of his neck. "I dinnae ken how you'd want te be touched." A partial truth.

Her smile turned precious, slightly shy yet exceedingly satisfied. Satisfaction won out, and she beamed at him. "Will you take me to your house now?"

She was everything. Her infectious happiness penetrated his anxiety, and he nodded. "Aye. Let's get the leftovers and go."

He followed her into the empty hall, and as they walked in silence, his heart skipped a beat. Her hand slipped into his, like a lost bird finally returning to last year's nest.

Chapter Twenty-Six

Riordan Private Estate
Lower Whitecraigs, Edinburgh—Scotland
Three years and Two Months Prior

This madness was not his life. Music blared over the pumping moans of tired women and pounding flesh as noses snorted up the cocaine cut on various flat surfaces throughout the house.

Rory was in high spirits tonight. He'd learned of a new drug lord, and sent Callan to invade their operation. The product he'd pilfered had been put to hard use, and everyone was blown out of their fucking minds except for him, Innis, Rhys, and the baby.

The work was gettin' sloppy. Not on his part, but on the parts of others.

Rory took so many drugs he rarely slept, which left everyone else walking on eggshells and forced to stay awake for his entertainment. Exhaustion made people stupid, and the careless injuries around the house seemed to double of late.

They were all tense. Even Rhys had abandoned the safe haven of Innis's room to keep an extra set of eyes on things.

Daylight poured through the windows. They'd been at it for hours, no end in sight.

Vapid shifts of tired conversation and delusional bouts of laughter set the wild tempo of the room. Up and down. Never a placid moment of silence.

The wain toddled through the house, pulling at Innis's clothes, shuffled away by Rhys. It had been weeks since Rory separated the two, but the lesson had left an impression, one Innis was careful not to forget.

Rory wanted Innis in his sight during waking hours. And whenever she was in his presence, her mask remained unmovable, even if the baby needed something. That's where Rhys came in handy.

But he wished Rhys would get the child out of here. It shouldnae have to see its mother so dehumanized. And Innis's silence likely confused it.

Uma.

Every once in a while, despite his efforts to ignore the obvious, her name slipped through his mind like a lost poem, fragile and small, but immensely meaningful.

He dinnae want to see the similarities, dinnae want to notice the precious way she had his sister's ebony waves or the way her giggles sang like music of lost years, so similar to the way Innis used to laugh when she was that age—when she'd been happy.

He dinnae want to recognize his best friend's features mingled with his sister's in the face of such innocence. But it was all there.

One glance at her faultless, wee face and he was lost. She was the seedling of life and purity that pushed through the cinders of ruin. She toddled around in such contrast to her surroundings. He understood why she should be hidden away.

She was the reason, during the dwindling hours of the day, when the uproarious guests could only slur their words and sway, he forced himself to stay awake. Rhys was the heart and Innis the sturdy shield, but Callan took it upon himself to be her sword. And he'd destroy anyone who harmed a single hair on the wee angel's body.

He hid his interest in the child, even from himself at times, because Rory could sniff out a lie like a starving dog could scent a freshly grilled steak. So long as Rory assumed him indifferent, the man couldnae use Uma against him. But the moment he realized Callan cared for the wain, Rory's interest would change into something dangerous.

"I feel like a game," Rory announced, staggering to his feet. "We need something te liven up this party. You there." He leaned forward and squinted. "Hamish. Fetch me a drink and my pistol."

Rory couldnae resist poking his finger in a tender wound. The temptation to make someone squirm called to him in moments of stillness. Callan felt the room tighten as if holding its collective breath, fearful of what might unfold. No one was safe.

Callan watched the room with sharp eyes, counting heads and hands, noting each person's degree of sobriety and calculating the overwhelming amount of drugs and empty bottles of alcohol.

Uma babbled as she worked the square corner of a block into a round hole on one of those cube puzzles toddlers enjoyed. She played on the floor. So long as she remained quiet, she was overlooked, but as her frustration with the block climbed so did her volume.

No one dared to quiet her, as that would only draw more attention to the child banging the plastic blocks in the corner. But Rhys saw her, and his concern matched Callan's.

Hamish returned and handed Rory a cocktail and a revolver. He sipped, sloshing the ice as he tipped back the glass. Dragging the back of his arm over his mouth, he emptied the bullets onto the table.

Several rolled to the floor. The chatter quieted. Everyone wore the same mask of pretended indifference, but not a single gaze left Rory since that gun appeared.

Rory equated attention with affection. So long as he remained center stage, he was satisfied, and he'd stop at nothing to keep the focus on him.

Violence came like first nature, whereas generosity or kindness would always be foreign concepts to him. His loyal subject's obedience kept him pleasant, but sometimes, even at his most pleasant moments, he got bored.

He slid a single bullet into the gun and shut the chamber with a click that penetrated the pulsing music.

"Who wants te play?" He spun the chamber, the rolling *tick-tick-tick-tick* too fast to know where the bullet hid. "Trinket?"

His sister's head twitched, her evident tension a testament to her fear. But she dinnae utter a word.

Rory clicked his fingers. "Come here."

The music lowered. Innis's hands pushed at the table, backing up her chair as she slowly stood.

Callan sensed her desire to look back at Uma, but she wouldnae dare. Even if this was her last chance to look in her child's eyes, she'd never risk alerting Rory to her daughter's presence.

Callan's discreet focus ricocheted between Uma, Innis, and the gun. Rhys's glare locked on the back of Rory's head as he stood behind him in the open doorway.

She approached Rory's side, her gaze lowering to the gun. The delicate feathers adorning her dressing gown trembled, the only tell of her nerves.

Rory placed the weapon on the table and nudged it closer to her. "Take the pistol, Trinket."

Her hesitation stretched into tense seconds, each one tingling like pins and needles.

"Take it," Rory whispered, his eyes wild with anticipation.

Her hand quivered as she reached for the handle. A sharp shift in the air chilled his lungs.

Callan recognized the moment she decided to shoot her tormentor. So did Rory.

"Careful, Trinket." He caught her wrist and Callan's knees softened as he prepared to spring into action at any second. "There's only one bullet loaded. But I have all night and many, many more."

Her shoulders shifted inelegantly, as if a chill chased up her spine. Rory released her arm and sat back, content with his warning.

"Good girl."

Innis kept her head low as her fingers curled around the metal. The gun looked heavy and wrong in her delicate grip.

Rory clapped his hands together. "Who else wants te play? Where's that squirrely fellow with the green eyes who's been leeching off me for the last year?"

Rhys.

Callan watched his sister's hold on the weapon tighten. When she sat unanimated, it was easy to mistake her stillness for calm, but the gun gave her away as it shook in her grip.

"Someone find him."

Innis's gaze, her unspoken plea, cut into him like an ax to the chest. Rhys stood just behind Rory, in the bordering doorway. Innis knew he was there, and her internal scream that dinnae make a sound shook Callan like the tremor of a seismic quake. She was panicking.

Callan shook his head, warning her not to do anything stupid. If she tried to shoot Rory, she had a one out of six chance of actually firing a shot. Five chances of failure and Rory would punish her beyond anything any of them wanted to imagine.

"I'm here," Rhys said, stepping forward and saving Innis from endangering herself.

Rory grinned. "The one thing about a squatter is tha' they're always around. Have a seat, leech. We're a player short." He kicked out the empty chair to his right, across from where Innis stood.

Rhys's gaze bounced between Innis and the gun, as he lowered himself to the chair.

"Trinket," Rory said, keeping his eyes on Rhys. "Put the gun in your mouth."

"No!" Rhys jumped up from the chair, toppling it to the ground. Two men grabbed his shoulders, and Callan took a jolting step forward before stopping himself.

His eyes shot to Uma, still playing with her blocks then back to his sister and Rhys. Rory glanced at him and smiled with slow, eel-like satisfaction.

"Did ye want te play, MacGregor?"

Despite everything he knew of Rory, he trusted this strange fascination he had with Innis. Why would he play a game that threatened to destroy something he loved?

Because he's incapable of love…

Nothing was sacred in this house. No one was safe. Callan quickly tried to switch his thinking to that of a psychopath.

This wasnae simply Russian roulette. Rory's motives were never that transparent. He wanted something. And it wasnae Innis's blood spattered all over the table—he had to believe that. But what?

He matched Rory's depravity with a cold calm. "What are ye doing, Rory?"

"We're playing a game."

Callan shook his head. "Ye dinnae want te play this game. This isnae the sort of game anyone wins."

Like an ill-behaved child incapable of gettin' the attention he needs, he argued, "Oh, someone always wins."

Aye, and that person was usually Rory. "You'll lose her. Who will ye play with if she dies?"

His eyes narrowed. "Toys break."

"Let's play a different game. One we all enjoy."

His glare tightened, seeping with challenge. "I want your sister te put the pistol in her mouth."

His jaw ticked.

Rhys surged forward, but they had him outnumbered, holding him back. He struggled. "Innis, don't listen te him!"

The more Rhys fought, the more it became a battle of choice, one where Innis would have to choose a side to take. And Rory never lost.

"Rhys, shut up," Callan snapped, but his friend had been pushed past his limit over the last year, watching her endure so much cruelty at the hands of this man.

"Fuck off, Callan! Innis, put the goddamn gun down!"

Giddy with warped joy, Rory laughed. "Trinket, last chance. Put the pistol in your mouth."

Her chest rose with rapid inhalations as everyone watched and waited for her to move. She hesitated too long, and Rory's delinquent amusement silenced. His fist slammed into the table. *"Put the fuckin' gun in yer mouth!"*

Her nostrils fluttered with panic as her face tightened and she looked at Rhys. Her arm holding the gun lowered to her side in unspoken defiance.

A harsh breath hissed past Rory's tiny teeth. "Fine. Bring me the child."

The gun was suddenly in Innis's mouth, her entire body trembling as her eye screwed shut. But Rory was already standing.

"Rory." Callan snapped, jerking the man's attention away as his sister shook hard enough to hit the damn trigger without even trying. "Play. Another. Game."

His cold, calculating stare burrowed into him, and his lips twitched. This was what he wanted. He dinnae want to kill her, his precious little plaything. He wanted to use her, just like he used everything else.

But Rory wasnae after the baby or his sister or even Rhys. He was after him.

Rory tipped his head back and breathed deep, the way he often did when scenting victory. "If I told her te pull the trigger, she would."

Callan slowly nodded, agreeing with him. "Aye. She'll do anything you tell her te do."

"I own everyone in this room."

Callan knew where this was headed. They'd treaded over this beaten path since the day he'd arrived. But today was the day Rory would demand an answer. He'd have it his way, or there would be blood.

Like he'd watched his sister do so many times before, Callan shut off his natural impulses and slipped into a shell. "You're a very powerful man, Rory."

"Aye." He preened, licking his lips and leaving them wet. "They might be free te roam, but they'll always obey. I own all of them, MacGregor. Including you."

He shoved his pride down as low as it would go, tucking it safely beside his dignity, and nodded.

Rory scowled. "You nod because you think you're smarter than me. But I see the self-righteous way ye view my world. You fight the truth. I might be a pile of shite, but you're the maggot that needs me te survive."

Callan kept his breathing level, his eyes locked with Rory's. "We're on the same side, Rory. I do everything ye ask of me."

"But ye always have an agenda, don't you, *Callan.*"

He dinnae know the significance of using his first name, nor did he want to waste time trying to figure out why it sounded so profane on his wet lips.

He spread his hands in front of him. "My agenda's irrelevant. I'm here. I'm not going anywhere." He glanced at his sister. "So long as ye do not hurt her, ye have my loyalty."

Rory scratched the back of his head, a strange show of uncertainty that concerned Callan more than any overreaction might. It was the drugs in his system, making him more dangerous than usual. Things were fraying too fast, and he'd grown used to an unemotional Rory. Anything else would be severely more disturbing.

"*Total* loyalty?" he asked.

Callan nodded, unable to speak the bitter lie.

"Say it. Say I have your *total* loyalty and obedience."

His brow hung heavy over his glaring eyes. "I'm here. I've been here. I'll continue te be here."

"Aye, you're here. That's not what I asked."

"Ye dinnae ask anything."

Frustration burned a red fog over his face. "Stop confusing matters! You're a lowly taxation officer, yet ye think you're somehow better than the rest of them."

"I'm no better than anyone else, Rory."

"That's right. You're no better! All that bulk and sinew and you're no stronger than any other man sitting in this room," he sneered. "Dae ye ken why she obeys me?"

He forced his knees to remain locked and still. She obeyed out of terror, but that wasnae the answer he wanted. "Respect."

Rory threw his head back and laughed. "That's what ye think I want te hear?" He slammed his fist on the table, and Innis flinched. "I dinnae give a fuck about her respect. It's her *fear* I crave. And the fact tha' ye have not kept your promise to kill me proves even you're afraid of what I might do. Ye probably jerk off to thoughts of murdering me. Fuck, ye outweigh me by a ton. You're nothin' but fine, chiseled masculinity, but you're as useless as a twat on a corpse when it comes down te it."

"Twat on a corpse still works in a pinch," someone yelled.

"Shut up," Rory snapped. His challenging glare burned into him. "Does the thought of me dead make ye hard, MacGregor? I know there's somethin' broke inside of you, maybe some wee part Da dinnae love. It's okay te admit ye get off on the pain of others."

The usual elocution of his finely dressed words slipped with each taunt, the heavy accusations stripping away all falsehoods and leaving everyone uncomfortably bare. It was a game, and Callan couldnae find an alternate end.

The *clank-clank-clank* of that block trying to make it into the hole filled the silence. The tip of the gun still rested inside Innis's mouth.

"What do ye want, Rory?" he growled, knowing there was an end game and this drawn-out torture of *guess-what-fucked-up-thing-I-have-in-mind* was all part of the sadistic foreplay.

"I want yer surrender. Yer obedience. I want you te admit I own you. I want te know I've broken

342

you so severely that the ugliness will always seep out, that I've left a wound so open you'll never be able te sew it shut. I want te know, that even if you kill me someday, I'll always be with you, a scar ye cannae shake."

He already was. This place and all the evil inside would linger like a cancer in all of them. No matter if they escaped alive or dead, they were changed the moment this place touched them.

"You're not one who's easily forgotten," he confessed.

"Not good enough." He stepped behind Innis, his hands fondling her trembling shoulders, tracing along her arms until his fingers closed over hers where they held the butt of the gun. He wedged it deeper down her throat. "That's a good girl."

"Get away from her!" Rhys shouted and lurched, earning a hard punch in the ribs that folded him in half. He moaned Innis's name as he gasped for breath.

Rory rolled his eyes. "You, sir, are on my last nerve." He turned his attention back to Callan. "*This* is true surrender, MacGregor. I could pull the trigger or tell her te do it for me. She'd blow her own brains out before daring te defy me."

"You've made your point," he snapped, sweat breaking out across his face.

"I've only begun."

Things were unraveling, and Uma still hadnae accepted that a square block would *never* fit in the damn round hole. Dinnae anyone, aside from them, have the instinct to get her the hell out of here?

"Enough of this," Callan growled.

"Oh, are we inconveniencing you? Sorry, no escaping work today, MacGregor. I've saved ye a front row seat." He jerked the gun out of Innis's mouth and shoved her forward, smashing her face to the satin finish of the table and positioning the pistol to the base of her skull. He glanced at Rhys. "You'll enjoy this, too."

A sharp gasp slipped from Innis as Rory shoved her gown up over her hips.

"Enough!" Callan threw over a chair and slammed his fist into the table. "Name it, and it's yours. Just get yer fucking hands off of her!"

"Yessssss," he hissed, letting Innis's gown fall back into place. "Let that beautiful rage out." He shut his eyes and shivered.

"What the fuck do ye want, *Riordan?*"

His eyes opened, and he smiled with a full show of little teeth. "I thought I made it clear. I want your total obedience, your absolute surrender."

Innis's body seized with fear. This needed to end. "Done."

Rory lifted a brow. "That easily?"

"The gun goes away, and ye let her up."

The metal clattered to the table. Innis's face crumpled around a silent sob as her body withered to the floor. Rory held out his hands and rounded the long dining table, his eyes never leaving Callan.

He stopped just in front of him. "Anything I want … you'll obey."

"I said yes."

He nodded, drawing in a slow, deep breath. "Shall we?"

Callan glanced at his sister. Rhys was already at her side. He looked back at Rory and nodded stiffly.

Of all the horrors Innis survived in this asylum, this one would be his. He'd take it, stuff it down, and grow stronger from the pain.

Callan followed Rory to the door, his eyes unseeing of anyone or anything around him.

Rory stopped at the threshold of the room and looked back. "Keep the baby away from her until I return. If I don't … drown it."

Callan dutifully followed him out of the room.

HURT

Chapter Twenty-Seven

Riordan Private Estate
Lower Whitecraigs, Edinburgh—Scotland

Callan followed Rory into his private quarters on the second floor, the tattering threads of his sanity unraveling fast.

Rory swayed to the glass cart that sat in front of the fireplace. Ice clinked. "Drink?"

"No." Callan stood by the door, arms crossed over his chest for fear that if he unballed his fists, he might strangle the life out of the fucking creep.

"Oh, have a drink, MacGregor. Live a little."

He watched with hooded eyes as Rory mixed two cocktails. Gone was the cold, calculating glare that had appeared below. The tension seemed lighter up here, replaced with a sort of implied kinship Callan dinnae feel.

"Where are my manners? Come in."

He obeyed only to avoid Rory coming any closer and touching him. His personal space would evaporate soon enough, but for now, he needed the distance to prepare himself.

A long couch hid the centre of the room where a sitting area clustered over an antique oriental rug. Wicker rockers angled to the sofa, their backs in front of the enormous four-poster bed draped with white lace that looked as if it hadnae been cleaned in decades. A marble-footed fireplace wore black soot up the front of its façade, and several glass birds decorated the mantle.

Callan would never be sure, but he wondered if the house and the things Rory dressed Innis in had once belonged to the man's mother. He wondered where she was now.

"Sit." Rory handed him a glass.

The weight of the crystal filling his hand seemed sturdy enough to kill a man. He envisioned himself doing just that, smashing the heavy crystal into Rory's face, bludgeoning him with the heavy heel of the glass until his skull caved in.

"You're not drinking your cocktail, MacGregor."

His grip tightened around the crystal as the toe of Rory's foot pressed into his knee. One snap and he could break the limb so severely it would never heal. He jerked his knee away.

"Uh, uh, uh," he tsked.

Callan's lips formed an airtight seal against his teeth, and he forced his legs to relax.

The foot returned to his knee, riding the thick seam of his jeans up the inner part of his thigh and only stopping when Rory fully extended his leg. "Ye promised total obedience."

His molars ground tight and his nostrils flared. "I'm here, am I not?" The words twisted through his clenched teeth.

Rory tipped back his glass and drank it down in several, fast swallows. The crystal clicked loudly as he set it aside. "Stand up."

Callan's gut twisted as he rose from the seat. He studied the room, seeking a focal point to target his pent up anger. He needed something to lock his eyes on, an interesting distraction to help him detach.

Any resistance would break the delicate truce keeping Innis and her baby temporarily safe downstairs. But as Rory's narrow finger danced across his chest, Callan questioned if he possessed the strength to endure whatever this next while would bring.

His eyes closed as an unfamiliar emptiness expanded inside of him, painfully stretching his chest until every beat of his heart hammered like an icepick chipping through stone. How did Innis do this? How did she turn everything off?

"Do ye think tha'll work?"

Callan opened his eyes, glaring at the man who now tugged open the buckle of his pants. Having never been touched there by anyone, he suffered a strange surge of curious tension in his loins. His veins washed with acid and grime. Everything inside of him wanted to pull away.

"You shut your eyes like a wee boy asked to stay after church with a grabby priest." Cool fingers snaked into his pants and Callan grunted as they coiled around his flaccid cock with entitled possession. "Do ye think the darkness can protect ye?"

His jaw remained wired shut as the tugging persisted and blood forcefully rushed lower, filling and stretching him until he filled the other man's grip.

"That's it now." Rory's other hand snaked under his shirt, gripping his hip as he pulled harder. "A man of your size has sizeable needs. Maybe there's a reason I never see ye with the women."

Callan held his breath, fighting back any response, but it backfired, bursting out of him in a hard grunt that gave away the physical release barreling through him.

Rory touched him with absolute purpose, the way a man handles himself in private. No wasted time on delicate gestures or lies about love. The goal was completion, and with every pull of Rory's fist, he brought him closer to that humiliating end.

"Dinnae fight it, Callan, not when it feels so delicious to give in."

Hot breath punched through his nose as his hands fisted at his side, his weight rocking on the desensitized soles of his feet.

Sweat beaded on his skin. The grip of Rory's fingers gathered moisture from the tip, smearing it down his shaft and his fist tightened. The punishing hold he had on Callan thrust him into a headspace that made this unforgivable act an unaccountable deed.

He dinnae want to give it, but Rory insisted on taking it.

"No," Callan gritted through clenched teeth, fighting back the release.

"Yes. Give it to me," Rory commanded, jerking harder.

He was a master of manipulation. Filthy and fearless in a way that could terrify the strongest men.

Mercilessly, Rory choked the pleasure out of him, twisting his hold with expert finesse until physical need toppled Callan's ethical will. An agonized moan tore from him as shame erupted in hot, white ribbons across his enemy's arm.

Shaken to the core, he panted and swallowed back a sob. Denial burned like a sharp, glowing poker through his soul.

Rory released his tortured flesh and stepped back. His eyes followed Callan's as he used the corner of the bed sheet to clean his fingers and arm.

"I think ye enjoyed that more than ye want to admit." His mouth curled into an approving grin. "Clothes off. And the weapons."

Callan staggered back as if he'd taken the hit of a lifetime. Glancing down at his spent erection, spotting the pearled markings clinging to his soiled shirt, a grotesque sense of failure tore through him.

He'd allowed Rory to do this to him while being armed to the teeth. His gaze jerked away. Bile burned his esophagus, and he had to swallow it down.

351

Rory clicked his fingers—the sharp snap he'd heard a hundred times before when he wanted Innis's attention—and Callan hated himself for responding.

"We had a deal, MacGregor. Don't make me find better entertainment."

Callan removed his shirt and tossed it aside. The sooner this was over, the better.

Stepping out of his boots, he stripped. He kept an arsenal of knives holstered on him at all times.

Unsheathing the trench knife from his thigh, he ripped the harness away and dropped the heavy brass handle to the floor. Then his dirk and bowie. He bent to remove his boot knife. Last, came the kukri, its long, slightly curved blade catching the flicker of the overhead chandelier as he tossed it to the carpet.

Rory sipped a fresh drink, appearing mesmerized by the show. Callan's gaze dropped to the floor, his focus shifting to his bare chest where the rosary hung.

Christ on the cross, his crucifixion now a poignant spike Callan could feel stabbing through his skin. In the end, it had come to inevitable sacrifice. How much pain could have been avoided if he'd only buckled sooner?

Ashamed of the moments ahead, he removed the rosary and set it with his clothes. When he wore nothin' more than his scars, he lifted his head, rising to his full height, and stared straight ahead. His cross to bear. Not theirs. But it would ruin him all the same.

"Jesus. You truly are a magnificent beast." The glass clicked against the table.

Callan stood for inspection, his stare drilling into the far wall as Rory's gaze crawled over him like centipede legs.

"Have you ever been with a man? Maybe fucked around after one of your fights when the adrenaline's runnin' high and no one's lookin'?"

"No."

Nor had he ever known the softness of a woman. His childhood propelled him full speed into adulthood. The day his father left, the nurturing part of their mother died. Gavin and Innis had been his number one concern ever since.

His soul ached with wild homesickness for a past that no longer existed. This evil man had taken everything from him. Beautiful Innis. Sweet, wee Gavin.

The reoccurring, ugly revelation knocked the wind out of him, the blinding punch of defeat turning his knees soft as he stood there naked, stripped of everything that made him strong—including his dignity.

He had no strength left. And the sharp perfume of surrender lured him like an opiate calls to pain.

He wanted to fight to the end. But more than anything, he wanted numb oblivion. He snatched up and guzzled the drink Rory had poured him, welcoming the burn.

"So primal." Rory circled him, and with every step, Callan's spine softened. "Savage."

Warm hands covered his back, stroking reverently. There was no cruelty to his touch, which made it all the more impossible to bear.

"You're a fuckin' animal." Damp lips pressed to his shoulders, wet and cold. "And I'm goin' te break ye."

Seething hatred burned white inside of him. He'd longed for the death of Oscar Riordan. Whittled that yearning to a sharp, stabbing point that pricked whenever he lost faith in his purpose. But perhaps it would be easier to simply run himself through.

His slithering touch trailed down his spine. Callan's hips jerked and his arse clenched.

"If ye fight me, it'll only hurt more."

It already hurt. The way he touched him added up to so much more than a physical violation.

His body's betrayal stung harder than any injury ever could. And as his cock lengthened again, like a snake charmed by a Grand Vizier, he feared Satan himself had compelled him here.

"Look at the size of you."

Rory wasnae molesting him as much as he was caressing him, teasing strokes awakening his body in ways that made him desire things he should never want. It was better when he'd aggressively grabbed him. At least then Callan could blame him.

"Ye like my hands on you." He cupped his sac, and Callan grunted.

Emotion lodged like a mountain in his throat, choking him until his eyes stung under the wash of shameful tears.

Stroking, fondling, it all collided into an inescapable pain he couldnae bear. The pain had no color or shape. It was dark and deep and hollow and full.

A dizzying need to thrust into Rory's hand swept over him. Sweat broke out across his chest. Then he was moving. It all started too quickly.

A fire snapped to life in his veins. His breath siphoned through clenched teeth as Rory's arm whipped harder, twisting and pulling his sensitized flesh, his fingers exploring below his spine, prodding tender tissue, breaching his flesh.

Need rolled through him like a hurricane set on destruction. Callan's hips thrust violently—shamelessly—into his palm, seeking more.

Shameful need rose, and he told himself it was because no one had ever done this to him before, because he'd been starved for human contact. Desperation pumped through his teeth. His lonesome life, so starved for physical affection, dragged him down like a fallen angel plunging to the pit of hell.

His head tipped back, and he growled at the tunneling relief about to set free. His bucking hips pumped faster, harder, as he panted to get out the poison inside, hissed through the hate-fueled lust.

Electricity zipped up his spine like a lit fuse, and he grunted. Rocking. Jerking. Thrusting. Needing. Screaming. Rory's grip contracted like a vise, cutting off his release, strangling the rushing flow of blood, and shooting bolts of startling, mind-numbing pain back into his body.

Callan howled in shocked agony, his knees buckling and slamming to the ground, the tight skin at his heels pulling painfully after the sharp collapse.

Rory followed him to the floor, his hold unbreakable, his nails puncturing swollen flesh and ripping an abused roar out of Callan's raw throat.

"Beg me. Beg me te let ye come."

His arms trembled, his head dropping between his quaking shoulders. His vision crossed and blurred as a fever shook his flesh off the bones.

Fuck. *Fuck.* He had to get it out.

"Please," he wheezed, tears burning his eyes as they squeezed shut.

Weak. Shameless. But keeping it would be like voluntarily swallowing poison. Rory put this sin inside of him, and he needed to get it out.

Never loosening his relentless hold, Rory shoved him forward, and Callan fell like a wounded stag. He climbed over him and jerked his head back.

"Look into my eyes."

Callan's unsteady gaze latched onto his malicious face, jerking over familiar features and landing on flat, soulless eyes. A visceral connection welded them together, a bone-deep hatred sewed through every coiled centimeter of his intestines. Nothing would ever claim his gut as totally as his malevolence for this man.

Rory peered into his soul. "I. Own. You."

His hand released him, and the pain reversed, only it wasnae pleasure. It was a backward sort of agony, his deprived flesh pulsing as blood rushed to the tip of his cock with enough force to knock him down. But he was already down, so he screamed, rolling to his back. Lost. Pinned as cold, wet lips covered him, sucking and licking.

"*No*," Callan cried, but his body was under a spell, drowning in rapids of hate too strong to fight. The current swallowed him, and he let go.

Icy hands petted over the passing of time. Clasped in prayer. Locked in trembling despair. Something held him to this life when desperation begged his physical self to drift away.

His surrender came at the cost of his soul. The sin of a mad man would always stain his skin, and Callan twitched with knowing awareness, that even after Rory finished with him, this would never end.

He'd see it in his reflection whenever he looked into his own shameful eyes. This nightmare would always be a part of him—exactly as Rory wanted.

"Stay just like that." The command drifted through a haze of confusion.

He rested on his side, limp and covered in things he dinnae dare name. His vision wobbled. His muscles twitched. Relief and phantom pain swirled amongst entrenched sorrow.

For a moment, nothing touched him at all, and he floated in the hands of God, praying the Almighty might take mercy on his soul and carry him to heaven.

Then he plummeted back to the cold earth like an orphaned angel clipped of its wings. Coldness blanketed him, and shivers wracked his body.

Rory rolled him to his chest. His forearms braced against the antique carpet. His damp brow lowered to the floor. The wiry press of hair scratching at the back of his legs forced a whimper past his lips, but he was too weak to make a sound, and only a hollow sob came out when something breached him.

Warm. He focused on the body heat, needing an anchor.

He tried to recall the last time anyone had laid a kind hand on him. His mother. His sister. His brother. No one had touched him in so long—and it pained him that he couldnae recall the feel of gentle hands now.

Rory was gentle. *He* would be the memory. The scar deep enough that Callan would carry it with him for the rest of his life.

Silent tears wet his cheeks.

And then came the searing pain.

His body locked, turning to cold, unwelcoming granite, but that dinnae stop Rory. Callan's bellowed cries ripped through the room in a voice he dinnae recognize.

"Aye. Scream for it, Callan. Let them hear how much ye adore them. How much ye'll sacrifice te save their ungrateful souls." Fingers dug into his sore hips, as he impaled him, stabbing hard and deep. "Would any of them do the same for you?"

Breath trembled through his burning throat past his dry lips. The searing pain anchored him. The truth was in the hurt.

In the hurt.

The hurt.

Hurt.

Truth.

The truth was in the hurt.

His eyes blinked hard against the consuming agony, some foreign sense of strength teasing the fringing edges of his battered mind. His teeth sank into the pain, grabbed it in a grip only death would break. He tasted the discomfort, drowned in the truth, and swallowed the hurt whole.

He bared his teeth and growled through the demoralizing shock, roared at the soreness until the welcomed slide of control knocked hard against his trembling knees, and his head gradually lifted.

No matter how much he wanted it to end, Callan could not be defeated. He bore the pain. Welcomed the hurt. And accepted the truth.

And once he accepted it, he had control again.

His eyes opened, his fists locking against the pain, inviting it. Grounded by the agony, he let his inner beast feed off it.

Retribution would come. He could bear this. He would survive it.

Dinnae scream.

Dinnae give him the satisfaction.

He cannae break what's already broken...

Rory's hips bucked out of rhythm, his plunging madness scorched with the sensation of tearing flesh. Callan welcomed the blood, hoping it would slicken his passage. And then Rory's guttural moan rent the air and the plunging cock throbbed inside of him, spilling venom into his soul.

He collapsed on top of him, his lungs heaving hard against Callan's back.

It was over.

Over.

Over…

He wanted to sleep but needed his clothes. Needed his weapons.

The eviscerating pull of Rory leaving his body took a part of Callan with it. Perhaps his dignity. It dinnae matter, so long as he left him his rage.

The need to move gnawed at him, but Callan couldnae feed the urge. Every muscle throbbed and twitched with disobedient relief. No matter how much he wanted to get up and leave, he lacked the strength to move.

Ice clinked, and his ears followed Rory's footfalls, the heavy pace of deep breathing matching his own.

"Now, I'll always have that part of you."

Callan shut his eyes and drew in a long, galvanizing breath. His hands objected as he planted his palms on the carpet, and his wrists shrieked as he pushed himself up.

Rory stood, back in his jeans, smirking over the crystal lip of his glass. "At least ye dinnae hate it." He snickered. "Ah, but that's what ye hoped." He winked.

Callan's legs trembled from heel to hip as he unfolded his limbs. He clumsily dragged on his clothes, his legs as useless as they'd been just after the fire.

He itched to collect his weapons and disappear from this place. Maybe disappear from the world.

Rory watched him dress with entitled curiosity. "Next time it will be easier."

Callan's glare cut across the room, sharp and unmistakable. There wouldnae be a next time.

Rory met his challenging scowl with one of his own. "I own you, MacGregor. I warned ye the job would be permanent."

Fire blazed through his skull, roaring so loud it overpowered the screaming logic forbidding him not to respond. Too late. This time his conscience wouldnae muzzle his hate.

"You dinnae *own* me," he sneered, years of seething rage spewing out of him in volcanic disgust. "And you dinnae *own* her. It's our resolve tha' owns *you*."

The words cut through the air and for once he believed he had the lunatic's full attention. Perhaps even a chunk of his elusive fear.

Callan cornered him with wild eyes, unleashing every pent up truth he knew could hurt.

"We are iron, and you are sand. We're everything you will never be, and you're sick with envy over it, obsessed with our mulish tenacity te care for one another, the way no one cares for you. *We* will be the death of you. It's why ye hold us so tightly. It's why it infuriates you te admit you'll never break us. Ye'll never sever our love for each other. Ye'll never compete with our bond—a bond forged of things ye envy but cannae feel."

Rory seethed with contempt. It beat out of him in waves, but he couldnae deny the truth.

Callan was already half dead. It was time to nail this coffin shut.

"Yer bullshite ownership is just a lie that helps ye sleep at night, Rory. We're no more yers than this house and all the stolen treasures in it. They're just pieces of the people ye wished ye could be— memories ye confiscated but never really owned. Trash. A castle of lies. And we all know its nothin' more than sand."

His words spilled like acid, burning through the illusions and baring the ugly truth. Rory's eyes brimmed with fury, the muscles of his face twitched with violent agitation and incarnate rage, as a storm of red indignation burned across his cheeks.

The air hummed like a kettle ready to blow, and he shook like an overwrought engine.

"Ye think I cannae hurt ye?"

He shrieked, and the walls shook under his shrill scream.

Like an atom split open, he exploded, shattering crystal across the room as he screeched obscenities, his fury splattered with menace and wrath.

Callan covered his head as more glass crashed against the wall. Rory barreled toward the door with demonic rage, his hands sweeping things off every surface and hurling them against the wall. Callan's wide eyes bounced between him and his scattered weapons. No time.

His battered body protested in frantic alarm as he raced after Rory as he tore into the hall.

"Rory, wait!" Terrorizing fear choked him. What had he done?

Everything outside of that room washed by in a flood of hideous reality and he wished he could eat his words. Rory rushed down the steps in a rampage of hungry fury, seeking a target.

Callan couldnae think beyond stopping him, beyond getting between Rory and his family.

His useless feet tripped down the stairs as Rory's agile steps gave him the speed advantage.

He gripped the banister, jerking toward the common rooms. Rory was several steps ahead. He'd never make it in time.

"Innis! Run!"

The wash of pumping music and baffled faces blurred as they tore through the den into the dining room. The world slowed and silenced as his gaze connected with his sister's, panic registering in her eyes and she shot to her feet, bolting to the other end of the room.

Her sweeping hair flew like a war flag into battle as she scooped Uma off the floor, sheltering her against her chest and pushing her wee body into the wall.

"Rory, no!" Callan shouted.

Innis used her body as a shield as Rory tore into the room, knocking into chairs and swiping the gun off the table. He aimed it at her.

"No!" Callan's scream echoed, accompanied by another.

Time slowed, passing in horrific slides he'd never forget as the gun clicked, failing to shoot. Rory snarled and spun to Rhys, and the world cracked into silence.

Blood splatted against the wall, but there was no sound, only the pop of his ears and his sister's blood-curdling scream.

Dripping pulp, red and thick with soaked tissue spattered on the moldings. Rhys's body collapsed to the table, limp and lifeless. A flood of crimson rushed from where his face had been. But he was gone. Nothing was real.

Surreal terror knocked Callan into the doorway. Denial hammered his chest hard enough to crack his ribs.

Innis's tortured howl ripped through the room, vibrating with Uma's frightened screams.

"What have you done?"

Callan couldnae move. He couldnae breathe. Rhys's face was gone.

His friend's blood pumped only a second more and then seeped slowly into the forgotten pile of stolen drugs. The metallic scent turned his stomach, and someone puked in the corner.

Rhys was dead. His mind refused everything his eyes saw. The percussive echo of the shot so loud his hearing still pulsed with a strange echo of irreversible permanence.

"Rhys!" His sister screamed, now cradling his limp body in her arms, his dark blood saturating the gossamer lace of her gown until it clung to her skin, matting all the little feathers.

"No. No…" Her ravaged sobs gutted him.

One of the whores held the screaming baby, trying to soothe her cries in all the chaos. Callan blinked. Numb.

The empty gun clattered to the floor. Rory met his stare, his face blank and his eyes flat.

Callan couldnae move. He couldnae breathe. His friend was dead, his sister devastated, the baby distraught. This wasnae their life.

Rory rounded the table and jerked Innis by the hair and wrenching her tear-streaked face away from Rhys. Blood coated her neck and hair. *"Use yer good eye and fucking look!"*

Her rough sobs ripped like jagged punches to the soul.

Holding his stare, Rory leaned close to her ear. "Yer *brother* did this." He thrust her head forward, releasing her. "Now, clean it up!"

Tension zipped across the room as Rory's gaze bore into him. His brutal possession still burned on Callan's skin, scored him from the inside out.

This bottomless hurt he couldnae feel—not yet.

Unarmed. No shoes. He reeked of his mortal enemy's sweat and semen. Perhaps he did own them because Callan could do nothing but flounder in shock.

Innis stood, her sobs chopping through the space, her motions jerky, her mind truly unwell.

"Shut that fuckin' baby up!" Rory snapped, and the half-dressed woman holding Uma raced out of the room.

But not far enough to silence the cries.

Innis returned, her ghostlike presence dragging the weight of a mop bucket and supplies. Would he really be so cruel as to make her clean up Rhys's remains? Everything was so fucked up he couldnae catch his breath, couldnae fathom how to intervene.

"Tell me again, MacGregor." Rory's voice penetrated the fog. "Say I don't own y—"

The broad side of a board smashed into the side of Rory's head. Callan flinched.

"Jesus fuck!"

Rory's eyes widened, his unfinished words seemingly trapped in his paralyzed mouth.

Callan's shocked stare landed on Innis as she clenched the end of a wooden club, the crude board shot through with rusted nails, several piercing the side of Rory's face as rivulets of blood drizzled from his eyes and ears.

"Innis…" They were all going to die.

She yanked the board, Rory's head jerked with it, impaled. Red flooded the whites of his eyes and spilled from his lips.

The board wrenched free with a slurp of wet tissue and hair. Her wild eye shined like a barometer of shrinking sanity.

Callan reached for his knives that werenae there.

"Again!" Rory needed to die. There was no coming back from this.

She swung the board but Rory stumbled, and she missed.

The disgusting wheeze of his rage drew in on a breath that pulled all the air from the room. He lunged at Innis. "Fuckin' cunt!" His garbled hate pierced the silence, and the room erupted into chaos.

Callan's fear exploded as Rory's bloodied eyes followed Innis with surprising accuracy, as he lurched forward.

"I'll fuckin' kill ye!"

How could he still speak and move?

"Kill them!"

Callan sprung into action when Rory bared his bloodstained teeth and lunged for her.

Innis screamed like a suicidal warrior and swung the board, missing Rory's head and slamming it into the table.

Rory choked and gagged, spitting a thick clot of blood as he lurched back, stumbling away from her. His hacking, wet cough rattled as he spewed blood and hate, swallowing down whatever choked him. "Kill ... her."

Hamish lunged at Innis. Callan flew after him without feeling the ground under his feet. "Dinnae fuckin' touch her!"

His fist crashed into Hamish's face, shattering bone and flinging his body away from the table. He ripped the board from the surface. Crooked nails punched through the end like a crude, homemade mace.

He dinnae think. Only acted. Slamming it down on Hamish's pocked face. The sickening smash left his legs twitching. Another blow and he stilled.

The room exploded in a flurry of howling chaos. Glass broke. Men shouted. There were too many.

Rory stumbled after Innis, a riot of murder seething from his soulless, red eyes.

"Grab that fucking bitch!" He hacked and spit, his voice crunching like crumpled cellophane as he wheezed out the command.

A guard snatched a fistful of Innis's hair, and she screamed like a possessed banshee. In a cloud of blood-drenched feathers and lace, she clawed her nails down the captor's face leaving rivulets of blood and biting his ear.

Bellowing screams howled out of the stumbling guard as he released her and covered his scored flesh.

Pain exploded in the back of Callan's head as something dropped him to his knees. He twisted, finding three men at his back. A booted kick slammed into his face, blinding him in a white burst. Another kick and the wind punted out of him. Too many.

They railed into him, tenderizing his muscle to mush, beating him until he tasted blood and his eyes swelled shut.

"Innis!" he screamed, unable to hear her anymore.

More men joined the fray, breaking chairs over his back as he tried to shelter his face from any more blows. He crawled, only to have their vicious kicking follow him. He couldnae escape them. His body became a bag of flesh, smashed to the bone.

They beat the fight out of him. The last of himself he had left.

He could no longer hold a thought. There was only pain. Only hurt.

Broken.

Defeated.

Finished.

He waited for merciful death to come. Someone dragged him, but he could only blindly moan.

"In … nis…" he rasped. Where was she? He had to protect her.

His eardrum sloshed with a disgusting crackle and crunch. Breathing was excruciating, as if water filled his lungs. Glass cut into his back as they dragged him.

Stolen from their drafty house and plunged into the fiery flames of hell. This was the end.

No more….

Please. No more.

The distant *pop-pop-pop* of a gun firing pierced his heart. *Innis…*

He needed to get to her.

But they dragged him away. They had her. He couldnae help her.

Maybe she'd be safe now. At peace. With Gavin.

Chapter Twenty-Eight

Somewhere dark.
No concept of time.

The throbbing of his skull around his brain shook the hinges of his jaw. His teeth rattled in a constant tapping that resembled the prattle of drizzle against a window. Cold. He was freezing cold.

A ruffle of cool air ransacked his exposed body, like icy needles piercing the skin. The twitch of his finger, strapped to something bulky, made it impossible to move.

His bare knees shifted under the crushing weight of the sheet. Sweat gathered like a blanket. His drenched flesh quivered. Scalding heat pushed into cold and a wheezed moan raked up his throat.

"Are ye finally awake?" The soft, muffled voice was too far away to hear.

Wet heat pressed to his ear. A shiver stabbed down his shoulders.

Tiny threads of pain traced to every point of his body. Even the insides of his ears screamed in agony.

Thirsty. Parched. But when he swallowed the swollen sides of his throat screamed.

Cool drops drizzled across his cracked lips. His tired tongue chased them into his mouth. Life.

"More," he rasped, hardly able to shape the word.

The damp cloth bathed his lips again, and his tongue greedily caught the droplets. He mentally told his arms to tell his fingers to move, to reach for the water, but straps held him down.

Where was he? Who fed him water?

Open your eyes...

The command hit a brick wall.

Open your eyes...

A small flash of light burned his retinas. A blurred figure wavered. The struggle to see knocked the strength out of him.

His consciousness jerked. The unforgiving taste of their boots and the lingering scent of blood had him tensing in fear.

"Dinnae tax yourself." A hand held him down, but he fought it.

His lungs stretched around a wheeze. He counted two, possibly three splintered ribs pushing back.

Open your fuckin' eyes. Now!

Light flickered, the tall, blurred figure bent closer. More muffled words.

He tried to ball his fist and failed. His strength sapped out of him and sleep pulled him under.

Sometime later his eyelashes pulled apart, and he was alone. Dark shadows and a cricked neck. Everything hurt. His search, enlisting only his roaming eyes, exhausted him.

The familiar ceiling he recognized. This was his space.

He dinnae blink. Rather, he awakened, again and again, unsure how long he slept in between. He waited for the person with the water, but she never returned.

For hours, possibly days, his thirst grew, and his mind spun. The pain ebbed and flowed with every pulsing beat of his heart.

He kept time with the muscle, counting off sixty beats and then sixty more—frustrated when he'd wake up, his count lost.

He coasted on a sea of hypnotic waves. Choppy water battled against the burning cold, submerging him in a fevered chill of thirst and shivers. No anchor. Lost.

The hot press of something solid to his lips woke him with a jerk that radiated down his spine. Metal clicked against his teeth.

He opened, stretching his battered jaw. The warm spill of broth filled the crevices of his mouth. He swallowed greedily and opened for more.

Another swallow. And then another.

A sweet, merciful angel cared for him, bathed and fed him. He'd swear fealty to her as soon as he had his strength back. Her figure sloshed in his blurred sight, but he needed to know who…

"Who are you, angel?"

"Elspeth." The muffled voice carried the soft tenor of a female.

"Els…"

"Try not to talk. You need to eat."

He swallowed another mouthful of broth. His mind sorted through the limited information he had. He was still in Rory's house. Still alive. Where was everyone else?

"Where…" The spoon interrupted his question, and he lost his train of thought. "Who…"

"I'm one of the tail."

A prostitute? He dinnae recognize her. Nor could he fully see her.

"That's my call." She stood, taking away the warm broth.

Panic gripped him. He dinnae want to be left alone again. "Wait. Please."

"The baby's crying. I'll be back."

The baby? Visions of Uma spun through the maze of his mind, twisting until relief settled in. Uma was still alive.

A cold drift of fear moved over him like a sheet of ice. He'd use the baby against him again. He kept it alive for a reason. He'd hurt her to hurt him.

"Elspeth," he rasped and coughed.

What if the whore's loyalty belonged to Rory? Could he ask her to take Uma and run? He was too weak to defend himself or the child.

Forcing his shoulder to lift from the bed, he screamed through his teeth at the deluge of pain. The broth in his gut swilled.

His elbow cracked with the reverberation of a rifle, and he collapsed.

Fast, panting breath hissed past his teeth as sweat beaded across his skin. He shut his eyes, sensing he might pass out from the pain. So weak.

Discomfort splintered from his back to his front, goaded by a hacking cough that tasted too much like blood to be a sign of healing.

"Are you mad?" Elspeth's voice softly reprimanded as she returned. Maybe he passed out.

No time for that. "The baby," he coughed. "Dinnae leave her…"

"Hush now. You've got yourself in a fit." She pressed a cool glass to his lips and held his head. "Sip slowly, so you dinnae choke."

The water quelled the coughing. He sagged into the bed and caught his breath.

Too weak to escape. Too feeble to walk. Too blind to see clearly. Too deaf to hear. Too dead inside to be certain he was alive.

He surrendered. Too beaten down to fight.

He lost any grasp of time. Days counted by the intermittent night, but he might have slept through some, so nothing seemed accurate or trustworthy.

The fever came when he was at his weakest, ravaging his already broken body. His depleted strength wrung out eventually, and his tattered mind simply begged for peace.

Elspeth tended to him on a random schedule he gave up trying to predict. He craved her when she wasnae there. Questioned her when she was.

She only ever whispered, which made hearing her especially difficult. He suspected both his eardrums had ruptured. The pressure from the fever and the congested ache in his head dinnae help matters.

He appreciated her gentleness, but dinnae trust it. He trusted nothing and no one. But as time passed, his yearning for Elspeth grew stronger. She represented survival.

"Your bruises are healing," she whispered, dragging a warm washcloth over his legs.

She took turns washing his skin and bending his muscles. He'd been in this bed so long his body started to atrophy. She even applied a soothing salve to his burn scars, which eased a great deal of the pain in his legs.

"Thank…" It was all he could manage.

She massaged the salve into his ruined heels. "Save your strength."

Consciousness wove in and out. "Innis?"

As he healed, his mind passed too many hours in silence, tortured by his thoughts. He needed to understand what was left out there.

Elspeth bent and unfolded his knee, hesitating to answer. "You're no help to anyone like this. Focus on healin' yourself."

He needed to know if they'd killed Innis— needed the closure of knowing she was finally at peace.

He knew the baby was alive and Rhys was dead. What of Rory? What would they do to him once he got out of this room?

"Rhys's body. And..." He couldnae get the question past the crushing lump in his throat.

Elspeth lowered his leg and covered it with the sheet. "All the bodies are gone. I'd appreciate no more speakin' of it." She washed his chest and left him alone with his thoughts.

Another length of time passed. He gave up speaking. Gave up searching for answers that might put his life in gruesome perspective. There was no sense in any of it. And the longer he lay in that bed, the less he understood why anyone would wish to live at all.

The slam of a door woke him with a start. His hands searched for protection, but he had no idea where his weapons were.

This was it. He'd been mentally preparing for the moment the end would finally come. At least the swelling in his face had gone down enough for him to open his eyes and face death like a man—fight with the last crumbled grain of his strength.

Footsteps raced back and forth, up and down the hall. Panicked patters and thudding objects collected on the other side of the wall.

More doors opened and slammed.

He forced himself into a seated position, adrenaline disguising his body's protests. Where was Elspeth? He needed her to find his weapons.

His trembling fingers curled around the bedpost. He pulled at the tape holding the cushioned metal splints to his hand, wincing when they tugged his damaged fingers. There was no time for self-pity.

His legs failed him when he stood, and he stumbled into the dresser. Remembering the way he'd relearned to walk after the fire, he found his balance and staggered closer to the door, listening. He searched the dark for anything he could use to defend himself. Nothing.

The door burst open. His fists flew to protect his face, his gnarled fingers unable to bend properly. Elspeth raced past him, opening drawers and tossing items on the floor.

"What's happening?" he hissed.

"We have to go." Her head shook as she frantically gathered up his clothes. "Or I do. You can come with me if you want. I assumed you would." Dumping the contents of his drawers onto the bed, she looked at him. "You need pants."

He caught the clothes she flung at his chest and staggered. His grip tightened on the bedpost. "I dinnae understand."

"I cannae stay here a second longer. 'Tis cursed. And no place for a child."

She was taking Uma? He stepped into the pants. "They'll catch us. I can barely stand."

She ushered him to the side of the bed. "Sit. I'll help you."

His head swam as she jerked a shirt over his shoulders. He grunted at her rough handling. "Easy. Tell me what's happened."

Her hands trembled as if she'd seen a ghost. "I'm takin' that child away from this madness."

His hand tightened on her thin arm and her frantic gaze jerked to his. He'd not allow her to steal away the last of his family. "The wain stays with me."

Her mouth opened and closed. "You'll come with me, too, then. But we have to go now."

He wasnae strong enough to leave, but also, not strong enough to survive without her. "I need my weapons."

"No. No weapons. I'm sick of blood and violence." Her words choked off, the backs of her fingers rushing to her lips as her eyes flooded with unshed tears.

Her tears were a beautiful pity, but his ability to comfort the fairer sex had died with the rest of him. He gripped her wrist, feeling the fragile bones beneath the surface. "I want my fucking knives. And you're going te bring them te me."

She yanked her arm back, breaking contact. Fire ignited in her eyes, drying up her tears. "Lay a hand on me again, Mr. MacGregor, and I'll leave ye here te rot with yer deranged sister."

His entire body tensed. "Innis is here? *Alive*?"

"Oh, Trinket's alive, the twisted bitch tried te kill me! If you're thinkin' about takin' her with us, ye can forget it."

Innis was alive? She lived?

He'd mourned her, believing her dead—again. Why had she not come to see him? Only one thing could have kept her from him—*Rory*.

Elspeth planned to steal Innis's child. It would break her. He couldnae allow that to happen.

"Where's Rory?" He needed to prepare. If they were leaving, so was Innis.

Elspeth's eyes widened as she shook her head. Fear mangled her features. "He's upstairs with Trinket."

He shoved off the bed, ignoring his body's protests. "Dinnae leave this room."

"Where are ye goin'?"

"Dinnae leave this room," he repeated, eyes threatening.

She'd cared for him, and he appreciated her kindness, but he wouldnae allow her to kidnap Uma from Innis. Their family needed to stay together.

"You open this door, and I'll hunt ye down and kill ye."

Her face paled as he shut her inside.

The house seemed quiet. Too quiet.

Gripping the banister, he peeked into the den. Furniture was flipped on end. Tables were shattered. Black smudges marked the carpet. His nose twitched. The air smelled cold, of bleach and emptiness, as if a fire hadnae been lit in days.

He strained to listen through the muffled churning of his eardrums. Nothing.

Sweat broke across his lips and nose at the sheer sight of the stairs. His fingers locked on the rail and he swallowed a growl, hoisting himself up the first step.

Fuck. He'd never have the strength to get to the top.

Again and again, he pulled his body upward. It took years to make it to the landing. His muscles shook, and dizziness stole through him. His body lowered on the top step, his back falling to the floor as he heaved for breath, his lungs protesting.

Eventually, he found the strength to stand. Every bedroom door was open. The hinges whined as he pushed into Innis's room. Empty. Where was Uma?

Calming his agitated breath, he shut his eyes outside of Rory's door. Hideous memories flooded him like a tsunami, visions of his last visit here knocking him off balance. He wasnae strong enough to beat him then, and he certainly wasnae strong enough now.

A cold surrender blanketed him as he understood he'd be trading his life for theirs. It was the only weapon he had left.

His ears searched for any sound, but all he heard was the hammering of his heart. Then he smelled it. Blood.

Dear God, what would he have done to her? Why could he not just let her die? It might be too late for a trade. He might have to end this himself, delivering her the quick, merciful death she deserved. He swallowed hard.

His soul trembled at the thought. Had this tragic journey always led to this end? Was this everything he'd fought for? To be the one to take her life, his sweet, fragile Innis?

His stomach twisted with empty knots. The unavoidable wish to see her in a happy home shifted to a place of golden gates and mercy.

If this was his only choice, he'd see it done. He'd bring her peace as she deserved.

Letting out a long breath, he turned the knob and flung the door open. Innis stared back at him and relief impaled his heart with such force he staggered back. His sister paused, watched him through her eye, rocking on a wicker chair.

"Innis," he breathed.

Her bare feet tucked under the billowing white of her nightgown. Her head tipped with curious caution.

She watched him like a wee creature watches a predator. Or maybe *she* was the predator and he was the prey.

"Innis, love, are ye all right?" He could see by her strange stare she wasnae.

He scanned the room, seeing no sign of Rory. Was she alone? He held a misshapen finger to his lips, warning her to be silent.

Her brow tightened and the chair rocked again. *"Bobby Shafto's gone to sea."* The singsong tempo of her childlike voice pealed through the silence in a haunting tone. *"Silver buckles at his knee..."*

The fringes of his mind ruffled as a sense of nostalgia stole through him. *Bobby Shafto* was a nursery rhyme Innis had loved as a child.

Something glinted in her hand, hidden by the billowy sleeves of her gown, and he squinted.

"What do ye have there, Innis?"

Buried in a cloud of white gossamer, she swayed slowly, her disjointed state of mind feathering through the room like a lonely wind.

She looked like a child. A broken doll entangled in a paradox of innocence and peril. Jumbled chaos swarmed around her like invisible bees, they protected her as much as they tortured her, forbidding anyone to come too close.

"He'll come back and marry me, Bonny Bobby Shafto..." she sang, rolling her head back and smiling at the ceiling. It was the truest show of joy he'd seen from her since arriving at this house.

What did she have to smile about? Her life had been nothing but tragic futility, a chain of unpardonable errors and unparalleled atrocities. She wasnae well.

"Innis, love," he spoke softly. "It's time te leave." He expected Rory to burst out from the closet at any second. "We have te go, now."

"Bobby Shafto's bright and fair—"

"Innis." He needed her to focus. "Listen te me. We have te go, right now, before Rory comes back."

Her eye widened, casting her broken parts in a demoralizing light. The chandelier cast a soft golden glow over her antique nightgown and making her porcelain skin appear urbanely plastic.

Her hand lifted from the billows of her gown, a slender finger tracing the empty socket of her missing eye. "Rory..."

The oppression of this place brooded in the shadows. Pillaged treasures surrounded her. She belonged to them. Another overlooked toy.

He couldnae fault her for the madness. "Yes, Innis. We need to go before he returns."

Her head rolled back, and a delicate laugh rang from her lips like a cracked bell. Her other hand lifted, revealing his kukri, the curved blade stained with blood.

He took a jagged step forward, and she pointed her arm with surprising accuracy, her gaze sharpening with the scorching promise that if he moved another inch, she wouldnae hesitate to hurt him.

He stood on thorns, waiting for her to lower the blade. His legs wobbled, and his hands stretched open in a show that he meant her no harm.

"Please, Innis. I want te take ye away from here. You and Uma. Come with me, now."

Her gaze dropped to the floor and bounced back to him. Separated by the seating area, he worried what hid behind the couch.

"Where's Uma, Innis?"

She frowned and lowered the knife. He crept forward. The wicker rocking chair moaned as it swayed over the creaking floor.

"Bobby Shafto's gettin' a bairn, to dangle on his arm..."

Another creeping step forward and the scent of blood intensified. The closer he stepped, the more it saturated the air.

"In his arm and on his knee, Bobby Shafto loves me..." Her disembodied words filled the silence as she stared at the wall, rocking in a mask of tranquility.

Moving closer, he noticed the spotted smears of bloody fingerprints peppering the mantle. And the dark stains saturating the hem of her gown and the bottoms of her feet.

A board creaked under his weight. Her words cut off, as did the rocking. He stilled.

"Innis, do ye know who I am, love?"

Her head tilted, ebony waves tumbling down her shoulder. "You're Callan."

"Dae ye ken where Uma is?"

She frowned again.

"Dae ye ken where Rory is?"

Her face lifted, her eye staring off as her lips pulled in a delicate smile. "I made him pretty."

Her palm dragged over her cheek, the lashes of her missing eye peeking through her fingers as she traced the hollow socket. "Just like me."

The blood rushed from his head as he rounded the sofa and stumbled, covering his mouth as he gagged on the sight and stench. He staggered back in horror.

What was left of Rory lay on the floor, stapled to the carpet with multiple knives. Mirrors, spattered with blood, angled against the sofa and foot of the bed. Flesh rotted around the massacred corpse, flayed from still bleeding muscle and stark white bone.

She'd made him watch—until she carved out his eyes.

"Innis!" Disturbed by the sight and stench he had to look away. "You're playin' with a corpse."

He searched for something to cover the body, yanking the blankets off of the bed. Then, through the muffled mess of his ears, he heard the unmistakable wheeze of a masculine groan.

The world stilled in a gruesome landscape of blood and tragedy. Rory was alive. She'd kept him alive because that was exactly what Rory would have done.

Falling against the wall, Callan gaped in horror. The gurgling rise of Rory's skinned chest pooled with blood like an overworked sponge. Flayed skin exposed pulpy, pink flesh, the rind of a wasted human.

"Innis, what have ye done?" he breathed, drawing a jagged sign of the cross over his chest.

He needed to kill him. They needed to leave this place.

She was back to rocking. Back to her disembodied nursery rhyme.

He couldnae think or breathe when the noises kept coming from the floor. Yes, Rory deserved to die. Callan fantasized of killing him since the day he learned his name. But this...

The tormented, mutilated, mass of a human being bleeding into the ground was beyond his penchant for cruelty. Even he took mercy on his depleted, sadistic soul.

His stare jolted to the table. Back to Rory. Crucified.

His crusty fingers twitched. Could he hear them? Should he speak to him? End him? He couldnae leave him like this, nor could he offer comfort.

She wasnae well. He needed to get her out of this room and away from here.

"Innis, I need ye te put down the knife."

She shook her head. "Not until he tells me."

"Tells ye what, love?" He was losing his grip. The stench of rotting man had seeped into every swallow of air, and he fought hard not to retch.

"Where he is." She twisted the tip of the kukri against her fingertip.

"Who?"

Her head tilted, and she smiled. Her feet dropped off the edge of the chair onto the ground, pressing into sticky blood. The gown flowed over her legs as she crossed the room, one hand holding the knife.

She snatched a small paper from the corner desk and brought it to Callan. "Him."

His eyes locked on the picture, a chill blooming over his skin. A teenage boy with a shaved head and a dark tattoo covering half his face glared at the camera. The eyes were unmistakably familiar. MacGregor eyes, but...

No. It wasnae him. Gavin had a wee build and couldnae have grown so much in such a short time. "Where did ye get this?"

Leaving him with the picture, she crept closer to the body and dragged the pointed tip of the blade down Rory's battered thigh. His leg twitched, and the sound that escaped his bloodied face was pure suffering.

"Innis, stop!"

She spun and glared at him. *"He did this to us!"*

He breathed fast, unsure of how to handle her. "He did a lot of things. He's wicked in every way, but you're not."

Her shoulders lowered. "I am what he made me."

Callan shook his head. "You don't have te be. We can leave here." He held up the photo. "We can find Gavin."

His stomach curdled at the lie. Gavin was dead. She watched him die, but now her mind had suffered too much torture, and she was confused, convinced the young boy in the picture was their deceased brother after all these years.

Her lost mind had created a cold and dangerous, vacant place. He needed to get her help. "We can start over."

"I'm not finished," she said, returning to her chair.

He staggered to the desk and yanked out a drawer. Banknotes spilled onto the floor. Property deeds and letters fluttered to his feet. Finally, his hand closed around cold steel. He checked the chamber—fully loaded—and stuffed it in his pocket. "This has te end. Now. Where's Uma?"

The chair creaked as her voice fluttered through the room in that same eerie melody. *"He'll come back and marry me, pretty Bobby Shaftoe…"*

"Innis! Where is yer daughter?"

She drew in a long breath and sighed. Leaning forward, she plunged the blade into Rory's leg, and a gurgling moan seeped from Rory as fresh blood flooded the sticky, twitching tendons.

"Fuckin' Christ! Enough!"

The body convulsed in a spasm of pain. She was torturing him for the sheer, sick pleasure of it.

"Enough, now," he pleaded with a trembling voice. He leveled the gun and pointed it at the suffering body on the floor, no longer a man.

The rocking chair stilled, and her haunted whisper pierced the silence like a hacksaw. "I'll kill ye if ye kill him."

He stared at her incredulously. "We cannae leave him like this—"

"I'm not leaving," she snarled. "You go."

"Innis, this isnae right!"

"Right? It's my right te make him suffer! He stole everything from me! My independence. My family. My freedom. My will. My *innocence*. My love! I'll never forgive ye if ye take away my vengeance." She bared her teeth. "It's all I have left, and I'll murder anyone who thinks te take one more fuckin' thing from me. Dae ye understand?"

This was not his sister. Gone was his beautiful, innocent Innis, replaced with a sick minded woman who could only speak in violent pleas.

She was a broken doll, wound too tight and abused too long to ever recover from the tragedy she'd become.

His wasted vision blurred, the ache choking him as he forced his heart to let her go.

But he couldnae leave the innocent baby behind—not with Innis. Not anymore.

Swallowing against the fierce stabbing that gored his heart, he rasped, "What about Uma?"

Her head shook slowly. "I cannae be what she needs anymore."

The last fractured bit of his heart broke. He lowered the gun. His breath tumbled out of him in a defeated gust.

Face pinched, he looked at her with tears in his eyes, his voice scraping over the one truth he knew. "I dinnae ken how to walk away from ye, Innis."

He'd fought for her. Avenged her death. Hunted her tormentor. Stayed with her. Watched over her. Sacrificed all he had left for her. And in the end, none of it had been enough to save her. Why would she trust him with her daughter?

"I'm no father."

Years of his life lost to vengeance and nothing but pain to show for it. He needed her to look at him, say *something*. But she just rocked and rambled on about Bobby Shafto.

His head lowered, the last of his strength leaving him. This would be the last thing he ever did for her. He needed to do everything in his power to do it right, even if that meant protecting the wain from a lunatic mother.

"I'll take Uma. But once I do, she's mine. I'll not let ye come collectin' her without gettin' help for yourself first. She deserves better than..." He lifted his arm, encompassing all the degradation and rotting life between them. "Better than this."

Even the mention of her daughter failed to provoke a reaction. Her entire focus burned into the bleeding enemy at her feet.

He spoke in hopes that if she ever got well, she might recall what he'd said, but he knew this would be the last time he'd ever see her. "I'll take her someplace safe, Innis. And when I get there, I'll send a postcard with only the address—adding three to every number so no one else can find us—me, you, and Gavin. Remember three by thinking of us. For the street name, I'll replace all the vowels with M for MacGregor. You must remember that, so you'll know what it is when it arrives. I'll send one every year until she's of age. Then the choice to find you will be hers."

She dinnae respond, and maybe that was for the best.

"Dinnae think te try and steal her away from whatever home we find. I want te help you, Innis, but ye have te come te me first. You asked this of me, and I'll do it as my last kindness te you. But from here on, the wain's my priority."

The unfinished goodbye lacked any sort of affection. Any physical contact wouldnae be welcomed. All this time since discovering she'd been alive, and he never once got to hug her.

The sentiment was lost anyway. He might never relearn how to touch another person without causing harm, so he kept his distance for both their sakes.

"I love ye, Innis. I'll never stop."

Turning, he hobbled to the door, shutting away the nightmare at his back, but knowing he'd never truly leave it behind.

Chapter Twenty-Nine

Saratoga Springs, New York—America
Present Day

Emery's belly turned and flipped like a tickling feather as Callan drove her down a street she'd never visited. They were near the hotel but off the beaten path. The charming Victorian homes mixed with Italian Renaissance architecture that dappled the historic town passed with increasing distance in between.

Saratoga Springs was once a bath town. Tourists no longer only came for the springs, but also for the quaint escape and equestrian hobbies. She loved their little town and thought she knew all its secrets, but as Callan turned the car, she realized some secrets hid in plain sight.

They approached a private road. Not a road. A driveway.

She frowned at the expansive stone wall. She'd pictured him living in a house, but this was clearly some sort of estate occupied by multiple renters. It had to be. It was huge.

The traditional, Tudor style home was revealed from the horizon like a hidden gem. The grand beauty had a sort of white elephant appeal, situated on the periphery of commercial real estate, only slightly removed from the bustling congestion a block away.

"This is where you live?"

Gabled dormers and lead framed windows attested to its genuine age. It must get drafty as hell in the winters. But Callan probably didn't mind the cold, being from a place that never got hotter than sixty degrees. The stone façade likely kept it cool in the summers as well.

He glanced at her, a strange, perhaps nervous, set to his eyes. "Aye."

"It's stunning. How many tenants are there?"

"Tenants?"

"It's apartments, right?" It had to be. It was far too large for one man, too costly for a bartender. Unless he'd inherited it.

"No apartments. It's my home. My house."

She gaped at him, her eyes drawn back to the sprawling front of the stone house. "You own this?"

His hands clenched the wheel, and he nodded slowly. "Aye."

How? "You bought it?"

He glanced at her, uncertainty flashing in his eyes. "Do ye not like it?"

"Callan, it's lovely. I just…" She was being rude. She wanted to understand how a man who worked as a bartender at a local hotel could afford something so grandiose. "What made you buy it?" Maybe he'd won the lottery.

"I liked the stone. Like the story of the three wee pigs. Stone's safe."

She frowned. That wasn't the sort of answer she expected. But she smiled at the simplicity of it.

He parked by the front door, beside a blue Toyota. The car was unfamiliar and not anything she recalled him driving.

"Does someone else live here with you?" It might not be an apartment, but it made sense for him to have a roommate in such a big place.

He shut off the car. "Aye."

He removed the key, closing his fist around the metal and sinking his hand to his lap. His gaze lowered and they just sat there.

"Callan?" Had he changed his mind? "Is something wrong?"

He swallowed, the dry sound of his throat clicking in the silence. "I've never brought someone te my home before."

Her mouth circled a silent "Oh." Now she was nervous. "If you want to go back to my place, we can."

He glanced at her then. "I want you te see where I live."

"O—okay." She believed him, but there was something he wasn't telling her. "You don't have to be nervous, Callan. I'm already in love with this place."

He took her hand and squeezed. His palms were warm. "I'm not legally in the States, Em'ry."

Now his hesitation made more sense. She laughed. "Do you think I'd report you?"

He studied her face, a soft smile turning his lips. "I cannae go back te Scotland. There's nothin' for me there. And I think it would kill me te leave this country. Te leave you."

Her heart skittered. Leaning across the cup holder, she pressed her lips to his cheek. "I think it would kill me if you left," she whispered, dropping back into her seat.

His fingers rushed to the place she'd kissed, and he blinked at her. Kissing was new, but it felt right. He'd somehow managed to appear as nervous as she was about it, and that had a way of leveling the playing field.

And despite his size and strength, he never frightened her. On the contrary, he made her feel safe and utterly protected. She trusted him completely.

"I want to know everything about you, Callan," she confessed softly, hoping her desire didn't frighten him. "I don't understand this connection I feel toward you, but … it's the nicest thing I've ever felt."

His lashes lowered, his eyes darkening like wet denim. "Dinnae look too hard, love. Ye might not like what ye find."

"I like everything I've found so far."

His shoulders lifted as he breathed. The stillness of what seemed forced composure no longer disarmed her as it once had. Callan was a thoughtful man, who moved with measured actions, seeming to always weigh the waves he might spread into the world. His patience was born of a care for others.

"There's...." His lips pressed tight. "You'll see when we get inside."

He exited the car and came around to her side just as the front door of the house opened, a woman with long, raven black hair and a slender body emerged from the shadows.

She looked at home. Barefoot and in cozy clothes. Emery knew immediately she lived there—with Callan.

Insecurity trembled up her spine as Callan led her up the front steps. "Em'ry, this is Elspeth. Elspeth, this is Em'ry."

The closer she fell into her orbit the more intimidating the woman's beauty became. "Callan's told me so much about you," Elspeth said.

Strange, because Emery hadn't known she'd existed until this very minute. She nodded shyly and followed the woman inside. Her accent put a timestamp on her relationship with Callan, dating back to his time in Scotland and jealousy slammed through her.

Callan's thumb rubbed softly against the back of her hand, soothing her nerves, but then he let go. A squeal pealed from the other room, reverberating in the acoustics of the open entryway, startling Emery.

She gasped as a young child, a little girl, with waves of ebony curls raced into his arms. Her little body catapulted off the ground, flung by trust, and he scooped her up in a way that made Emery yearn for someone to always catch her so unflinchingly, so reliably.

Whoever this child was, she obviously adored Callan.

"And this is Uma," he introduced, clutching her little body to his.

"I painted a picture of a ladybug!" The brash yet dainty Scottish lilt that belted out of her melted something inside of Emery.

Bright green eyes stared up at Callan—contrasting with his blue eyes. But there was no mistaking their shared lineage. The child's dark hair matched his and Elspeth's. And while his nose wore the markings of a few boyhood scuffles, the narrow shape of it matched hers.

Emery's focus skipped to the other woman's face, noting her thin bone structure and finding no resemblance aside from their dark hair.

Callan had a child. The realization settled over her with unexpected ease. And as he clutched the little girl to his hip, her eyes glittering like tinsel as she prattled on about her painting of a ladybug, Emery could see how deeply he adored her.

His gaze drifted to her, the proof of his affection for the little girl radiating from his smile. His lips firmed, but nothing could hide his adoration for the people in this room—people she had no clue existed.

"Hi there," she finally greeted. "I'm a friend of your daddy's."

Her elfin features creased, and Emery immediately regretted her assumption.

"Uma's my niece."

"Oh. I just assumed… You look alike."

The girl appeared around the age of five. Was Elspeth his sister? That would be a relief.

"This is Em'ry."

"Pleased te meet ye, Em'ry."

Elspeth stepped forward and lifted Uma out of Callan's arms. "We still have a few lessons te finish so we'll leave you two alone."

A thousand questions raced through her head as she watched them leave. The details of the house now an afterthought.

Dark tones, rich fabrics, and antique furnishings washed away as she stared at Callan. "Your niece?"

He flushed. "I'm her guardian."

"And … Elspeth?"

"Uma's au pair. And a trusted family friend."

The way he inserted the word trusted made her believe he didn't apply it to others easily. It made her crave his trust all the more.

"What happened to Uma's parents?" Perhaps he had an estranged brother or sister.

"Gone." The single word cleaved through the air, cutting off any further questions.

"I'm sorry. Your brother?"

"My sister. And my best friend."

A hundred questions craved answers, but she sensed this was a subject he didn't like to discuss. "Will you give me a tour?"

He nodded and took her hand. The weight of his fingers entwining with hers sent heat blooming in her chest.

He led her through an open room, so large the furniture seemed an afterthought to the architecture. Cascading shelves climbed the walls, covered in cloth spines and hardback classics.

"You have so many books."

"They came with the house."

How did one afford all this on a bartender's salary? The question echoed with every glimpse of luxury.

While some women might find this level of wealth alluring, Emery found it intimidating. She'd assumed they were the same, financially speaking, but now she questioned all the times he'd been to her house. What he must have thought of her second-hand lamps and trash picked end tables.

"Callan," she said quietly, trying to take in all this opulence. "You're rich."

He looked at her as though she told a lie. "Material possessions don't measure a man's worth. I've met men with twenty-times as much, but they were broke from a bankrupt soul. I dinnae have as much as ye assume."

Yet this place had to be worth over a million dollars. "What did you do before you were a bartender?"

His glance turned away. "I fought for money."

"Like boxing?"

"Aye. Sort of. A wee bit grittier."

"You must have been very good."

"I was undefeated. But in the end, I lost everything that mattered."

The humble sadness of his words tugged at her heart. She noticed a pattern. Every time Callan opened up and unveiled a secret about his private life, it came with a painful truth.

He seemed no stranger to adversity. His sister, Uma's mother, was gone—along with his best friend. It must have been a tragic accident. He spent the first half of his life fighting and lost everything important to him. His journey had definitely taken a toll on him, but it made him who he was today.

Under the vaulted ceilings and high wood frames that swallowed her, he towered like a gentle giant. His fragility shook her to the core, beautiful and precious, something to guard close to her heart.

Dust particles danced in rays of light seeping from the large windows. An enormous desk, not from this century or the last, sat in the center of the room facing the mammoth fireplace. Did he sit there?

Her fingers trailed over the corner, wanting to touch everything he put his hands on in a typical day. She wanted to feel him through the objects he held.

She inspected the books lining the lower shelves, but not all titles were written in English. "What language are these?"

"French, I believe. Some might be German."

"Do you speak French or German?"

He smirked. "I have a hard enough time gettin' people te understand my English."

She laughed. "I love the way you speak."

His eyes lit. "Ye do?"

She loved everything about him. Her gaze fell on familiar red leather, and she stepped closer. Nothing written on the soft spines.

"These are yours." His journals. At least two dozen. She dragged her fingers over the spines, deeply curious about what hid inside.

"Your fingers are teasin' over my most private thoughts, love."

She stilled and pulled back her hand. "Oh."

"Would you like somethin' to drink?"

Worried she might be intruding on more than his thoughts, she eagerly left the library and followed him to the kitchen. Ornate, wooden cabinetry covered the walls, but the appliances were state of the art.

"Em'ry?"

He caught her staring. More than staring. She'd never been inside such a house, and her face seemed set on ogle. "Sorry. This place is just … unexpected."

"Things, love. They're just things."

"But this is a part of you." And she didn't recognize these parts. A strange panic to know all of him climbed into her chest.

Callan's quiet mannerisms led them back to the library. Sitting beside him on the oxblood leather couch, she clutched her glass of iced tea in both hands, body perched on the edge of the cushion, knees drawn together.

"Does it make ye nervous bein' here with me, love?"

Her stare lifted from the overwhelming collection of books and turned to him. "I'm never nervous around you—not in a bad way."

"But in some way?"

Concerns churned, and she pushed out a shaky breath, nodding. The back of his index finger made a slow glide along the top of her hand, and she watched the gentle way he touched her, fascinated.

Shallow breaths tightened her lungs as heat swirled low in her belly the way it hadn't swirled in a long time. Flecks of emerald and sapphire danced in the icy blue seas of his eyes. And she was lost, drowning in an ocean of Callan.

"What has ye thinkin' so hard?"

Transfixed, she stared at him. She coveted his secrets, wanted to know every part of him. Why he sometimes looked as though sorrow had swallowed parts of him and he'd always be somewhat incomplete. How he looked like a rugged warrior with a first-hand account of hell but spoke like an eloquent poet and acted like a guardian angel.

"I want to know you, Callan. I want to know all of you, and then I want to learn the parts of you that you've yet to learn."

An invisible force field fell over his face, shielding his expression in an imperceptible veil, couture and well-worn. And while he barely moved, she saw in his stillness that he tried to hide from her.

She placed her glass aside and turned to face him on the leather sofa. His hands were cold when she took them in hers—chilled.

"I'm not asking you to tell me anything you don't want to share. I just want you to know the curiosity's there. More than curiosity." Her gaze dropped to her lap. "So much of what's inside of me feels broken. But when I'm with you, the jagged edges don't seem so sharp and the hurt sort of subsides. When we're apart, I long for you to come back, I count the hours, and then I count the minutes. And I feel you before I see you."

She swallowed against the sense of self-imposed exposure but pushed more truth out. "I've never felt that way about anyone before. You settle the riot inside of me, but at the same time, you start something even wilder." Her palm lowered, flattening over her belly. "I feel you here, with every breath. An ache I can't soothe."

Her eyes prickled against the sharp pinch of tears, but they weren't tears of sadness or fear. They were tears of truth, the brutal honesty she'd buried for so long now slipping out. And her body mourned the passing of the words, knowing the second she let them go she'd never be able to draw them back again.

"I'm in love with you, Callan. I've been secretly in love with you since…"

He severed their eye contact, and she dropped his hands when he gave the slightest pull. His shoulders rocked with audible, insubstantial breaths.

"Dinnae love me, Em'ry."

Her chest pained as if a knife delivered the command. The request stabbed into her most tender parts, gutting her courage and humiliating her.

"Oh," she breathed, perhaps because she could think of nothing else to say, or maybe the word fell out as the hurt pushed in. She'd massively misread the situation. Or had she? "I thought…"

Her gaze combed the vintage carpet, seeking an anchor that wasn't there. The kiss at the hotel was only a kiss, not a relationship. Just like when he touched her before, he reached for her only to pull away. Now, the gulf between them stretched like a vacant land of barren hopes.

She glanced out the lead-paned windows. Laden clouds gathered over a huddle of kelly green hills in the distance, bloated with dreary grays. A storm was coming. She hated driving in the rain.

"Maybe I should go." But she hadn't driven. He'd brought her here, and she was trapped. Trapped like a girl who walked into the wrong bathroom. Or was this worse? She couldn't recall a pain so sharp. His rejection of her greatest secret punctured the last of her confidence. "I have to go home."

She stood, and he caught her hand. "Em'ry wait."

Her frantic breathing cluttered the quiet library with ineloquent sounds that didn't belong. "It's okay, Callan. I get it. I…" She stared at his shoes, recalling the way it always came down to shoes. Her gaze tore away as she recalled another man's shoes walking away from her as if she were no more than trash. "I'm ... baggage."

He jerked her arm—harder than expected—and she dropped to the sofa cushion. Her eyes flew to his, panicked by his palpable frustration. "Ye. Are *not*. Baggage."

Her vision blurred. She didn't need his pity or coddling. She was a grown woman, and she'd put herself out there too soon.

Her frivolous attempt to form an intimacy with the man she loved and somehow outsmart the physical now seemed like the stupidest, half-hatched plan in the world. Of course, she wouldn't be enough for a man like Callan MacGregor.

"I think you should take me home now."

His eyes searched hers. Soft winds murmured against the glass. A stronger gust pushed the antique windows against the frames like a sail filling with wind. Seeking sanctuary, she turned her gaze to the darkening sky, resting heavily on the horizon. That looked like a good place to hide.

"I dinnae want ye to love me because I ken the moment ye do I'll not be able to save ye from myself anymore," he whispered, his words so low they competed with the sighing wind.

Her eyes slowly returned to him. He stared at her in stark, masculine simplicity.

"What?"

Deep regret stole over his eyes and his mouth pressed into a tight line of worry. The scent of rain tickled her nose. Then came the heavy downpour against the glass.

She actively tried to listen harder, to not miss whatever he might say, but his lashes dropped, and his brow pinched. So much pain and she didn't understand why.

"Callan, please…" She needed to understand what he meant. "Why would you have to save me from yourself?" Didn't he know he was her hero?

His gaze turned away, and his jaw ticked, his mouth opening but no words escaping. He glanced everywhere but at her face, his full, black lashes curtaining the windows to his soul.

Maybe this is how men cried, she thought. Perhaps their pain was too big for tears, too obstinate and heavy. It felt like he was crying, but he fought hard not to shed a tear. And Callan, her warrior poet, won the battle.

"Shh," she whispered, pulling his heaving shoulders into her arms the way he often collected her. "It's okay. Whatever it is, it's okay." She couldn't bear to see him suffer—not even an intangible thought.

His hands wrapped around her lower back, holding her with surprising tightness as he burrowed his face in her hair. His panted breaths beat at her neck, warm and intense. His emotions terrified her because she wasn't sure she could match the level of friendship he'd shown her.

"God, Em'ry…" he breathed, the words slipping out in a tortured rasp. "Forgive me."

Her hand petted over his hair, stroking. Her brow hardened as she stared at the sheet of opaque rain now hiding them away from the outside world.

"There's nothing to forgive."

His arms tightened. "Aye, there is. I want ye with a fierceness I've no right to feel. I've not had an easy life, but denyin' myself the right to talk to ye, touch ye, kiss your sweet lips… It's an ache I have no comparison for."

Wretched inadequacy bloomed in her chest. If she wasn't broken, he wouldn't have to deny himself. "I'm sorry."

"It's not your fault, love."

"Of course it is. If I wasn't so damaged, we'd be able to have a normal relationship—"

"You are *not* the damaged one." He drew back, holding her by the ribs and looking at her with glassy eyes. "I've done terrible things, things that should never touch you. And I wear my sins like a second skin of scars. I'm tarnished by the wicked things I've done. There's no more penance left for me in this world, and I've been hurting for so long, I dinnae remember *how* to love." His gaze shifted and when he looked at her again, she felt the hooks of his soul latching onto hers, thrown in an almost desperate attempt to trap her, yet his words were meant to push her away. "You, Em'ry, deserve a flawless love, not a stingy one."

"Callan." She breathed in and held it as if she might never draw a full breath again. "Are you in love with me?"

More regret filled his eyes, pouring from him in waves. "I love ye like Hemingway loves the sea, with enough comprehension to fear it, respect it, and admit that it's bigger than me by a million miles and too deep to ever know all its secrets. Every dawn I wake, grabbed by the desire to hold it to me. But these hands cannae hold love any more than they can hold the sea."

Her heart pounded as if hit by a battering ram. She grasped those beautiful, scarred hands and pressed her lips to his broad knuckles. "You can hold me, Callan."

"I dinnae want to break you."

Her tears dampened her fingers as she kissed the heel of his palm and pressed his hand to her cheek. "You won't. I trust you."

"Em'ry, there're a lot of parts of me you cannae trust. I need it that way. And ye have te believe I know what's best here."

She trusted him. But he needed to trust her on this. Her hand held his to her face. "I don't want you to fear your feelings for me. And when you're grabbed by the desire to hold me, I want you to take it. I know I don't always have the right reactions, but I trust you, Callan. You're the only person who makes me feel safe and normal. You're the only person strong enough *to* hold me, and careful enough *not* to break me."

His fingers slipped into her hair, his grip tightening. "I'm not as gentle as ye assume."

She nodded her understanding. "I know. I feel you holding back. Maybe it's time you stop."

He jerked his hand away, a frown chiseling heavy divots between his eyes. "All I've ever done is fight. It's the only thing I'm good at. And when it comes to love, all I've ever done is lost."

"You won't lose me, Callan."

He shook his head, refusing to look at her.

She couldn't bear his doubt. She climbed onto his lap, wreathed her arms around his strong shoulders and brushed her lips over his hard jaw. "You're not going to lose me. And you won't break me. You think your past is all you are, but I see you, Callan MacGregor. You're kind." She kissed his ear. "You're gentle." His other ear. "You're patient." His temple. "And you're strong. Stop fighting." Her eyes searched his. "If you love me, I'll love you back."

His hand caught the back of her neck and his mouth crushed to hers. Weight pressed over her as he turned and dropped her back to the couch. She kissed him hard, shoving down the nip of fear and proving to him that she could handle this, that she could handle him.

His tongue stole into her mouth, demanding and seeking. The press of his muscled form sank her deeper into the sofa until it was all she could feel. Blanketing. Sheltering. Safe.

Her fingers pulled through his hair as her body cushioned his. The defined jab of his erection digging into her belly made her still. He tore his mouth from hers and tucked his face over her shoulder, hiding in her hair. His breath panted in the silence.

"I'm sorry." He shifted, his weight pulling away from her, and she caught the back of his neck.

"Wait." They needed to get through this, or they'd continue to run into the same wall. "Just … stay."

His body trembled over her, the rigid weight of him shaking with restraint. Her hand stroked down his spine, over the warm cotton of his shirt.

"It's okay, Callan." If only he knew the way her body responded to him, but a woman's tells were always a bit more disguised.

The spasm of her thoughts threatened to drag her into a dark place, but she kept her head rooted in the now. She needed this, needed the contact and the help to break through this wall.

Her lips pressed tight as she considered how long it might take to be normal again, the possibility that it might never happen. She couldn't bear the thought.

Swallowing tightly, her throat parched, she said, "Sink your weight into me."

His muscles tensed. "Em'ry—"

"Please. I trust you."

He hesitated, but little by little she felt his tension melt away, and soon his bulk pressed down. Her heart raced, and her breathing pulled in erratic jerks. His arms still held some of his weight, but his lower body rested over her, molded to every curve, the inescapable proof of his desire jamming into her hip.

The warm caress of his lips to her ear softened the punch of nerves. "I'm here," he whispered. "I'm with you."

His voice settled her mind, and she shut her eyes. Callan. This was Callan. Her next swallow came a little easier, though neither of them seemed to handle intimacy the right way.

Her lungs deepened, more air getting where it needed to go. "Now what?" she whispered.

"I dinnae ken," he rasped, his mouth close to her ear and his face hidden by her hair. The warm tickle of his breath sent a shiver through her.

"Maybe you should kiss me again."

He didn't move. "I'm afraid if I kiss ye, I willnae be able te stop."

"Maybe that's okay." She bit her lip. "I like when you kiss me."

He eased up, rising over her. "Dinnae panic."

She froze, her lashes fluttering shut as he closed the distance. The heat of his mouth captured hers. Warm, sensual lips caressed hers like feathering clouds. Slow licks delved, exploring with exquisite leisure.

Her breast grew heavy, her chest pressing into his in search of an anchor. The moment she moved under him, gliding and arching, his hips rocked against her.

"Em'ry…" Her name was a plea, a secret told, a gift from his lips to hers.

Her knees lifted, bracketing his hips and rising against him. They found a rhythm, a shared ebb and flow. Heat pooled and melted her insides. The kiss deepened. His hands on her body, on her clothes, tightened.

They lost their rhythm. The kiss grew frantic, needy. Greedy.

Panic nipped as she sensed his control slipping, but she forced herself to remain present. This was Callan. They could only move forward as a couple if she proved she could handle this, not because he required it, but because they both wanted it.

His fist closed over her shirt just at the shoulder, pulling her collar tight. His hips jerked, and she gasped. He'd found a niche of heat in the cradle of her hips, and he thrust like he could somehow bury himself beneath her clothes.

Her heart ripped out of rhythm as he thrust again, groaning into her mouth, taking pleasure, abusing the delicate threads of her shirt.

She turned her face away, breaking the kiss, and his lips closed over her frantic pulse. "Callan?"

His other hand caressed the underside of her jaw, angling her face away so he could press open-mouthed kisses down the entire length of her throat.

The pop of threads preceded his groan as he dropped his mouth to the shallow dip of her shoulder, his hot tongue tracing the wing of her collarbone as he stretched the seams of her shirt.

His hips stabbed, no longer rocking or gliding, but seeking. Her brave exploration suddenly became an endpoint for his pleasure, her panic a silenced backdrop she'd obscured with her insistent lies that she could handle this.

He'd warned her, and she didn't listen. Her chest tightened, her body cushioning his every thrust, and her mind spiraling.

"I love ye, so much," he rasped fiercely, shaking, trembling, groaning no matter how he tried to mask the desperations taking over him. "I'm sorry."

His weight sank into her again, this time without an ounce of restraint. He crushed her to the sofa. *Trapped.*

Her erratic heart thundered in her ears as she tried to make sense of what just happened. She'd survived it. And while her fear had spiked, his muttered confession removed any regrets.

But her memory told her this was not the way a man Callan's age touched a woman. His desperate need and frantic grip spoke of innocence and inexperience. His apology and pained finish told of torment.

Confused, she brushed a hand down his back, aiming to comfort him from whatever this was. "It's okay," she whispered.

His breath sucked in, and a tortured sob trembled out with lacerating force. His body shook over hers, his arms sliding beneath her back to hold her tight. The gasping sound of his weeping sawed into the silence.

"It's okay," she repeated, her own fear and confusion now second to his.

"I'm sorry," he rasped and choked, hugging her to him with heartbreaking affection.

414

"You don't have to be sorry. You didn't do anything wrong."

A ravaged sob escaped, partially stifled, but not enough to hide whatever pain he suffered. "I love you," he whispered, his damp lashes flicking against her skin. "I love you." The words repeated on a loop as he pulled her closer, as if seeking a sort of intimacy beyond a sexual connection.

She stroked his back, whispering promises that everything was fine and she loved him too. But deep down she knew whatever hid inside of him was not fine. Yet it belonged to him, would always be in him, and therefore, it was also part of her.

Chapter Thirty

Saratoga Springs, New York—America
Present Day

They'd fallen asleep, and when she awoke, Callan's warm body stretched beside hers in a tangle of limbs. The rain had stopped, and darkness flooded the library. She needed to pee and tried to remember where the bathroom had been on their earlier tour.

His arm tightened around her when she tried to slide out from under his weight. He tugged her back to him and nestled his face deeper into her shoulder. "No."

Her lips twitched at his defiant protest. "I have to use the bathroom."

He seemed to debate her request and then sighed, loosening his hold. "Promise you'll come back."

She sat up and glanced at him, startled by the honest worry she found in his eyes. "I promise."

417

She found the bathroom down the hall and stared at her reflection as she washed her hands. Her tousled hair lifted in teased waves, the telltale sign of a man's hands having been there.

She smiled. Callan's hands.

Drying her fingers on the soft towel, she paused. A little pink stool was tucked under the pedestal sink.

She opened the door, confused by the quiet house. Children were typically noisy. Where was everyone?

She glanced down the hall to the library and back the other way to where the kitchen and other rooms were. The soft golden glow of lights beckoned where they spilled into the hall. As she approached, the gentle clatter of cookware met her ears, followed by the thick, roll of rhotic R's pitched in a little sing-song voice.

"Dae ye think Uncle Callan's friend will like this?"

"Oh, Aye. How can she not? You've made it with such attention te detail and tender lovin' care."

Emery shifted silent feet closer, staying out of view but catching sight of Uma sitting on the counter using a spatula to spread the batter Elspeth poured into a pan. The scent of something savory teased her nose.

The hair rose on the back of her neck, and she turned. Her breath sucked in as her gaze collided with Callan's. He smiled and slowly approached.

"Have I caught ye spyin'?"

She leaned into him, her head resting on his chest as her eyes continued to watch them put the cake in the oven. "You have a little girl."

His smile curved against her temple. "Aye. Does that complicate matters?"

She shook her head. "Not at all."

For the first time, her mind touched on the things the doctors had warned her about, uncertainties she hadn't been prepared to hear. She watched Uma lick the spatula and laugh with such childish abandon at something Elspeth said.

"You're very lucky," she whispered.

He kissed her temple and tightened his arms around her. "They'll be a while longer. I want te show ye something."

When they returned to the library, she noted that his shoes were gone and he'd changed his jeans. There was something enchanting about Callan walking around in white, cotton socks—surreal.

He led her to the sofa again, and when she sat, he opened his hand in a staying motion as if she might run away. He moved to the desk and collected a leather-bound journal.

"You said you wanted to know me."

She sat up and nodded. "I do."

"I dinnae want you te ken the Callan I was in Scotland. I want te be better for you."

"Okay." But she would always wonder who that Callan was and what brought him here. "I just want to know you—whoever you are right now."

His lashes lowered. His fingers clutched the leather cover of the book in his hands, his thumb running an affectionate stroke along the spine. Sublime anticipation sweetened the air as he opened the journal.

She waited silently as he turned several pages. His lips pressed and he cleared his throat, his voice working through a web of gravel as he softly read.

"One day, I hope to be the rain, sliding down her skin, washing away whatever came before. Should I be the salt on her cheeks, the cause of just one tear, I'd fall like a wave into my grave on the edge of my own spear. But to be the rain dancing over her skin, too wee for any memory, inconspicuous to my Emery, I'd give all I have ever been."

Startled by his words so delicately wrapped around her name, she was struck too dumb to even formulate a reply.

His eyes met hers, and a deep flush washed across his cheeks, his gaze dropping back to the pages. His fingers moved backward, working closer to the start of the book. He drew in a deep breath.

"I cannot figure out why I'm so drawn to her. Perhaps it's her beauty, the way I'm envious of the air she breathes and the clothes that have permission to touch her skin. But it's deeper than wanting, heavier than simple petulant lust. And no matter how wretched I ken I am, I long for her to see me. Yet, it's for her, that I hide."

"When did you write that?"

His brows pulled together, and he swallowed. "Just after we met—a little over three years ago."

Her jaw unhinged and she gaped at him. All this time? She felt ripped off, deprived of something radiant. "Why didn't you ever say anything?"

"I did. I said it every day since the minute I met you." He shut the book. "In here."

Her head shook. She would have known if he felt this way—*should* have known. The collision of so many missed opportunities made her motion sick. "Callan, I've..." They could have been happy. They could have avoided so much. "I've had a crush on you since the day you started working at the hotel. I can't believe neither of us had the guts to say anything. What's wrong with us?"

"Sometimes, we know when to back away, love. Even if we dinnae always trust the scream."

She scowled. "I don't know what you mean by that."

He tossed the journal on the desk and closed his fists, pressing them into the surface until they popped. The corded muscles of his back stretched the worn cotton of his shirt as he turned away from her.

"You're my sacrosanct fetish, my obsession too valuable to touch. From the first time I saw ye, I've not been able to look away. I dinnae ken how to love you, but I know I feel somethin' deeper for you than I've ever felt for anyone. And I know, earlier, on the couch, you felt..." He cleared his throat. "Well, ye see I dinnae ken how to always be delicate. And I fear, now more than ever, ye need a man with a delicate touch."

She rose from the couch, crossing the carpet with silent steps. He flinched when she pressed her hand to his back.

"I don't want lies between us, Callan. You might not always be gentle, but there's truth in the way you touch me." Something worried her, warned her that truth came from hurt and hurt might be all he knew. "Maybe we need to stop being so gentle with each other. Maybe that's what trust is."

He turned and cupped her face, a war raging in the deep blue depths of his eyes. "I'd never forgive myself if I crossed a line with ye."

"You won't."

"Ye put too much trust in me, love. Ye have te stop."

She rose on her tippy toes and brushed her lips to his. "I don't want to go through the rest of my life afraid of someone hurting me. I want to remember how to trust again. I trust you, Callan. Don't talk me out of it."

His eyes closed and his brow pressed to hers. "The lengths I would go for ye…" His warm breath puffed across her cheek as his arms closed around her. "I want ye to be sure this is what ye want, Em'ry. Because once I have ye, I dinnae ken if I'll ever be able to let ye go."

She rested her head on his chest, pressing her ear over the steady beat of his heart. "I don't want you to let go."

She didn't know where the courage came from or if she was being foolish and biting off more than she could chew, but she wanted him to hold her so tight that her mind stopped fighting. She needed his strength until she found hers.

And despite his warnings, he'd only convinced her all the more of his good heart. His words, his poetic scribblings, other men didn't see her the way he did. Why should they hide from such intense feelings?

From the beginning, when he'd appeared at her place of work, she'd noticed him, noticed some indistinguishable difference in the way his mind processed the world. She'd been trapped in his orbit ever since. It was time they stopped hiding from the truth and confronted it.

Her lips pressed to his chest. "I don't want you to hold back with me anymore. I love you. It's a relief to say it out loud. I'm exhausted from holding it in."

A sad smile crested his lips as the fingers of his hand softly teased down her cheek. "Aye, here ye are, standin' in my house, tellin' me ye love me. I dinnae take those words lightly, Em'ry."

No one said love was light. Its heavy presence in her life had weighed on her since the moment her feelings coalesced. "Me neither."

He tipped up her chin, forcing her to meet his gaze. "I've not a lot in my life. The few things I've cared about most were the first to go. I'll never assume to own ye, but I cannae stop myself from being a possessive man, not after every experience has taught me the permanence of loss. If this is truly what ye want, I need to know you understand what you're gettin'."

Her heart already belonged to him. She would give him her soul if he asked. All of it.

So when his possessive hold closed around her like a fist, a hand holding onto her with an unbreakable grip, she welcomed it. Savored every dependable inch of his strength that touched her.

She smiled up at him, then pressing a kiss to the dark stubble of his jaw. "You keep trying to dissuade me, but all you're doing in making me want you more."

"I'm serious, Em'ry—"

"So am I, Callan. You can't scare me away—not from you."

He moved out of her reach, pacing to the other side of the room, his steps agitated. His fingers forked through his dark hair. "I've givin' ye more honesty than I've ever given anyone, but ye refuse to listen. There are ruthless, cold parts to me, Em'ry. Places ye cannae touch, places where I'm dead inside."

"Callan, you're not—"

"Listen to me," he snapped. His head bowed, and his voice lowered. "I've hurt people."

"What people?"

"Bad people, but people all the same."

Bad was a rather relative term. She thought of the little girl in the other room, the woman who took care of her. Neither of them seemed to fear him. "Give me an example."

His shoulders bunched and shifted. He wasn't going to answer.

"Children?" she asked.

His eyes flashed. *"Never."*

"Women?"

"No."

"Animals?"

His head shook.

So only men. "Did these men hurt other people?"

He nodded. "They... They would have continued to hurt others."

A chill raced over her body. *Would have.* As in past tense. "Are they still alive?" she asked, her words whispered, carrying enough significance to cross the distance.

His naked gaze drilled into hers, unshielded honesty staring back, and she had her answer before he spoke the words. "Not the truly evil ones."

"Uncle Callan?"

Emery pivoted, startled by the appearance of his niece as much as his words. Uma wore a hand-sewn silk gown over her regular clothes and a pair of purple fairy wings. The picture of innocence, combined with the unblinking challenge in Callan's eyes painted an absolute contradiction her mind couldn't decipher. She broke eye contact, and Callan addressed the child.

"What did ye need, my wee angel?"

"Dinner is ready. Elspeth tol' me te come find ye."

He ran a loving hand over her tangled waves, the motion so achingly paternal and protective Emery had to look away. "We'll be right there. Go wash up."

Uma pranced away as if her wings might actually fly if she got the lift-off right. He turned back to her, regret pulling at the corner of his eyes.

"I imagine you want to go home now," he rasped. "She'll be disappointed—"

"Don't blame it on her."

His lips pressed into a thin line. "I'll be disappointed. But I'll understand."

She didn't know what she wanted to do. But that little girl dressed as a princess fairy made her a cake, and she intended to taste it and fuss over how delicious it was regardless of the flavor. Everything else could wait.

Lifting her chin, she walked to the door. "I'll go wash my hands for dinner."

Chapter Thirty-One

Saratoga Springs, New York—America
Present Day

Callan kept to himself through the meal, watching Emery converse with Uma in a way that tugged at his heart. She had a natural instinct for putting anyone at ease, and Uma instantly took to her.

He'd made a mess of things. First, losing control with her on the couch, then confessing the depth of his feelings only to push her away. He was drunk on emotion, feeling things he'd never felt and torn by the throbbing warning that love only brought pain.

But he loved her. And the moment she confessed loving him too, he was doomed. His reanimated heart became a rushing stream, breaking through the waste that plugged him like a dam.

Deep, gutting truths spewed from him. And as he'd rutted into her, seeking any sort of relief from the painful truth bursting out of him, he understood the intrepid danger of unguarded love. It enslaved

427

him. Humiliated him. And it would eventually destroy him, if not her.

But as he continued to sabotage his hard-earned privacy, she knocked down his walls and touched places in his soul that were starved for affection, desperate for love. Then he'd done the unthinkable and told her the sort of monster he was.

He saw the moment she understood how deep his depravity reached, caught the slight recoil of her spine, and the catch of her breath. Exactly why he'd told her the truth, so she'd stay away. But here she was eating cake and laughing with his niece.

"Callan, why have you never taken Uma te this carousel Em'ry raves about?" Elspeth asked, drawing him back into the conversation.

He blinked. "I dinnae ken of a carousel."

"Of course you do. It's in Congress Park. We have brochures for it all around the hotel."

Did she not hear his confession before dinner? "I never noticed."

Elspeth rose from the table and collected their dessert plates. "Well, we should visit it. Uma loves anything to do with horses."

"Not the races, Elsie."

Elspeth smiled. "No, not the races."

Emery frowned. "How come?"

"Uncle Callan says it's cruel te use a beautiful animal for its strength and never let it run free."

Emery's gaze drifted to his. "I suppose it is." Her focus returned to Uma and she smiled. "You're a very strong-willed little girl. I hope that never changes."

"That's 'cause MacGregors are made of strength and will and a fuck-ton of morals that get in their ever-lovin' way." She smiled cheekily up at him. "Is tha' not what ye say, Uncle Callan?"

Seeing Emery's shock, he narrowed his eyes at Uma but had to give credit where credit was due. "Aye. Though wee angels should watch their mouths in front of company." He messed up her hair. "Go help Elsie dry the dishes."

She slid off the chair and pranced to the stool in front of the sink where Elspeth stood scrubbing the plates. He looked at Emery, catching the laughter in her eyes. She wasnae supposed to find him amusing.

"Shall I drive ye home, now?"

Her amusement visibly died. "Sure."

He stood, carrying the last of the dishes to the sink and pressing a kiss to Uma's head. "I'll see you in the morning, angel."

She twisted and threw her wee arms around him. He shut his eyes as she squeezed tight, lifting her feet off the stool and hanging from him like a clinging monkey wearing fairy wings.

"Love you, Uncle Callan."

"I love ye, too." He put her back on the stool and Emery said goodnight, thanking them for a lovely dinner and seeming all too comfortable in his home. He liked it but wanted to hate it.

When they got to her house, he hesitated, unsure if he should walk her to the door, or give her space to digest everything he'd said before dinner. He typically liked to give the house a sweep whenever he dropped her off, but that usually led to him staying longer than intended.

"I think I'll say goodnight then," he said, gripping the steering wheel. Leaving would be safer.

"I've thought about what you said."

He frowned. "You've hardly had time to think it over—"

"Whatever you did, it doesn't make you evil in my eyes, Callan. It makes you safe."

"You're believin' what ye want to hear rather than the truth."

"Why are you pushing me away?"

His shoulders slowly heaved as he reined in his fraying patience. How much longer would he have to fight himself from taking everything he wanted, everything she continued to offer him?

"Because touchin' you makes me feel like a thief."

"You can't steal what's freely given."

He shut his eyes. The jigsaw edges of his past formed a crude picture of love, one where every kindness was stolen and any weakness crushed.

Their da loved their mother so much he beat his feelings into her. Innis loved Rhys but hid it from everyone, never giving away how deeply she needed him until he was gone. Rory loved beautiful things. He loved them so much he eventually destroyed them. And Callan loved Uma so much, she hardly ever left the property—not even to visit a carousel that she'd undoubtedly adore.

"I don't want to leave things like this, Callan."

He glanced at her, trying to find the answers, but a storm raged in his heart, and he couldnae see two steps in front of him. "I dinnae ken what I want."

The hurt that flashed in her eyes broke him. She reached for the door handle, and he caught her arm.

"That was a shite thing for me to say."

She wouldnae look at him. He loosened his hold on her, dragging his thumb over her sleeve.

"Do you want me or not, Callan?"

It wouldnae matter either way. She wasnae ready. "They say if you love something, you let it go."

She glared over her shoulder, a sheen of tears trembling in her eyes. "And if it comes back, it's yours. Forever." Her lashes flicked, and a tear tumbled down her cheek. "But they never say what happens to the love not let in."

"Do ye know?"

Her head shook. "I suppose it suffers because true love never dies." She glanced away then back to him. "I fell in love with you the day you fixed my buttons. Everything before then was only a crush. But when you told me to be careful and fixed my coat... I felt cherished. I spent years wanting you, wishing I had the courage to say all the things I felt. And then when you found me in that hall—"

Her voice seized, and more tears fell. His chest tightened to the point of physical pain. "You dinnae have to—"

"When you found me in that hall," she forced the words out, her voice ravaged but strong. "I truly fell in love with you. I thought you were gone. I thought, let me find a phone or Marco, but deep down, as I crawled to that door, I only wanted you. And then you were there." She sucked in a shaken breath. "And you saved me."

He pulled her into his arms, unable to bear her tears. "Please, dinnae cry, love."

She came to him, climbing onto him and clinging like a lost child suddenly found. "So you see." She sniffled. "You can push me away and tell me not to love you, but I already do. And it's a true love that'll never die, no matter how many times you try to kill it. No matter what you did before I knew you. No matter what sort of man you think you are. So please stop pushing me away, because it hurts every time and I don't know how to stop coming back to you."

He caught her face in his hands and pulled her to him, his lips trembling against hers. "I'm sorry. I'm so sorry."

She kissed him, tugging at his collar and crawling inside of him with every staggered breath. "No more pulling away, Callan. I need to know you'll be there."

"I'm not goin' anywhere," he rasped, knowing it for a fact. Even if she broke things off with him, he'd never be able to stay away. "I'm here."

Her mouth opened against his, tasting of tears. "I love you."

"I love you, too. So much."

They eventually made it inside, her shy glances drifting back to him as if to make sure he dinnae run. He tried to warn her off, tried to protect her, but like most women, she had a will of her own and dinnae take kindly to others tryin' to bend it.

They shared a cup of chamomile tea, and when her eyes grew heavy, he walked her upstairs to her room. The cat purred with enthusiasm as she reclined in bed. He drew the covers to her shoulders like he'd done a dozen times before, and tucked the plush dog by her cheek.

She blinked up at him, all too trusting and innocent. "You don't have to leave. You could stay. The sofa bed…" She flushed a soft pink.

He brushed a knuckle down her cheek. "How about I surprise ye with breakfast in the mornin'?"

She smiled. "If I'm expecting it, it's not a surprise."

Then he'd surprise her with flowers. "Get some sleep, love. Be safe." He dropped his hand and forced himself to step away.

"Are you coming for breakfast?"

He glanced over his shoulder, one hand on the door. "It's a surprise." But he knew she knew he'd be there. Trusted it. And he sort of liked that she believed in him that way.

A short drive from Emery's house, just outside of town and far enough removed from the tourists and natives, hid a rural stretch of land mostly consisting of boggy forests and fields cultivated for agriculture. The country roads and sporadic rental homes—many on wheels—seemed at complete odds with the picturesque town.

He'd moved to Saratoga Springs for its low crime rate and quaint charm, wanting a safe place for Uma to grow. But even seemingly safe places had bad people. More dangerous than if they occupied the most hazardous cities. Because in safe places people often let their guards down and that was when evil men did their worst.

He turned down a forgotten road, too far for college students to live, yet close enough for a person to visit the campus parties at night and still return home before anyone suspected where they'd been.

Killing his headlights, he rolled to a stop on the empty dirt road and watched the blue glow of a television set flicker in the windows of the doublewide. The rental met all the requirements imposed by the authorities—more than three hundred feet away from Emery's grocery store, post office, home, and work, yet within the jurisdiction of the law—but still somehow too close for comfort.

The state of New York was large enough that the bastard dinnae need to stay right on top of them, but it did make Callan's job a little easier.

He could have gone to the border of Canada or the city. But he decided to stay here. Why? Why not disappear as much as he could until his time to take the stand? Why risk screwing up again and damaging the well-cultivated image his family fed the media? Why risk running into a crazed Scot on a dark country road where no one would hear a scream for miles?

Callan understood hunting. He recognized the skills needed, the patience, the grace, the ability to spot vulnerable prey.

Wesley Blaine thought he was a lion, king of his domain and admired by all in his pride. But sometimes even a lion grew negligent, peacocking about and taking without thinking of others, drunk on its own power and blind to its surroundings. It assumed it was unbeatable, cozy in its natural habitat, picking off its usual prey until the true master of the food chain arrived. The one foreign animal that dinnae belong, but came armed to the teeth and got the final word every time.

The lion was nothing compared to man. And for all his glory, in the end, man—the truest hunter of all—would use the lion for a rug and wipe the shite off his boots onto its back. Aye, the lion was going to die.

HURT

Chapter Thirty-Two

Saratoga Springs, New York—America
Present day

Emery heard the phone ringing from the shower and let it go to voicemail. After drying off, and twisting a towel around her head, she slid into her robe and listened to the message from her advocate.

Now that Wesley Blaine had been indicted things were starting to move. She wished she had a different name for him. His name made him sound like some sort of superhero. And Wesley was too … human. Too boy next door. Too charming. Too *Princess Bride*. Too … ruined.

He'd been accused of rape in the first degree, aggravated assault, and predatory sexual assault. All of which he'd done and pled not guilty to.

Her advocate said it was typical in cases like this for the accused to claim innocence. And while the news had her name, they liked to say Wesley's much more. It was twisted of her to envy his ill-gotten fame, especially when she wished they only knew her as a Jane Doe.

437

The media referred to the case as *Blaine versus The People*. She was *The People*, yet she'd been utterly alone in that bathroom. Just a person. Just a victim. Just a girl. A girl alone with a monster.

The relief of not having to attend the trial waged a tug of war in her chest. She wanted to see him go down, needed to see that look in his eye when the freedom he so arrogantly flaunted got stolen away. But what if that didn't happen? What if all he ever got was a slap on the wrist while she was sentenced to a lifetime of living with these emotional scars?

She debated if putting a face to the victim might help her case. She'd turned down the offers from journalists so far, but maybe being more than a name would show the world that she was just like them. And Wesley Blaine was nothing but a beautiful monster.

The bad guy already knew who she was. Who was she hiding from? What did she care if the rest of the world knew this happened to *her*?

Turned out, she cared a lot.

In Harold's voicemail, he asked her to write a letter, addressing the emotional damage not conveyed in the police or medical reports. He'd made the request several times before, and too many unfinished drafts hid in her dresser drawer.

Seeing her truth jotted down on paper had a way of minimizing the pain she still needed to feel. She didn't enjoy suffering or being tied up in knots, but she needed the pressure, needed to feel the cut sliding into her skin. She needed the hurt.

She feared if she forgot the pain, all the craziness left in the wake of Wesley Blaine would seem irrational and misplaced. The pain focused her blame. But trying to fit her feelings into words diluted something. It mitigated the horror of what actually took place, reduced it down to an abbreviated letter. It was so much more than a letter. It was her story, her pain, her endless hurt.

Besides, she wasn't a good writer, and her inability to evoke emotion or think up powerful verbs shouldn't sway the verdict one way or another. But it would.

Like a broken metronome, every day another statement from some influential person in Wesley Blaine's life hit the news, singing his praises, and the scales tipped more in his favor.

Folding her hands around her cell, she lowered it to her lap. It felt like a lifetime had passed. She still thought about it every hour of every day—some hours tortured her with thoughts every minute. But she was getting better.

She wasn't having as many breakdowns or panic attacks. She and Callan were spending a lot of time together, kissing and facing their feelings. Things were on an upswing for her, but moments like this, moments when her phone rang with messages essentially telling her victimization wasn't enough to earn justice, that she needed to publicly crucify herself, again and again, to make the world see she could bleed, to prove rape is rape is rape... Yes, these were the moments that really knocked her down.

Why should it matter how he grabbed her or which bones he broke? He put his hands on her when she said *no*. He forced himself into her hard enough to make her scream and bleed from the searing pain. He hit her. He hurt her. He *raped* her.

And no matter how civilized the world pretended to be, she somehow felt as much on trial as him.

What if they interviewed people from her high school and found out she gave that guy a blowjob after the senior bonfire that one time? Would that somehow detract from the horrible things Wesley did? Would it make her more deserving of his crime? Soften his penalty?

Those were the details the media sharks wanted. They had their picture of perfect Wesley Blaine in their heads. Now they needed a picture perfect victim.

Or a woman deserving of the crime.

They wanted a story more than the truth. And the deeper they dug, the more she realized how self-serving the media's loyalty was. A vilified victim would sell more headlines in the end. Her only other option would be to publicly bleed, show she'd been wounded just enough so as not to get accused of lies.

The sound of a car on the street pulled her out of her thoughts, but not enough. She couldn't get herself moving, the pressure to produce some sort of written voucher for her self-worth weighing her down.

"Someone order breakfast?"

She smiled. "I'm upstairs."

"Are ye comin' down?"

She stared at her phone and then at the drawer that hid all her failed attempts. The door creaked.

"Em'ry?" Callan stepped into the room and abruptly turned around. "I shouldae knocked. Are ye all right, love?"

He was so modest it made her laugh. She was in a robe. And he was holding a bouquet of ruby and pink roses.

"Callan, turn around. I'm not naked."

He slowly pivoted, his cheeks wearing a splotch of red to match the roses. His gaze clung to the floor.

"Are they for me?" She stood and touched the petals to her nose, breathing their soft scent in. "They're beautiful."

"I dinnae ken which colors ye liked, but I thought these were the prettiest."

"I love them." She lifted on her toes, pressing a kiss to his jaw. "Thank you."

He finally glanced down at her. He shifted the towel on her head, and it unraveled, falling to the floor. Damp, tangled snarls of hair fell just past her shoulders.

"Sorry."

"It's okay." Since Callan became more of a fixture in her life, her confidence had grown, and her stress seemed lighter. Her hair no longer fell out in clumps.

"I should let ye get dressed." He didn't move.

"Is that what *ye* want, for me to get dressed?"

His gaze jumped to hers, questioning her teasing tone but not reciprocating. "That's what's wise, and we both know it, Em'ry."

Her humor faded. Her confused desires no longer recognizable, but still very much alive. As were his. "But it's not what you want."

"Em'ry—"

Taking the decision away from both of them, she unraveled the belt of her robe with one tug, and the material fell open. His stare locked with hers and his nostrils flared.

"What do ye think you're doin'?"

God only knew. Her body tingled with anticipation—nervous, but not afraid. She shook with temerity but remained miles away from panic.

She lifted a shoulder. "I ... thought you might want to look at me."

The weight of his gaze sometimes felt like heaven. She wanted to feel it on her naked skin.

One day I hope to be the rain, sliding down her skin, washing away whatever came before...

None of this was premeditated. All of it a result of him catching her by surprise at this exact place in time. But his words from last night stuck in her mind. Could he actually wash away whatever came before?

She stepped back, broadening his view of her, and dropped her robe off her shoulders until it pooled at her feet. The cool air teased her bare hips, and a chill skated up her spine, tightening her nipples. His lips parted on a sharp inhalation, and he cursed, something ancient and possibly Gaelic.

She turned and placed the roses on the bed, then stood before him completely naked. She'd never let anyone just look at her like this before. She didn't suck in her tummy or cross her legs to hide the dimpled scar she hated on her left knee. She just stood there—honest, unrefined, and imperfectly whole.

"You're ... radiant."

Warmth exploded in her. Her lashes lowered, and she bit down on her lips, but they pulled free in a smile. When she looked at him again, she noted the way his breathing had changed and his eyes had darkened.

Heat rushed from her chest to her face. "I hadn't really thought this through." Her nipples tightened as the room temperature cooled. "I forget what to do next."

His lashes lifted and he stared at her. Slowly, he stepped further into the room. He closed the door, then seemed to think better of it, and left it half open.

She took a quick step back, her thighs grazing the comforter of the bed. He followed and the heat of his body burned through his clothes, warming her chilled skin. His gaze held hers and he traced a calming stroke down the side of her face with one finger.

"I'd like, very much, to kiss ye, Em'ry."

She swallowed and nodded. "Okay."

He dropped to his knees and cupped her hips. "Wait..."

He looked up at her, his face eye level with her sex.

"I thought you meant…"

Sliding his hand from her hips, he kept his stare on her eyes and ruffled the soft hair at her apex with the same finger he'd used to touch her face. Warm breath teased her wet folds, and she considered actually letting him kiss her there.

He left the decision to her, waiting patiently, no longer stroking. Not even touching. Just looking up at her with those hungry eyes.

She nodded, and he drew in a full breath, leaning forward and pressing a kiss to the peak of her sex. She sucked in a gasp as his lips pressed more firmly. The soft, probing tip of his tongue swirled around her clit and teased with tentative licks.

Her stance widened, and his hands caught her hips. His lips closed over her flesh, and he pulled softly. She gripped his shoulders for balance, a keening cry escaping her throat.

He groaned and pulled her hips closer, angling her more toward his mouth. The first penetrating swipe of his tongue that separated her folds nearly dropped her to her knees. His mouth opened and closed, kissing, tasting, and sucking every tender part of her.

It was delicate and divine. Torturous and wonderful. She swallowed, her mouth going dry as she breathed through the intensifying pleasure, her hands combing softly through his hair.

He returned to her clit, swiping and swirling all that delicious heat over her sensitive bud. His hands never moved from her hips. He used only his mouth, and he used it in a way that told her he had all day just to kiss her there.

When he tentatively sucked her clit between his lips, nibbling softly, she cried out. Her hand clutched the back of his head, holding her to him as her muscles shook.

"More," she breathed, her fingers lost in his soft hair and her mind spinning for that one out of reach push.

His tongue shot between her folds, stabbing softly, as arousal wept from her. She needed more, and at the same time, it was too much.

Reaching back for the bed, her body angled and she sank onto the covers, her toes still pointed into the floor and his hands tight at her hips. His mouth closed over her clit again, and this time he suckled the little knot with determined purpose.

She cried out, her hand gripping the foot of the bed as her knees lifted, her thighs encircling his head. She shamelessly rocked against his working lips as her moans shifted to high-pitched cries.

He burrowed deeper, worked faster. It was the most selfless act she'd ever shared with a man. Yet, he behaved as if the pleasure she received was solely for him.

Her voice peaked in a crescendo of bliss, and she crested that elusive wave, falling into a sea of wild tremors and trembles as every muscle in her body skipped about, dancing right down to her bones.

Her legs fell open, and she panted, little aftershocks tripping over her skin and jolting her supine limbs with tiny shivers.

Callan's cheek rested on her thigh, his hair and breath a welcome weight and tickle against her quivering skin. "Tis like biting into a lush tomato, fresh from the garden and still warm from the sun." He turned his face and pressed a kiss to her damp curls. "I dinnae ken a woman could be so juicy. So ripe and full of taste."

Her entire body flushed with heat. "Thank you?"

He chuckled. "I think I should be the one thankin' you. Ye might be my new favorite snack."

She laughed and sank deeper into the bedding, her head lolling to the side and her gaze stilling at the sight of her roses. She traced a finger over the silky petals. "I hope you haven't spoiled your appetite for breakfast."

He rose, sliding up her body and smiling like a cat with a mouth full of canary feathers. "Hardly." His gaze dropped to her breasts. "May I?"

Her arms slowly lifted, offering her body to him, a wave of confidence born in the fire of his gentle manners and palpable desire. His eyes followed hers as he lowered his head.

She gasped at the first swipe of his tongue, her body still sensitive. He teased her nipples softly, licking and testing out various ways to find pleasure or draw hers. He might be disappointed, as he'd started lower and worked his way up instead of the other way around.

Drawing back, he frowned at her chest. Her confidence wavered, and she wondered if she should cover herself. "You're going to give me a complex if you keep looking at them like that."

His face, awash with guilt, stared at her. "I dinnae mean—"

"I'm teasing." She shrugged, making light of his response. "Not all men are into boobs."

"I dinnae care about other men. And it's not about your *boobs*," he said the word as if he'd never used it before. "It's about you."

Her mouth made a silent *oh*.

He cupped her, giving them a little jiggle. "Does that hurt?"

She shook her head. What was happening? This was turning into more of an exam than any sort of foreplay. It was like he never played with boobs before.

Oh, my God, he's never played with boobs before.

She scooted back on the bed, sitting up and knocking him off of her. She grabbed a pillow and covered her body. "Callan, are you a virgin?"

He looked away and stood, turning his back to her.

"Callan—"

He reached for the flowers. "These should be in water." Before she could think of something to say, he was gone.

She scrambled off the bed and shoved her arms into her robe, knotting the belt quickly. He was already in the kitchen when she caught up to him.

"Callan, you don't have to be embarrassed."

"I'm not."

"It's not a big deal. I mean, if you can overlook…" A chill locked in her bones. She didn't want to devalue herself, but it seemed unrealistic to ignore the damage she'd suffered. "Who am I to judge anybody for being a virgin?"

He thrust the bouquet in the sink and spun, grabbing her shoulders and lowering his stance to look her in the eye. "First, I'm no virgin. Second, you have every right to judge. What happened to ye, happened without consent. It will never tarnish who you are in my eyes. And last…" His lips closed as he rose to his full height. "Last…"

She waited, wanting to know what the last detail might be.

"Lastly…" He drew in a deep breath. "I'm no virgin, but I've never been with a woman."

Chapter Thirty-Three

Saratoga Springs, New York—America
Present day

He'd never said the words out loud and as they left him an internal shell cracked and something toxic burned from the inside out. Putting words to such a vile truth was like setting a needle to the vein. His heart hammered, vibrating his entire skeleton, and he dropped into a seat at the table, his stare working rivets into the surface.

"What?" Her question breathed through the air. "But… You're not gay. Are you?"

If there was judgment in her voice, he dinnae hear it. Why was he telling her this?

Maybe on some level, he thought to take away her shame by exposing his own. Or maybe his ego couldnae chance her misreading his inexperience as lack of skill. But even the memory of Rory made him shiver.

Mostly, he ached to confide in her because she was his friend. And after years of solitary living, he wanted to tell someone the horror he survived.

He swallowed and looked across the table. Her image swirled, his eyes wet and his throat full. "I've never told…" Tongue tied, the words sank into him like led balloons, refusing to get out. "I dinnae want it."

The tension in her face softened as the color rushed out. "What?"

Shallow breaths tightened his chest. His skin prickled with phantom weight. He could smell Rory. The bite of his sweet aftershave, the tang of his cum.

His stomach churned, and he folded his hand into a tight fist. "When I was in Scotland, there was a man… A very powerful man. He was my boss. And he was pure evil. Corrupt and malevolent, vicious. He took great pleasure in using his power to manipulate others. He loved to force others to commit the most depraved acts."

As he heard himself speaking of a man he'd tried fruitlessly to forget, he understood there were no words vile enough to paint an accurate picture.

"Ye have to understand, I take no issue with those who favor the same sex. I never gave it much thought, as my life moved accordin' to circumstances. My da left, and I needed to help out my ma. Then she got sick and eventually we were alone, me, Innis, and Gavin."

"Your siblings?"

"Aye." He nodded, his stare burrowing into the napkin holder resting in the center of the table. "I was the oldest, and Innis was gettin' bullied once she … filled out. My sister was a stunning creature, smart and sharp and burstin' with potential."

He swallowed, all that potential seeming to fall back on him like shrapnel whenever he tried to measure all she'd lost. Innis was his surrender, his sorrowful white flag. His failure.

"And Gavin…" He still couldnae go there. "My wee brother."

Her delicate fingers closed over his fist, squeezing softly, lending him strength. He swallowed again at the lump growing in his throat.

"When our ma passed, we hardly had the money to pay the coroner. No funeral. No grave. And when Innis came home, cryin' that some boys were harassin' her, I knew I had to do somethin', get her to a safer school. Rhys, my best friend, had overheard men talkin' about underground fights. They were somethin' to gamble on, but the contenders got paid. It was fast money and I'd always been built like an ox, so we asked around."

He glanced down at her pretty hand holding his mangled fist and his skin burned under his collar. She never seemed to stare at his scars or focus on them.

He pointed to his nose. "That's how this masterpiece happened."

"You're a masterpiece," she whispered. "I think you're beautiful."

He frowned at her, trying to see through the words and pinpoint the lie, but her eyes showed such sincerity he couldnae make sense of it. He knew what he looked like.

"Ye dinnae see all the scars. There are more that my clothes hide."

"They're just scars, Callan."

He nodded, considering how some still hurt. The tight skin at his ankles prickled. On days when he overlooked caring for his burn scars, they could pain him something fierce. But all that pain was nothing compared to the damage he carried inside.

He drew in an unsteady breath. A valve had been opened, and the only way to shut it off was to finish expelling the toxins inside.

"I put Innis and Gavin in a private school with the money I made havin' the shite kicked out of me on a weekly basis, so it was worth it. My da was not a kind man, and every time I won—*every time*—I saw more of him in myself. I hated it, but we were finally able to save a little and eventually we'd move. But there was a house fire. We dinnae have much, but the things we did have…"

"Callan, if this is too difficult to talk about—"

His fist opened, and he caught her fingers, squeezing. He instantly softened his grip and kissed her knuckles. "I left Gavin and Innis home. After that…"

He couldnae bring himself to share the stories of Innis. He dinnae want those haunting images lingering in Emery's head.

"I lost everything. I lost them."

Her chair scraped over the floor, and she caught his face in her hands, pressing her lips to his cheek. "Oh, Callan…"

Her sympathy was a jagged pill he couldnae swallow, so he nodded and nudged her back to her chair. Understanding and deep sorrow swirled in her glittering eyes.

"It was all tied together. The fights, the gambling, the corruption, and the man behind it all."

The cold, expansive ache in his chest started to warm, and then it started to burn as his words up to this point ignited like a bed of kindling for the fire of hate that now blazed in his gut.

"My world was a dark place." He pulled his hand away from her touch as if his hands still wore the blood he'd spilled. "I killed the men who started the fire." His eyes stared, no longer seeing the surface of the table, but recalling the towering flames and screams as he'd watched them burn alive. "I wanted vengeance. I wanted my family back. And after that, I planned to die."

Silence enveloped the kitchen for a long time. He dinnae look at her. Couldnae. But he felt her next to him. The markings on his arm came alive on his skin, each one quivering just beneath the surface with a memory.

He saw himself on a rampage, slashing through flesh, hacking apart bone, bathing in rivulets of blood. He'd buried bodies from one end of Scotland to the other.

His sins went to God and God alone. But she needed to understand his hands were far from clean. "They were all bad men, Em'ry. Men who had stolen guiltless lives, ripped the innocence away from the weak. I acted as judge and executioner, never regretting my ... actions."

"They deserved to die."

His head jerked up, his memories splashing away as he looked in her eyes, unsure he'd heard her or imagined the conviction in her voice. "Pardon?"

Something cold flashed in her stare as if she was seeing her own nightmares. Her lashes flicked, and she looked at him. "Some animals just need to be put down, Callan. Especially if they're putting innocent people in danger."

Thrown by the assertion of her uncompromising vengeance, he was unsure if he should celebrate her comprehension or mourn whatever part of her goodness that died to make room for it.

"The man who ... touched you... Is he still alive?"

Of course, she'd want to know about Rory. "No."

It had been more than three years since he'd left him rotting on the floor, nothing more than a bloodied pile of bone and tissue. Though he hadn't been the last person Rory saw before leaving this world, Callan should have taken some sort of peace from knowing his tormentor had died. But peace dinnae exist after something as horrific as what they survived, only a strange sort of inner quiet that could be just as unnerving as the endless noise.

Innis had every right to take his eyes. In the end, his death was hers.

"Could you not have gone to the cops?" she asked.

He drew in a long breath and let it out slowly. "The polis dinnae help criminals, and that's what these men were. It's what I became the moment I was forced into a job workin' for them. Life got complicated, some days all I could feel..." His lips worked as he tried to put a name to that dark feeling that owned him. "Hurt."

He covered his jaw, massaging slowly and working his fingers over his mouth, so his teeth dinnae chatter and his hands dinnae shake. The hurt still anchored him. But so did she. He needed to balance the two, show her this side of himself. It was the only way he could accept her love. She had to truly know the darkness inside of him to truly accept him, even if he could only reveal a wee bit at a time.

He knew nothing about love but knew everything about pain. Violence could lift the skin right from the muscle, tearing it back from the bone. It was tangible, messy, and palpable. When a man fought, and he got his arse pummeled, he couldnae forget he was trapped in that battered bag of flesh. But when the bruises healed and the exterior pain was gone, the hurt remained, and the real ache began.

But hurt was different. Hurt lay beneath flesh and blood, within the hollow of the bone. Hurt was dark and lonesome.

Hurt was the phantom slap of God that knocked a man to his knees when the rest of the world only felt a breeze. He had so much hurt inside of him when he came to this country, he'd been nothing but a sack of shattered glass.

Elspeth had taken care of both him and Uma, acted as an accomplice when they robbed the estate, proving herself a trustworthy friend—his only friend—until he met Emery. His world was small by choice. His home a fortress and his heart a vault.

But little by little, his guard dropped. Uma, with her wee fingers, and her laugh that curled into him... It was the little things that first slipped past his watch.

His appreciation for Elspeth grew with his respect. Women knew things, like when a tooth was loose or how to get knots out of little tangles without making Uma cry. He needed her, and she proved a devoted companion for his niece.

But Emery, she was different. He coveted her since the day he set eyes on her, knowing he had no right to even look her way. But her beauty tempted him, and her laughter intoxicated something inside of him, something that quieted the hurt.

Addicted to watching her, wanting that strange sense of peace she brought, he changed his shifts to make sure they matched hers. Even on his worst days, when the memories were inescapable, and the hurt pushed him close to ending it all, she had the power to settle him. She quelled the storm, quieted the beast inside, and quickened his heart.

He hadnae killed a man since making her acquaintance. It seemed ironic that her circumstances had awakened the beast she'd so effortlessly tamed. But he would see to her justice in the end. It would be the poetic finish to his sorry life. And while it would disturb his sanctuary, possibly stir up trouble he couldnae outrun, he knew loving a woman meant slaying her demons and not becoming one.

Uma would have Elspeth and Emery would have peace.

Her sniffle dragged him out of his head. Damp streaks cut through her beauty, shredding his heart. He'd given those tears to her. "Please dinnae waste tears on me, love."

"I hate that you had to go through that. I hate knowing you suffered."

Once again, he couldnae bear her tears. Pulling her into his lap, he pressed his lips to her hair. "Dinnae waste yer tears on me, love. I was built for pain." Because pain hit the exterior. The thing that ate at him most was the hurt. That's what rotted him from the inside out—but she couldnae see that. It was good to keep it hidden. In the end, it would serve his purpose well.

She burrowed into his strength, her silent tears leaving damp stains on his shirt. "When I look at you, I see this unstoppable force. I can feel power thrumming from you and sense you before I know you're there. I can't imagine anyone hurting you. And that man who…" Her voice faltered. "I just can't, Callan."

He softly brushed her hair away from her eyes and tucked it behind her ear, pressing a kiss to her temple. "It wasnae like what happened to you, *leannán.* As much as I hated it, I never lost complete control. He had my body, but he never touched my mind." Yet, he'd wrecked his soul.

For several minutes, only their soft breathing broke the silence. Both of them lost in their own memories, unforgettable nightmares that had more sides than a kaleidoscope. That was the tricky part of trauma. You never saw it twice from the same angle, and every viewing hurt.

"I remember," she whispered. "Hiding in my head. I was there, in the bathroom, the sink, my screaming reflection all I could see. But there's also this other memory. I'm just sitting, in a dark corner. My knees are up, and I'm hugging them, but no one's touching me. It's like the pain's at the door, banging hard enough to rattle the walls, but it isn't touching me."

She lifted her head from his chest and looked him in the eyes. "It's not a real place. But I've been there. I went there when he went inside of me. And the walls would suddenly vanish, but then they'd come back." She blinked, her brow knit into a frown. "I can see myself clear as day, like it was a real place. But it wasn't. He had me all along."

His arms tightened around her. "I did the same. I tried to become as empty as I could. It sort of flickered but never held. I just remember the pain." He swallowed. "And the shame."

Her eyes closed and her weight sagged into him. "I know the shame."

No more words. They sat in a timeless silence, drowning in the hurt with no urge to struggle.

Sometimes hurt just needed to do its thing, so they let it drag them down.

Her hurt seeped into him. And his into her. Together they weighed each other down, and that hadnae been his intention. He never wanted to add to her burden.

"Ye help me, Em'ry."

She sniffed and lifted her face. "I do?"

He nodded. "Maybe love is the glue that puts a broken man back together. When I'm near you, I feel ye in my soul, like every look from your eyes is somehow sewing me back onto the bone."

Her lips parted as she breathed against him, the soft heaves of her chest pressing with each inhalation.

Her eyes wore a mask of pain, one he'd seen before. "I tell myself it can be *everything* or *nothing.*" She shook her head. "Like, I didn't have a choice then, but I do have the choice now. And I get to decide what I make of it."

He understood what she meant, if she'd let it ruin her or if she'd rise from the pain, bury the hurt. For him, it was everything. The vengeance, the hate, the drive, it all started and ended with one person. But in the end, it hadnae been a loop that came full circle, it was just a messy labyrinth of derailed turns that confused his past and left him more lost than he'd started. But it led him to Emery.

"I think that's the difference between men and women. On most days, most men believe themselves at least half-gods. When our power's ripped away, and the truth of our vulnerability is all we have left to feel, it turns us into something ugly. But women… I dinnae ken why so many women take that blame and put it on themselves."

A small gasp slipped past her lips like a deformed laugh made without humor. "I still blame myself for going into that bathroom."

"That's insane."

"I know. But it's true."

His lips formed a thin line. "I blame myself for Innis and Gavin. I even blame myself for leavin' you tha' night. Had I been there…"

She stared up at him with stunned comprehension. "Callan, no—"

"Let's not argue the irrational logic of blame. I know better than to try to convince ye out of yours. You'll not convince me out of mine."

Her mouth closed, though he sensed her lingering need to argue with him. He kissed her softly, needing to feel her lips but pulling away before any expectation could be drawn.

"Do you believe in destiny?" she asked.

"No. I believe in very little these days. Even God seems to have turned his back on me."

"Has He? Maybe we were brought into each other's lives for a reason. Maybe I was always supposed to walk into that bathroom, and you were always supposed to pick me up off the floor. What if all the pain prepares us for a bigger reason? Struggles harden us in ways nothing else can."

"I think that would be a nice belief if one could actually believe it."

Her lips pressed to his, firm and meaningful. "Maybe we're meant to heal each other, Callan. You say I help you. Well, you help me, too. Maybe we're here to ease each other's burdens the way only you and I can because on some level we share the same pain. We know the weight and shape and ache of the hurt that's inside."

"I dinnae ken if I can be healed, love. Sometimes things break, and help takes too long to arrive. They have to be broken again to reset. I dinnae have enough left in me to break again."

"I think you're wrong. I think we have to push through it. Every minute I spend thinking about the past feels like days stolen from my future. I refuse to let him win, Callan." She shook her head, a spike of hostility in her voice. "He took from me without asking. He took so much. I refuse to give him one more piece of me. I won't let him rob me of this." Her fists closed around his shirt, shaking him like a caterpillar shakes a tree.

"What are ye sayin', love?"

Her eyes screamed what she struggled to say, but he needed to hear it from her lips. She slipped off his lap and stood, the robe tumbling over her bare legs and swallowing her petite form.

"Let's be the rain, sliding down each other's skin, washing away whatever came before." Her fingers laced with his. "Come upstairs with me."

His head shook before his brain could form the word *no.* "It's too soon."

"No, it's not," she argued. "We need this. Both of us. And it needs to be now."

461

"Em'ry, it's been only a few months since—"

"Don't put him in this, Callan. He's not a part of the equation any more than the monster that hurt you is a part of it. This is about us. We love each other. We've been pining for three years and our time's finally here. I want to show you that love can heal. And I need you to let me show you so that I can prove it to myself—prove that I'm not permanently broken." Her chin trembled as she waited for him to respond. "Please."

Every panic attack she'd had flashed through his mind. The way he'd handled her like a rutting bull the other day, finishing in his pants with uncontainable lust. Everything inside of him said they shouldnae do this, that this would be a well-intentioned mistake that might ruin everything they had.

"Please, Callan. I need this. So do you."

She spoke those magic words and he couldnae bear to turn her down. Not for him, but for her. He could never refuse her needs. He'd die trying to meet them. "All right, love."

Chapter Thirty-Four

Saratoga Springs, New York—America
Present day

Emery led him into the bedroom, not unlacing their fingers until she approached the bed. Callan's gaze dropped to the floor, and she sensed his reluctance.

Drawing in a galvanizing breath, she flattened her palm over his pounding heart. "Callan." She waited for him to look at her, flinching at the uncertainty in his eyes. "I want this. I want you to have this part of me."

His finger traced down the side of her face, achingly tender. "I could never forgive myself for hurtin' you, Em'ry. And I dinnae ken how to do this." The last of his words ripped from his throat as if drenched in acidic shame.

She shook her head, swallowing down her nerves. "You do it the way you know how. No one else is here but us, Callan. This is *ours*. There's no right or wrong to it, okay?"

He glanced away, jaw ticking with tension. When he looked back, his lips were bleached of color. "I cannae tolerate bein' touched... I dinnae know what I'll do if ye put your hands on me, love."

"Where?" Her ability to gather the needed facts surprised her. "Tell me where I shouldn't touch you."

He swallowed. "Where he got inside of me."

"Okay. Anywhere else?"

"I dinnae ken." Her heart cracked with his voice.

Her eyes prickled with the onset of fresh tears, but she hardened her jaw and blinked them away. "I can't... Don't grab me from behind. I need to face you at all times, okay?"

He nodded. "Aye."

Neither of them seemed to know how to begin. She pivoted and opened her drawers, digging around until she located the box she needed. She pressed it into his hands and shrugged. "For pregnancy." She didn't know if she could have kids, but she knew she wasn't ready for that conversation.

He stared at the box, finally pulling the cardboard flap and removing a foil covered condom. He placed the box on the bedside table and drew back the covers. It was a strangely gallant gesture.

His dependable chivalry numbed her nerves, a gentle anesthetic that boosted her courage and built her confidence. She gave him a shaky smile and unbelted her robe.

They'd done this dance before. He often walked her to bed and tucked her in, but now she was naked, and soon he would be too. Lowering herself to the pillows, she watched him.

"Wait." She grabbed Max and tossed him into the bedside drawer and smirked. He silently chuckled and the moment suddenly seemed lighter.

Pulling the covers over her bare chest, he stared into her eyes. His finger dragged slowly from her eyebrow to the tip of her chin, and her nipples tightened under the cool weight of the sheet.

He glanced at his clothes. "I have scars."

Her heart ached at the proof that even a man as stunning as Callan could have body image issues. "They're just the surface, Callan. I don't see them when I look at you."

His brow tightened, his face twisting with pinching emotion. "My legs... From the fire..."

Understanding spread through her like a heavy wind pushing a vessel out to see. How silly of her to assume the extent of his scars were on his hands and face. She reached for his fingers and squeezed.

"I want to see you, but if you can't, we can—"

"I can. I just want to prepare you."

Uncertainty knifed through her. If she reacted in any way that hurt him, it would crush both of them. But she'd never seen a burn victim before, and she didn't know what to expect. Didn't know how her mind and eyes would respond. She forced herself to be still.

"I'm ready."

First, he reached to his back and pulled off his shirt. Her jaw unhinged as sheer glory unveiled before her. Breath rushed from her lungs as she stared, unblinking.

Hard, angular curves carved into his hips. Muscles stacked like the rungs of a Jacob's ladder climbed up his flat abdomen. Swells of sinew and tendons bulged beneath his skin. The flat pigment of his nipples and the corded thickness of his ribs seemed all the more menacing with Christ on the Cross hanging down over his chest where the rosary fell. He had bulges in places she couldn't name, muscles where she didn't know muscles hid.

"Holy..." She blinked in awe at his physique. "Wow."

He had the modesty to flush, and as his lashes swept low over his blush, she fell a thousand feet deeper in love with him. She smiled with pure, female admiration.

"You know you're beautiful."

His blue eyes flashed and the side of his mouth hooked. "I show ye the good parts first, to help ye overlook the bad."

She laughed. It was a solid plan. "Keep going."

The playful smile on his face vanished, and he set to work on the buckle of his belt. His breathing turned noticeably jagged, and his fingers fumbled with the button of his jeans. He paused when he had the belt undone, finger on the zipper, and then he yanked them down, toeing out of his boots and socks and shoving his pants into a crushed pile of denim on the floor before she could fully look at him.

She caught the flash of some marks on his back. Deep divots of reformed flesh that didn't quite match his other skin.

He stood, and her confidence wavered. He was thick everywhere, but not hard. Her gaze dropped to her chest, a terrible thought stabbing into her.

What if she was pushing too hard, forcing too much too soon? What if he was too much of a gentleman to say no to her? What if the flaccid proof of his nerves was the same as a swallowed scream?

The wretched sense that she might be bullying him into this gutted her. She couldn't do it. Her courage toppled.

The words weren't easy, but she had to get them out. "If you don't want to do this, we can stop."

There had never been a silence as ear-splitting as the one that followed.

"I want to do this. I want to know the touch of your hands on me and the feel of my body in yours."

Her gaze lifted and she recognized the desire in his stormy eyes. She glanced down the front of him and relief spread through her as his length hardened. She smiled, and he stepped back.

She forgot to prepare, too sidetracked by her concern that he didn't want this, and when his legs came into view, her jaw unhinged. "Oh, Callan."

She swallowed, the evident pain the injuries must have caused stabbing into her empty stomach. Beneath his knees, the muscle of his calves twisted around the bone. The flesh was smooth, without hair, and darker than the rest of his legs. The definition of his shins showed beneath the almost iridescent scar tissue, delineated by crossing veins. Blotches of dark and light pigment swirled around his feet.

"I know it isn't pretty to look at."

Her eyes lifted, her heart so full of sadness. "Do they still hurt?" They looked painful, even if they were only scars.

"Not like they did. The scars itch and I have to tend to them, but there are worse things. When they pain me it slows me down a bit, but..." He shrugged. "I'm sorry ye have to look at it."

She scowled at him. "Don't. There's nothing wrong with the way you look, Callan. We all have imperfections."

"Imperfections. That's a big word with a small meaning. I know I'm mangled, Em'ry. And yer immeasurable beauty only makes the truth more clear."

"Stop. No matter what you think you look like, in my head, you'll always be better looking than me. So when you put yourself down, know that I'm still several rungs below."

"But you're not—"

"In my head I am. So let's not do that to ourselves. We've got enough damage on the inside that we don't need the pressure of our shortcomings on the outside, too. Deal?"

"Deal." He shifted his feet and his hands fisted at his sides. "Should I join you?"

"Yes." She flipped back the covers, and he rounded the bed, sliding in beside her.

They both lowered to their backs and stared at the ceiling.

"Your bed's soft."

"Thanks." Silence unfolded, like a napkin turning into a blanket until it enveloped them and was all she could feel. "You can kiss me."

She could hear each breath passing through his nose. The covers lifted, and she gasped as his body pressed over hers, his lips surprising her and seeking before she had time to acclimate.

A soft sound left her throat as his tongue stole into her mouth with deliberate purpose. The heat of his erection weighed heavily against her hip, its implication burning through her skin.

Fumbling to find the emotional balance she seemed to have lost, she put her fingers in his hair and slowed the kiss. His hips moved, nudging her thighs apart.

"Can I put my hands on ye?"

"Yes," she whispered, taking control of the kiss and slowing it to a pace she liked.

Heat covered her breast as he cupped her. She moaned, and his fingers teased the tip. His mouth broke from hers, his breathing heavy as he traced his lips along the edge of her jaw, finding the frantic beat of her pulse.

Her body arched into the warmth of his touch and, when his fingers flexed against her skin, she caught his hand, dragging it lower and pressing it to the wet folds hidden between her thighs.

"Touch me, Callan."

He stilled and then softly petted over her curls, teasing her sensitive clit. Her knees fell open, and as he leaned back, the covers fell away.

"You're so soft here." His gaze held hers as the tip of his finger traced the edge of her slit, gathering moisture and spreading her wider. He slowly pressed the finger inside of her, and she inhaled sharply.

Panic flashed in his eyes. "Did I hurt you?"

"No. It's good. Keep going."

He drew back his touch, frowned, and shoved the finger deep.

"Ah—" Cool air covered her as he withdrew his touch and jerked his body away.

"I'm sorry. I dinnae ken how to touch you. I'm no gentle touch, Em'ry—"

"Callan," she snapped, her voice breaking through the hysteria ganging up on him. She caught his arm and pulled him back over her, pushing his hand back between her legs. "Just not as rough. You'll get me there. Gentle."

Tension carved deep lines into his face as he hesitantly touched her again. The now tender way he pushed his thick fingers in and out of her had heat spreading through her limbs and warming her core.

"Yes," she whispered, her eyes closing and her pelvis softening under his touch. "Like that."

His confidence shined in his efforts as he lowered his mouth to her breasts. The tight pull of his lips closing around the tip of her nipple unleashed another moan. His wet fingers slipped out of her sex, and closed around her breasts, plumping the soft flesh.

She smiled, her body tipping back as he spent time getting to know her breasts. No hesitation like before. Now, he couldn't seem to get enough of them.

"I want te drink from them," he rasped. "Do you think if I suck long enough I could?"

A hot blush rushed down her front. There was a strange innocence to his question. "I don't think it works that way."

His mouth closed over the turgid tip, and he pulled the nipple deep into his mouth, suckling hard as if he didn't believe her. Her breath caught as a surprising knot of pleasure tightened in her womb.

The cool beads of the rosary gathered on her stomach. She gasped as pleasure spiked downward, triggering the sharp twinge of an orgasm, but he wasn't touching her sex. She arched, and he lifted her to him, feasting on her breasts.

Her fingers dug into his shoulders. How was this happening? She typically took lots of patience and skill, but Callan seemed on to something.

471

Her body gushed with desire. Her voice climbed with needy cries as she clung to him, holding him tighter to her chest with every shoot of pleasure. Her feet pressed into the bed, lifting her hips as the building swells broke, crashing over her in an astonishing shock of glitter and shivers.

He wasn't done. He moved to her other breast, cupping and pulling and suckling hard.

"Callan," she rasped. She had no idea her breasts could provoke such interest—or such a response.

His hips moved against hers, the slick trail of pre-cum dragging across her thigh. The fact that he loved touching her so much only added to her pleasure.

"More," she whispered. "Yes."

Her nipples had never been so adored. The tight, swollen tips throbbed with wet sensation. The more he nibbled and twisted and pulled the more she felt. Wave after wave, pleasure crashed over her. And when his fingers found their way between her legs again, she shattered, her drenched sex welcoming him.

"Now," she gasped, her body trembling in a rush of sensation and euphoric chills.

His mouth broke from her nipple, her flesh deliciously abused and divinely sore. He fumbled with the condom, and she considered telling him to forget it, but he had it on before she made up her mind.

He stroked a large hand down his latex covered cock, and her eyes widened. He was bigger than before, bigger than—

That door in her mind slammed shut. Only her and Callan. Nothing else. She wanted no bitter thoughts to intrude on this moment.

Swallowing tightly, she forced her knees to fall open. "Come here."

His jaw twitched, a hard line of concentration carved into his brow as he crawled over her. She cupped his face, needing to look into his eyes.

"I love you, Callan."

Always one to measure his words, he drew in a slow breath and let it out completely. "I love you, too, Em'ry. I'll love you always."

Her body stretched as he entered her slowly, the broad crown of his cock trying tender tissue with such gentleness that the fragile reed of her womanhood, the spine of her broken confidence, trembled. Tears gathered in her eyes, distorting her view of his beautiful face and she panicked, swiping them away.

His lips pressed to her cheeks, his mouth whispering against the damp skin where her tears had fallen. "I love you. I love you…"

Breath filled her as he pressed completely inside. Her eyes closed at the intrusion, welcoming the weight of his body over hers and soaking up his tender affection.

"Don't let go," she begged, needing him to hold her so tight she wouldn't fall apart.

"Never," he rasped, crushing his chest to hers. His breath beat against her ear, his lips pressing to her cheek. "Nothing has ever felt so g—good."

His voice broke, and she caught his face, turning it to hers so she could kiss him. Only then did she notice his tears. They fell from his eyes, and she kissed away the trails.

"I have you," she whispered. "Just like you have me, Callan, I won't let go."

Tension twisted in his face, an agonizing show of his need for physical affection. She tentatively lowered a hand to his back and tried to soothe him with gentle strokes.

"Shh, it's okay."

The force of the sob he tried to hide from her wracked his body. He dropped his head to her shoulders as the terrible sound ripped from his lips, flowing into her with such force she could no longer control her own tears.

He didn't move, but he filled her. And she held him. It was the most intimate moment of her entire life, perhaps the precipice of her purpose. She wished she could take his pain away, eradicate all the hurt.

As her hands traveled over his arms and shoulders and down his back, he gasped, shaken by the contact and nuzzling into her touch for more. She wasn't sure how long they held each other like that. And it wasn't always clear who was holding whom. But they never let go.

She never knew such a sense of oneness could exist. The way he completed her, filled her, softened all her jagged edges, it was spiritual, existential, and life-altering. No empty places of her soul left unfilled. So brutally broken when alone, yet beautifully complete when together.

She didn't need his verbal confirmation to know he felt it too. They communicated through something stronger than words and more permanent than any promise.

Drenched in dispersed emotion and exercised pain, their first movements were clumsy, but soon they found their way. Callan, despite his efforts to handle her like the frailest glass, wore intensity like a second skin and couldn't always manage gentle.

She welcomed his passion. Met every forceful thrust like the shore meets the sea, resilient and true. He was a large man, but he was hers, and she wanted all of him.

He pounded into her, his thick erection not only thrusting between her tender folds, but his body opening her, stretching her to accommodate each heavy fall of his hips. Their bodies glistened with slickened haste as his physical demands challenged them to the point of exertion.

Her strength waned long before his, but she wanted him to keep going. She wanted him to take all of her until there was nothing left untouched.

Eventually, his rhythm slowed and his head lowered to her chest. His mouth closed over her nipple, and she moaned, her fingers combing softly through his hair. Part of her wished they could stay like that forever, but she sensed him fighting back his release.

His hips flexed slowly, never letting her forget they were connected. When he lifted his chest from hers, she remembered how it felt to draw a full breath, but she hadn't missed it. On the contrary, she missed his weight and wanted to pull him back to her.

"You're radiant," he whispered, with that intoxicating rhotic accent.

Heat tickled her cheeks, and she tipped her face to look at him, silently begging for a kiss. A sort of language had been constructed, and they no longer hesitated to take what they wanted. His tongue delved deep into the crevices of her mouth, and she sparred with him, playfully nipping at his lips and jaw.

His hips thrust, asserting his dominance, and she grinned, handing it over. He growled and bit at her neck, driving his erection deep with renewed speed. His thick length stroked her insides, and her body wept with a warm welcome.

His mouth pressed to hers as his body lowered, his chest crushing deliciously against her breasts and his hands pushing the hair away from her face to stare into her eyes.

"Dinnae look away, love." His breath hitched with jagged jolts of pleasure. His mouth pushed to hers as they rocked as one.

And the last of the veil fell away. His unearthed secrets showed in every fleck of his crystal blue eyes as she stared into his open soul. He trembled with completion, shivering over her and then letting his body blanket hers.

Chapter Thirty-Five

Saratoga Springs, New York—America
Present day

They stayed in bed all day, talking more openly than they'd ever talked. Em'ry nibbled on the pancakes Callan had brought that morning, not caring that they were cold and dry. Not caring that she hadn't worn a stitch of clothing all day.

"And what about yer parents?" he asked.

Hugging a pillow to her front, she tore the floppy pancake with her teeth and shrugged. "They're very literal in their faith. I was raised in a Christian Science household, so I was never vaccinated, and we weren't allowed to watch much television. Suffice it to say, the second I could get out, I did. I only applied to colleges in other states and sold anything I had of value my senior year of high school so I could afford a place to stay."

"You dinnae speak to them?"

"I do. I mean, I love my mom and dad, but as an only child, I can't take their magnified,

477

undivided focus on my life. They're very … critical. And we don't share the same views."

"Do they know what happened to ye?"

She shook her head. "There's the chance they might hear it on the news, but they're all the way in Kentucky. And my mother and father stopped watching the news after Nine-Eleven."

Lying on his side, his long body twisted in her blankets, he lovingly traced a finger over her knee. "I'm sorry. I'd think, goin' through all ye been through, it would be nice te have the support of loved ones."

She forced a smile. "When they found out I wasn't a virgin they threatened to throw me out. I wouldn't be able to handle their scrutiny on top of everything else." She didn't like discussing her parents. "Besides, I have you."

She pushed the Styrofoam container of pancakes onto the bedside table. "Tell me about Uma."

His eyes became alert at the mention of his niece. "What do ye want te know?"

She squirmed under the covers beside him. He pulled her close, tucking her against his hips and cupping her breast. The heat of his chest burned into her back and she let it warm her.

"You love her like a daughter." It wasn't a question because she knew the answer. She could see how much he cared for her the second she saw them together.

"Aye. She's like that to me, I suppose."

"Does she remember your sister?" Trying not to overstep, she kept her voice tentative, leaving him the option not to answer.

"I hope not. My sister wasnae well at the end, but she loved Uma the best she could."

Her hand tightened over his arm. "I'm sorry."

His sister must have been very young when she had the baby. Frowning, she wondered how Uma had avoided the fire. Maybe the au pair had been with her when the fire happened.

"Has Elspeth always been her nanny?"

"Since she was two."

He didn't seem to enjoy discussing this, so she changed the subject. "Do you think Matt will eventually have a dark enough spray tan to get cast in the next Willy Wonka remake?"

Callan snorted, his laughter shaking from his chest into her back. "That or possibly a future as a spokesperson for cheese puffs."

She laughed. "Someone should tell him."

"I think Marco tried."

She rolled to her other side so she could face him. "Do you think they know we're dating?"

He lifted a brow. "I dinnae care either way." His hand gripped her ass and yanked her closer. "You're mine, and I'll not try te hide it."

His lips pressed to hers as he turned her, pulling her under him. She moaned as he deepened the kiss, her hands lowering to fondle him.

His hips lifted and he broke the kiss. She stilled, wondering if that might be one of his rules.

"I don't have to touch you," she said.

479

Gaze still turned away, he blinked as if working through an internal battle. "It's not that I dinnae want your hands on me, love."

"I know. When you're ready."

He frowned, appearing disappointed in himself.

"Really, Callan, it's fine."

Reluctantly, he nodded and rolled off of her, his head lowering to her chest as if she was his favorite pillow. "I'm not sure it's possible to cover scars enough that we forget they're there."

"What do you mean?"

"What ye said earlier about washin' away what came before."

"They were your words, the ones you read me from your journal."

He glanced at her, and she laughed at his surprise.

"Mine?"

"Yes. Couldn't you tell?"

He lowered his head back to her chest. "What a trite windbag I am, mutterin' on with such fanciful bullshite."

She shoved his shoulder. "Hey! I love your words. Hearing you read them the other day was like … looking into a poet's soul. I can hardly write a grocery list."

"Remind me not to share any more excerpts if you're gonna go rememberin' them and quotin' them for all the world te hear," he teased.

"Please."

His fingers drifted over the thatch of curls between her legs. "Please what?"

"Please share your writing with me again. I really love it."

He sighed and gently pulled her thighs apart. "I suppose I could. But only the best of my drivel and I'll ask that you not quote it back to anyone."

"Deal."

His finger sank into her sex, delving softly with shallow dips. Soon she was breathing fast, and he replaced his hand with his body. Like before, they clung to each other with an unmatched intensity.

By the time the sun started to set, and shadows stretched across the room, they admitted they were both going to be late for work. They shared a shower and dressed in front of each other with a novel comfort that still fit a little awkwardly, like a new pair of running shoes.

"You didn't get to spend any time with Uma today." She felt guilty for taking up so much of his free time now that she knew he had a little girl at home.

"Her days are spent with Elspeth. They have school."

"Is she in kindergarten?"

He nodded and helped her make the bed. "Home school."

"Oh. How come?" The local schools were fantastic in this area. Not a large population of homeschooled kids.

His eyes shifted away. He sat on the bed, presenting her with his back, as he laced up his black combat boots.

"Callan?"

"Aye?"

She frowned and rounded the bed. "If there's something you'd rather not discuss then say so. Don't just ignore me."

He dropped his leg and sighed. "Uma's taught at home because she's not registered with the schools. The house is under Elspeth's name. Everything is, but I own it."

"Why?"

"I told ye we aren't here legally and we cannae go back."

Her lips parted. "If you were caught, would they deport you back to Scotland?" Fear clutched her heart with sharp claws.

"Aye. But no one knows we're here. Matt pays me under the table, and cash tips are untraceable. We're very careful, love. No one's caught us yet."

She lowered to sit beside him on the edge of the bed, knowing they were already late. "Do you have legal custody of her?"

"She's my responsibility."

Her stare jumped to his face. "It doesn't work that way here. If they find you living here illegally and you have no proof she's yours—"

"Hush," he kissed her. "She's mine, love. They'll never get close enough to take her from me, nor would I let them go pokin' around in our DNA.

Elspeth understands how protective I am. I trust her to keep Uma safe."

But what sort of life was that for a child? Kids needed to play with other kids. "You said the men you used to associate with are gone."

His eyes hardened. "Aye."

"Then why not try to live a normal life? You could change your name if you think someone's still looking for you, become a citizen, and raise Uma here." She knew it was much more complicated, but it was still worth trying.

He stood. "This isnae a part of my life I need help figurin' out, Em'ry."

"When does she play with other kids, Callan?"

"She's not yer concern. And we're late." His temper snapped like a plucked fiddle string, cutting sharply through the air and knocking everything out of key.

"Okay." She'd overstepped, and now he was upset. She should have never pressed the issue.

"I'll wait for ye downstairs."

Left alone in her room, she stared at the empty doorway. The sudden void between them crushed the wind out of her. She wished she could take all her stupid questions back.

Her eyes prickled and she forced herself to stand, sliding her stocking covered feet into her black pumps. Head bowed, she stepped into the hall.

Callan's body collided with hers, and she gasped as his arms closed around her, his face pressing into the collar of her shirt.

"I'm sorry," he rasped. "I know ye mean well and I dinnae mean te snap at you."

Her hands fluttered to his back, and her eyes closed in relief. "I shouldn't have overstepped. The way you raise Uma is none of my business."

He shook his head. "I want it te be your business, Em'ry. My walls are down with you."

She sucked in a breath, emotion choking her. "My walls are down with you, too."

He nodded and traced his thumb over her lower lip. "Then we forgive each other."

She nodded. "I'm sorry."

He kissed her. Her fingers pulled at his shirt wanting to drag him back to bed. Reluctantly, they broke apart and made it to the car.

He might think his words were trite, but there was something to the things he said. And while they might not ever fully hide their scars, love had a way of washing the pain away.

Chapter Thirty-Six

Saratoga Springs, New York—America
Present day

In the weeks that followed, as the trial drew near, Callan continued to follow Wesley Blaine. Though he'd decided the second he saw Emery stumbling from the bathroom that ill-fated night he would see this through to the end with her, he now questioned if vengeance was for her or him.

She dinnae know his plans, and he had no intention of burdening her with them as the end crept closer. There was a strong chance her assailant's end would be his own.

Wesley Blaine was a beloved member of his community where his crimes were voluntarily ignored. Killing him would not be as easily overlooked as the murder of a lowly drug dealer or a flesh peddler or pedophile or even a kingpin.

His family had a powerful attorney, one that would make certain the outcome of his trial would not match the crime. But that's what boyfriends were for.

He'd see that vengeance got delivered in the end. He'd see that she found peace and her demons downed. But the Blaine family would not rest until their son's murderer was apprehended and punished.

Maybe he'd run. It had been his plan when he understood he might not have the option of simply drifting back into the shadows unnoticed. Everyone, including the polis, would be doing their very best to close the case of the murdered Boy Scout who only occasionally violated women between swim meets and feeding the poor. Not because they loved him, but because the world would be watching.

He had no stomach for the shite lies pumping out of the media about the bastard. He was a vile, Godless cunt who should have his bollocks chopped off and sewn to his face for the world to see. But the masses loved to debate the motive rather than review the facts in cases of rape. Probably because they couldnae face the truth of it, couldnae fathom the bottomless hurt that never went away.

As he refilled the drinks of a business party sidled around his bar, his glance drifted across the lobby to Emery. Her head was bowed over a yellow legal pad, her pen working hard to put together some letter her advocate suggested she write.

He'd offered to help her with it, but every time he brought it up, she tore the top page away and crumpled it in her hand, never letting him see what the letter said. He suspected she was putting so much work into it so it could double as her impact statement to the court, a vignette detailing her assault and the lingering repercussions with enough gut-wrenching truth and evocative prose to sway the judge in her favor when it came to sentencing.

Not exactly the self-healing process she needed to find satisfaction after the crime. For others like himself, writing could be a cathartic way of healing, but not for his Emery.

But Blaine had dozens of people singing his praises and proclaiming his infallible innocence, so it made sense that part of her wanted to fight back. How sad that paper and ink were the only weapons she thought she had.

He hated to see her struggle, hated that she kept reliving those horrendous moments in order to twist them into words that outsiders could never feel as precisely as she had.

Her pain should have ended that night. But he knew better. The bruises would heal, the skin would mend, but the interior hurt never fully went away.

He delivered the drinks to his patrons, his gaze once again seeking her out. She lifted her head and smiled, her fingers waving before blowing him a kiss.

Believing a woman could actually throw a kiss from such a distance ranked with the belief that a fairy collected Uma's missing teeth from under her pillow. Yet he felt Emery's love hit him square in the chest like a punch.

His palm rubbed over the mark, and he grinned. An ache of worry spread beneath the target and tightened his heart.

What would he do without her?

He never considered his life coming to this. Never actually believed he'd know her in an intimate way. But what he shared with her now went beyond his comprehension of love. It was deeper and sharper than anything he'd felt before.

Uma—his wee angel—would adapt to a life without him. She'd cry, but Elspeth would get her through. He'd set up several secret funds to ensure neither girls ever wanted for anything. One of the many benefits of robbing Scotland's most lucrative criminals before fleeing the country.

But leaving Emery... Who would she have? Would she ever forgive him? And if he wasn't dead, would he actually be able to keep away?

He stowed his worry for another time as she crossed the lobby, a secret smile tucked in the corner of her mouth as she rounded the bar.

"Looking for something?" he asked, as she hardly acknowledged him as she passed the patrons.

"I think I left my book in the back."

He frowned. She'd been reading her book an hour ago—at the reception desk.

He glanced at Peter who had his nose buried in another spy novel by the front door. His customers all had full glasses. Slipping into the back, he nearly crashed into Emery, waiting just around the corner on the other side of the wall.

She laughed and pulled him by the shirt, yanking him down for a kiss. He sank into her softness, smiling against her pillowy lips.

His hands burrowed under her blazer, finding the warm curve of her hips. Blood rushed to his cock, and he nudged his hips into hers and growled. "What did I tell ye about gettin' me fired up at work? Now, I'll have to go pour drinks with my cock standin' at full salute for the world to see."

She laughed, the witch. He was tempted to drag her deeper in the back, but that's not what this was. Work was more than their place of employment. It was the place of her nightmares, so they only ever kissed when in the hotel, nothing more.

Perhaps it was a distraction for her. Or maybe she just wanted to sneak a wee bit of closeness in. It dinnae matter. He liked that she'd recovered her confidence enough to speak her mind and ask for what she wanted. Her boldness with him was a welcome surprise.

"I have to get back."

"Witch," he hissed, reaching in his pants to try to hide the evidence.

She snickered. "Only a few more hours until closing."

And then two more waiting for her shift to end. His journal entries were turning rather pornographic of late.

She skipped away, but not before he grabbed a fistful of her arse and pulled a squeak from her. "You'll be payin' for that later."

"I'm counting on it," she called. As she looked over her shoulder, the world stilled.

The whisky brown of her eyes danced with teasing promise, the white corners glittering like the sea. Her laughter drifted through the air like falling dew, lighter than a snowflake and as impactful as a blizzard.

A wayward strand of fawn colored hair clung to her lips as she smiled in playful abandon. And his heart beat with frenzied haste as he subdued the urge to go after her.

His mind froze at the thought of abandoning her. How blissful it would be to simply exist in this tumultuous rapture with her, losing himself day after day in the marvelous allure of her body, the breathtaking palace of her mind.

His eyes glazed with carnal fire, a savage need to hold her close, hide her away and keep her all to himself. Standing as impassive as a statue, he nearly buckled under the weight of the world spinning back into its rapid orbit as her gaze pulled away.

Ripped from the spell she cast, he plunged back into cold reality.

Two business associates tried their luck in an unspoken competition to take their one female colleague to bed. The woman had stopped drinking hours ago, unknowingly to her male companions, as she'd subtly asked Callan to switch her over to club soda and lime.

As their voices grew louder and their manners more sloppy, the woman smiled shrewdly, a look of corporate poise flashing in her eyes and a devotion to her career keeping that false smile pressed to her lips.

The things women sometimes suffered to even the playing field... He dinnae care to see how far she'd let them drink themselves under the table.

Noting it was almost midnight, he passed by their glasses. "Last call. Can I get ye anything else?"

The men carried on, but Callan caught the look of relief in her eyes. He'd addressed situations like this with Matt, and while it wasnae the hotel's policy to impose on guest privacy, the hotel now had security cameras in every hall and outside of every bathroom and alcove.

He glanced across the hall and sighed. Unfortunately, Peter, the bibliophile was supposed to be watching the cameras.

When the group left, and the bar was empty, he dialed over to the front desk, alerting Peter to make sure the woman made it to her room safely.

When the bar was empty, and the tables cleaned, he settled in with a whisky and his journal. His gaze sought out Emery and the prose simply poured.

Chapter Thirty-Seven

Saratoga Springs, New York—America
Present day

Callan's mind stirred under the heavy haze of sleep as Uma's melodic voice chatted over her dolls. His body protested as he stretched, and the book he'd fallen asleep reading tumbled to the floor.

Damn, he'd slept in his library again. He needed to stop doing that.

He always drove down the country road after leaving Emery's at night, and last night the car hadn't been parked in front of the trailer that led to a ride past the local college. For a man set to be sentenced in a week, Wesley Blaine sure had an active social life.

He'd found him stumbling around a fraternity party, pawing his way through the crowd, which reeked of desperation and naivety. So many young, trusting girls looking for some sort of vindication they'd never find there. He stayed long enough to make sure Blaine dinnae put a hand on a single one.

By the time he got home, he'd been both wired and exhausted. If God had any mercy left for him, he'd see the man put away for at least a few years, giving Callan a break from his grueling post of trying to sever the inseparable nature from the beast.

Blaine seemed to be somewhat aware of his actions in light of the upcoming trial. Several times Callan saw the flash of entitlement in his eyes, but he never acted on the impulse. But it was in him to do it again and eventually, he would. As sure as Callan would kill again, Blaine would take.

"What do ye have there, my angel?"

Uma turned and flashed him a heart-melting grin. Her front teeth were slightly parted in a way that reminded him of her father. "A tea party. Want some?"

He stifled a groan as he forced his legs to the floor and sat up. "Ye know I cannae resist yer magical tea. I'll take it in my usual cup, please."

She gathered up her dollies and the wee kettle and plastic cups. Dropping her treasures on the carpet by his feet, she set up the saucers and cups again, pretending to carefully fill each one.

"Careful, it's very hot," she warned, handing him the wee pink cup and saucer.

He pinched the handle between two gnarled fingers and sipped gingerly, pretending to burn his lips. "Mmm, delicious."

She giggled, her green eyes dancing over the rim of her own cup. "How come ye slept down here again?"

"I fell asleep readin' a book."

"It must not 'ave been anythin' good then."

He chuckled. "Must not 'ave been."

She refilled their tea and fluffed the ruffles of her dolly's dress. He frowned, not recalling the name of that one, or seeing it before.

"And who is this?" He was used to having tea with Mr. Ruffington and Honeypot—the bears. They were married but going through some troubles, according to Uma.

"This is LeeLee."

"Oh. Pleased to meet you, LeeLee."

Uma lifted the doll to shake his hands, its eyes fluttered, and he frowned, noting the vintage porcelain face and somewhat ratty hair. It dinnae look new.

"Nice to meet ye, Uncle Callan," Uma said, speaking for the doll. Its clothing looked hand-made, different from anything they sold in American toy stores.

"Where did you say LeeLee came from?"

"The lady gave her to me."

"Which lady?" Elspeth sometimes took Uma to the market with her. Perhaps a woman at the store sold them the doll.

"The lady who visits me."

A cold chill settled in his veins. He gently hooked a finger under Uma's chin, drawing her gaze up to his. "What lady?"

Wide green eyes blinked up at him, wavering with uncertainty. "The one who sings to me?"

"Someone comes to the house?" He scowled and yelled, "Elspeth?"

"Uncle Callan, am I in trouble?"

"No. Where's Elsie?"

Uma's lip trembled. "She's makin' lunch. Do I have to give LeeLee back?"

He stood and went to the library door, shouting for Elspeth again. "No, angel. But ye need te tell me who gave ye the dolly. Did she have a name?"

"I dinnae ken her name. She just comes here every once in a while and plays with me."

"She comes to the house?"

With fidgeting impatience, he marched into the hall. "Elspeth, I need you in here. Now." Returning to Uma, he crouched low, putting himself on her eye level. "Listen to me, Uma. I need to know what the lady who gave you the dolly looked like. What color hair did she have? What color skin? Was she inside the house? When was she here? Who let her in?"

Her eyes widened as he overwhelmed her with questions. The bright green pupils swam behind a wall of tears as two large drops fell down her fair cheeks.

"Callan, what is it?"

He stood and took the doll from Uma, marching it to Elspeth. "Where did she get this?"

"LeeLee!" Uma cried.

Elspeth shook her head. "I've never seen it before a few days ago. I assumed you gave it to her."

"I dinnae give her this doll. She says a lady did. Has someone been to the house?" he shouted.

"No." Elspeth appeared genuinely shocked by this information.

Uma continued to cry, so he handed her back the doll, only slightly consoling her. Trying to control his temper, he dragged a hand through his hair.

"Is it possible she found it in the house? It looks like an antique."

He shook his head. He'd searched the house when they moved in. He would have found it and probably given it to her himself. And he believed Uma wouldnae lie to him.

"...Silver buckles at his knee. He'll come back and marry me, Bonny Bobby Shafto."

Callan turned to Uma who sang softly to the doll, his eyes unblinking and his head swimming with a disembodied sense of déjà vu. His heart thundered, and his blood ran cold. "Who taught her that rhyme?"

"I dinnae ken," Elspeth answered.

Uma looked up at him and smiled tremulously. "The lady taught me it."

"Jesus fuckin' Christ." He grabbed Uma off the floor and shoved her into Elspeth's arms. "Leave. Get her out of the house. Take your mobile and dinnae stop drivin' until I call you."

Elspeth's panicked stare widened. "What's the matter?"

"It's Innis. She's been here."

"What?" Her arms closed protectively around Uma.

"Just go. I'll search the house." He reached to the top of the hutch and pulled down a revolver, checking that the chamber was full. "Now!"

She raced out the door with Uma on her hip, and he watched as the car sped away, his thumb unlocking the safety on the gun as he crept silently through the hall. At the grandfather clock, he swiped his bowie knife hidden in the compartment with the clock face and held it at his hip.

"Innis?" His eyes scanned the empty den, his feet walking the perimeter and flicking the heavy drapes as he inspected the locks on each window.

"I dinnae want to hurt ye, love. Just come out, and we'll talk."

He moved slowly, his eyes alert. The library was empty, as was the dining room and parlor.

"I want to help ye, Innis."

Keeping his back to the wall, he worked his way up the stairs to the second floor. His socked foot pushed open the door to the first bedroom. He worked his way through all the rooms and closets and bathrooms, finding no window unlocked and no traces of her.

When he reached Uma's bedroom, the last place she could be, he prepared himself for anything. "We can talk about ye seeing Uma, but ye have to talk to me first." That was the agreement.

He angled his head, peeking under the bed, spotting only a few tumbles of dust and Honeypot the bear.

Keeping his breathing calm, he clutched the bowie knife in his teeth and reached for the closet doorknob. The second it clicked, he yanked it open.

He let out a breath and pulled the knife from his mouth. Pivoting, he faced the bedroom door. "Innis," he yelled. "Enough of this."

He'd told her not to come back unless she wanted help, told her Uma would be his first priority and she'd have to go through him first. This was not part of the plan.

Something caught his ear, and he stilled. A soft clatter from downstairs.

He raced out of the room, taking the steps two at a time and following the noise to the kitchen. His feet slipped over the polished floor, his legs kicking out from under him as he came crashing down on his hip and nearly stabbing himself as the gun flung out of his grip. He lunged to his feet and bolted toward the kitchen, swiping up his revolver from where it spun on the floor.

A clatter of pots and pans slammed like thunder, and he burst into the kitchen, catching a flash of motion behind the island. He cocked the gun.

"*Dinnae fuckin' move* or I'll put a bullet through yer fuckin' skull, ye crazy bitch."

The blood rushed from his lips as a pale-faced Emery rose from behind the counter, hands spread and shaking. The knife clattered to the ground, and he lowered the muzzle of the gun.

"What the hell…"

"The front door was open." Hands still in the air, she glanced at the groceries on the counter. "I was going to surprise you with breakfast in bed."

Her eyes welled with tears, and he cursed, stashing the gun on the counter and rushing around the island to gather her in his arms. She dinnae go easily, her body stiff and unyielding as he pressed his face into her shoulder.

"I'm sorry, love. I thought ye were someone else." How could he have left the door unlocked?

"Who?" she choked.

"It makes no difference." Jesus, he'd almost shot her.

She was trembling from head to toe. He pressed his lips to her pulse.

"Is that a real gun?"

He shut his eyes, wishing he could rewind his life. "Aye."

"You need to put it away before Uma finds it."

Sometimes her thought processes surprised him. "She's out with Elspeth." He needed to call her and let her know it was safe to come home. He reluctantly let Emery go and held out a staying hand. "Wait here."

He returned the weapons to their hiding spots, but grabbed a smaller knife on the way back, sheathing it and tucking it inside his jeans. Emery hadnae moved an inch.

He tried to act casual, rubbing his hands together and peeking in the brown paper bag on the counter. "What are we making for breakfast?"

She stared at him, eyes wide and unblinking. He gave up any hope of acting like this hadn't happened and sighed.

"I wouldnae have shot ye, Em'ry. I've never accidentally hurt someone."

She blinked. "But if I was the *crazy bitch* you were expecting?"

His gaze dropped to the carton of eggs. "I wouldnae have shot her either."

Her eyes narrowed. "Callan, why did you think a *crazy bitch* was in your house? Who is she?"

Was that jealousy he sensed in her voice? The sharp glare in her eyes held enough fire to wither a man's bollocks right off the stem.

He swallowed, knowing he had to tell her more unflattering truth. "My sister."

Her jaw unhinged and she gawked at him. "Your sister's dead."

"Not … truly. The Innis I grew up with is gone, but the woman she became is still very much alive and very much insane. And possibly lurking around the house."

Her head shook. "I don't understand."

His lips firmed. "I think she came to see Uma, possibly gave her a doll."

"But Uma rarely leaves… Oh, my God, you think she was in your house?"

He nodded, brows lifted. Now she was gettin' it. "Aye. Last I saw her, she was covered in blood and singing songs like a lunatic, starin' into space."

She gasped. "Can you call someone?"

"She's my responsibility. I'll find her. Or I willnae. But she cannae see Uma again without coming to me first. She should know I'd never allow that."

"Is Uma in danger? Should you guys come to my house—"

He caught her hand and smiled, appreciating her concern, but certain if Innis was around, she already figured out Emery and where she lived. "That willnae be necessary. But I'd like ye te stay here with us for a while. With the trial coming up, it might be a good idea te spend the nights together."

"What about Ernie?"

"Bring him. Uma would love it."

She blinked up at him, a strange look in her eyes he'd never seen before. "O—kay. But … this is just temporary, right?"

He stilled, now understanding the look. Would she be opposed to something more than temporary? Would he? It all depended on how much time they had before he had to take care of Blaine.

"Let's play it by ear."

She nodded. "How do you like your eggs?"

Chapter Thirty-Eight

Saratoga Springs, New York—America
Present day

She might be a little bit crazy. Callan pointed a gun at her, and five minutes later she agreed to temporarily move in with him. Her and her cat. Yeah, she definitely wasn't making sensible choices, but her gut told her this was right.

If his sister was unstable enough to freak him out to the point that he needed a gun and a big Crocodile Dundee knife, then Emery knew enough to be afraid. And when life got scary, she turned to Callan.

It didn't matter that he had weapons and a track record of killing bad guys. How was that any different than a celebrated veteran who made the world a little safer?

She trusted him. She trusted his moral compass and his conviction to protect those he loved. She counted herself lucky to be one of those people, which was why she'd packed a bag and her cat and spent the night.

She'd been excited to finally have a full sleepover with him, but it turned out Callan rarely slept. He followed her to bed, they fooled around, he read, and when she opened her eyes, he was gone.

She'd slipped downstairs to get a glass of water, thinking he might be in the library, but the house was dark and unfamiliar, so she quickly returned upstairs, never figuring out where he'd run off to.

"Where were you last night?" she asked, sliding a noodle onto a long thread of yarn.

"This one next," Uma said, handing her another macaroni for the necklace they were making.

Soft wind murmured through the trees where they sat, enjoying a hidden pocket of beauty on Callan's property. The sweet scent of smoke and burning twigs tinged the air.

"I couldnae sleep, and I dinnae want te wake ye with the light, so I went downstairs te read."

A golden riot of leaves spun up from the ground as a breeze burst through the garden, lifting the corners of the tartan blanket. Long strands of Uma's black hair elevated like silk cobwebs as she focused intently on stringing the macaroni necklace.

Emery fixed the blanket and returned her stare to Callan. "When I got up to get a glass of water you weren't in the library."

He sipped coffee from a vintage thermos, silently watching Uma thread the necklace. "Sometimes I walk the yard at night. Ye must have just missed me." His lashes hung low over his eyes—hiding something.

"Can I eat a noodle?"

Emery looked back at Uma. "Sure. It won't taste good."

She bit into the hard shell and crunched, her little face scrunching with disappointment.

Emery laughed. "How is it?"

"It tastes like shite!" She spat the hard, crushed noodle into the grass.

She never heard a little girl swear so much, but Callan and Elspeth never seemed to correct her, so she rarely commented.

"There." Emery tied a knot at the end of the string, closing the necklace. She slipped it over Uma's head. She admired the new jewelry, lifting the whistle dangling from the front.

Callan sat up and inspected the whistle, giving it a blow. "Now, when do you use it?"

"When I see the lady or a stranger at the house."

He brushed a hand over her head. "Very good, angel."

The whistle was only one change after Callan learned his sister had visited the house uninvited. New locks had been installed on all the windows and doors, and he'd stashed several hidden cameras around the property. Safety measures shouldn't make her feel less safe, but they sort of did because they made her more aware of danger.

"Are we done now?" Uma asked.

"One more thing." Callan lunged forward, tumbled her to the blanket, and she squealed as he lifted her shirt and blew raspberries on her belly.

Uma's laughter vibrated the open air, and Emery's face pulled with a smile. The way he played with his niece and adored her, protected her so completely, made her fall a hundred feet deeper in love with him.

"Do Em'ry!" Uma shouted.

Callan shot her a sidelong glance, and her heart skipped a beat. "No, no—*ah!*"

He tackled her to her back, and she laughed as he yanked up her shirt. Wet bubbles blew into her stomach, tickling and vibrating. She laughed and tried to squirm away, but he had her pinned, tucked safely in the lighthearted moment, captured in a way she never wanted to escape. Safe.

Uma's infectious laugh rose until she couldn't contain her joy and started to cough out of excitement.

"Uma!" Elspeth called from the house. "Time te come in for yer lesson."

They froze, and Uma pouted. "I have te go, now."

Callan held Emery's wrists at her side, and she panted, out of breath. "We can play some more after your lessons," she promised.

"Go on, now," Callan pushed, and Uma obediently ran off. He glanced down at her, and something shifted in his gaze. "You're twice as beautiful when you're tousled." His hips rocked suggestively.

"We're out in the open."

"No one can see us. Uma's classroom's on the other side of the house." He dropped his head, catching the hem of her shirt between his lips and lifting it over her breasts. "I want you."

Her breathing shifted, a hungry ache forming at her core. It only took one look from him, and she was on fire.

His mouth closed over the lace of her bra, a wet mark seeping through the thin material to her puckering skin. "Callan."

"Hush. Let me have you."

She tried to relax, knowing anyone could catch them. She shut her eyes, giving over to the pleasure as his body shifted over hers and his familiar weight anchored her to the ground.

His arousal pressed into her, and she lifted her hips, craving the friction. He moved her arms over her head and pressed them into the blanket, an unspoken warning for her to stay like that.

Sliding the cups of her bra down, the material cradled her breasts, and he suckled and bit, teasing the tips in a way that drove her wild. By the time he pressed his fingers into the front of her pants, she was sopping wet.

He groaned, sliding a finger through the soft seam of her sex. "You're always so warm here."

She moaned, lifting her hips and opening for him to press deeper. He teased and rubbed, and soon her cries bullied the wind. She shattered, right there on a blanket in the middle of his yard.

He had her pants off before her brain caught on. "Callan! We can't."

"I need you." His hips pressed between her thighs and while he appeared fully dressed, her legs were bare. He nudged her tender folds, sliding the broad tip in and teasing her.

Her head fell back, too much temptation to care about the consequences. "Hurry," she begged.

He thrust and filled her. Her nails dug through his shirt, pressing into the solid muscle of his back. He pulled out, nearly leaving her, and jabbed forward again.

Sometimes he took her with aching tenderness. Other times he hardly took at all, lavishing attention on her body in ways she innately knew men didn't typically do. And then there were times like this, times when he took nothing but gave her everything. It was as if he wanted—no *needed*—to get so deep inside of her she'd never get him out.

He gripped her shoulders, pulling her into his thrusts. He didn't kiss her or look at her, but he held her in an unbreakable grip. Intense need rolled off of him like waves of thunder, rumbling to her core.

His hips slammed forward, harder and deeper. She'd be tender after, maybe even bruised, but his desperate possession awakened something inside of her she needed to face. This was Callan, and she wanted to experience the true him.

Gentle, savage, brave, shy, thoughtful, and sometimes harsh. She wanted every ounce of him—and craved belonging to him.

Callan's prior life existed before them. Whatever went into that recipe had come before she knew him. His crimes were from a prior life, separate from the one they shared now and irrelevant to how deeply she loved him.

With one final thrust, he filled her and trembled. His breath rushed to her ear as he buried his face in her hair and held her to him.

"My Emery."

Her heart swelled with a sense of belonging, her softer sides molding perfectly to all his jagged edges until they were one. "My Callan," she whispered, dragging a loving hand down the back of his head.

She shivered as he pulled out, wishing they could stay like that forever. He closed his jeans and tossed her pants over his shoulder.

"What are you doing? I need them back."

"Let me take care of my woman." He folded the blanket over her legs and gathered her in his arms, carrying her toward the house. His strength never stopped surprising her. Even with his scarred legs, he had enough hardheaded determination to make up for any muscle mass he'd lost.

He carried her through the quiet house, Elspeth and Uma's voice a distant vibration through the walls. When he put her back on her feet, they were in the master bath.

Water rushed from the modernized showerhead, and he stripped off her shirt and bra, then removed his own clothes. Pulling her under the spray, he washed her with attentive affection. Suds danced over her skin, and she watched his mesmerizing hands caress her.

She turned to face him, looping her arms around his neck. "I love you."

He looked at her, his words unnecessary as raw adoration poured from his stare. He tucked a wet strand behind her ear and kissed her with desperate abandon.

He took her again, against the tile wall before leaving the shower. Her body was deliciously sore and her mind wrapped in gauzy softness.

"Now, I want a nap." She rolled over his large bed, loving the scent of his skin on the sheets.

"So take one. We have hours until work." He climbed in behind her, enhancing the tempting comfort of the bed as he tugged her into his body and held her tight. "Aye. A nap sounds perfect."

Just as she started to doze off, her phone vibrated. She groaned, and Callan mumbled something that sounded like ignore it. She did, but then the phone beeped, alerting her of a voicemail.

She had to testify in four days, and that voicemail gnawed at her. What if it was Harold Wong, her advocate, with a change of plans? She'd written the letter he'd requested, knowing it wasn't as poignant as he would have liked, but it was the best she could do.

Harold suggested she write something up because victims usually found the task cathartic. But his mention of so many *others* only made her feel like nothing more than a drop in an overflowing bucket.

It wasn't cathartic. Not for her. And now, the implication that it should have helped, made her feel like she wasn't appropriately filling the role of victim. Just another tick in the defective column of her life.

But she was the victim, and that letter made her feel like *she* was the one on trial. Harold had mentioned something that—if they went to trial—her letter could also double as an impact statement for the judge during sentencing.

Her lack of confidence in her persuasive writing skills should play no part in the conviction of her assailant. Others might feel validation, as if given a voice, but she wasn't a writer, and the weight of the pen crippled her.

Why should she have to convince the world that sexual assault was an unthinkable, damaging crime? Wesley Blaine did horrible, horrifying things to her and he should rot in a prison cell until she no longer thought about it, until she no longer flinched when a man shared her aisle at the grocery store, or panicked at a traffic light, or woke up in a cold sweat.

A judge, or anyone else, shouldn't need a statement from an already victimized victim on top of all the other reports to measure out a fair sentence. How was this even a common practice?

She knew why. Things like "impact statements" came from centuries of victims fighting for justice without being fairly protected. They were a way for sexually assaulted women, men, and children to be heard. Yet, the longer this nightmare went on, the more she felt ignored.

From beginning to end, this experience had gutted and gored her, objectified her, and withered her down to a statistic. She was no longer Emery Tanner. She was victim number four-hundred-*thousand*-X-Y-whatever of the year.

Her stomach hollowed. Four-hundred-thousand...

Feeling sick, she needed to check her phone. She climbed out of bed. As anticipated, it was her advocate. She pushed the command to listen to his message and brought the phone to her ear.

"Emery, it's Harold Wong. I have some news. Blaine's lawyer is now open to discuss a plea bargain, but we can't move forward without your consent. I'm going to be completely honest. With your willingness to testify and worries about the cross-examination, it might not be a bad angle to take. With the police report and medical records, there's enough evidence to assure he serves *some* time. We can offer your letter to the judge, as well.

"The defense will want the rape charges dropped first, but you'd still get him for assault and the other charges. Their motive's going to be saving Blaine from future public shaming. Under the penal code, if he's convicted of a sexual offense, he'd go on the registered sex offender list for life. That's what his lawyer will want to avoid. That, and a lengthy sentencing.

"Give me a call as soon as you can. I'm at the office until four. But think about it. Admission of guilt takes a lot of the guesswork out of the equation."

The message ended, and she lowered the phone, blinking and not seeing anything in front of her.

How did someone claim innocence but entertain the idea of a plea bargain? Didn't that automatically prove their guilt?

"Who was that?" Callan asked, still lying on the bed behind her.

She didn't turn around. "Harold Wong. They want to negotiate a plea bargain."

He was supposed to be her advocate. She felt like an infant tossed into a pool expected to instinctively swim. She felt like she was drowning in front of a frozen audience.

Callan's silence made her turn. He'd heard her, and by the hard glare in his crystal blue eyes, he appeared displeased.

"What should I do?"

"What do ye want to do?"

She wanted to live a normal life. She wanted to stop feeling afraid. She wanted to feel connected to her body again—*all the time* not just sometimes. She wanted to make this go away, undo everything that happened. She wanted Wesley Blaine to know what he did was wrong and unacceptable and make it so he could never do it again—to anyone.

"I want it to be over."

"What does yer advocate suggest?" His voice remained soft and unobtrusive as if spoken from behind a mask of calm the way he always spoke whenever she verged on a meltdown.

"He says this is a fast angle that will guarantee an outcome in our favor—to *some* degree." But not all.

All signs pointed to her total destruction and only a partial repercussion. She felt increasingly devalued when she foolishly assumed her self-deprecating feelings couldn't drop lower than they'd already plunged.

Her chest burned with acid as it fluxed into her throat. "They want to keep him off the predator list." She knew what *Megan's Law* was, a public list of registered sex offenders. But she never checked it.

How irresponsible of her to have a security measure at her disposal, but not the instinct to see who lived on her street. And what if there was a blue dot or whatever they used to mark sexual offenders? She couldn't afford a therapist, let alone a new house.

This was what he worried about? Being on a list that most of the world never read. This was his so-called *public shame*?

Her hand tightened around her phone. He knew nothing about shame.

He didn't know what it was like to worry that her boyfriend might enter her from behind and trigger a waterfall of terror. He didn't know how it felt to face everyone she worked with and have them look at her with pity, envisioning her having sex in the vilest manner possible. He didn't know what it was like to fall into the arms of the man she loved wearing torn clothes, vomit in her hair, blood on her skin, and a monster's semen dripping down her burning thighs.

He didn't know a fucking thing about shame.

"I should have had you help me with the letter," she whispered, heart heavy with regret. "You're a good writer. You could have helped me make it stronger."

His hand pressed into her back, stroking with silent support. "I'm sure what ye wrote was fine, Em'ry."

She shook her head. "It's not enough. I told the police what happened. They saw me. The doctors, the nurses, the psychologist at the clinic... They all saw what he did to me. Then I had to write it out because emotion doesn't show on x-rays. It's bad enough I have to keep reliving it in my head, but they wanted me to write it down, come up with the right word to describe what it feels like to have a stranger shove his way inside of you. *Well, there isn't a word for that!*"

A sob jerked out of her, and his arms closed around her, his lips pressing to her hair as he whispered, "I know, love. Dinnae beat yourself up. You did everything right. It's the system that's wrong, not you."

It didn't matter what they negotiated, or if they turned down the plea and went to trial. She was already defeated. She lost the day she walked into that bathroom—maybe the day she was born female.

"Do you know that only thirty percent of sexual assault cases are reported?"

"I'd heard something like that."

The heel of her palm crushed her lashes as she angrily wiped away her tears. "And did you know that out of every one thousand rapes less than five rapists are actually incarcerated. Less. Than. Five." She sniffed. "They're *rapists*."

He didn't reply, and she appreciated his silence. Any comment would have cheapened the truth. The statistics didn't lie. The criminal justice system was failing, not just her, but hundreds of thousands every year.

She swallowed, her shoulders sagging under the immense expectation that she continue to rise after being so emotionally and physically beaten down.

"One in four," she whispered, her head shaking as defeat weighed on her shoulders. She was just another number.

"One in four?"

"That's how many girls are sexually assaulted before they even reach eighteen. And one out of every five women will get raped in their lifetime." She choked on an unamused laugh, the sound raw and disgusted, devoid of any humor or hope. "We're like those little paper dolls, a line of statistics too chopped apart to function and too fragile from the start. Scraps. That's how they treat us when we're torn apart. We're just scraps that need to get swept under the rug and out of sight before the truth of our hurt gets noticed, and others realize how prevalent and systemic and absolutely fucked up this world is. Before they realize they could be next."

"He will get what's comin' te him, Em'ry."

She wanted to believe the hard rumble of his voice might somehow provoke an unbreakable promise, but these were the facts. Wesley Blaine would get a slap on the wrist compared to the life long sentence assigned to her.

Voice detached, she blinked through a fresh wall of tears. "There's always some equivocal punishment, but never an equal one."

She called Harold Wong and told him to tell them to negotiate a plea, do whatever he thought was best. She was done fighting a battle she'd never win. Tapped out, she had to ring the emotional bell.

Then she called out of work and changed into softer clothes and climbed back into Callan's bed. Since the beginning, she'd tried not to wallow in self-pity. Yes, it sometimes got ahead of her, but she always forced herself to keep moving.

She was sick of forcing herself. Sick of trying to appear strong when everything inside of her felt weak and horribly flimsy. She wanted to be brittle and hard, so she could break rather than tear, but no matter what hit her next, she knew she'd have to just take it and keep moving.

The system was set to fail as easily as the poor weapons meant to arm little girls. Nothing more than fragile, little words. Two tiny letters. *No.* What a joke.

No, thank you.

No, not interested.
No more…
I said no.
No.
No!
No…

No, she didn't want to do this anymore. But no one listened.

Purple stained the sky outside of Callan's window next time she opened her eyes. She heard him whispering, on the phone with someone.

"I'll be in tomorrow night."

He bent over a trunk in the corner of the room. She shut her eyes, forcing down the cold dread of what tomorrow would bring.

This was her fight? A bargaining chip for a partial win? Even her rage was too browbeaten to rouse much of a response. Her pulse thrummed like a slow faucet drip. She just couldn't care anymore.

"Love?" A feather-light touch drifted over her forehead. "Ye should eat somethin'."

She groaned and frowned. "Not hungry."

"You've slept all day, and havenae had anything since early this mornin'."

She blinked, surprised to find the bedroom doused in shadows, the black windows devoid of stars. Ernie slept soundly, curled into her side. "Why aren't you at work?"

"I called out. Dinnae feel like goin'."

Translation, he didn't want to leave her alone. "You should have gone. I just want to sleep."

"Can I make ye tea?"

She hated that he worried, but also loved it. At least *he* cared.

Guilt that her pathetic wallowing might somehow be punishing him had her agreeing. "Sure. Tea would be great."

He silently left, and she fell back to sleep before he returned.

"Em'ry, I have your tea."

"Just put it on the table," she mumbled without opening her eyes.

He sighed and set it down. Warm lips pressed to her forehead and the mattress compressed. He lay next to her, his concern rolling over her like an inescapable fog, blanketing her until it filled every crevice.

"It'll be all right, love. I promise it'll be all right."

Chapter Thirty-Nine

Saratoga Springs, New York—America
Present day

A loud crash awoke Emery, and she sat up with a start. It took her a moment to recall where she was and how long she'd been sleeping.

"Callan?"

Light flashed outside of the window, and a boom of thunder startled Ernie. Shivers chased up her spine. She pulled at the collar of her loose sweatshirt, covering her exposed shoulder.

Where was he?

She slipped out of bed, her bare toes pressing into the worn wood floor and her feet flattening against the cold planks. Her hands chafed up her arms as she squinted into the shadows illuminated again by the lightning.

Rain pummeled the slate roof, overtaking the silence in a steady, unfamiliar clatter. She had to pee, and she was incredibly thirsty. Spotting the cold tea on the table, she took a sip, just to wet her mouth.

"Callan?" Nothing.

She used the bathroom and slipped into her wool-lined boots, if only to have something on her feet. The floor creaked as she navigated the dark hallway. Elspeth's door was closed, and Uma's was cracked.

She peeked inside, a blooming warmth spreading through her chest at the sight of her pale, cherub cheeks and tumbling black curls. Her little foot poked out of the blankets, so Emery crept in and carefully covered it.

Her fingers brushed over her curls, and she smiled. "Sweet angel," she whispered, lightly pressing a kiss to her cheek.

Something creaked, and she flinched, turning toward the closet, but nothing was there. Just some hanging princess gowns and a pair of dilapidated fairy wings.

Finding her way into the kitchen, she poured a glass of water, sipping it silently as she stared out the window at the rain. The garden beds close to the house flooded with water and the rushing gutter spouts dumped into them with relentless overflow. No way Callan would be out walking in this.

She placed her glass in the sink and went to find him. The downstairs was empty, including the library.

She frowned, wondering where he could be. Her head tipped as she stared at the front door. She walked slowly through the foyer, staring out the glass through the rain. Her car and the blue Toyota were there, but Callan's car was missing.

She touched her hip, reaching for her phone, but she must have left it upstairs. Where would he have gone at this time of night in this weather? What was open?

The grandfather clock in the hall proclaimed it was four thirty in the morning. She stared at the face, noting the way the minute hand clicked but didn't move as if stuck on something.

The glass front of the clock had a tiny brass key. She turned it and the frame opened with a soft whine. She lifted her arm and felt around, something smooth and cold meeting her fingers.

Her hand closed around a rounded edge, and she pulled, freeing the captive minute hand. A knife. A big one. The kind she'd seen Callan carrying only days ago.

She put it back and went upstairs to get her phone. But when she made it to the room, she didn't call him. She sat on the bed and stared at the trunk in the corner.

Leaving the phone on the bed, she crossed the room and kneeled in front of the chest, watching her fingers pop the clamps and lift the heavy lid open.

She frowned and lifted the sheets of colorful paper, paging through them.

"The Royal Bank of Scotland," she read, realizing they were money.

Some had the euro symbol, which she recognized. There were thousands of them. And most of them emblazoned with the number one hundred.

She shuffled around the piles, digging to the bottom of the case and her hand stilled when she spotted one of his journals resting beneath a scary knife with a wicked curved blade.

She tipped the book, knocking the knife into the pile of money without touching it and sat back on her heels. Her gaze darted to the door, and she bit her lip.

With a twisting knot in her stomach, she unraveled the leather cord wrapped around the book and opened it to a random page.

I started with his tongue, breaking his jaw as easily as Christ broke bread. He gurgled, choking on my blade as I sliced through the muscle. His screams turned inside out, swallowed by the inability to speak, choking on blood and terror. Gagging. Voice stolen, just like hers.

Next I took his teeth, kneeling over him and yanking hard with the pliers I stole from the shed. His eyes begged, but I only saw Innis, the way her withered pride collapsed after Smithy had finished with her. I had no mercy in me.

I left him alive as I peeled back his fingernails, reminding him all the while that he'd never lay a hand on her again. When he passed out from the pain, I stabbed him in the chest, twisting my blade, but he was done.

I cut him into pieces, giving his favorite parts to Rory's dogs and burying the rest of him deep in the woods. His teeth I dropped in the river and his fingers I burned.

Innis never knew what happened to him, but

I can see, when I look in her eye, that she trusts he'll never bother her again. I made sure of it. And she knows I did so, in a way that will never be undone.

The book fell from her trembling hands and her gaze shot to the empty bed. Her pulse thumped with unsteady guesses, rattling with Poe-like echoes as haunting as the tell-tale heart. Building, until the thrumming was all she could hear.

Her brain throbbed. Her knees pressed into the hardwood floor. Awareness closed around her like a cold blanket sewn of ice.

She threw the book back in the chest and slammed it shut, her feet racing down the hall as a panicked wind seemed to rush her along. Her feet barely touched the steps as her hand burned down the banister, her arm nearly pulling from the socket as she cut the turn close at the last step and ran into the library.

The clean surface of his desk sang of guilty intention. Items were turned with precision, not a single thing out of place. She yanked open the top drawer and found another journal, this one only partially full.

The pages fluttered as she sought the last entry, her breath rushing from her lungs in chopping terror. Spotting blank pages, she dropped the leather book to the desk and paged backward, her fingers trembling.

Today's date. Her cold fingertip rushed under his beautifully scrolled words, her eyes unblinking as she only read every other word. *Tonight. Vengeance. Emery. Love. Peace. Avenge. Monster. Wesley.*

Panting, she eyed the window, her frantic stare lost in the rain. Callan was going to kill him. He was going to go to jail because of her. She was going to lose him.

She tore through the pages of the journal, flipping backward, searching for any sign of an address. She knew Blaine was required to stay nearby for the trial but had no idea where, only that he was required to keep his distance from her.

She gasped, spotting the name of a road, her mind doing a rough sketch of where she thought it was.

Ripping the page from the book, she grabbed her car keys and rushed out the door. The laden skies poured over the earth, leaving the ground soggy and drenched in splattering puddles. By the time she got behind the wheel, she was soaked and chilled to the bone.

She shivered, turning over the engine and spraying mud as she backed away from the house. Her body jostled as she plowed the back end of her car into the lawn. Her tires burned over the soft ground, humming with effort until enough friction set them free.

The lines of the road were hardly visible under the heavy onslaught of rain. She sped over a flat sheet of water, her car hydroplaning several times on the way to that country road.

She didn't think beyond getting to Callan. He couldn't do this. She couldn't let him sacrifice his life for hers. He had Uma to think about.

She screamed as the wheels spun through a puddle, sliding her nearly off the road. Her hands tightened, and she panted, body huddled close to the wheel as she squinted through the windshield.

The heavy, rapid beating of the wipers couldn't keep up with her heart. The drive took years and yet she registered none of it aside from her terror.

She bounced in her seat, slamming to a stop when she spotted Callan's car parked behind some trees. Squinting through the foggy glass, she saw the silhouette of a building up ahead. Small and narrow. No lights.

Where was Callan?

She jerked open the door, her foot sinking into a puddle and saturating the wool interior of her boot, but not slowing her. Rain doused her hair, its incessant pattering making it impossible to hear.

She ran as fast as she could, sloshing over the wet ground and slamming her body into Callan's car door. When she yanked it open, it was empty.

"Fuck!" She turned to the house, horrific doubt crushing her lungs.

What if she was too late? What if he wasn't in there, but Wesley was?

LYDIA MICHAELS

A paralyzing fear that she was there all alone had her back pressing into Callan's car and her body sliding closer to the ground. All she could see was the house. A small mobile home. No sign of Callan anywhere.

She had to find him. Her palms flattened over the metal exterior, slipping like wet hands glide over Formica.

She was back in the bathroom. Her screams all she could hear as he shoved inside of her.

Her eyes squeezed shut, and she shook her head violently, once again staring into the rain. She forced her legs to straighten.

She looked in Callan's car again, searching for some kind of weapon but finding none. Was this his car? It smelled of smoke, and a crumpled pack of cigarettes sat in the cup holder, but everything else was exactly as it should be. Did he smoke?

She didn't even have her phone to use for a flashlight. Her brain worked on some alternate track she never used.

She grabbed an ice scraper from behind the driver seat and crossed the road, creeping in the shadow, closer to the house.

Lightning lit the sky, and she froze like a burglar caught under a spotlight. She raced to a nearby tree, praying it didn't get struck by a bolt.

A sharp crack ripped a startled cry from her throat, and the sky webbed with white light, breaking like a teacup against the hidden stars. Something caught her eye—a shadow, moving on the porch.

She squinted through the curtain of rain. Fought back the propelling impulse to run back to her car and hide. Her feet sank into the soggy ground as she panicked, unsure what to do.

She couldn't move. Paralyzed by fear, she could only watch the shadows, waiting for another bolt of lightning to give her a clue.

Her drenched, frozen arms shook violently as she clutched the plastic ice scraper in both hands, holding it out blindly in front of her chest, shaking like a leaf. Her hair clung to her face and her back pressed into the hard bark of the tree.

Thunder rumbled, the storm moving away. She counted in her head, remembering something about the distance of a storm being measured by the space between thunder and lightning.

She blinked rapidly, so she wouldn't blink when it happened. Her eyes widened against the rain, and she focused on the porch. Then it came, another flash of white light illuminating the empty fields and highlighting the tiny trailer, and she recognized Callan's familiar build. But then it was gone like a mirage in a dessert.

She needed to stop him. "Callan!" She ran, her feet carrying her as her voice screamed through the rain.

Her feet plunged over the swampy ground as her arms pumped at her sides, the ice scraper in a death grip. But when she reached the trailer, fear slowed her steps. She raced around the side, looking for Callan, and finding nothing but an empty rocking chair swaying in the wind.

A hand slapped over her mouth, and she screamed. Wesley's hard arms held hers down, lifting her wet feet off the ground in a pinwheel of kicks. His hold so tight against her face she couldn't let out her breath and her cheeks inflated with the pressure of her terrified scream. Her stifled, useless scream.

Chapter Forty

Saratoga Springs, New York—America
Present day

Callan shook Emery with bone-rattling force, trying to penetrate her panic. *"Stop screaming,"* he hissed, jerking her off her feet and away from the house. "It's me, Em'ry. I have you."

Her body quaked violently, soaked through, and her hot breath pressed hard against his fingers covering her mouth. He dragged her into the trees and shook her again.

"Hush, love. Take a breath."

Her head and neck quaked with a spasm of terror, and she silenced.

"Dinnae scream, Em'ry." He slowly unclenched her fingers, the shallow pants of her breath jerking into the air with wee puffs of vapor. He set her on her feet and turned her around, scowling hard in her panicked face. "What the bloody fuck are ye doin' here?"

Her brow pinched as she stared up at him. "Don't kill him."

His jaw locked, his nostrils flaring with menace. He grabbed her hand and jerked her behind him, not slowing his steps as he marched her to his car. He opened the passenger side and shoved her in, slamming the door.

He got behind the wheel and ignored her shivering, backing up the dark road without the help of his headlights in the rain, and gripping the wheel so hard he was surprised he didn't bend it.

Once off the country road, he parked behind a copse of trees. Half a mile down was an abandoned gas station. "Lock the doors, and dinnae fuckin' get out of this car."

"Where are you going?" she shouted as he opened the door.

"I'm going to move your car. Where are the keys?"

She looked down and back at him. "I left them in there."

"Dinnae fuckin' move." He slammed the door and ran back to the house.

His clothes were drenched, his muscles pulsing, and his heart a violent battle sound. What the hell was she thinking, coming here? He'd had enough of the women in his life thinkin' they knew better than him.

He climbed into her car, yanking the seat back and his eyes caught on the torn piece of paper sitting on the passenger seat. He stilled, recognizing his handwriting.

His wet hands lifted the paper, the familiar thickness belonging to his journals. She'd stolen this from him, violated his privacy and nearly gotten herself killed trying to interfere in his plans.

His fingers crumpled the paper, the ink bleeding onto his wet fingers as he backed the car up and sped to the gas station. He parked behind the building and used the walk back to try to calm his temper. It wasnae working.

Wrath boiled under his surface. The rain slowed to a quieter downpour, but a storm still raged on his insides. His long steps crossed the muddied shoulder with frenzied fury as the black sky softened to a deep amethyst.

It was too late. Dawn was coming, and by the time he got her out of here, his opportunity to end Blaine would be gone. How could she take this away from him? Away from her? This was his last chance to avenge her before the courts intervened.

He pounded a fist on the window, saw a flash of movement and heard the snick of the loosening lock. He yanked it open and dinnae spare her a word or a glance, afraid of what he might say if he spoke.

She dinnae speak either. But he could hear her shivering and her teeth chattering between the swiping blades of the wipers, so he turned up the heat and pointed the vents at her.

His molars locked. The weapons strapped to his body pressed into him, their cold metal mocking him for the dim-witted sod he'd become. He could have handled this for her had she not interfered. He needed to do this thing for her and couldnae ignore the thought of another monster on the loose.

"Ye had no right to come here tonight!" he spat, not preparing his argument with anything more than rage.

"You were going to kill him!"

"So what? He deserves to die! Do ye think I have any sympathy for that Godless cunt? I'd enjoy makin' him scream."

Her body turned, her back to the door as he drove through the wet vacant streets of Saratoga Springs, its quaint, still life charm at complete odds with the situation.

"And what about when you get caught? What then, Callan? What would happen to Uma? Your house? Your life? What would happen to us?"

Her voice broke in a way he dinnae want to hear right now, so he sneered at her. "I wouldnae get caught. I know what I'm doin'."

"Like you knew with Smithy?"

Ice twisted in his veins and he nearly swerved off the road. "Where did ye learn that name?" he asked with menacing calm.

"It doesn't matter. I know he did something terrible to your sister and you cut him up and fed him to dogs."

A quelling silence enveloped him. This was it then, the way it would end. She finally saw the monster he was.

"I'll not apologize for doin' what needed to be done." He kept his eyes on the road ahead, his speed dropping back as if he could somehow hold her in his life a little longer. "Ye violated my privacy, trespassed in my personal things. Serves ye right for findin' somethin' ye dinnae want to see."

"This is where you went the other night. You were stalking him, planning this all along."

"He *raped* you!" he roared, the curling menace of the rolling word penetrating the safety of the car. "I'll not apologize for defendin' your honor and seeing vengeance served." His breath labored as his muscles tightened. "I learned long ago, there's no justice in this world for the meek. We must protect ourselves, protect what's ours. You're my woman, and that filthy scunner put his hands on you—"

"And this is protecting me?" she shrilled. "This isn't the underbelly of Scotland, and that vigilante shit doesn't fly here! If you touch him, they'll catch you. They'll put you in jail or deport you. I'd be left all alone and—" Her small fist slammed into his arm with a soft swat, and he flinched. "You swore you wouldn't leave me," she sobbed.

He debated pulling over but wanted to get her home. "At least you'd be safe from him."

"He's one person, Callan, and once he's sentenced, he'll never come back here again."

He scoffed. "Sentenced. He'll be out in less than four years. I know his type. You aren't his last victim."

"Killing him doesn't nullify my chance of getting hurt again. I need *you*."

Her words hung like the echo of a gong, and neither of them spoke for the next mile. His temper cooled, but he knew he'd go back. He'd see to her and get her car out of there, then he'd figure out a way to get to him before they took him into custody for some flimsy retreat they called a sentence.

When he pulled up at the house, he shut his eyes and waited for her to get out of the car. She dinnae move. "Go inside."

"No."

"Em'ry," he snapped. "I'm this close to losin' the fine hold I've left on my temper. Get your arse inside the house. Now."

"Where are you going?"

"I have to go get yer car." It would take him hours to move it and jog back to his car then move hers a little more. But he refused to let her get anywhere near that road again.

"I'm not leaving you."

His fist slammed into the steering wheel, and he practically kicked his way out of the car, snarling vicious profanities as he rounded the vehicle.

Snatching her door open, he grabbed for her, and she hit him, harmless little swats flicking at his damp sleeves as he hoisted her over his shoulder and landed a firm hand on her arse. *"Enough!"*

She punched his back and then sagged, accepting he had her beat. He pushed into the silent house and hauled her upstairs, dumping her like a wet kitten onto the bed.

"Now, stay there until I get back." He turned and paused. "And change into some dry clothes before you catch yer death."

She bolted off the bed and scrambled to the door, throwing her back into the wood and blocking his exit. "I'm not letting you go back there, Callan."

His eyes lit with fury. "Dinnae piss me off more than I already am!"

"Why?" she challenged, pointing her chin up at him. "I know you won't hurt me. The most you'll do is yell at me, because you're a *good man*, Callan."

"Ye dinnae ken the kind of man I am."

"I do. I know that you love that little girl down the hall so much it scares you. You think you'll lose her because you associate love with loss. I know you're still not over Gavin and no matter how terrible Innis has become, you'd still fight to the death for her if she needed you. I know that man hurt you, and the only reason you let him was to protect those you love."

Her eyes shimmered as she stared up at him, her body trembling as her wet clothes clung to her skin.

"And I know you love me. You think if you kill Wesley, the hurt will go away, but deep down you know nothing can erase it." Her fist closed, pressing against her heaving chest. "It'll always be a part of me, like it'll always be a part of you. A life sentence we just have to live with. But Callan, I can live with it. I swear I can. But I can't live without you."

He stared at her, his voice buried under years of grief, his heart shaking with the weight of the bitter truth.

"They'll let him walk, Em'ry. Maybe he'll serve a year or two, but he'll walk away from this long before ye." His heart broke. "How is that justice? After what he did to ye…"

"I can't let you walk out this door, Callan," she whispered. "I can't risk losing you. Not … to him. Not when he already stole so much from me."

A crushing pain exploded in his chest, and he stumbled back, his hand rubbing with slow swirls over the ache. "I dinnae ken how to bear it," he rasped, his lashes thickening as his vision wavered. "I see ye cry, and it breaks me so severely I feel ripped in two. I can stand a dozen men beatin' me into the ground, but I cannae seem to survive your sufferin'. I cannae sit idly by and watch him walk away. The only control I've ever had, I've had to fight for. Let me fight this for you, the way I know how."

"No." Her voice wavered, but her glare hardened as she stared at him through glassy eyes.

He threw his hands in the air. "Yer makin' me fight you, and tha' is the last thing I want."

Her head shook, and her lips pressed tight. "Then don't. We can just walk away. I don't care about him, Callan. I care about you—about us."

His brow pinched as frustration burned across the ache in his chest. "Knowin' he hurt you… It stirs a sorrow deeper than anything I've ever known, a crushin' hurt in me I dinnae ken if I've the strength to survive. I just…" He blinked at her through a wall of wavering tears. "I love ye so much it hurts, Em'ry."

"I love you too. And your pain hurts me too, Callan. I wish I could take it away, but I can't. And you killing him will only make matters worse."

His hands fisted at his sides, his head bowing between his shoulders. "All my life, people treated me like a weapon. My da used to beat it out of me before I even knew it was in me. Then they paid me to beat bigger men. And then… I became part of *his* collection, the only good I ever served was in punishin' others."

"That's not true."

"Aye, it is." He shoved up his wet sleeve, baring the marks of his kills for her to see. "I slaughtered all of them. Every last one. And I itch to make his mark here."

"No."

He met her stare, seeing the relentless determination in her eyes as she pressed her back into the door, flattening her palms to the surface and refusing to move out of his way.

"We will not let the evil define us, Callan. We're better than that. Stronger. And we have to let it go. We have to accept what happened and rise from the ashes." Her shirt clung to her curves, drips of rain dropping to the floor. "You're not that person anymore."

"Then who am I?" The pain had defined him for so long, letting it go felt like ripping open a partially healed wound. "I dinnae ken how to be anything else."

She drew in a full breath and let it out with a breathy huff. "You're mine. And Uma's. And I'm yours. That's all you need to be."

Her ownership did not abrade the tender exterior of him. Rather, it slid into place like a well-worn glove, fitting over every jagged edge like couture armor made specifically for him, for his very soul.

He staggered forward, not stopping until his arms lifted her and her body clung to his. His lips pressed to the cold flesh of her throat, and he breathed her in.

"I'm yours," he rasped. "And you're mine."

Her legs wrapped around his hips and she hugged him tightly. "I won't let you leave me," she vowed. "And I'll never leave you."

Her lips kissed over his jaw, her hands holding his face as she marked him with frantic possession.

"I need you," she begged, her lips pressing to his cheeks and eyes. "Now. I need you inside of me. Stay with me."

He dropped her to the bed, following her down as she pawed at his wet clothes.

"Easy." He removed his shirt, revealing his weapons. They clattered to the floor in a frenzied rush as he kicked off his boots and peeled away her pants. Their bodies were frozen, and they shivered, their damp, chilled skin needing each other's warmth to survive.

Her hand closed around him, gripping his hardening flesh with entitled surety. He pushed through the panic and let the soft caress of her

542

fingers whisk away the cruel memories. He trembled with the sense of vulnerable exposure, but she was there, whispering his name, pulling him to the bed, replacing the nightmares with the inevitable pleasure she bestowed.

"I love you," she rasped, her mouth lowering to his hardened flesh.

Heat engulfed him and his body arched against the bed. His eyes rolled back in pleasure as her hot, wet mouth dragged over him, sucking and pulling. She was after his soul, and he freely surrendered it to her.

"You're mine," she whispered, stroking a tight fist up his taut skin as she continued to milk him.

"Yours," he agreed, his body coiling so tight he feared the pleasure might break him. "Forever yours, *leannán.*"

She released him, crawling over his legs where muscles bunched and danced. Her body stretched over him, her mouth planting kisses on every expanse of exposed flesh as she straddled him.

She looked into his eyes, and he saw, not a victim of cruelty, but a survivor of adversity, a woman warrior who refused to die on the battlefield and forced herself to rise. His savior who would always come back for him.

He caught her hips, stilling her as she lifted her body over him. "You're glorious."

A fragile smile pulled at her kiss provoking lips, and a radiant blush stole over her ivory skin. Her exquisiteness countered his savageness perfectly. Where he was weak, she was strong and vice versa. Together they were whole.

She took him without shame, loved him with pure abandon, and he did the same. They belonged to each other, not because condition or circumstance demanded it, but because they chose to give parts of themselves, the most delicate fragments of all, to the other for safekeeping.

Chapter Forty-One

Saratoga Springs, New York—America
Present day

In the days that followed, they gathered his journals. Callan kept the portions worth keeping and burned the removed entries he ached to forget. It was a cleansing experience for both of them, one that allowed him to unburden his soul, truly giving Emery the chance to hold his hands and soothe all his jagged scars.

His past, his secrets, his sins vanished in the flames, and for the first time in years, the remaining hurt inside of him shifted, making room for love. For the first time in his life, there was more happiness than sorrow, more laughter than tears. The hurt, though enduring, never permanently removed those pleasant emotions. It only temporarily obstructed his ability to feel them. But Emery brought them back.

Apart, they'd been alone, incomplete, broken. Together they were happy and whole.

Blaine took the plea bargain. Two years and six months with good behavior. A fraction of a fraction of a fraction of what he deserved. It should have been an additional five with the proof of her broken hand, but the D.A. seemed reluctant to push—possibly because of his association with Blaine's hometown.

Emery dinnae want to talk about the case anymore. She only wanted to focus on the future, so that was what they did.

Callan applied for citizenship, and she signed up for a writing class at the local college. Two complicated goals they each feared for their own reasons, but both obstacles they each longed to overcome. Living was meant to be done in the open, and they both decided to no longer hide in fear.

Her house went on the market and sold within two months. He loved seeing her belongings mingled with his, loved the scent of her in his house, the feel of her in his bed. He finally felt like he had a home, a place to be happy, a place to feel safe.

He proposed to her on New Year's Eve, and they were married January fifth. The winter kept them inside, but they dinnae seem to mind as they found lots of ways to entertain themselves.

The recent blizzard had buried them in three feet of snow, and the roads were closed for a state of emergency, meaning he could drag her up to bed for days if she'd stop lingering by the window.

"Look how pretty it is," she sighed as he wrapped his arms around her, resting his chin on her shoulder.

His fingers slipped into the front of her robe, taking a possessive hold of what he now considered his. He stared at the window, ignoring the downy view, fixated on her reflection in the glass.

"Aye. Stunning."

Her weight sank into him until the coffee pot beeped, alerting them that it was finished brewing. She was like a beggar in the mornings, waiting by the machine with her empty mug clutched between both hands.

The television chattered on at a low volume, an old set taking up a big chunk of the countertop beside the coffee pot. Emery liked to hear it in the background, claiming it made her mornings less lonesome when she'd lived alone.

He pressed a kiss to her cheek as she swirled a spot of cream in her coffee, then dropped the spoon in his as a way of teasing him. He hung back, content just to watch her move.

She carried her mug to the table where Uma slurped soggy cereal off her spoon. Emery dabbed her mouth with a napkin, acting so much like a mother he ached to see her body ripen with a baby of their own.

"Why don't you scoot closer, so you don't have to lift the spoon so far?" She dragged Uma's chair up to the edge of the table.

He leaned against the counter, watching the pretty picture they made—his girls.

547

The newscasters prattling from the set about the ongoing snow seemed to mimic the cheery winter feel in the air until something sent a chill down his spine. "In other news, last night, at a New York State correction facility located just outside of Ottsville, inmate Wesley Blaine was found dead. Police are forming an investigation, but have no leads…"

The room stilled and Emery was suddenly beside him. They faced the tiny TV set. Numb. Until her hand closed around his and squeezed.

His mind retraced his steps over the last few days. He hadn't left her side since the snow started. Yet… He questioned if he'd done it.

With a shaky hand, he twisted the dial and turned up the volume. His fingers tightened around hers, needing an anchor.

"Witnesses at the prison claim they heard screams an hour after lockdown, but when the guards arrived, it was too late. Blaine was serving a sentence for aggravated assault. His cellmate had been temporarily removed from the cell for reasons the police wouldn't share. Family and state officials are actively investigating the death and calling it a first degree, pre-meditated homicide. The victim's eyes had been forcibly removed from the sockets before other parts of the body were severed. The mystery remains how the suspect was able to enter and exit the cell without detection or alerting authorities. Stay tuned for a statement from the chief investigator on the…"

He looked at Emery, her face bleached of color and her eyes wide as she watched the screen. His heart jerked about in his chest as he pulled her to face him.

He stared at her, blatantly exposing his lack of secrets for her to see. "It wasnae me, love."

"I know," she said, glancing back at the dated television set. "Missing eyes."

Another chill. He'd felt Innis's presence since the moment he'd seen that doll, but he never found her, nor had she shown up on any of the cameras he'd hidden.

Glancing over his shoulder at Uma who drank the milk from her cereal bowl, not a care in the world, he wondered if his niece was safe. Emery now knew what happened to Innis, and some of how he'd left her—left Rory. She loved Uma like a daughter and kept a close eye on her safety as well.

"She did it for me," Emery whispered, her back still to Uma. She swallowed, and a smile teased her lips but lacked the conviction to fully form. Her gaze lifted to him, a spark of awe in her eyes. "She *likes* me."

He frowned, but dinnae argue. Perhaps this was Innis's way of watching over them, perhaps paying them back for taking care of her only child when she was incapable of doing so.

Callan reached forward and shut off the TV. A sense of peace blanketed him as he caught the satisfaction shining in Emery's eyes. In the end, vengeance had been served.

Her shoulders shifted as she let out a sigh, the small breath a long-awaited exhale she'd held for far too long. Then her full smile came. It was like watching her meld back together before his eyes. But he never saw her as incomplete in any way. To him, she'd always been perfect.

He pulled her into his arms and kissed her temple. She sank into him like a lost shell drops to the bottom of the sea, returning to the secret garden where it belonged. She glanced up, and the love in her eyes rocked him.

Their bodies slowly untangled. "Who wants to build a snowman?" she asked, and Uma bounced off her chair, rushing to the door.

Callan smiled, believing everything was as it should be. "I'll get the shovel. You two get bundled."

Uma raced out of the kitchen and Emery followed, pausing to look back at him, her smile the absolute sum of all his happiness.

"I love you," she said, never failing to remind him of the one truth he'd always know.

"I love you more."

Affection warmed her gaze, as radiant as twilight and as dependable as the dawn. Her eloquence disarmed him, dismantled his mind, and combined all the broken pieces into something whole again. She was the fastening of his world, the hinges of his soul, and the beauty of his life. His Em'ry. His *leannán.*

THE END

*If you enjoyed HURT,
please leave a review!*

#HURT

www.LydiaMichaelsBooks.com

DID YOU KNOW?

The 2016 National Crime Victimization Survey *estimated...*

431,830 *sexual assaults and rapes in the United States during 2015*

1 in 5 *women experience rape or an attempted rape in their lifetime*

1 in 71 *men experience rape or an attempted rape*

Only ***34.8%*** *of sexual assaults are reported (348/1000 cases)*

And of those...

Only a tragic 0.6% result in incarceration (6/1000 cases)

Speak out.

Protect victims, not predators.

LYDIA MICHAELS

Other Books by Lydia Michaels

La Vie en Rose

Breaking Perfect

Blind

Untied

First Comes Love

If I Fall

Something Borrowed

Protégé

Simple Man

Falling In

Breaking Out

Coming Home

Sacrifice of the Pawn

Queen of the Knight

The McCullough Mountain Series

The Degrees of Separation Trilogy

The Calamity Rayne Series

Hurt

HURT

Special Thanks

I would like to thank those that supported me during the creation of this novel. I've never been so overwhelmed by such enthusiasm for my work. You all felt *this* was the exact time for this book to fall into readers' hands and I couldn't agree more. But it takes courage to write the truth, especially when it hurts. Thank you for reminding me that difficult words are sometimes necessary, for challenging me to keep it raw, so not to diminish the realism, and, above all, thank you for your faith in my work.

To my greatest champions of HURT, Salima Headley, Allyson Young, A.J. Marks, Amo, Pam Godwin, Stephanie Sab, D.D. Lorenzo, and Ms. Good, your encouraging words motivated mine in a way nothing else could. You truly made this an epic experience. And for that and so much more, I thank you.

XO,
Lydia

About the Author

Lydia Michaels is the Award Winning author of over thirty-five contemporary romance novels. Her favorite things are coffee, the Jersey shore during the off-season, snuggling, and unforgettable love stories inspired by real people.

Lydia is the two-time winner of the 2018 & 2019 *Author of the Year Award* by *Happenings Media,* as well as the 2014 *Best Author Award* from the *Courier Times*. Her work has been featured in *USA Today, Romantic Times Magazine*, and more. As the host and founder of the *East Coast Author Convention*, the *Behind the Keys Author Retreat*, and *Read Between the Wines*, she continues to celebrate her growing love for readers and romance novels around the world.

Follow Lydia Michaels

Facebook

www.facebook.com/LydiaMichaels

Instagram

www.instagram.com/lydia_michaels_books

Twitter

www.twitter.com/Lydia_Michaels

Join Lydia's Reader Group

https://www.facebook.com/groups/ReadBetweenTh
eWinesStreetTeam/

Join Lydia's Book Club!

http://bit.ly/Pimps_and_Bookers_SIGNUP

HURT

LYDIA MICHAELS

CPSIA information can be obtained
at www.ICGtesting.com
Printed in the USA
BVHW030259110919
558010BV00001B/1/P

9 780999 523636